THOMAS CRANE PUBLIC LIBRARY

QUINCY , MA

CITY APPROPRIATION

The Peppered Moth

Also by Margaret Drabble

FICTION
A Summer Bird-Cage
The Garrick Year
The Millstone
Jerusalem the Golden
The Waterfall
The Needle's Eye
The Realms of Gold
The Ice Age
The Middle Ground
The Radiant Way
A Natural Curiosity
The Gates of Ivory
The Witch of Exmoor

OTHER WORKS
Arnold Bennett: A Biography
A Writer's Britain
The Oxford Companion to
English Literature (editor)
Angus Wilson: A Biography

The
Peppered Moth

Margaret Drabble

Harcourt, Inc.
New York   San Diego   London

Copyright © 2001 by Margaret Drabble

All rights reserved. No part of this publication may be reproduced or transmitted in any form or by any means, electronic or mechanical, including photocopy, recording, or any information storage and retrieval system, without permission in writing from the publisher.

Requests for permission to make copies of any part of the work should be mailed to the following address: Permissions Department, Harcourt, Inc., 6277 Sea Harbor Drive, Orlando, Florida 32887-6777.

www.harcourt.com

Library of Congress Cataloging-in-Publication Data
Drabble, Margaret, 1939–
The peppered moth/Margaret Drabble.—1st U.S. ed.
p.   cm.
ISBN 0-15-100521-4
I. Title.
PR6054.R25 P4 2001
823'.914—dc21   00-050568

Text set in Sabon
Designed by Linda Lockowitz

First U.S. edition
K J I H G F E D C B A

Printed in the United States of America

For Kathleen Marie Bloor

On Remembering Getting Into Bed with Grandparents

It's amazing we got that far, loveless,
As you were supposed to be, yet suddenly
I have a longing for your tripeish thigh;
Swallows, thronging to the eaves; a teasmade
Playing boring Sunday news and all sorts of
Rites and rituals which seemed noteable but
Were really just trips in and out of the
Bathroom, the neurotic pulling back of
Curtains, stained-glass window at the top of
Hall stairs; dark chocolate like the secret
Meaning of the world in a corner cupboard:
Three-quarter circle smooth as a child's
Dreams and as far above reach . . .
'Loveless', the daughters said, years later when
The slow-lack peppered in their brains like a dust,
And life had grown as troublesome as thought.
Yet just tonight, I am dreaming of your thigh,
And of the unconscious swallows thronging to the eaves.

Rebecca Swift, 1993

The Peppered Moth

Prologue

It is a hot summer afternoon, in the hall of a Wesleyan Methodist chapel in South Yorkshire. Here they gather, the descendants. Where have they all come from, and who has summoned them? Is this a religious occasion? Are we about to hear a sermon? Sermons hang heavy in the air, for in this hall the ancestors endured decades of almost intolerable boredom. But we don't have to put up with that kind of thing these days. We have moved on. If it's a sermon, we'll leave quickly, by the side door.

It's surprising this chapel is still available for functions at all. It's surprising it hasn't been privatized. The Primitive Methodists down the road in Bank Street have been turned into a modest dress shop, and the chapel at Cotterhall is now a warehouse. In other parts of England, churches and chapels have been deconsecrated and turned into private houses, public houses, restaurants. But there isn't the money for that kind of thing round here. There isn't the call.

It's quite a large gathering. There are sixty or so people here, many but not all of them elderly. Tables are spread with refreshments concealed beneath white cloths, just as they might have been in the nineteenth century. But it's not the nineteenth century. It's the present, or possibly even the future. The hall is dominated by a large screen, set up for communal viewing, but this isn't going to be an illustrated talk with slides on 'Flora and Fauna of the Rocky Mountains' or 'The Life Cycle of the Honey Bee', such as the ancestors used to watch before television was invented. It's much more modern than that. This is the electronic, digital age, and that screen is the very latest of its kind.

The walls, if you look more closely, appear to be covered with charts and family trees. Diagrams of brightly coloured molecules and double helices are on view. This is some sort of genealogical assembly. The letters DNA appear upon a large banner. It is a computer-designed and computer-printed banner. Nobody has time for cross-stitch and herringbone and tapestry now. There may still be some worn dusty old hassocks amongst the pews next door, and some of those gathered together here may once have knelt and prayed upon them. But the mood of this meeting has nothing to do with prayer. It is a scientific meeting, and microbiologist Dr Robert Hawthorn is about to address his flock upon the subject of mitochondrial DNA and matrilineal descent.

The descendants have been lured here by free refreshments and by curiosity and by boredom. There is not much to do of an afternoon in Breaseborough, and they are willing to give Dr Hawthorn a hearing. Some of them are locals who have dropped in on the off chance of hearing something interesting about their own family backgrounds, or about the discovery in the cave. Others have come from further afield, summoned by Mr Cudworth, convenor of the Cudworth One-Name Society. A few look as though they have no place here at all.

Cast your eye around, and see if you can discern a pattern amongst these descendants. Can you tell from whom they may descend, can you discern the form of their common ancestor? Will Dr Hawthorn be able to reveal their origins to them, and if he can, will they want to know?

It's wonderful what science can tell you these days. It can tell you all sorts of things you'd be better off not knowing. That's what some of the old folk are thinking. You were better off in ignorance. But you can't turn the clock back, can you?

The big old plain-faced wind-up clock on the wall, which had seemed to stand still through long hours of tedious Sunday school during Bessie Bawtry's long-ago childhood at the beginning of the century, now stands still for ever. It is stuck at twenty-eight minutes to eleven. Nobody bothers to wind it now, though it might start ticking again if someone were to bother to try. They made things to last, in the old days. You could probably get it to go again. But why bother, when everyone has a watch or a mobile telephone? When you can tell the time from the microwave on the draining board in the kitchenette? When Dr Hawthorn's computer screen tells you in large glowing green digits that it is 15.27 hours precisely?

The seconds pulse onwards towards the next minute, and the digits flick slickly and silently to 15.28 hours. The show is due to begin at half past three, and most of the descendants are already waiting expectantly. The side door opens, and in shuffles a short stout old woman. She has been out to the toilet. People nod at her as she makes her way back to her seat. She is well known to most of the congregation. She ignores their signs of recognition and concentrates on regaining her chair at the end of the second row. She sits down on it, heavily.

Next to the stout old woman sits a beautiful young woman. What on earth is she doing here? She is radiant with light. She dazzles. She is a bobby-dazzler. She has surely walked in out of some other plot. She cannot be the daughter of that old woman, can she, although they are sitting close together and whispering to one another? She is too young. The granddaughter, perhaps? But the old woman is single, and has no children. Her spinster status is both known and manifest.

So who is the beauty with the huge eyes and the golden earrings and the lipstick? Is she the one from London? Is she one who got away? Is she a freak, or is she the future?

Back in the slow past, Bessie Bawtry crouched under the table, in an odour of hot plush and coal dust. Her painted bobbin perched upon its secret shelf, and she alone could see it. It was her friend. She was safe in her wooden cave. She could look up at a roof of nails and notches and splinters. They could not see her here. She was doing no wrong here. They were not angry with her when she sat in here. Beyond the bronze tasselled fringe of the cloth, a dull gleam of brass shone from the fender. The firelight reflected from the wicked tall fire-irons, and glinted upwards from the safe smooth blunt pedals of the silent piano. A thick dirty warmth filled the small close room and her smaller cavern.

This was the coal belt, and coal was its bed and being. Coal seamed the earth, coal darkened the daytime air, coal reddened the night skies. Bessie hated the coal. She was fastidious and rare. Smells offended her, grit irritated her. How could they live, up there, in such coarse comforts, so unknowingly? She was alien. She was a changeling. She was of a finer breed. She could hear her father sucking on his pipe. Spittle, dottle, wet lungs, wet lips, wet whiskers. Unutterable revulsion had set up its court in her small body. She was hiding in her underground cell with its fluted pillars, and already she was plotting her escape.

Would she make it? The odds would seem to be against her. Her ancestors had bred upon this spot for eight thousand years of as yet unrecorded time. The recording angel will attend, with folded wings, by the glimmering screen, waiting for Dr Robert Hawthorn to press the Start Button. Dr Robert Hawthorn, a little shining man of the future, as yet unborn, will be a direct matrilineal connection of Bessie Bawtry, however unlikely that connection might seem. Dr Hawthorn will make it part of his mission to track the Bawtrys back to pre-history, taking in on the way Bessie herself, and all her de-scendants and ancestors. They will cluster, the Bawtrys, one day in the future, to hear the tidings from the past. Technology will glitter and reveal them to themselves. But little Bessie, under the table, knows nothing of this, though she smells the deep thick primeval mud of the past. Bessie does not like mud.

The Bawtrys had stuck in Hammervale for millennia, mother and daughter, through the long mitochondrial matri-archy. Already Bessie sensed this, and already she feared it. She sensed inertia in the Bawtry marrowbone. Others had shoul-dered their packs, taken to the road, fled with dark strangers, enlisted, crossed the seas, crossed their bloodlines, died for-eign deaths, spawned foreign broods. The Bawtrys had stuck here through the ages. Cautious and slow, they had not even crossed the grimy brook. And how should she, a puny sickly child, find the strength to loosen the grip of this hard land, these programmed cells? Yet already she knew that, whatever the cost, she must escape or die.

The structure of DNA had not been discovered when Bessie Bawtry crouched under the table and brooded upon flight and murder. Genes were not then the fashion, as they are now. The Oedipus complex, in contrast, was already much discussed, in Vienna, in Paris, in London, if not yet in the South Yorkshire coal belt. (The son of a Midlands coal miner was even then writing about the Oedipus complex, but his works would not reach Bessie Bawtry for some years.) Both parent-murder and genes, however, had been around for a very long time, awaiting formal recognition. The revolutionary discoveries of molecular biology and digital electronics would, in a matter of decades, bring Dr Hawthorn to his Start But-ton, as he waited to impress the wonders of genes and geneal-ogy upon his patient audience. Bessie Bawtry could not foresee this future, or this past. But under that table her infant mole-cules yearned and jostled and desired. Or so we may, retro-

6

spectively, fancifully, suppose. Something had set her apart, had implanted in her needs and desires beyond her station, beyond her class. Will Dr Hawthorn diagnose and analyse the very gene that provoked her to attempt mutation? And will she succeed in her escape? To answer these questions we must try to rediscover that long-ago infant in her vanished world.

⁍⁍⁍

Bessie Bawtry, from her earliest memories, thought of herself as special. And so she was. Most children are special to themselves. But Bessie had an unusual determination, and an unusually strong desire to impose her own view of herself upon others.

She had a precocious intelligence, but she was also a delicate child. She enjoyed ill health. It was her earliest source of pleasure and indulgence. She suffered, as did many of the inhabitants of that small town, from the usual respiratory diseases that plague an industrial population. Each winter they inflamed her throat and constricted her skinny chest and infected her sinuses and bronchioles. Bessie was also endowed with an unusually refined digestive system, and a sense of smell so acute that an unpleasant odour could make her retch and gag and on occasions vomit. Bessie, as her mother complained with forced and grudging pride, was always being sick. These sensitive attributes may have seemed ill-suited to survival in South Yorkshire in the early years of the twentieth century, when pollution was so pervasive that it provoked no comment. Only strangers from the soft south or the rural northern dales noticed its pall. The natives lived in it, coughed in it, spat it out, scrubbed at it, and frequently died of it. They did not much question it. A delicate child like Bessie Bawtry might be expected to die young. Perhaps only the coarser strains had bred and multiplied amongst the slag heaps and the quarries and the pitheads. Bessie may be an evolutionary mistake, a dead end, a throwback to the clear valleys. Natural selection may deselect her. Time will tell. Dr Hawthorn, with his electronic trees and tables, will tell.

Meanwhile, under the tablecloth, Bessie Bawtry sat and rotated her painted cotton bobbin and rehearsed phrases from hymns and from the lessons from the Bible. She could already read, for she was precocious, and had learned several skills at Morley Mixed Infants on the Oxford Road. But the words she now muttered to herself were not the short clean words from the school primer, nor the jingling little verses that accompanied Sunday school collection at chapel—

> *Hear the pennies dropping*
> *Listen as they fall*
> *Every one for Jesus*
> *He shall have them all.*

Already, though yet an infant, she despised such stuff, as she despised Mr Beever's sermons, which took on the mean colouring of the mean streets. Mr Beever preached docility, acceptance, littleness, the second-rate. But the Bible was different. It was grand, extreme and horrid. It spoke damnation and darkness, it sounded cymbals and trumpets, it flared its nostrils and it sniffed another air. Deserts and mountains, valleys and springs, pits and entombments, cedars of Lebanon and roses of Sharon, fishpools of Heshbon and vineyards of Samaria. Its polysyllables had nourished famished poets and wandering Jews and political prisoners and religious fanatics for centuries, and now they nourished Bessie Bawtry. She would turn against the Bible, in years to come, but now, as an infant, she invoked it. 'Watchman, what of the night?' 'His anger endureth but a moment: weeping may endure for a night, but joy cometh in the morning.'

We must find our sustenance where we may.

The texts of the Hebrews travelled by strange routes to the

South Yorkshire coalfields. God's Sacred Word, though not in the form or language known to Bessie, had been heard in the hamlets of Hammervale since the Dark Ages. It had brought a new strain to the genetic sloth of the valley dwellers. Those who had ears to hear, let them hear. Not many listened, it must be said, and those who did listen came up with some unorthodox interpretations. Nevertheless, the sounds rolled on, *in saecula saeculorum,* intoned from the pulpit, and in times of stress and heresy yelled forth in the market place amidst the rotting stinking inland fish. In ditches and dungeons dwelled the Word of the Lord, with tinkers and cobblers and all manner of dissidents, and now it muttered itself to itself in a cavern beneath a wooden table with fluted legs in a back living room in Slotton Road, Breaseborough, which is on the way out to Bednerby Main.

'Joy cometh in the morning.' Will it come? Will it ever come?

The Jesus pennies dropped into the bottom of a specially adapted ginger-beer bottle. When the bottle was full, it was smashed and the pennies were released for Jesus. What he spent them on, nobody knew or dared to ask. The extortion was resented, especially as it was coyly described in the chapel records as a 'Glad Offering', but the moment of smashing did provide a thrill of rebellious, destructive delight, prefiguring the delight that Bawtry descendants may take in hurling their bottles into bottle banks and listening to the purge of their splintering.

The bottle factory was then the second-largest employer in town. Glass predated coal as an industry here. But the bottles produced were not wine bottles. Wine had disappeared with the Romans. It will make a comeback, but not for some decades.

The Rose of Sharon, when Bessie eventually came to identify it as a plant, was to prove a great disappointment to her. 'I am the Rose of Sharon, and the Lily of the Valley.' Was this the excellency of Carmel and the glory of Lebanon? Surely not. It was a weedy, untidy, scruffy suburban undershrub, with leaves that curled and turned brown at the edges, with undistinguished yellow flowers, disorganized straggling spotty red anthers, and patchy inadequate gloss. She found it hard to believe that this was the flower that had bloomed in glory in the plains and on the slopes of the Holy Land. It must, she decided, be some inferior, second-rate, Yorkshire variety. She banned it for ever from any of her imagined gardens, along with the privet and the laurel. She banned, by association, the perfume of the lily of the valley, which, she was to maintain, had a vulgar shop-girl smell. Maybe words are always more beautiful than things, and reality but a pale shadow of the Word?

'Joy cometh in the morning.' Will it ever come?

Bessie Bawtry rocked a little, with her short arms round her thin knees, and nodded in private ritual to her cotton bobbin. A professional observer from a later age—for one cannot suppose that Freud and his contemporaries would have found this modest, undeveloped case of much interest—might have diagnosed a problem in the making. A withdrawal, perhaps a psychosis. Why was this child not out on the street with her playmates, throwing her bit of slate at the chalked hopscotch grid, or skipping, or winding through the branched arms of in-and-out-the-windows, or creeping up on her friends in a scary game of grandmother's footsteps? Was she afraid she might always be It? For she was not very strong, nor very agile, though she was not clumsy. (Pelmanism, the memory game, is the only game at which she will excel.) Why did she choose this secondary cavelight, when out there on Slotton Road the sun shone bright, and at night the moon's brightness glimmered through the smoky air? Other children played on the street. Why was Bessie sitting there intoning verses to a cotton bobbin instead of sitting by her mother's knee and helping her with the peg rug? Did her parents abuse her? Did they neglect her? Was she jealous of her harmless little sister?

No, her parents did not abuse her. And they were attentive, in their own ways. But their ways, one might now say, were not very good. Bessie Bawtry's mother Ellen did not know how to play and did not understand children. She did not like children, as a class. Nobody had played with her when she was a child, for in those days childhood had hardly been invented, and now she did not play with her own children. She sometimes rocked the baby when she woke and cried, but Bessie was now, at the age of five, considered far too big to sit on her knee. Ellen never sang to her children, for once upon a time, or so it was said, her husband had mocked her—once, once only—for singing out of tune. And she had never attempted a lullaby since. She kept an apologetic, a vindictive silence, and never sang again.

Dora, Bessie's sister, was sleeping now, in a corner, in the Moses basket which she was fast outgrowing. Ellen Bawtry, born Ellen Cudworth, was happy with this, for Ellen liked her children to be quiet and good. She did not like Bessie to play on the street with the rough ones. She claimed that the street was dirty. And she was right. Anything beyond her own carefully whitened doorstep was dirty. Ellen, like her daughter Bessie, disliked dirt. They were at one on this. Ellen had always been at war with dirt. She lost, but she fought on. Bessie would not respect her for these battles, because she was to observe only the defeat, not the struggle. Therefore she was to despise her mother. That is the way it is with mothers and daughters.

Dora, unlike Bessie, was a robust and placid baby. She was never much trouble. There was not room in one family for two delicate children. One was quite enough. Dora chose her destiny wisely.

Mrs Bawtry, if asked, would have said that she loved her daughters. But she would not have expected the question, nor would she have liked it, and indeed in all her life it was never to be put to her. Emotions were not her forte. It was hard to say what her forte was. She is not even very good at pegging that peg rug. One cannot go far wrong with a peg rug made of coarse strips of old trousers and worn-out jackets, in shades of navy and grey and brown. One cannot go far right either. And she went wrong.

Bert Bawtry—his christened name was George, but for some forgotten reason he was always addressed as Bert—had a talent or two. He was good with the electrics. This was just as well, for he was by trade an electrical engineer. He worked at Bednerby Main, but was on call in many local domestic crises, and achieved popularity by his ability to fix, for free, the power failures at the cinema down the road. He loved his motorbike and sidecar, and belonged to the Automobile Association Motorcycle Club. He also wrote in a good, clear copperplate script which would have put the illegible scribblings of his grandchildren to shame. And, unlike his wife, he could sing. He liked to raise his voice in chapel, and he attended the choral society's weekly meetings to sing the praises of the Lord. He cared nothing for the Lord, for he was not a religious man, but he liked the sound of the singing. Every Christmas, he sang his way through the bass parts of *The Messiah*, assuring Breaseborough that the Saviour's yoke was easy and his burden light, bellowing forth the Hallelujah Chorus, and chanting to the gates to lift up their heads. *Lift up your heads, O ye gates, and be ye lifted up, ye everlasting portals!*

He was not allowed to sing at home.

He had a mildly sadistic nature, though he would have been astonished had anyone tried to tell him so, for his sadism took the socially acceptable form of pinching his elder daughter's cheeks until tears came into her eyes, and of burning the back of her hand with a teaspoon hot from his tea. He also described with too much relish the deaths of cats and dogs in the burning fiery furnace of the Destructor at the Electrical

Works, and the injuries sustained by miners down the pit. But he never hit anyone. Ellen Bawtry would not have put up with being hit. Mr Bawtry was not a violent or a drinking man, unlike many of the men of the families whose clogs tramped their way each dawn to Bednerby Main. The Bawtrys were a cut above that kind of thing. They were overground, not underground people, and meant to stay that way. Ellen Bawtry considered herself lucky in Bert Bawtry. And, all things considered, she was. She had married late, and cautiously, and she was satisfied with what she had got.

Ellen and Bert Bawtry were not bad people or bad parents. They tried. They were respectable. They did not hurt their children, but they did not indulge or pet them. Their normal mode was repressive. The normal mode of Breaseborough was repressive, and Ellen and Bert were not innovative. They went along with it. Their children, when small, were afraid of them. Most children, in those days, were afraid of their parents.

It is not pleasant to use this tone about Bert and Ellen Bawtry. They cannot help their stony lives. But if we were to find another tone, the heart might break. And then where would we be? What good would *that* do, Ellen Bawtry herself would be the first to ask.

We might find ourselves obliged to weep. We might not be able to stop weeping. And what *would* be the point of *that*?

Bessie sat under the table, Dora sucked her thumb as she slept in her cradle, Ellen Bawtry hooked and pulled at her length of brown sacking, and Bert Bawtry read the racing results, then a motorcycle magazine. He did not gamble himself, except for an annual flutter on the legendary St Leger, but he liked to know what was what. He liked the names of the horses, and something of spirit in him liked it when one won against the odds. A disagreeable smell of boiled meat issued mournfully from the blackened kitchen range. The Bawtrys, in these prewar years, did not go hungry. They did not eat well, but they ate a lot. Both Bert and Ellen were stout, as people of their age were in those days.

Prospects for young Bessie, with her refined nature and her great expectations, did not seem too good on that October evening long ago. It seemed that nothing would ever change. It seemed she would never get out of here.

It was lucky, really, that Mrs Bawtry did not let Bessie play on the street. It was more dangerous out there than any of them knew, than any of them could have known.

Against known dangers, Ellen Bawtry warned and protected her daughters. The world beyond the wooden cave was full of menace. Steep steps, runaway horses, spiked railings, epidemics of whooping cough and measles and diphtheria. The gormless gaslighter, the loiterer on the corner, the cracks in the pavement, the poisonous coloured icing on those gross Whitsuntide buns. Glucose, germs, splinters. Boiled sweets. The very earth was mined. Beneath the streets, a mile down, toiled the employees of Bednerby Main, in dark tunnels supported by wooden pit props. The ground might give at any moment and let one down into the darkness. The crust was thin. It was easy to fall through. Dawn by dawn the miners tramped their way to the pithead. They were of another race, an underground race. They were the scum of the earth, the dregs of the earth. (This is how Ellen Bawtry spoke of her neighbours.) The streets might at any moment crack and open in terrible fissures, and the menace beneath would grab one's ankle and pull one down, however clean one's ankle socks. It was not safe to venture far. Between the scum and the dregs one might hope, by keeping still, to survive, in some kind of suspension. Do not rise with the scum, do not sink with the dregs. Stay safe. Stay where you are. Keep your mean place.

No wonder Bessie Bawtry hid.

Bessie's earliest memory was of a steep and narrow staircase. Strait was the way. A narrow, steep incline, of steps too high for her short legs, and herself midway, on the seventh step, crouching, unable to climb up, afraid to fall down. The drugget-protected carpet runner was tethered with cruel rods and clamped down with brass teeth. Its abrasive weave attacked her knees and her fingers. She was afraid to let out a whimper. The great sharp edges towered above her, the geometric cliffs plunged down beneath her. How had she got there? It was forbidden. And now she must stay there for ever, trapped, between two perils, in utter terror of wrath or of unbeing. She had been paralysed with fear. How had she got there? She had been unable to move. What had rescued her? She could never remember. Had she been slapped or scolded for climbing the stairs? She did not know. And were the stairs in her birth-home, in Slotton Road, or in some stranger's house? Again, she did not know. Could that puny little staircase even have seemed so long, so steep, so high? Did the memory belong to her grandmother's house in Leeds, of which she had no other recollection? She would never know, would never work it out.

But again and again, throughout her life, she would dream of that staircase. A birth trauma, we now might call it. Will Bessie Bawtry ever learn this term? It seems unlikely, as she crouches in her cave. But so much is unlikely. Bessie Bawtry herself is unlikely, and so are her imaginings. ('Where *did* she get those notions from?' will be an indignant, often dismissive, but occasionally proud refrain.) Nobody taught Bessie to recoil from stale fish, from over-boiled meat, from suet, from dank lavatory moss on the steps of the outside privy, from the silt that stiffened the curtains. Nobody had taught her that the town's unmade streets were unsightly, nor that its patches of wasteland were an affront to order and to common sense. She had never seen a handsome building or a well-planned town. Had she constructed for herself some image of the Ideal City from photographs in newspapers and magazines, from paintings, from descriptions in books? And if she had, what gave her the notion that she had a right to inhabit it?

The house in Slotton Road had been built in 1904, not long before Bessie was born, but she was not to remember it as a new house, for the dirt had invaded it so rapidly. But new it had been, and not so long ago. It was a corner house, and of that the Bawtrys were proud, for corner houses were desirable. The street itself straggled along in a haphazard, low, creeping, speculative manner. Fern Villas, a semi-detached double-fronted building, had been built first, and was dated 1902 in crude Art Nouveau script: this was followed in 1903, if the runes spoke true, by Hurst House, marginally detached. Then came the rapid march of unnamed numbers, of two-storey houses in red brick with shallow projecting bays, not quite regular or uniform in design, but showing small signs of not always very happy or confident decorative independence—a fretted eave, a patterned airbrick, a rudimentary floral motif in fired clay over a doorway. The little town had grown from a population of four hundred in 1800 to fourteen thousand in 1900, and was still growing. The streets marched, met a dead end, turned a corner, then groped and wandered blindly on. The streets marched over Gorse Croft and Cat Balk and Chapel Pit and Coally Pond and Longdoles. They marched right up to Gospel Well. They marched over field and fell. People had to be housed. Lot converged on lot, unplanned, undesigned, parcelled out. Small tenants paid small rents to small landlords, and bigger tenants paid slightly bigger rents to bigger landlords. The lucky ones were those that found they owned the coalfields. The unlucky ones were those that worked the coalfields. A thin grassy layer of agriculture continued to cover the wide basin of the valley, but the riches lay below.

Slotton Road was undistinguished, but it was better than some of the other new streets. At least the Bawtry house did not front straight on to the pavement. Each house in Slotton Road had a small area, a yard or so across, beneath its bay, fenced off by a low wall or railings with a wrought-iron gate.

Not quite a garden, not quite a yard. 'A waste of space,' as Bessie might have described it, in her caustic later vein. But as a child she was proud of it. She despised those whose unprotected houses lined the roadway, whose front-parlour windows were shrouded by grimy Nottingham lace.

Contempt was common currency in Breaseborough. Those with little are trained to despise those with less. Contempt marks off an area, it marks you off from the common street. You are protected from the common by a small, useless, ugly, proud, discriminatory little asphalt patch.

Canal Street, Cemetery Road, Coal Pit Lane, Quarry Bank, Clay Pit Way, Gashouse Lane, Goosebutt Terrace. They didn't mince words round Breaseborough. At least Slotton didn't mean anything dirty or rude. Slotton Road was called after a fishmonger, but that wasn't too obvious. And there wouldn't have been any point in calling it Belle Vue or Rosemount or Mount Pleasant, would there? People in Breaseborough liked to call a spade a spade.

Bessie Bawtry sat under the table and watched the glowing coals. She watched the coals and the shadow of the firelight as it flickered on the wall and on the sheen of the disproportionately large mahogany sideboard for which her father had paid five pounds and ten shillings. In the red heart of the fire, palaces and castles blossomed, blushed and crumbled, caverns opened and pulsed, and flaming ferns of fossilized forests branched. Bessie's clean white little bobbin sat safely in its place and nobody but she knew it was there.

Her father read the paper. Her mother pegged a rug. Her sister Dora quietly slept.

Is Bessie to be our heroine? Something of interest must happen to her, or we would not have wasted all this time making her acquaintance. Something must surely single her out from all those other statistics that Dr Hawthorn has fed into his computer. But to her, as yet, the future was unimaginably opaque, although it was more real than the present. Bessie had decided at an early age that Breaseborough was not real. It was a mistake.

She was not alone in this view. The exodus from Breaseborough is part of our plot. Some stayed, some left, and, decades on, some were gathered back into the hall of the Wesleyan chapel to try to retrace these journeys.

ꙮ

Months passed, years passed. Bessie came out from under the table, and forgot her cotton bobbin, and Dora woke up and began to try to make a noise. Ellen and Bessie between them soon put a stop to that. Bessie had decided that she was the most important member of the family, and had already managed to impose her conception and her will on others. Dora must learn to stay in second place. Bessie was determined to occupy the centre of the story, and she did not want a competitor. She had not yet perfected her techniques for subordinating others, but she was working on them.

It would be tedious to follow Bessie through all the stages and stopping places of her infancy, through those interminable Sunday school classes and Whitsuntide processions. Those days are dead and gone, and so is the dullness that went with them, the slow prose that described them. Bessie Bawtry prayed for acceleration, before she even knew what she was praying for, and in the end she got it. Whether she was grateful for what she got remains to be seen. But we can, at this stage in the story, predict that despite her delicate constitution, she may well live to a ripe—or perhaps an unripe?—old age.

There was a month or two in her early life when she looked as though she was not going to make it, for Bessie, like millions of others around the world, nearly died of the Spanish flu in the autumn of 1918. Before this crisis, she had been making what school reports describe as Steady Progress. She had graduated from Morley Mixed Infants (sums, letters, clay and pencils), where the motherly Miss George sometimes let you sit on her knee. She had moved on to Morley Girls (knitting, sums, letters and ink) and had said good-bye with relief to the stout and ailing alpaca-clad headmistress there, whose chief educational principle had consisted of 'knocking it into them', and who was forever sending children on pointless errands to look for her pills or her spectacles. Under her regime Bessie had been a failure as a knitter of socks and a turner of seams, but had mastered the names of the Books of the Bible and the rivers of Europe, and was good at reciting by rote.

She had, by the age of ten, exhausted the limited supply of reading matter in the Morley Girls Library, and had read over and over again the small collection of books in Slotton Road, most of which were Sunday school prizes which had been awarded to various Victorian Cudworths and Bawtrys for chapel attendance. Most of these Bessie found as contemptible as Mr Beever's bathetic sermons. A characteristic example was *The Dairyman's Daughter; an Authentic Narrative from Real Life* by the late Rev. Legh Richmond, A.M., Rector of Turvey, Bedfordshire, reprinted by William Walker in Otley, which had been given to one of her Cudworth aunts, Selina, by Bessie's grandmother in 1861. This doll-sized pocket volume, four inches by three, had looked promising when discovered in the bottom of her mother's sewing drawer. Its yellow endpapers, its tiny print, its gold-engraved title, its vaguely Oriental embossed red-brown cover, and its frontispiece of deathbed and medicine bottles might well have attracted a hypochondriac child. But the text was excessively religious, and Bessie at once saw through its condescending equation of servile rustic poverty with virtue. She could not identify with the abject piety of its heroine Elizabeth, even though they shared a name, and the clergyman-narrator's profound self-satisfaction irritated her intensely. His praise of humble cottages seemed compromised by his delight in grand mansions and fair prospects. She could not have provided a Marxist critique of it at the age of nine, but she could and did react with honest indignation. Such stuff! She wondered what Great-Aunt Selina had made of it.

Great-Aunt Selina had qualified as a nurse of insane persons under the auspices of the Medico-Psychological Association of Great Britain and Ireland, and had worked for some years in the asylum at Wakefield, where the legendary misogynist psychologist Henry Maudsley had recently been assistant medical officer. She must have seen some sights there, but Bessie could not ask her about them, because she was dead. Great-Aunt Selina had spent her spare time crocheting lace edges for pillowcases with a finger-punishing small steel hook. The pillowcases survive.

No, Bessie did not care for *The Dairyman's Daughter*, that once-so-popular tract. In contrast, however, she felt a strange and disquieting affection for Mrs Sherwood's *Little Henry and His Bearer*, a slightly larger volume in slightly larger print, and with more numerous and more lively illustrations. This had been presented as a Christmas gift to a long-forgotten Samuel Cudworth on 25 December 1859. (What had he been? Butcher, baker, or pattern maker?) Bessie read it many times. It was the story of a neglected little English orphan, brought up in India by his devoted bearer Boosie as a happy heathen Hindoo, then converted to Christianity by a visiting lady of missionary and Methodist leanings. This lady had easily convinced little Henry of the inefficacy of the Hindoo faith by shattering a little Hindoo god of baked earth into a hundred pieces, and pointing out that it could not then get up and move or do anything useful. From this it proved an easy step to turn Henry into a devout Christian, conscious of sin and afraid of hell. ('They shall look upon the carcasses of the men that have transgressed against me; for their worm shall not die, neither shall their fire be quenched, and they shall be an abhorring unto all flesh', Isaiah 66:24). It was as well that Henry had repented his sins and assured himself of immortal life, for at the age of eight years and seven months he sickened and died, as children did in India. But he did not die before he had converted his bearer Boosie and persuaded him to lose caste by becoming a Christian, with the new name of John.

This little tale intrigued Bessie Bawtry. It was a stimulating study in what would soon be known as comparative religion: the unredeemed Boosie at one point delivered himself of the challenging, albeit incorrect view that 'There are many brooks and rivers of water, but they all run into the sea at last: there is the Mussulman's way to heaven, and the Hindoo's way, and the Christian's way, and one way is as good as another.' It also provided an interesting picture of a way of life quite unlike that in Breaseborough, where English ladies smoked hookahs at tiffin, where Indians consulted gooroos and ground mussala, where the Ganges (not a river of Europe, but an important river none the less) wound its way around the curving shore to lose itself behind the Rajmahal Hills.

Satisfying though this fable had proved in its own curious and unintended way (though perhaps we cannot be utterly sure of Mrs Sherwood's intentions), Bessie, at the age of eleven, felt herself ready for stronger fare. And at Breaseborough Secondary School, before she fell ill of the influenza, she was beginning to find it. She had been introduced to English Language and Literature, Reading and Recitation, History, Geography, French, Arithmetic, Algebra, Science, Scripture, Art, Needlework and Nature Study. Riches of learning spread themselves before her. (The subjects of Music and Laundry, although listed as options upon her terminal report, do not seem to have engaged her scholarly attention. Like her mother, Bessie was tone deaf, and she already knew about laundry. She had learned the subject young, by the side of her mother's copper and her mother's oak peggy tub, in the hot steaming fug worked up from yellow bars of Perfection Soap, where she played with her own little doll's washtub and her own little toy wringer.) Bessie was entranced by this brave new world of adult study. And just as it opened up to her, she fell ill.

Bessie Bawtry fell ill in October 1918. She, who caught every passing germ as punctually and diligently as though her invalid honour depended upon it, could not fail this great opportunity. The avenging virus of influenza settled upon her just as she was attempting to caption and colour in a map showing the pattern of medieval strip farming. It struck her much more rapidly than malaria had settled upon the slowly fading little Henry, or consumption on the virtuous dairy-maid. One moment she was feeling fine, but the next moment, even as she dipped her pen into the inkwell, the flu assailed her with peremptory violence. It occupied her nose and throat, it poured hotly through her bloodstream, and speeded up her pulse to fever pitch. She was the first child in the school to surrender: she had that distinction. Others followed rapidly. By the time she got home that afternoon, her temperature was 104, and she was mildly delirious. She was conscious of a pride in her status. But, though proud, she was very, very ill.

As this was the first moment in which her private history clocks in with that of public recorded time, we may spend a paragraph or two upon the topic of the outbreak of what was known as Spanish flu.

The influenza pandemic of 1918–1919 was responsible, we are told, for the highest mortality rate of any pandemic since the Black Death of the fourteenth century. According to some authorities, it originated in the spring of 1918—in San Sebastián? in Almería? The Spanish, who, unlike much of the rest of the world, were not at war, and therefore did not censor their press, rashly admitted the existence of their infection. Thus they had the doubtful honour of giving their name to the sickness and being blamed for it by posterity. Other authorities claimed that the first cases were identified in March 1918 amongst the troops of the United States at Fort Riley in Kansas. Be that as it may, the illness swept across America and Europe, and by July of 1918 had spread 'in a tidal wave' to Asia, China and Japan. Chicago succumbed, and so did London, Liverpool and Glasgow. George the Fifth of England, Emperor Wilhelm of Germany and Alfonso the Thirteenth of Spain contracted it, and recovered. Round the world, thirty million died in three months, more than three times the military casualties of the Great War itself: of these influenza victims, two million died in Europe, and 183,000 in Britain. Or so it is said: the figures are hardly likely to be very precise.

In Britain, schools and cinemas and libraries emptied spontaneously, and some were closed by decree: children drooped at their desks, as one medical officer reported, 'like plants whose roots had been poisoned', and died by the end of the week. A single case could infect a whole school. Coffins were in short supply, and so were reliable remedies. Muslin masks and gargling became the fashion. Some tried oil of garlic, and others relied on permanganate of potash or quinine or arsenic compounds. Some doctors prescribed whisky: other doctors forbade it. Dover's Powder was popular, and so was iodine of lime. Various vaccines proved useless. A good nosebleed or a heavy menstrual period was thought beneficial. Tobacco was proclaimed an effective germicide. Some swore by fresh air, others by isolation in darkened rooms. Despairing doctors of the fresh-air persuasion dramatically broke their patients' bedroom windows with rolling pins. It was safer to stay at home than to go into hospital, where the mortality rates rose and rose.

Was influenza connected with swine, or with dogs, or with ferrets, or with pigeons? Was it caused by a bacterium? (Yes, argued Sir Paul Gordon Fildes, who mistakenly backed *bacterium Haemophilus influenzae*.) Was it a virus? (Yes, argued Sir Patrick Playfair Laidlaw, who was right.)

The course of the disease was as mysterious as its source. In Britain, the second wave of the epidemic, the autumnal wave that claimed Bessie, proved the most severe. It subsided

abruptly in November, with the signing of the Armistice—
only to swell up again, equally mysteriously, in a third attack,
in a final cathartic roundup, in the spring of 1919. To this day
experts declare that 'the extreme violence of the fall wave has
never been explained,' and now perhaps it never will be,
though the whole episode continues to arouse curiosity. Sev-
enty years later scientists were still as yet unsuccessfully attempting to analyse the nature of the virus by exhuming the
bodies and examining the lungs of four influenza victims, all
coal miners, who were buried and preserved at Spitsbergen in
the permafrost of the Norwegian Arctic Circle.

Was the Spanish flu a judgement? Was it a purge? Was it a
sign of the wrath of God? Various little Spanish sufferers endured affliction so patiently that they became candidates for
sainthood, so they did well out of their early deaths.

Let us return to Bessie Bawtry, who survived the first four
crucial days, but remained ill for twenty days and twenty
nights. She was, during this period, promoted to the bed in
her parents' bedroom, though she was never to be sure why:
was it for convenience, was it through a superstitious respect?
There she lay, as empires crumbled, as fateful peace treaties
were negotiated, listening to the echoes of their death throes
and to the rapid beatings of her little childish heart. There she
felt both safe and happy. Her mind wandered, and she babbled
of Dickens's *Pickwick Papers* and Charles Reade's *The Clois-
ter and the Hearth,* both novels that she had devoured that
September: the characters of Sam Weller and the abandoned
Margaret seemed to stand in person by her bedside. She knew
them: they were her friends: they spoke to her. Occasionally
she would lapse back into her earlier biblical phase, for the
language of the Bible had long outlived its content in her
imagination, but fortunately no Mrs Sherwood was waiting by
her sickbed to pounce like a vulture of salvation upon these
signs of weakness and of grace. The Bawtrys, chapel-goers
though they were, were not a religious family.

The Bawtry bed was the best piece of furniture in the

house, and it offered Bessie its own interior world, a haven such as once, aeons ago, the cave beneath the parlour table had provided. Her father said he had bought it secondhand from Arthur Cook's in Leeds, along with all his household furniture. He liked to boast, with an uncharacteristically romantic flourish, that he had paid for the lot with 'a handful of golden sovereigns'—the drawing-room suite, the grandfather clock, the bentwood chairs and rocker, the walnut bedroom suite, the mahogany sideboard, the oak table with castors, the hair mattress, and the *pièce de résistance,* the mahogany 'Tudor' bedstead itself. Many of the neighbours had cheap new furniture—chip oak, veneer—although several also possessed the silent, never-to-be-played status symbol of a piano. Bert Bawtry alone had ventured far into the past, and he had chosen well, for the bed was an object of virtue. (It is a pity Bert did not live to see *The Antiques Roadshow.* He would have enjoyed it. He was a man of curious interests.)

The bed was a four-poster, far too large for the room, but never mind that: it was a room of its own. Its hangings (original, and antique) were of a pale fawn green with a woven design of dark blue flowers and yellow stars, and pinned into the back curtains were watch pockets of a rubbed and faded crimson velvet embroidered with birds of pearl beading. These watch pockets filled Bessie with inexpressible delight. They were aristocratic, they were poetic, they were historic, they spoke of Sir Walter Scott, whose novels Bessie much admired. (Walter Scott had once, astonishingly, visited their neighbourhood, and had exclaimed upon its great natural beauty—'there are few more beautiful and striking scenes in England...the soft and gentle river Hammer sweeps through an amphitheatre in which cultivation is richly blended with woodland'—so had the great Wizard of the North bizarrely described their paltry spoil tips.)

Above Bessie's fevered head was a half-tester, also of green and blue: she gazed up into this heavenly canopy, and muttered cajolingly to herself that Assyria would fall, yea, that

Damascus and Babylon and the whole of the Austro-Hungarian Empire would be given over to the thorn and the wilderness, and that the vine and all its silverlings would perish. (Bessie did not know what silverlings were. But that made them all the more attractive to her, for in the Beginning was the Word. Miss Hackett at Big Sunday School did not know what they were either, though she had pretended that she did, and had spitefully and fruitlessly warned Bessie against too much random reading of the Old Testament.)

Bessie rambled on about trumpets in the wilderness, and held conversations with Mr Pickwick and Mr Tupman over gallons of beer and oysters, in smoky snuggeries and hostelries. This should have worried her parents, and it did. Her mother waited on her, and her little sister Dora eagerly ran errands for her. Dora, insensitive, sturdy, a little carthorse, not a highly strung thoroughbred, failed to catch the virus. Dora would have felt proud of her resistance and resilience had not Bessie by now managed to persuade her that they were somehow contemptible. Health, in Bessie's view, was rude, and therefore the healthy Dora was inferior. Dora, who looked up to her big sister, had come to believe this. Her earlier moments of rebellion had been crushed. No longer would she dare or even wish to dare to tear a page out of one of Bessie's precious books. Gone were the days when she would plead with Bessie to play with her instead of sitting there endlessly reading. She took her big sister at her own estimate, and accepted her superiority. So we cast ourselves in castes, even when our society fails to provide them.

Bessie's mother Ellen waited and watched, for the shame of a dead daughter would have been a black mark, a distress, a pointing finger. Did Ellen suffer during this crisis? Maybe she did, but honestly one would not have been able to tell the difference.

Bessie tossed and turned in the vast bed, which did not creak under her wasted body as it creaked under the weight of her stout parents. She could think of worse fates than dying here, admired and lamented by all. The Dairyman's Daughter, by such means, had achieved fame, if not immortality, but Bessie was not yet ready to depart happily and to leave a shining track behind her. She decided that on balance it would be better to survive. If life took a turn for the worse, she could always fall back on her old familiar, bronchitis, as she already did every winter, and regain this lassitude, this luxury, this queenly attendance.

And so she recovered, slowly regaining her strength through an exceptionally cold winter, pampered by a fire in the grate and a solid round hot-water bottle of cream and brown stone. Dr Marr, who paid regular and courteous attendance, was impressed by her steady progress: in the first four days he had despaired of her. But one of the oddest features of this epidemic was that it killed more healthy adults than it killed children and old people. Again, this has never been explained, though it certainly puzzled Dr Marr. He was particularly attentive to Bessie, for he already knew her well, through her many previous illnesses, and, like the staff of Breaseborough Secondary School, he had a fondness for her. He supplemented the meagre wartime diet by malted milk, and beef tea from his own larder.

Dora in the meantime made do with bread and cheese. Dora liked bread and cheese. In fact, Dora was a stubborn little eater, and in her early years ate nothing but bread and cheese. She was labelled Mousie by her mother: the nickname was not intended as a compliment, but Dora seized on this small crumb of differentiation as a mark of affection, and she may have been right to do so. Not many compliments came her way, and she had to make the best of what was on offer.

It is surprising that Dora did not contract scurvy, if her recollections of her own early diet are accurate.

It was a small town, in those days. (It is still a small town.) In those days, Dr Marr knew all his patients, and paid them home visits when he was needed. It did not cross his mind that there was any other way of conducting his professional life. He saw most of his flock through the flu. Breaseborough did not suffer as badly as Leeds, Glasgow and Manchester. It did not suffer as badly as Chicago, Peking and Bombay.

Dr Marr's daughter Ada was a particular friend of Bessie Bawtry, and although she was forbidden access to the important sickroom many messages, doubtfully fumigated, were carried between the two girls by sister Dora in the weeks of quarantine and convalescence. Ada did not fall ill, perhaps rendered immune by her father's regular contacts with the disease: she envied Bessie her status, for martyrdom of one sort or another was one of the few attractive prospects to an imaginative girl child in those days. But, like Dora, Ada made the best of keeping well. She reported school activities back to Bessie (who was annoyed to have missed the lesson on Babylonian mythology) and pasted carefully saved and cherished little prewar brightly coloured scraps on cards for her—flower baskets, butterflies, nymphs in flimsy array, ponies and puppy dogs. She also collected autographs from her classmates in a little velvety autograph book—some adorned with crude little drawings of Dutch dolls or sailor boys or coy Mabel Lucie Attwell–inspired pouting babies, some with elegant and uplifting verses from Ella Wheeler Wilcox or from Anon.—

> *No star is ever lost*
> *That we have seen*
> *We always may be*
> *What we might have been.*

The popular conundrum

Y Y U R
Y Y U B
I C U R
Y Y for ME

was copied out in various colours by two contributors. And, on 11 November, Armistice Day, equipped with a small patriotic paper flag and a whistle, Ada Marr came and stood under Bessie's bedroom window and shouted up through the drizzling rain: 'Bess, the war's over!' and Bessie, with unusual boldness, crept out of bed and crossed to the cracked and sooty pane and croaked back to her friend below, 'Yes, I know.'

⟨✺⟩

The war was over, and the sun shone down on Breaseborough. We move to May 1922, and rejoin Bessie Bawtry and Ada Marr, taking the short cut home from school through the cemetery. At this time of year, even the windy plateau of the cemetery seemed cheerful. The distant rim of low hills was green, the chestnuts were in bloom, and dark emerald fairy rings of mushroom enlivened the yellowing graveyard grass. The cemetery, conveniently placed next to the grim fortress of the turn-of-the-century hospital, was a favourite walk for courting couples, for old men with dogs, for mothers with perambulators. Breaseborough was not well provided with recreational spaces, but the cemetery served. Bessie, word-addicted, knew most of its inscriptions by heart: she had noted how many had 'borne the cross', or been 'anchored by the veil', or discovered, often prematurely, that 'in the midst of life we are in death'. She had wondered about the many 'beloved daughters'—would she merit the epithet 'beloved' when dead? She had read the names of those who had died in colliery disasters. The most eloquent of these epitaphs read, disturbingly, not quite grammatically:

> *A sudden shock which did appear*
> *And took my life away.*
> *At morn I was in health and strength*
> *At night as cold as clay.*

29

The uncertainty of the grammar seemed to intensify the uncertainty of life.

Bessie had overcome her childish fear of the alarming apocalyptic tilt of some of the headstones, the cracked and uneven kerbs of the grave plots: she no longer expected the dead to burst forth through these cracks and crevices, nor did she think that she herself was about to fall through into the underworld. (Though this latter fear was far from irrational: like most of the neighbourhood, the cemetery was deeply undermined and subject to subsidence. A thousand yards below the dead laboured the living.) But she preserved her deep early distaste for some of the funerary materials. She particularly deplored the mottled red and green granite tombstone which surmounted Reuben and Esther Twigg, who had passed away in 1902 and 1906 respectively: it was of a horrible colour and a vile uncertain spotted brawny texture which made her want to gag. She hated mottles and spawns and blotches. How could anyone think such a finish attractive? Had the Twiggs been *mad*?

But today, in May, not even the tomb of the Twiggs annoyed her. She and Ada were in high spirits. They were in fine form, and they were in the fine fifth form, and they were doing well. The world was all before them, as they tripped down Cemetery Road, and on, down Swinton Road, under the lime trees, and across the triangle between the Rialto, the bus station and the public library. They forgave the weeds that burst through the asphalt. They jumped across a paving stone, avoided a pile of dry crotted chalk-white dog dirt, and headed downhill, deep in discussion, towards the footbridge over the canal. They had cheese sandwiches and a bottle of pop and a couple of currant buns, and their homework, and they were off for a picnic on the riverbank. They were happy. Bold yellow dandelions, democratic daisies, escaped wallflowers, and blossoming twigs of elder had fought back against the pit-pall and grew in every crevice. The girls too had fought back.

Their breasts were budding beneath their striped cotton shirts and gymslips, and a pretty down sprang from their shapely arms. They made a striking couple, and they knew it. Bessie Bawtry was Angle-angel fair, her hair as soft as a silver-gold dying celandine or as sun-touched thistledown, and Ada Marr was as dark as a gypsy, with heavy plaits and olive skin and raven plumage. The light and the dark were they, the princesses of a Walter Scott romance. They bounced along: even the delicate and often listless Bessie had sap and spring in her step.

They paused at the canal bridge, and looked down at the barges. Their names were poetry, said Bessie, momentarily distracted from the theme of their discussion. There they lay— *Guiding Star, Providence, Persephone, Perseverance, Hope, Only Daughter* and *Fred.*

They laughed at *Fred.* 'You shouldn't call a boat *Fred*,' declared Bessie censoriously. 'You should never give a boat a boy's name. It's wrong.'

Bessie knew her grammar, Bessie knew her genders and her declensions. Bessie knew what was what.

Fred lurked, guilty, insulted, male, on the oily water.

Would Bessie rather have been an Only Daughter? Did she think she would have got more attention had Dora never been born? Bessie spent much energy negating Dora. But Bessie was not thinking of Dora as she gazed at the pretty, cherished blue and white longboat, with its pots of scarlet geraniums. She was thinking of romance.

Ada and Bessie were speaking of romance, as they hung briefly over the barrier of the bridge, then made their way on, across the canal, to the riverbank, to look for a picnic clearing. (The canal and the river met here, in confluence.) They were speaking, however, not of Philip Walters, nor of George Bellew, nor of Jimmie Otley, nor of Reggie Oldroyd, nor of Joe Barron, nor of any of the other stars of Form Five: they were speaking of literary romance. They had long outgrown Walter

Scott, who had engaged them when they were twelve and thirteen: they now regarded him as hopelessly old-fashioned. They had moved on, under the purifying influence of senior mistress and English mistress, Miss Heald, to the study of Elizabeth Barrett Browning. Miss Heald had been speaking of Mrs Browning's strange fate that very afternoon, and Bessie and Ada had been much taken by her story. Its strangeness defied the laws of probability. It defied sense.

Bessie and Ada were fortunate in their teacher Miss Heald, and they knew it. Miss Heald, with her Leeds degree, her long neck, her braided earphones of hair, and her pleasant, short-sighted, calmly efficient expression, was a marvel. Lest you should think it odd that Breaseborough Secondary School should employ a marvel, let it be said at once that this school, albeit in a later manifestation as Breaseborough Grammar School, was to produce within the next half-century a Nobel Prize winner, a Poet Laureate, a matinée idol, a champion racing driver and a couple of cabinet ministers. Such schools should not be written off. Talent cracks the asphalt, talent will not stay underground.

It is true that handsome red-haired freckled Joe Barron had recently added to Bessie's tiny autograph book the following lines:

> *Full many a gem of purest ray serene*
> *The dark unfathomed caves of ocean bear,*
> *Full many a flower is born to blush unseen*
> *And waste its sweetness on the desert air.*

But he had inscribed these lines because that was the kind of thing that nice boys used to inscribe in the autograph books of nice fifteen-year-old girls. Joe Barron had no intention at that stage of blushing unseen. Nor did he expect the enchantingly pretty Bessie Bawtry to do so either. It would be up and out for him, it would be up and out for her. Particularly if

Miss Heald had anything to do with it. Miss Heald was an ambitious woman.

The Great War and the Spanish influenza had murdered the lovers of Miss Heald and her generation, and therefore the energy and passion of Miss Heald and her generation poured forth like fierce ennobling rays on the young people of Breaseborough, of Doncaster, of Bingley, of Selby, of Grimsby, of York. They must move on, they must gain a better world, they must never slip through the cracks into the slough, the pit, the trenches. They must march into glory. So urged Miss Heald.

It was not so much the love story or the poetry that had animated Miss Heald, as she spoke of Elizabeth and Robert Browning. It was the miracle of the resurrection, the daring of the escape. From her sickbed Elizabeth Barrett, at the age of forty, had arisen. She had defied her father, and gone forth, and married, and eloped to Italy, and made love, and given birth to a child. Miss Heald found this sequence of events unlikely and astonishing. Miss Heald herself, in 1922, was forty-two years old, and it was unlikely that any Robert Browning would stretch out his hand to lead her like Eurydice from the grimy underworld of Breaseborough. Nor would she have wished for such a deliverance, for, despite the sociological accuracy of that statement about murdered lovers, it is not a statement that applied to the particular fate or inclinations of Miss Heald. She was happy single. She had a good job, and a position of power and influence. She had worked hard and travelled far to acquire superior qualifications, certificates and diplomas, and was in receipt of a more than adequate income. Her salary had risen steadily from £135 a year in 1908 to more than £300 a year by 1920: she was not as well paid as the male staff, naturally, but she had a higher salary than any of the other women teachers.

What would she want with a man? If she married, she would have to give up her job. That was then the rule. She was happier teaching. She enjoyed the respect of a town where the members of the middle class could be numbered in named dozens. She was independent. The daughter of a Unitarian minister who had warmly supported her in her career, she had a strong sense of mission and was fulfilling it. She was not lonely. She shared a home with Miss Haworth, who taught Latin, and had a First Class Honours degree from Leeds. On their joint incomes they lived comfortably and companionably. What more could they want?

As it happened, Miss Heald did not think much of Elizabeth Barrett Browning's poetry. She preferred Robert's. She was inclined to make fun of *Sonnets from the Portuguese,* and had never read *Aurora Leigh.* She was of the wrong generation—too late, too early—for *Aurora Leigh.* But she had discovered that one of Mrs Browning's most famous anthology pieces, 'A Musical Instrument', was a very successful teaching device. The younger children loved its pounding, repetitive rhythm, and its gloomy romantic rhetoric. It was a favourite for recitation choice.

> *What was he doing, the great god Pan,*
>   *Down in the reeds by the river?*
> *Spreading ruin and scattering ban,*
> *Splashing and paddling with hoofs of a goat,*
> *And breaking the golden lilies afloat*
>   *With the dragon-fly on the river...*

There was something touching and painful and pleasing to her in the sight of the young unformed faces, reciting, unapprehending, reverent, solemn, the painful lines of metamorphosis:

> *Yet half a beast is the great god Pan,*
>   *To laugh as he sits by the river,*
> *Making a poet out of a man:*
> *The true gods sigh for the cost and pain,—*
> *For the reed which grows nevermore again*
>   *As a reed with the reeds in the river.*

And then, with the older pupils one could discuss the weaknesses of the work—what, she would demand of them, was that odd word 'ban' doing there, apart from filling in a rhyme? Discuss. One could even, in the sixth form, prompted by the classical Miss Haworth, look at Ovid's version of the rape of Syrinx, who was transformed upon Pan's approach not into a poet but into a reed, or perhaps into a whole reed-bed? Into a plurality of about-to-be-raped maidens, a swaying generation of maidens awaiting the scythe?

But on balance Miss Heald preferred Robert Browning to Elizabeth. She was modern, and she favoured the masculine, because she was a feminist. She commended the virile intellect of Robert Browning, and had read some of the early dramatic monologues of T. S. Eliot. (She will be one of the earliest readers of *The Waste Land,* which will be published later in the year in Eliot's new magazine.) On the whole, Miss Heald tended to shy away from the romantic and the ladylike, and to go for the strong. But she was moved by the story of Elizabeth Barrett. E. B. B. had not been content to waste her sweetness on the desert air. With a quite unladylike determination she had sought pollination and borne fruit.

Miss Heald did not put it to her mixed-sex class in those terms, but that is how she saw the matter. And a sense of her perception had reached the highly receptive Bessie and Ada, who were now strolling along the riverbank, hoping to see fish lurking in the grimy water, and admiring the brave wayside flowers, the speedwell, the marguerite, the purple vetch. They were too delicate to speak of sexual matters very directly, but the story of the Brownings provided a convenient metaphor for speculation. What had it been like, to be so rapt, so ravished, after waiting for so long, after lying on a couch for so many years of waiting, like the Lady of Shallot? Had it been a shock to the nervous system? Had it *hurt*? What had it felt like, to escape from a darkened overfurnished Victorian sickroom in a tall dreary forbidding London street to the dazzling light of Florence? Neither of them had been to London or

Florence, but Miss Heald was familiar with both, and had tantalized them with vivid descriptions of these two contrasted cities. Bessie and Ada longed to visit London and Florence, and in the confidence of their youth they believed that one day they would. What would it be like, to escape from Breaseborough to Cambridge, to London, to Paris? To Jerusalem, to Jaffa, to Constantinople, to Ceylon? Would it all be glory and awakening? Or would it *hurt*? Prurience, innocence and desire struggled in their budding breasts as they walked along the verdant riverbank.

They were walking towards the neighbouring town of Cotterhall, which lay a couple of miles upstream. It was smaller than Breaseborough, and considered itself a cut above it socially as well as geologically. It was possessed of limestone cliffs, an ancient ruined castle and a bluebell wood. It housed fewer miners than Breaseborough, for it stood further from the pithead at Bednerby Main: its residents numbered schoolteachers, railway clerks, a piano tuner, a colliery manager, brewers, maltsters, confectioners, glass manufacturers and other prosperous tradesmen. The air was said to be good, up in Cotterhall. Oh, it had been pretty here once, when Bessie Bawtry's maternal ancestors had planted their crops and fed their beasts and drawn their water from Gospel Well: when they had milked their cows and churned their butter and winnowed their grain in the distant forgotten pastoral past. Now the whole landscape was mined and undermined, apart from this stretch of river green. Who owned this earth? Nobody that Bessie or Ada knew. They did not think of such matters. They took no interest in the means of production, though they were well versed in iambic pentameters, trochees and heroic couplets. Maybe it all belonged to the lord of the manor, as in the days of Robin Hood and the greenwood. Maybe it belonged to an absentee landlord. Maybe it belonged to the Wadsworths at Highcross.

For whom did the miners extract the coal? Bessie and Ada

did not know. It burned in their own grates, and they knew it did not come for free. Their parents paid good money to have it shunted down their coal holes and into their coal cellars, but they did not know who received that money. Was it the colliery manager, Mr Barlow, whose son was in the sixth form? That seemed unlikely. But they did not think much about these issues. They thought about Miss Heald, and Elizabeth Barrett Browning, and deferred pleasures, and School Certificate, and self-advancement. Whatever self-advancement meant for them, it had nothing to do with coal.

Miss Heald spoke sternly of the necessity of deferring pleasure. Work hard now, she said to her young people, and reap the rewards later. Do not grab the instant, like the sluts of Bednerby. The reason why those people live in such squalor is because they have not learned to defer pleasure. They cannot plan. They spend, they borrow, they waste. They are bad managers.

Can one defer pleasure for too long, so that it withers and dries up and tastes sour? No, said Miss Heald. That is the lesson we learn from the Brownings. There shall be a reward on earth, not the martyr's heavenly crown of gold. Work hard, and pass your examination, and it shall be yours. You too shall be happy and serene, like that wise Minerva, the clear-skinned, clear-eyed, bespectacled Miss Heald. Your pleasures will mature, like fine wine. A good education is never wasted. Poetry and prose will never fail you. A foreign language will never desert you. You will inherit the earth.

Did they believe her? The diligent and clever ones listened and believed. Their pleasure, she assured them, would be her pleasure. How proud she was of Keith Badger (do not titter, Badger is a good Yorkshire name, and not to be ridiculed)—of Keith Badger, who took a top County Scholarship and matriculated last year at the University of Northam. He will do well.

Certificates, matriculation, examinations, graduation. Difficult words, difficult concepts, a hill of difficulties, a ladder of steep steps, reaching upwards. Climb, climb, do not look backwards, do not stumble, do not lose heart, do not freeze with fear. Ignore the grazed knee, the scabs, the vertigo. Never look back, and never, ever look down.

Ada and Bessie turned a corner, ducking under a green branch that bowed heavily towards the water, and surprised three naked boys swimming in the murk. Little white frogs splashing. Ada and Bessie backed and froze, hiding in the dense leaves, but the boys sensed them, and giggled and hooted and waved cheekily, knee deep in the dirty river, splashing and flapping, throwing out showers of water drops, and through the water drops Bessie could see their little winkles, their chickenmeat legs, their white bodies streaked with black. Dirty water, filthy water. Too small to be frightening, but boys, naked boys. Carrot-topped little Saxons, white-skinned, underexposed, undeveloped. Escaped from underground, and frisking briefly in the sunlight. Bessie had never seen a naked boy, and hardly saw one now, through the sparkle and the confusion and the leaves. Ada, who had brothers, had seen many, and anyway, was she not a doctor's daughter? She was not to be turned back. 'Shoo!' she cried, advancing from her leafy retreat, waving her hands before her, protected by the striped carapace of her school shirt. 'Shoo, you boys, shoo, scram, shoo!' And the boys dog-paddled their way to the far bank, where their boots and heaps of grey garments lay, and waved and whistled and sniggered, hopping like little savages in sooty warpaint, as Bessie and Ada, eyes averted, themselves on the edge of nervous laughter, gathered themselves together, and braved the gauntlet, and marched on with their noses in the air.

Little doomed free spirits, coal babies, urchins.

'Whatever next?' said Bessie, demurely, maturely, once they were out of earshot of treble catcall and piercing wolf whistle.

'You can't blame them, it's hot,' said Ada, fanning herself

with a swatch of long grasses. She was perspiring and her school shirt was scratchy.

Bessie, who did not perspire, shuddered slightly. 'But still, the filth in that river,' she objected. 'How could they? They'll catch diseases.'

Bessie, on her first day trip to the seaside resort of Mablethorpe, had declared that the sand was 'dirty'. Which in those days it was not.

Now, on the banks of the Hammer, she was finding it hard to find a suitably hygienic picnic spot: those wild boys had disturbed her. But she agreed that they had walked far enough, and allowed Ada to select a clearing under a willow tree, where they spread out their cardigans as groundsheets. A marbled white butterfly settled on a tufted purple blossom and spread its wings for them. And there they sat, eating their doorstep sandwiches, watching the flow of the water and the dance of the insects, keeping an eye open for intruders and passersby, while they tested one another on French irregular verbs. 'Fear, Doubt, Shame, Pleasure, Regret, Surprise,' chanted Ada dutifully, as they revised the subjunctive. And so they were discovered, prettily disposed, by Joe Barron himself, who was wheeling his new Hercules bicycle from Gurney's.

He was accompanied by Alice Vestrey.

Joe, when he saw Bessie and Ada, blushed red under his freckles to the roots of his red hair. Alice Vestrey, in contrast, remained unnaturally cool, and pretended that there was nothing out of the way going on. And maybe there was not, for both Joe and Alice lived in Cotterhall, and there was no reason why he should not be walking Alice home on a fine summer afternoon. The four young people greeted one another: they were obliged to do so, for a couple of hours earlier they had all been studying Robert Browning in the same room, and therefore could hardly pretend not to know one another. Nevertheless, there was a mutual embarrassment. Perhaps Ada and Bessie thought that Joe might think that they had been lying in wait for him. Perhaps Joe felt that he should not be walking alone with Alice Vestrey after offering earlier that day to teach Bessie to ride his new bike. It was strange that they were all so confused, for Breaseborough Secondary School prided itself on its coeducational Yorkshire common sense. It did not go in for innuendo, flirtation or 'smut'. Yet confused they were, for a few moments, before bold Ada took the lead, and offered Alice a bite from her bun. No, no, demurred Alice, she had to get home, her mother would be wondering. So on upstream went Joe and Alice, at a slightly faster pace, and at a slightly greater distance from one another, separated by the shining chrome antlers of the Hercules, and after a while Bessie and Ada gathered themselves together and shook off the crumbs and thoughtfully made their way back to Breaseborough. Fear, doubt, shame, pleasure, regret, surprise... tentative half-feelings, subdued subjunctive feelings, rose and fell in their tentative half-grown bodies and undeveloped hearts. O poor young girls in flower, you poor frail darlings, who will watch over you, who will guide and protect you, and will you ever safely reach the happy bourn? Happy you have been this afternoon, but with so tentative, so frail, so pedantic a happiness, and now you are confused and disturbed even by that small happiness you have enjoyed. What chances have you of survival? Will the wind blow you away? Will you land on stony ground?

Ada will survive, we may feel sure, for she is robust, and she has confidence and courage: had she not, even in extremity, offered Alice a bite of her bun? Well may she dare and risk and conquer and multiply. But Bessie is delicate and she may wilt and fade before she reaches her goal. Is there enough persistence in her for the hard road ahead, for the steep climb and the airless altitudes, for the as yet undreamed of perils of those heady upper reaches?

They walk home, along the riverbank and the towpath. And the weeks pass, and the months pass, and the summers pass, and their bodies bloom: see them as they walk, the school blouse lifting, the ankles narrowing, the hips swaying, the lips reddening through art or nature, the little bead neck- let added to the throat, the butterfly brooch to the lapel, the bracelet to the wrist, as they walk through the seasons of their young life and their young hope (does hope too take the subjunctive?) towards whatever it is that awaits them—fame, love, loss, triumph, distress. And still it takes no shape as they walk towards it, it will not show its features to them, they wonder if it will ever show its features. Maybe it will for ever vanish out of sight, just ahead of them, around the corner, be- yond the branches, behind the trees, lost in the reeds and the willows. What is it, what will it be, will they ever see it face-to-face? Along this stretch and other stretches they will walk in constant flux towards it: their glands secrete and be- tray and settle, they lose weight and gain it and lose it again, they tan and they pale, they skip, they loiter, they recite Vir- gil and Verlaine and Lamartine, they quarrel and are recon- ciled, they laugh and they weep and they sulk, they crop their hair and then try to grow it again, they experiment with hem- lines and covet forbidden nail varnish and lipstick and smart sandals, they break out in spots and are suddenly smooth again, they blow hot and they blow cold, they catch trolley buses and trains and see silent movies and go to a theatre mat- inée and appear as Helena and Hermia in the school play and they write verse and join a debating society and win prizes and honourable mentions and receive decorous floral valentines. See them now, as they walk into view again along the banks of the Hammer, as they pass the clearing where two long years ago Joe Barron and Alice Vestrey surprised them at their French verbs.

⌇

Do they remember that distant afternoon? Perhaps they do, for it is towards Joe Barron's house that they now are walk- ing, where he now awaits them. They are grown girls now, and they no longer wear striped school shirts. They have just taken their School Certificate, in History, Latin, English and French, and school may no longer be their refuge and their sole field of endeavour and display. It is summer still, and the sun still shines, and the water curls and the midges hover, and spikes of foxglove lean to the water in this semi-rustic semi-industrial hinterland between townships, in this pause between past and future. The marbled white survives, and so does the friendship of Bessie and Ada. They have survived coolnesses and rivalry and the increasingly relentless ratcheting of Bessie's superior intellectual performance. They have chosen their own paths, and those paths will now diverge. Ada, obligingly, has an out-of-town admirer: she has met a young man down south with whom she corresponds. She will go to teacher training college in Saffron Walden. She will teach for two or three years, then she will marry her admirer. This is what she plans. Her future has a face. If her exam results are adequate, which they will be, she will cut free from Breaseborough, and rear her children in a more pleasant environment. She will do well in her School Certificate. She has not worked as hard as Bessie, but who has? Ada has worked hard enough. She has worked for freedom. She can parse and prose.

The Barrons still live in Cotterhall, of course, and will remain there for decades to come. And it is towards Laburnum House, the home of the Barron family, that Ada and Bessie now make their way, not as shy schoolgirls, but as invited guests. Mrs Barron has invited them to tea. It is a Saturday in late June. The weather is uncertain: as they walk, the sun clouds over. Perhaps it will rain. The girls are walking to Cotterhall by choice, but it is understood that one of the boys will escort them back. Perhaps they will be offered a lift in the new Morris Minor. (It has been rumoured that Elsie Scrimshaw has been seen on the back of Phil Barron's brand-new BSA motorbike: can this be true?) The girls are honoured by this invitation, and are dressed in their best: Ada colourful in a bright floral pink frock, Bessie ladylike in a pale blue and cream two-piece.

The Barrons are one of the most important families in unimportant Cotterhall. This is a neighbourhood without an aristocracy, and with very little of a middle class: there is a public house in Breaseborough called the Wardale Arms, and the hospital, built in 1906, is called the Wardale Hospital, but nobody ever spares much of a thought for the mythical and absent Lord Wardale, whereas there is much talk in town and roundabout about the Barrons. They have done well for themselves. Old Grandpa Bill Barron, recently deceased, had started work at the age of fourteen at Gospel Well Brewery, owned in those days by the Clarksons: he had become a foreman, married a Clarkson, and set up his own little bottle-making business in a warehouse and yard behind the stone quarry. It was long known as Barron's Yard. The business had prospered, and at this period prospers still. Under Bill's son Ebenezer (Ben) Barron the firm had diversified from beer and pop bottles to a range of cheap fancyware: cake stands, jugs, fruit dishes, sugar bowls, tumblers. These are attractive, tubby, friendly pieces, pleasing and familiar to the eyes of most of the locals, and the range does well. Should Ben think of introducing new lines, or should he stick with the old faithfuls? Eldest son Bennett Barron is keen on innovation, but so far he has not had much clout. Bennett has gone into the family business with vigour and ideas, and now he is beginning to get a little impatient with the old man, who is stubborn and will not listen to anything new. Bennett has been to London, to a trade fair at Wembley, where he has fallen in love with the new celluloids and phenolics, and with a magical semi-synthetic milk stone which he longs to manufacture and develop. He is sure it is the thing of the future. His father thinks celluloid is trash, and will not last. He will be certain that polymers are a dead end.

There are four boys in the family. There is go-ahead, industrious Bennett, a chip off the old block. Then comes philandering Phil, in theory in partnership with haulage contractor Stan Lomax, but in practice in love with his motorbike; he spends too much time roaring around the country lanes and over the moors and drinking in the Fox, the Three Horseshoes, and the Ferry Boat Inn. Alfred works for Castle Confections, for a maternal uncle: they specialize in liquorice toffee. Then comes Joe, the afterthought, who hopes, unlike his brothers, to be allowed to go to university. There are two sisters, Rowena and Ivy. Rowena works as bookkeeper for Ben and Bennett, having volunteered to replace a character known as Ratty Red who had been fiddling the figures. She is not very good at figures, but she is much better at them than Ben. She sits in a dark little office filling in ledgers, and is said to be saving up her earnings for a trip to the Holy Land. Ivy left school two years ago, and has done nothing much since, although she reads a great deal, writes poetry, has corresponded with Vita Sackville-West, and published radical verses about colliery disasters in the local paper. She would like to have gone to university, but nobody even thought of it. She intends to make something of her life, does Ivy, but when? How long, O Lord, how long?

Joe Barron is the baby of the family, the youngest of them all, and it is Joe who is now watching out for Ada and Bessie as they approach the gateposts and high walls of Laburnum House and make their way up its short drive. The walls are surmounted with a nasty boy-proof ridge of sharp-angled black crozzle, a waste by-product of the mining industry: this is decorated with dangerous splinters of broken glass, another product of which there is no shortage. This double defence is intended to prevent boys from breaking into the small orchard and raiding the apple trees and soft-fruit plot. But the house, behind its wall, is not hostile. Its porch is full of scarlet geraniums, and its doors stand open.

There Joe greeted his guests. He was past the blushing stage, and was now quite the young man, in his white shirt and grey flannel trousers. Quite the 'Anyone for tennis?' young man—and he was indeed good at tennis, which he played at the club with Ada's brother Richard, his brother Phil, and Ernie Nicholson from Sprotbrough. But tennis was far from his mind as he ushered the girls into the large drawing room, into the presence of his mother and Ivy. Joe was thought to be sweet on Bessie Bawtry, and Bessie was thought to return his admiration. Nothing serious, of course—they were too young for that. They were just practising.

Mrs Barron presided over her second-best teapot with nervous affability. Flora Barron was only in her fifties, though she thought of herself as an old woman, and looked and dressed like an old woman. Unlike Bessie's mother Ellen, she was thin, not stout: she was a bony, upright figure, and she sat forward on the edge of the chair, her back stiff to attention. She was dressed in a dark patterned maroon artificial silk which reached nearly to her ankles, for she had not even thought of adopting the shorter skirts of the younger generation. Her chest was flat, and seemed to sink and recede from her prominent collarbones. Her hair was grey and abundant: she wore it scraped back into a large bun, secured by a heavy imitation-tortoiseshell clasp and pin. This ornament was, in fact, made of celluloid, as many hair ornaments of the period were. The new plastic technology pierced Mrs Barron's bun, but despite Bennett's enthusiasm it had not penetrated many other corners of that predominantly Edwardian drawing room.

Mrs Barron poured tea for Ada and Bessie, for Rowena and Ivy, for herself and Joe. Bessie politely admired the teacups—botanical Spode, with an ornate pink patterning of twining foliage and stylized carnations and roses. Each cup had within its bowl, opposite the sipping lips of the drinker, a passionflower, though Bessie did not recognize it as a specimen of a species she had never seen. Passionflowers were not much cultivated in South Yorkshire. Bessie admired the Spode very much, and thought it in better taste than the Bawtry best, which consisted of a bright and vulgar Crown Derby with too much purple and gold and a lot of random spots. It must be said that Bessie also had a contempt for the Cotterhall-crafted Barron fancy glassware, which she thought horribly common. She was relieved not to find it on the Barron table.

(Where *did* Bessie get these notions? Who *did* she think she was?)

It appeared that Rowena was indeed planning to take herself off to sea on a luxury cruise. This year, next year, sometime. She was off to the Holy Land, though not for any very holy reasons, and would proceed thence through the Suez Canal and back round the Cape. Rowena went to look for the atlas, when the girls showed an interest, and traced her route with a thin white finger, pointing a sharpened manicured nail. It would be a lark. She would fly south like a swallow. On board was a swimming pool, a gymnasium, an orchestra. She had been saving up for ages and ages and ages. Father said he might chip in. Gertie Thomson from Broom Hill was hoping to go too, and they would share a cabin. Would the girls like to see the brochures? Yes, the girls certainly would. Bessie and Ada wiped their fingers delicately on lace-edged napkins, brushing off the crumbs of scone and jam sponge, and took in hand the lovely leaflets with their bathing belles and young men in boaters, and a promotional photograph of the Yorkshire cricket team and their lady wives playing quoits on the deck of the *Ormonde* as they sailed away to Australia.

Even Bessie and Ada, who had not yet reached this level of aspiration, were aware that ocean passages were advertised regularly in the pages of the *Breaseborough and Cotterhall Times*: tickets were available to 'all parts of the world' from the *Times* office in Bank Street. You could book yourself from here to there. From the dark hole of Breaseborough itself you could buy your voyage on the White Star Line or the Canadian Pacific, on the *Caronia* or the *Carmania* or the *Empress of Australia* or the captured *Berengaria* (once the German *Imperator*). You could embark for New York, Vancouver, Yokohama, Shanghai, Honolulu, Suva.

Will Rowena really sail away, or was this a daydream, a fantasy? Time will tell. The world was speeding up, and the great ocean liners were competing for custom and cutting their prices, eager to forget the Great War, eager to forget the sinkings of the *Titanic* and the *Lusitania* and the *Waratah*. This was the dawning age of the third-class traveller, now reclassified as a tourist. Steerage was no more. The schoolteacher, the student, the clerk and the shop assistant were being tempted onto voyages where they could simultaneously imitate and make fun of the idle rich. Restlessness was sweeping round the globe like influenza. In a few weeks, you could be in Australia, in New Zealand, on the far side of the pink Empire and the turning globe. Bands would play for you, and artistes would perform for you, and you could dance beneath the silvery moon as you were transported across the tepid tropical oceans. Or that was the idea.

Meanwhile, Joe Barron and the girls would wait for their examination results. All were expected to do well, but Mrs Barron, a kindly, diffident and self-effacing woman, was aware that for Bessie these results were of particular importance. Bessie was to stay on at school that autumn to sit her Cambridge entrance, and she would need a County Major Scholarship to finance her, if she were fortunate enough to get a place. It did not matter much what happened to Joe, for the family business could absorb him whatever happened, and Ada's family was willing and able to support her through teacher training college. But Bessie had nothing to fall back on. She was on her own, and she had to do well. How would this teacher's pet fare in open competition with the county and the country? Did she have time enough for study? inquired Mrs Barron. Oh yes, said Bessie, her parents were very understanding. She had her own little corner, her own worktable. She had plenty of encouragement at home, said shy, hard-working, pretty, tender little Bessie Bawtry.

Joe Barron had no intention of spending the rest of his life peddling cheap glass. But he was lying low, waiting for the right moment to confront his father. His father thought education a waste of time—he'd done all right without certificates, and set little store by schooling. In Ben Barron's view, the universities were overproducing, and creating a generation of idlers. Joe listened, but said nothing, as his mother gently probed Bessie about her prospects. He thought he could count on his mother to take his side if it came to a showdown. Joe was still his mother's pet. She had nursed him through a dangerous childhood bout of meningitis, and regarded him as her special baby. Mrs Barron did not approve of brother Phil's motorbike. She would stand by Joe.

Ivy, grumbling slightly, cleared the tea things onto the wooden trolley, and Ada helped her to wheel it away into the back regions. Rowena, in Ivy's view, never did anything to help. Rowena took out a violent-hued raffia basket of purple and acid-green which she was constructing, and Mrs Barron took up her embroidery—yet another linen tablecloth, which would join its companions in a drawer full of unused linen tablecloths and tray cloths and napkins and cushion covers. Joe Barron went over to the piano, and began to fool around to amuse the girls—'On wings of so-ong I'll bear thee,' he crooned, in his pleasant tenor, as he picked out the notes with two fingers,

> *Enchanted realms to see*
> *Come, O my love, prepare thee*
> *In dreamland to wander with me...*

'Oh, belt up, Joe,' said Ivy fondly, and she pushed him from the crimson velvet piano stool. Seating herself, arranging her skirt, wiping her fingers on her skirt, she took over from him and started them all off on 'Ye banks and braes of bonny Doon'. Bessie sat silent, for like her mother she could not sing, but she listened sweetly, perhaps a little too sweetly, as Ada, Rowena, Joe and Ivy raised their voices in mock lament and mock Scots accents: 'But my false lo-over sto-ole my rose, and a-ah he le-eft the thorn wi' me...'

Bessie glimpsed the banks of the Hammer, starred with white stitchwort and oxeye daisies. She saw white boy-bodies in the eel-dark water. She blinked and banished them.

They hammed it up, the young people, and Mrs Barron, proud matriarch, nodded and smiled.

Picture them there, in that airy but overfurnished Edwardian drawing room, with its low bow window, its stained and frosted and slightly phallic sub–Art Nouveau cock-and-balls grape-and-vine glass panels, its swagged plaster frieze, and its central plaster ceiling rose from which depended an inverted opaque frosted flower-stencilled glass bowl of a lampshade. In the glass bowl reposed a few fly corpses. Add large chairs, antimacassars, cushions, an embroidered firescreen displaying a peacock and lilies. Aspidistras, ferns, a curvaceous green-and-ochre pottery jardiniere. A busy floral carpet of blues and reds, and heavily fringed curtains of a goldish velvet. Occasional tables, highly polished. Bookcases with glass fronts, containing sets of Scott and Dickens, and well-read volumes of Victorian poetry. A tinted print of Cotterhall Castle, a Chinese screen, a sampler, a brass bell from Benares. A cluttered, old-fashioned, cumulative sort of room. The styles of the 1920s had not yet reached the drawing rooms of Cotterhall, and indeed seemed likely to bypass them altogether. There was no place here for the white and the straight and the pale, for the geometric, for the angles of Deco. All here was bulge and fringe. No wonder Rowena Barron was off to the Plain of Sharon and the dashing bounding remittance men of the Cape.

Slender Bessie Bawtry was not daydreaming. She was alert and tense, as she sat neatly on the edge of her chair, leaning slightly forward, listening to Ada's rendering of 'Pale Hands I

Loved Beside the Shalimar'. Her large periwinkle eyes were attentive, her knees and feet were carefully aligned and clamped together. She was a model of decorum, a little blue-eyed Dutch doll. Her soft straight silver-blond hair fell prettily from a low side parting, and was cropped at the nape of the thin stem of her neck in a short smart fashionably tapering shingle. Why was Bessie so anxious, so carefully censored, why was she sitting so much to attention? Nobody threatened Bessie here, nobody attacked her, nobody criticized her. Why could she not drop her guard for a moment? Why did she not dare to let her mind wander? Was she afraid of betraying some social ineptitude in this superior home? Did she suspect that Rowena thought she might be pursuing eligible brother Joe? Such a vulgarity would have appalled the delicate Bessie.

Ada Marr was stronger, thicker-set, more developed, more confident. She threw her head back as she belted out the Indian love song. There was a touch of the Indian in her dark colouring, and she thought it would be glamorous to have Indian or Spanish blood. Maybe she had: she sometimes voiced this hope to her other close schoolfriend and confidante, Leila Das, daughter of Dr Das of Sprotbrough, who was a bona fide Indian and the only coloured young person within a radius of thirty miles or so. How the Das family had made its way to Sprotbrough God alone knew, but there it was, well settled and respected. Leila did very well at school too, and was, unlike Ada, determined to follow in her father's footsteps and study medicine. This was not impossible, even in those days: one woman student from Breaseborough Secondary, a Dr Flora Hattersley, had already been practising for a couple of years in Jarrow. Leila had a double obstacle to overcome, of race and sex, but she did not seem to be aware of this.

Rather those hands were clasped round my throat
Crushing out life, than bidding me farewell!

yelled Yorkshire Ada, making eyes as she sang, by way of practice, at Joe Barron. But Joe Barron, handsome, clean-cut, blue-eyed ginger-haired Saxon Joe, had eyes only for pretty Bessie, perched anxious and vulnerable on the edge of her chair. Her neck was so thin it seemed to invite assault. It looked as though it would snap if you touched it. A blow from the side of a man's hand, and all would be over.

Joe Barron and Bessie Bawtry echoed one another in their fair tones and colouring. Had they evolved together through the centuries from this soil? And if so, would it not show greater genetic wisdom on Joe's part to pursue his opposite, and to make advances to the swarthy, thick-browed, lightly moustached Ada? In short, to marry out?

Mrs Barron seemed unaware of these dangerous undercurrents as she tapped her foot to the rhythms of the unseemly but drawing-room-accepted music that her younger daughter Ivy was bashing out from the slightly out-of-tune walnut upright with its little mauve pleated silk vest. Mrs Barron was stitching evenly and with satisfaction at a circle of brownish-cream linen trapped in a round wooden frame: she had chosen the transfer, of a Jacobean-style wreath of roses, from the excellent selection in the stall in Northam covered market, and was now filling in a leaf with a particularly delightful shade of moss-green silk. Stitch after stitch, strand after strand, she covered the linen. She could not have said why her embroidery gave her such pleasure. It distracted her from her worries about Phil and the motorbike and the girls. Phil had threatened to race on the Isle of Man. He had threatened to learn to fly an aeroplane. Stitch on, and choose a strand of carmine. Mrs Barron knew the numbers of the colours of all these silks. They repeated themselves in her innocent dreams like a litany.

Rowena was not sitting upright. She had dropped out of the group round the piano, leaving Joe and Ada to a duet. She was lounging, examining the cuticles of her oval nails. Hours of each day she spent examining her nails, pushing at the skin with an orange stick, filing, buffing, polishing. She would gaze at the little crescent moons as though she could read in them some augury, and would turn her ring finger slowly in the light as though displaying the refractions of an imagined diamond. Rowena lusted for a solitaire. She was lounging, one leg curled beneath her, the other provocatively extended. But there is nobody here to provoke. She twisted her ankle, admired its angles. Lord, how she loved her own legs. There were no legs like them in the whole of Hammervale.

Rowena was wearing a powder-blue Celanese dress with embroidery-garnished sleeves and embroidered panels in the bodice. She had thought it set off her fair complexion. But maybe, she now considered, it made her look insipid? Like that pale little Bessie Nobody? Perhaps she should try a bolder shade next time she went to Cole's? Elsie Scrimshaw was said to have been seen at the Rialto in red. Rowena Barron would be the talk of the town if she were to sally forth in red, for she was in a different class from Elsie Scrimshaw. What could Phil see in small-time small-town Elsie? Rowena hoped Phil would not let himself be trapped by scheming Elsie from Wath. He could do better than Elsie. Would red suit Rowena? Breaseborough and Cotterhall are brown and grey and navy and brown and fawn and tan. A splash of red would cheer things up. Scarlet town, scarlet woman, Californian poppy. The Vamp, the Temptress.

She yawned, as Joe came to the end of his rendering of 'Barbara Allen'. 'Hey, sister dear,' she said commandingly, to Ivy, who was leafing through the sheet music looking for yet another ballad of broken hearts, 'let's have something a bit more lively. This is the twentieth century, you know.'

But Ivy could not find anything more lively. The Charleston and the tango and the Black Bottom had not yet reached sedate Cotterhall. The Barrons had not yet purchased a gramophone. The raucous strains of 'California, here I come!' had, it is true, been heard in neighbouring Breaseborough, which to its own surprise had once boasted three music halls, of which two had recently been converted into picture palaces: but Bessie, Ada, Ivy and Joe did not frequent the music hall. So they were not well up in modern music, though they knew *The Messiah* and *Elijah* by heart. The wireless had not yet become a common household object, and the one remaining live theatre of Breaseborough, the Hippodrome, was more likely in those days to stage *Brigadoon,* or the works of Gilbert and Sullivan, or the Sequins and the Sunbeams, or the Merry Arcadians—already dreadfully old-fashioned nostalgic acts. The people of Hammervale, it was said, did not know how to enjoy themselves. Breaseborough was known in the business as the comedian's grave, and even the hardened Carl Rosa Opera Company dreaded it. The legendary Gracie Fields said Breaseborough was the worst town she'd ever played, and that was saying something.

At least it was saying *something,* not nothing. Breaseborough could be proud of being the pits.

How had this come about? Could one blame a chapel-going puritanism, a contempt for and fear of the life of the senses, which had seeped into the soul and soil of the land, leaching out colour, poisoning the wells? Respectable people did not sing and dance. And if they must sing, let them sing hymns, or sacred oratorio, or lovesick ballads of betrayal and death.

Perhaps this spirit was imposed from above, as a convenience, as an opiate for a depressed populace. Those that may not enjoy, let them not seek enjoyment. That thousand-fold increase in the nineteenth-century population of Breaseborough had not come there to have fun. It had been dragged in by need, as a servile workforce. Meekly it had taken itself underground to dig. Those who may not enjoy, let them not even wish to enjoy. No wonder the preachers born of the industrial revolution found texts in Isaiah, in Jeremiah, in Ezekiel. For what had the prophets said of Hammervale? 'I will give it into the hands of strangers for a prey, and to the wicked of the earth for a spoil; and they shall pollute it. My face will I turn from them, and they shall pollute my secret place' (Ezekiel 7:21–2). 'And it shall come to pass, that instead of a sweet smell there shall be stink; and instead of a girdle a rent; and instead of glossy hair there shall be baldness; and instead of fine embroidery there shall be sackcloth; and burning instead of beauty' (Isaiah 3:24). Why, the Old Testament must have been written with a denunciatory finger pointing at South Yorkshire.

So it was not surprising that Rowena Barron, as she admired her own fine-turned ankles and rounded calves, as she caught the late-afternoon light on her shell-pink nails, should have nurtured strange fantasies of the Promised Land. She would escape from this vale of abomination and dullness, this cesspool of boredom, where there were no dance tunes, and she would set sail for the Land of Milk and Honey, for Cyprus and Damascus, for Salamis and Ashqelon. Aboard a Cunard or a White Star liner, beneath an orange moon, she would swoon and spoon and flirt amidst the scents of cedar and jasmine. Behold, thou art fair, my love: thy two breasts are like two young roes which feed among the lilies. Thou hast ravished my heart, my sister, my spouse: how much better is thy love than wine! A fountain of gardens, a well of living waters, and streams from Lebanon . . . How beautiful are thy feet with shoes, O prince's daughter!

Little red shoes, perhaps, from Cole's or Cockayne's?

Yes, Rowena had ransacked the Bible for its erotic spoils, she had confounded her own body with the body of the Church. She had searched through *Cruden's Complete Concordance,* gilt-edged and bound in blue leather, for breasts, of which there were many (though not all of them very attractive), and for ankles, of which there were none. Like Bessie Bawtry, even the vain and fun-loving Rowena had been driven to the Bible. For we must find our sustenance where we may.

The rain continued to fall upon the garden, and Mrs Barron expressed regret that the young people would not be able to go out to pick the raspberries which were ripe and dropping from the cane. (Bessie glanced at the darkening sky gratefully: raspberries were full of maggots and infested by blue flies and rudely copulating metallic green hoppers, raspberries were soft and squashy and disintegrated in the fingers into little bloody sacs, raspberries stained one's best dress and got one into trouble. Bessie had had bad experiences with raspberries.)

The afternoon was turning awkward, as it moved towards evening. The young people did not know how to get out of Mrs Barron's presence, and she seemed reluctant or unable to release them. Ivy slammed down the piano lid, irritated by her sister's yawning and stretching, irritated by Bessie's meekness. Rowena yawned again and picked up her raffia basket. Where were the boys with the motorbikes, where were the big brothers? Rain fell, and raspberries rotted. Silence seeped into the room, and Ada involuntarily looked at her watch: it was twenty past the hour, the time of an angel's passing. Into the silence, Mrs Barron suddenly said, addressing Bessie, 'And how's your sister Dora?'

Bessie opened her big blue eyes in surprise and turned her head slowly towards Mrs Barron. Nobody ever asked after Dora. What could Mrs Barron possibly want to know about Dora?

⌒ɯɯɔ

How slow life was in the past. How it dragged. How heavily those silences fell. A sermon could last a lifetime, a forty-minute algebra lesson could eke itself out for centuries. A baby, left to cry itself to sleep, as babies so often were, could endure an extended agony of bereavement in half an hour, and a small child could count the seconds through a long night-watch of terror, and nobody thought to comfort or to care.

Hell was on earth, and it was the common lot, and it was to be endured.

But, in the early years of the twentieth century, things were at last beginning to speed up. Machinery had begun to click and whizz, and in the wake of the Industrial Revolution came movement, displacement for its own sake and global travel. One short generation took the industrialized world from horse and cart and pony and trap to railroad and steamship, and from that point we had galloped onwards, to bicycle and motorcycle and trolley bus and tram car, to motorcoach, motorcar, airship and aeroplane. Movement grew cheaper and cheaper. There was no need now to stay stuck in the same valley for centuries, for millennia. You could clamber out now, however steep the sides. Phil Barron dreamed of flying, and fly he will. Ellen and Bert Bawtry fell in love with their phallic Royal Enfield and its rattling sidecar: Bert would polish and tinker for hours of happiness, and mending punctures was to him a joy. Already, in Bessie's young womanhood, the heroic journeys of Dickens and Twain, of Trollope and Matthew Arnold and Oscar Wilde, were beginning to look commonplace rather than heroic. The world was on the move, and the age was dawning when our astral bodies would flap wearily behind speeding jumbo jets, never able to catch up with ourselves. Successful authors would be forced to circle the globe on unceasingly repeating biennial book tours as though the convenience of the written word had never been invented. One form of restlessness begets another.

Speed would reach even Hammervale, Breaseborough and Cotterhall. The slow years would be no more. If you didn't like it where you were, you could go somewhere else. Couldn't you?

Dr Hawthorn, who is now at last about to be discovered, some decades later, in Breaseborough, beside his giant computer screen, is not interested in the long, slow, unpleasant past, that dull past from which we will now take a period of leave. He is a post-Gutenberg, post-word, up-to-date Internet man. He is interested in migrations, but not in the migrations of words or ideas. He operates, across time, with unimaginable celerity. His subject could be said to be a form of that old-fashioned pursuit called genealogy, but Dr Hawthorn does not have to waste time on handwritten records illegibly transferred to microfilm, he does not have to sweat it out in public record offices inspecting census returns and birth, marriage and death certificates. He does not have to battle foolishly and noisily with faulty machines and snappy, bad-tempered, snaking spools of slippery sepia, attracting disapproving stares from those who have laboriously mastered the interim technology of ancestor retrieval. Dr Hawthorn has already left all that behind him. When he wants to find out where somebody comes from, all he has to do is to plunge a needle into bone or tissue, and extract some DNA. You can be six thousand years in your grave, but Dr Hawthorn will track you down.

Well, perhaps it's not quite as easy as that, though he is so thrilled by the implications of the new developments in molecular biology that he would like you to think it is. He is a champion of the new, a proselytizer, a prophet. Behold him as he stands there, in the now largely disused hall of the Wesleyan Methodists—it is that very room where bored little Bessie Bawtry once sat listening angrily to children's Sunday school sermons about virtuous little boys saving drowning babies from canals, while she idly popped the varnished blisters on the bench in front. Behold him, proud and powerful, as he prepares to unfold the wonders of his genealogical research! He is slight and light of stature, and grey of hair, but that grey hair bounds in exuberant curls irrepressibly from his small neat round head, a thick springing crop, borne upwards by its own momentum: he is a man of fire and wire and sinew, and his slightly protuberant blue-grey eyes flash with fervour at his audience while he propounds the amazing capacities of his computer, the novelty of his project and the implications of his experiment, and describes the help which he wishes to enlist from those who are gathered here together on this significant Saturday in June. 'We're all in this together!' he cries happily, with boyish, impish, gnomelike fun. His face shines with manic happiness. He talks too fast for some of his slow audience, but most of them, even those who can hardly follow him at all, are carried along by his high spirits. 'This is a grand opportunity,' he keeps repeating, 'a grand opportunity' (does that usage of the word 'grand' loop back to link him to his Yorkshire heritage?) 'and we're all about to make history. We *are* history, every man, woman and child of us, every grandmother, every niece, every auntie, every babe in arms! We're all part of one big happy family! I know a lot of you may have groaned when people went on about happy families—*I* used to groan myself, believe you me, and family duty was never a strong suit with me—but this business has given a whole new fascinating, fascinating, *fascinating* meaning to the family! Thanks to Mr Cudworth' (here familiar, friendly Mr Cudworth, a quieter-mannered gentleman, more the sort that most of them were used to, smiled in acknowledgement), 'thanks to Mr Cudworth, I've been able to assemble you all here—all the Cudworths, all the Bawtrys, all the Badgers, and all the rest of you that fit into this astonishing pattern of kinship, and we're going to compile a historic survey that will stand beside the Domesday Book! The new Book of Doom is being written even now, here and now!'

And Dr Hawthorn presses yet another button on his machine, and brings up yet another array of chemical formulae, of double helices, of arrows and circles and flashing conjunctions, more thrilling to Dr Hawthorn than any one-armed bandit in Las Vegas or in the floating casinos of the Midwest, more childishly exciting than any game of road revenge in the Happy Eaters and Little Chefs of the roadway, than any pinball machine in any smoky pub of the West Riding. This machine means more to Dr Hawthorn, and, in his view, to

humanity, than the sophisticated computerized defence pro-
grammes of the Pentagon. This machine will answer the riddles
of time itself!

The watchers blink in bewilderment, and some of them
giggle nervously, but they are impressed. Dr Robert Hawthorn
is impressive. He is the real thing. He is a millionaire and a genius and he is on his way, with their help, to win the Nobel
Prize for Molecular Biology. He may sound like a salesman—
he may even, in his smart casuals and his bright light brown
suede shoes, *look* just a little like a travelling salesman—but
he is not trying to sell them anything, as far as they can tell.
He is, instead, trying to take something from them—though
with, he assures and reassures them, their full cooperation and
consent. He begs swabs from their cheeks, he beseeches tissue
from their grandmothers' skeletons, he pleads for their secret
formulae, he wants their DNA. He is flash, he is brilliant, he
is light on his feet, he is eloquent: but he does come from
Yorkshire. This little pocket wizard with his mid-Atlantic
accent is a grandson of Breaseborough by maternal descent.
His mother had known its back alleys and its waste lots and
its cinder paths and its recreation grounds, and he himself
had often been to stay with his Breaseborough granny. As a
naughty thieving boy he had scaled the forbidding high
crozzle-topped walls of Mrs Barron's orchard, and skinned his
knees to steal the Barron apples, and been bawled out for the
offence. Mr and Mrs Barron are long, long dead, and at rest,
if rest it be, in the Nonconformist cemetery on Swinton Road,
but one of their direct descendants is here now, ready to offer
her secretions in the name of science.

Dr Hawthorn does not at first glance look very like a
grandson of Breaseborough, nor does he appear to have much
in common with most of this commonplace congregation.
Strong tea, powdered instant coffee, egg and cress sandwiches,
bridge rolls and squares of Madeira and fruit cake are not his
daily fare, and sharp-eyed young Faro Gaulden, who hopes

that she herself also sticks out like a sore thumb from this assembly, can almost see a think-balloon hanging over his head which says 'Jesus, do they *still* eat iced buns up here?' Though the spread, in fact, had been carefully judged by the thoughtful master of ceremonies, Bill Cudworth, who knows that the older folk here—and there are a lot of those, in the nature of the exercise—would not appreciate anything too newfangled.

Faro Gaulden is glad she came. Unlike most of those here, she is not a local, though she has local roots. She is here with a dual purpose, in part to accompany her Great-Aunt Dora, and in part to find out about Dr Hawthorn's project, in which she has a professional as well as a personal interest. And she is also here in order to get away from London and from her onetime so-called ex-partner Seb. She will have to ring Seb when she gets back to her hotel room. At least she will have something new to tell him about. Seb has been getting her down horribly of late. She does not know what to do about Seb. She doesn't know how she could have let him become such a problem to her. She shuts the thought of him from her mind, and concentrates on what is around her.

The genetic pattern manifested in the clever Dr Hawthorn—thick curly grey hair, slight bones, short stature, a large nose in a small face—does not seem to be repeated anywhere else in the room. Dr Hawthorn must inherit his genius and his physique from the non-Breaseborough branch. On the other hand, the Cudworth-Bawtry type is well represented here. Faro notes the obese, waistless, bosom-heavy, thick-jowled, loose-skinned, round-nosed, double-chinned and stolid Cudworths, and knows that she is of them. She has Cudworth-Bawtry blood in her veins and their DNA throughout her structure. She cannot pretend that she has not got a big bust. Is that what she will look like if she lives to be fifty? God, she hopes not. Pity she ate that second egg sandwich. Faro shuts her eyes for a moment and conjures up the image of her red-haired mother, still a presentable woman, and the memory of her dead and dissolute father, famed as the most handsome man in Europe. Then she glances, sideways, at stout Auntie Dora with her swollen legs. Quite a genetic battle to be fought, between the Bawtry-Cudworths and the Gauldens. Can one *will* oneself to favour one side of the family rather than the other? What would Lamarck have said? In Faro's case, she has to admit, there is bad blood on both sides. Pity she has to take after any of them. The weight of the flesh, the breeding in the bone. Pity one cannot spring from nowhere, or from fire or wind, like a phoenix or a flower.

That good-looking Indian in the back row, hiding behind tinted glasses and making notes in his notebook, seems to have sprung more or less from nowhere. He can't be a Breaseborough man, can he? What is he doing here? Is he a reporter, or a spy? wonders Faro. Or is he an archaeologist from Northam? He looks vaguely familiar, like someone she might have seen on telly. Perhaps he's a cricketer? Perhaps he's a Cudworth by marriage?

The Cudworths are the largest named group in the assembly, for the meeting has been organized by Bill Cudworth, who happens to be the president of the Cudworth One-Name Society. You can't tell much from looking at Bill Cudworth, as he is almost aggressively nondescript and average. He is Mr Everyman, five foot ten, eleven stone, brown-haired, fair-skinned, lightly freckled, round-faced, bespectacled, affable, comfortable, comforting and utterly English, in his grey weekend trousers, his checked Viyella shirt, his sports jacket. He is the respectable essence of respectable Cudworth. Unfortunately, bearing the name of Cudworth does not in itself guarantee one an important place in the new Domesday Book, for, as Dr Hawthorn has tried to explain, he is primarily interested in matrilineal descent, which in Britain at least has little to do with naming. Nevertheless, the Cudworths and their ready-made groundwork network will come in very handy for research purposes, and they can all look forward to the day when they will be invited by the Cudworth chapter in Argentina, or requested as guests by the Cudworth Congress in Iowa City.

Iowa City is represented here today, as those who have consulted the charts and read the labels have already discovered. Some of the locals have introduced themselves to Iowa Man, who has appeared here in the shape of a curly-headed young-middle-aged Cudworth who teaches business studies at the University of Iowa. He has come here to visit his roots. (He is also here in a professional capacity to explore the possibility of setting up a joint degree course with the University of Loughborough, but nobody here has shown much interest in that. Some of them have been to Loughborough, but they do not speak highly of it. Nothing much goes on in Loughborough, according to the parochial people of Breaseborough, though one of them concedes that it is 'a nice clean town'.)

Argentina, in contrast, has not made it to this reunion, for Argentina is a very long way away, almost as far as Australia, and the airfares are a good deal more expensive. Dr Hawthorn has been interested to learn that the legend of the black sheep of the Bawtrys, who emigrated to Buenos Aires, is still remembered here, a century and a half later. He'll try to catch the Argentinian Bawtrys next time he's flying through. Australians and New Zealanders are here, but then Australians and New Zealanders are everywhere these days. They seem to spend their lives on the wing, taking after their native albatross, restless, round the world with unshut eye, unable to settle, back and forth, on cut-price tickets bought in bargain bucket shops, trying to find out more about why their ancestors had to get away in the first place.

A rum mixture of people, in this hot chapel hall. Rum, but not at all random. They are carefully selected. There ought to be some meaning here, if only one could read it. Faro looks around, with an eye for dress codes rather than physique, and notes a quaint variety of English summer wear—

flower-patterned skirts worn with contrasting flower-patterned blouses, lace collars and shapeless cardigans, plimsolls patterned with flowers, scarves patterned with flowers, handbags and tote bags decorated with flowers. The Cudworths seem fond of flowers. Paisley is also in evidence. Faro's grandma had favoured paisley. Several of them wear what she guesses to be old National Health glasses with identically tinted pinkish-blue frames—does that represent a deep genetic pattern of taste, or merely the stock once favoured by the local optician?

Dr Hawthorn now tells them that one of the most interesting riddles facing humanity lies not in the future but in the past. 'How did we get *here* from *there*?' This is the question which, in its many aspects, obsesses him, and it must interest them, or they would not be here at all, would they? The future lies in the past, argues Dr Hawthorn. (He speaks very fluently, perhaps too fluently: Faro Gaulden from London and Peter Cudworth from Iowa City, who are more accustomed to listening to public speakers than most of those here today, wonder if there is not perhaps a touch of the charlatan about him, but both, independently—for they have not yet been introduced—dismiss this suspicion as unworthy: the gift of the gab does not necessarily make one a bad scientist, does it?) The very future of our species may lie, repeats Dr Hawthorn, in our correct interpretation, with all the new tools now available, of the data of the past. Where we come *from* is the most interesting thing that we can know about ourselves.

Some look doubtful at this suggestion. Of more immediate interest to some here is the result of the Yorkshire versus Australia cricket match currently being played at Headingley, or an anticipated pint of beer at the Glassblowers Arms, or a smoke on Castle Hill, or a coupling with some other Bawtry or Barron or Cudworth. Indeed, some may even have been contemplating a coupling with a far-flung Walters in Mexborough, or a Melia in Rotherham, or an Applebaum in Sheffield, or a Woolfson in Wath. They are not all stick-in-the-muds, not all stay-at-home slugabed intermarried untravelled folk. Some of them have been to places and seen the world. Some of them have come from places, and are wishing they were back there.

For Dora Bawtry, the distant past is of very little interest, and she is half sorry she was persuaded to come and listen to all this claptrap. She wouldn't have come if Faro hadn't chivvied her. Her immediate preoccupation is how and when to try to get back to the ladies' toilet, and whether she can get there before anyone else does. She hates a queue. She cannot wait in a queue. How annoying it is, she reflects—the older she gets, the more frequently she has to 'go', and the slower she is at getting there. It's not right. No more quick nips to the outside lav in the yard during the commercials—it's the slow hobble now on treacherous ankles, the leaking bladder, the soggy knickers, the wet tights. She can't smell the smell, because she can't smell anything now, but she fears others may. She just hopes she can last out, but this little chap seems able to talk for ever. He could talk the hind leg off a donkey. What's that he's got up there now? A skull, it looks like. She shuts her eyes, and tries to tighten her slack and aged pelvic muscles.

A skull does now fill the screen, a virtual, ancient skull, projected and rotating as it were in three dimensions—how do they do *that*? It is all very clever. (Auntie Dora's mind drifts back, semiconsciously, for a thousandth of a second, to a wonderful wooden machine—was it called an epidiascope?—which Ada Marr's mother had found in the attic when they bought the new house at the top of Ardwick Street. It was a sort of magic lantern. She'd let the girls play with it. You put postcard views in it—the front at Scarborough, Filey Brigg, the bandstand at Harrogate—and turned a handle, and it all went 3-D and the little characters along the promenade or the pier almost seemed to move.) It is all very clever, and Dr Hawthorn is explaining that although the skull is very ancient, you can't tell it's ancient from its shape, or from the slope of its forehead. This isn't a Neanderthal skull, with a heavy brow-ridge and a receding chin. Anatomically, it is a modern cranium, a *Homo sapiens* specimen. 'There was plenty of room in that dome,' Dr Hawthorn points out, 'for a Breaseborough Grammar School–worthy brain.' (Polite laughter, though all the locals note that this comment dates Dr Hawthorn, whose cranium contents belong to the period before the school went comprehensive and was renamed plain Breaseborough School.) 'Yes,' repeats Dr Hawthorn, 'this, before you, is Stone Age Man.' A twenty-two-year-old, eighty-centuries-old Stone Age Man, killed eight thousand years ago, in approximately 6000 B.C., by a blow to the back of the head, and laid to rest in a limestone cavern beneath the cliffs of Cotterhall. Peacefully he had reposed there through the Stone Age, the Bronze Age, the Iron Age and the Age of Coal: by chance neither miners nor potholers had disturbed him, and he might never have been discovered, had not a combination of circumstances brought him to the light of modern day. 'Many of you here will re-member,' he urged, 'the proposal to turn old Bednerby Main and the lower stretch of the Hammervale Valley into a landfill site, for many of you were involved in the successful campaign to arrest and stop it, and many of you supported the rival pro-posal to reclaim the land, in what has now become known as the Hammervale Millennium Earth Recovery Project. Stone Age Man might have been blasted to pieces by the landfill operation, or he might have lain secretly in his sealed tomb for ever, above the new wetland gardens, the new school centre, the (as yet unfinished) sculpture garden, the recently opened organic restaurant. But, as most of you have heard—you saw the headlines—a young worker on the Earth Project, scrambling around up there of an evening, put his foot through a chim-ney and discovered the hollow chamber and the miraculously preserved skeleton, of which this is the skull.' (He clicks a but-ton.) 'And here, here we have the whole man, as he was found by Steve Nieman last year. Here he is, as he was found, resting on his shelf of stone.'

The site had been opened up, and excavated, Dr Hawthorn continues. The skeleton had caused a small sensation, for such finds were rare so far south in Yorkshire. He had been brought to the light of day and the electronic age by a team from the Natural History Museum and Northam University. He had been nicknamed Steve by the popular press, after his discoverer, Steve Nieman. More scientifically, he is now known as Cotterhall Man, and now he lies in state in superfine atmospheric conditions in a glass coffin in Northam. Like Sleeping Beauty, awaiting the Resurrection.

Who was he? From what tribe, from what people, from what culture? He cannot be of the tribe of Nieman, for Steve Nieman is Jewish, and his family come from Riga. But he might be related, Dr Hawthorn explains, to many people in this room.

Cotterhall Man, according to Dr Hawthorn, is physically not very different from the Cudworths and Badgers and Bawtrys of today. If you were to dress him up in Breaseborough School uniform, he would pass muster. But what could have been his world picture, what landscapes would he have surveyed? Dr Hawthorn spoke of ice ages and pre-Celtic cultures and the Indo-European names of rivers, encoding languages and peoples now for ever forgotten—unless memories lingered on in the bone, in the tissue, in the DNA of the Cudworths, the Barrons, the Badgers?

In the year 8000 B.C., at the end of the last Ice Age, Yorkshire, said Dr Hawthorn, must have been intolerably cold. (That drew an appreciative laugh, on this warm early-summer day.) The landscape had been of the utmost desolation. He conjured up wastes of miry clay strewn with ice-borne boulders, ridged with mounds and sprinkled with tarns in the hollows. Frost-riven highlands, great sheets of water drowning the vales. But slowly the climate had relented, and the earth had begun to blossom with bracken, dog's mercury and cow wheat, with nettles and rosebay willowherb, with ash and hazel and lime and birch. Red deer, roe deer, wild pig, wolves, aurochs and Cotterhall Man had roamed the hillside. Pike and salmon had bred in the rivers. Utmost desolation had given way to milder climes, to biodiversity, to hunting and gathering, to burial rites, to long barrows and round barrows, to flints and pots and beakers. Wildwood had yielded to coppiced oak on the clayland of the Coal Measures. Cultures had succeeded cultures. Fire, charcoal, bronze, iron, glass, coal. The earth had given up its secrets. 'BUT,' said Dr Hawthorn, his eyes luminous and prominent with the passion of his query. 'BUT—how were *we* linked with *him*? Which of us here grew from him? What impulse propelled us forth from him? Newcomers poured into Hammervale, during and after the Industrial Revolution, and some left Hammervale—for Iowa, for Argentina, for Sydney, for Wellington, for Tottenham and Southend. Some had even crossed the Pennines.' (Mild, obedient laughter.) 'But some of us stayed on! Which, and why?'

Faro Gaulden, at the unnatural clamour of his insistence (for why does *he* care so much?), felt a shiver go through her, as though someone had stepped on her grave. What was it to him? He, like herself, was only a grandchild of Breaseborough. She found Dr Hawthorn unsettling. He had issued a call to arms. She really didn't much want to respond.

Dora Bawtry, like many of the older folk, had been mildly distressed by the too-present, too-pressing apparition of the skull, too obviously a *memento mori* at her advanced age. She struggled to her feet, reached for her stick, and began to make her slow way back to the ladies' toilet. 'Shall I come with you?' whispered great-niece Faro. 'I'll manage,' grunted Dora ungraciously, as she stumped off.

Faro Gaulden pulled herself together. She sat upright on her wooden chapel chair, pulled in her belly, straightened her shoulders and blinked several times, rapidly. Her eyes, like Dr

Hawthorn's, were large and shining, though much darker in tint than his: his are hazel, whereas hers are a deep, unreal, violet blue. (Could she, others often wondered, be wearing dyed contact lenses?) Faro Gaulden, all glowing O eyes, all round breasts, Faro Gaulden, with purple-painted toes and straining poppers on her bright cyclamen shirt, Faro with indigo-outlined eyes and dark-blue-painted lashes, Faro with curls and bedazzle and golden hoop earrings, all expectation and vigour, in the prime of her middle youth—how did Faro Gaulden get here from there? Why is she sitting in the dusty hall of a dying cult on a fine spring afternoon, instead of being out at play? And how did she get to be called a damn silly name like Faro?

To find the answer, we must track backwards down a winding path. We need not go as far as Cotterhall Man, nicknamed Steve, but we must return to Bessie Bawtry, back in the 1920s. Bessie Bawtry was, you will recall, anxiously waiting for news of her Higher Certificate examination results, and preparing, if they are good enough (as Miss Heald assures her they will be), to go back to school for one further term to sit her Oxford and Cambridge examinations in November. As we rediscover her, in late summer, she has made progress: she has matriculated with distinction (Joint Matriculation Board) in four subjects, and has been awarded a State Scholarship and a County Major Scholarship from the West Riding County Council, which will pay her way through university: £190, *per annum,* will be hers for four years. The school as a whole has done well and the *Breaseborough Times* has written a congratulatory leader, declaring that 'clever boys and girls abound amongst us, chiefly in the humblest homes'. It has also issued warnings about the overcrowding of the teaching profession and the expensive training that is going to waste as young people fail to find suitable jobs. The Depression looms, even for the newly educated, though not many realize it is on the way. Few of the teachers at Breaseborough are yet much concerned about the unemployment figures (rapidly mounting) of glassworkers and miners, though many of their own pupils are the sons and daughters of glassworkers and miners, and will expect to find work at the pit or the pithead, on the railways, in the bottle factories. The teachers are understandably more concerned with their best products, their sixth-formers, their university candidates, than with the rank and file.

Joe Barron, incidentally, has had an unpleasant surprise. He has unaccountably failed to get a County grant, and his father, pointing at the lazy overqualified youth of Cotterhall (well, at one lazy scapegoat youth of Cotterhall called Ivan Watson, who has done nothing with his Leeds degree but loaf about and play tennis at his father's expense), Joe's father, pointing at Ivan, insists that he has no intention of supporting Joe while he goes to university. Joe can go into the family business, like his brother Bennett. Barron Glass needs a travelling salesman. Let Joe get on his bike or into the family van and sell glass.

No such halfway fate is in store or indeed on offer for Bessie. Nor will she be claimed, as will many of her female classmates, by a future of 'home duties'. For her, it is college or death. Much has already been expected of her, and now yet more is at stake. Her parents, unlike Joe's, back her. Why? Is it because they are humbler and poorer than Joe's father, and therefore more trusting? They have faith in the headmaster, Mr Farnsworth, and in the senior mistress, Miss Heald, for they are important people in the town. These two have faith in Bessie, therefore Ellen and Bert have faith in them. If Mr Farnsworth and Miss Heald think Bessie can make it, then she can. Mr Farnsworth and Miss Heald know the ropes. They know all about admissions policies, and grants, and interviews, and examination boards. Mr Farnsworth himself has a

Cambridge degree. Leeds and Sheffield and Northam and Bingley are not good enough for Bessie, their prodigy. (They alone know that in the secret national register of marks, 'never on any account to be seen by the pupil', Bessie has scored some marks so high that they are almost off the map.) Bessie must go forth like a dove from the ark across the swollen waters. She may come back to visit, to attend reunions, to present prizes on speech days, but forth she must go. Dissatisfaction is slumpily brewing in South Yorkshire, and Bessie must depart.

The strain of all this makes Bessie feel sick. But she cannot resist the pressure. She accepts it, gives in to it. She is taken over by it.

Her parents are a little in awe of their daughter, though they try not to show it. How can they have produced this swan child? Is she a freak, a throwback, a throw-forward? They support her. They might well not have done, but they do. Breaseborough Secondary School has indoctrinated them well.

Nobody has any high expectations of little sister Dora. Dora, of course, is not as clever as Bessie, or so everyone assumes. She has to struggle to keep up at school, and finds Latin and Botany difficult, though she manages a Pass in both, she cannot think how. (She passes with Credit in English, French, Mathematics and Geography, but thinks that too must have been a bit of a mistake—or perhaps everyone gets a Credit?) Dora prefers needlework, and is disappointed not to receive higher praise and higher marks for her collars and buttonholes and garment repairs. When Dora thinks about her future, she thinks she might like to be a dressmaker, like her Ferrybridge aunt or Auntie Florrie in Makin Street, or to run a little corner shop and sell potted meat and jelly babies, like Auntie Clara. Or she might like to marry and have some real babies. She likes babies. She walks a neighbour's baby round the cemetery on a Sunday afternoon. (Bessie thinks this is mad, and says so.) She also likes to borrow Auntie Florrie's dog. She likes dogs, and cats, and canaries, and all small pet creatures. She has small, domestic dreams. Dora is at home in Breaseborough. Breaseborough is quite good enough for her, and she often wishes Bessie wouldn't sneer at it so much. Dora looks up to Bessie, but Bessie does have a way of trying to spoil things for other people. Bessie never says anything nice to Dora, or about her. She shouldn't expect it, but she can't help hoping that one day Bessie will praise her for something. For anything. That's all she asks.

Bessie hardly ever thinks about Dora at all. She had successfully neutralized Dora years ago, as soon as she started to pose any kind of threat, and now her mind is on more serious things. Bessie Bawtry has nightmares about examinations. She will have nightmares about examinations for the rest of her life. She will remember for the rest of her life the questions, the set texts, her answers, her mistakes. The examinations now upon her are the most important ordeal of her life. If she fails now, she fails for ever.

Her granddaughter Faro will not see life in these melodramatic terms. Will she? Things will ease up. For everyone.

Bessie swots and revises. Shakespeare, Browning and Keats. French verbs. Lamartine and Verlaine. General Knowledge. The League of Nations. Universal Suffrage and the Women's Vote. John Stuart Mill on Liberty, Ruskin on Manufacturing. Miss Heald ponders: perhaps a touch of the moderns? May one admit to reading D. H. Lawrence, Edith Sitwell?

The nightmare of the forced brain trapped in its skullcage. Bessie sits in the corner by the fire at a low little hexagonal wooden glass-topped table, which they call a vitrine: it serves her as desk. There is nowhere to put her legs, but she ignores the discomfort. She is lucky that her parents recognize her need to work, and give her this space. Her brain stitches and stitches, her pen scratches and loops. Outside in the smutty street the children shout and play, but indoors Bessie works for the future. Pleasure deferred, pleasure interrupted. Shall she be initiated? Failure she dreads more than she dares think. At night she dreams she is writing about Browning, she dreams she is translating Virgil. *The Aeneid,* Book IV. Creusa, O Creusa! O hollow, hollow, hollow. Her eyes are hot. She sleeps badly. Her friend Ada has already departed for Saffron Walden, and she writes letters to Bessie about her happy days there, letters full of little jokes and boastings. But she knows and we know that the Saffron Walden life is not good enough for Bessie Bawtry. She must slog on and on. The cave is dark, her eyes are hot and dim, her head aches. Shall she be ill? O, the comfort of illness! Let her lie down again in that large bed, let her sleep there for eight thousand years, let little jellies and broths be brought to her, let her be sealed up for all time behind a large stone, with the grave trophies, the offerings, the Virgil, the French Grammar and *Palgrave's Golden Treasury*! Let them light a heathen candle by her and let her fail and gutter and die and be forgotten. Let them not come searching for her with their needles and their probes.

But she does not die. She struggles on, supported, encouraged, forced by Miss Heald and Mr Farnsworth. She sits her examinations. She covers the pages with careful and well-shaped scriptings. She answers every question in order. Her pages are carefully named and numbered. Her handwriting is calm and free. She lays down her pen. She breathes deeply and waits. She is summoned for interview. She is interviewed. She will learn she has passed. She will be offered her place in paradise. In Cambridge, where gracious buildings of yellow stone have been built for the eye and the mind's delight.

Why then does she come home to Breaseborough from her college interview in so subdued a manner? (The return fare had been paid for her by her father, counted out at the station with serious, meticulous care: that fare must be justified.) Why does she sit on the train so rigidly, holding so anxiously on to the handle of her cheap little suitcase? Why does she not return triumphant? Why is she so pale? Is she sickly, is she ailing, has she 'overdone' it, is she one of those delicate young women who will justify the current male view that the health of the female is not suited to higher education? Will she become a dangerous statistic in one of Mrs Sidgwick's sociological surveys? The news that she has won not only a place but also a small college scholarship, quaintly known as an Exhibition, does not seem to revive her as it should. All are proud of her, but she remains anxious and downcast.

There can be nothing to worry about, she has just worked too hard, 'crammed' too much, and now she must take things easy, take a little exercise, learn to ride a bicycle, learn to swim. There is a new public swimming bath at Bednerby, which is proving immensely popular with the young people. Bessie must learn to relax.

Bessie hates the fresh air. Bessie hates exercise. Bessie cannot learn to ride a bicycle. Bessie will not learn to swim. And anyway, says Bessie fretfully, what's the point of telling her to get out and enjoy some fresh air. There *is* no fresh air in Breaseborough.

Bessie mooches and fades. Christmas comes and goes, and Bessie smiles faintly at her college-geared presents from parents, uncles, aunts, Miss Heald. The New Year comes in, the year that will usher Bessie into her own fuller life. Still she cannot sleep quietly. Dreams and riddles haunt her. Formidable escarpments of examinations rise before her, and she cannot believe she has scaled them. Even though she has been accepted in person as well as on the page, still she dreams of those papers, haunted by the blank sheet, the margins, the ruled lines. The unwritten script, the unwritten life, the unanswered question. Begin again, begin again. But you cannot begin again. It is done now. You cannot go back. The gap has opened. You have crossed the boundary and leaped across a widening crevasse. You cannot go back. You are on the far side, for better or for worse.

Dora is puzzled. Dora cannot see why Bessie does not rejoice. Bessie has her exit visa, which is what she has always said she wanted. Why is not Bessie happy now, now that she has only a few months to wait before she takes up her rightful place and enters on her inheritance?

For Bessie, these empty months prove an eternity of self-doubt. She lives now in Doubting Castle, and she tries to clean it up. Bessie scrubs at the back step in Slotton Road. Bessie disposes of a dead rat that she finds lying in the drain. She picks it up with fire tongs and wraps it in rags and throws it in the dustbin. Bessie takes down the curtains and washes them in the tub and stares at the sooty water. Viciously she mangles them through a heavy wringer and hangs them in the backyard to dry. They sag heavily on the line, and dark smuts descend upon them as they hang. They brush darkly against the dirty wood of the clothes prop. It is impossible to get them clean or to keep them clean.

Her mother Ellen is not wholly pleased to see her clever daughter scrubbing the step. She smells criticism. Ellen is no slut. She does her best. It is the place that is at fault, and Bessie will learn that she cannot conquer place.

⌒∭⌒

Although Bessie had now formally left school, Miss Heald kept in touch with her prodigy. At first she was not too disturbed by her low spirits. It was natural to suffer a reaction. Such moods were common in young people. Once Bessie got to college in October, and found herself among her peers, in young and lively company, then all would be well. Nevertheless, she knew that Bessie was a delicate plant, and she was concerned enough to make suggestions to cheer her and to help fill this dormant phase. She encouraged Bessie to go to the Gilchrist Lectures at the chapel, on 'Stars and Nebulae', on 'Mediterranean Flora', on 'The Life Cycle of the Honey

Bee', on 'Darwin's Finches', on the 'Pessimism of Thomas Hardy', on 'The Romans in Ancient Britain'. Bessie stared, in a mixture of horror and boredom, at the reconstructed image of fragments of a bronze diploma awarded to a Roman soldier in A.D. 124 to commemorate his discharge after twenty-five years in the service of his Divine Emperor: it had been dug up near Sheffield in A.D. 1760, and the original, like most such spoils, had been removed to the British Museum in London. So even the wretched Romans had needed diplomas and certificates and documents to validate them. This soldier had been of the first cohort of the Sunuci; he had been honourably discharged at last, and allowed, at last, his citizenship and one legal marriage (but only one, according to the bowed and barely audible Professor Harding). Twenty-five years was a long haul, thought Bessie, and perhaps that was why she sighed and shivered.

Miss Heald persevered. (Was she sexually attracted to Bessie? Certainly not, she would confidently have answered. And she would have known what the question meant.) In a lighter vein, Miss Heald invited Bessie to listen to Mendelssohn and Melba and Caruso on her new Gramola Table Grand. Bessie hated the Gramola, though of course she did not say so, and Miss Heald had to conclude that Bessie, for all her gifts, was not very musical. The Debating Society in Northam and the Reading Room of the Literary and Philosophical Society were more successful. But Bessie remained oddly lacklustre. Was it boy trouble? Or had she found her first sighting of Cambridge a little—well, intimidating? If the latter was the problem, Miss Heald could sympathize. She herself had felt very much up against it when she had first left her parents' home in little Rawmarsh for the big city of Leeds, and it had taken her a whole term to make real friends there. And as for her first weeks at the University of Toulouse, studying for her diploma—they had seemed a long dark night of loneliness and misunderstanding and ostracism. Sylvia Heald had felt out of place and conspicuous, attracting nothing but un-favourable attention. But she had worked hard at Toulouse, and had learned to love it, and to love the French language. She had learned to adapt and to fit in. Her delight in the language was never to fail her. She had stored up treasures for heaven as well as on earth. On her painful deathbed, she was to cheer herself up by reciting Lamartine lugubriously to her visitors—

O temps, suspends ton vol! et vous, heures propices
  Suspendez votre cours:
Laissez-nous savourer les rapides délices
Des plus beaux de nos jours!

Assez de malheureux ici-bas vous implorent,
  Coulez, coulez pour eux...

Miss Heald had even learned to like Toulouse sausages, which had at first struck her Yorkshire palate as an abomination. She had broadened her horizons, and had brought her new tastes and her discoveries back with her to Breaseborough, to her happy modern home with Miss Haworth, from which she spread sweetness and light and slices of foreign sausage.

Surely Bessie too would overcome her difficulties. She could not be as tender as she looked. There was determination in her as well as fear. She would survive. What she needed was a little help, a little encouragement. Of course she had found Cambridge intimidating, on her first visit. But she too would adapt.

So reasoned Miss Heald, and it was with the best of intentions that she asked permission to take Bessie Bawtry with her to the Easter party at Highcross House. She had for some years been favoured with open invitations to this annual event—'Do bring some amusing young things along with you, Sylvia!' had been the cry from Gertrude Wadsworth, to which

Miss Heald had over the years responded with a relay of the best of Breaseborough and beyond. It was an honour to be honoured by Miss Wadsworth, and Miss Heald was sure Bessie would be pleased to be included. It would do her good to see a bit of the wider world.

⟨⟨⟨⟩⟩⟩

Gertrude Wadsworth was the queen of Hammervale, or would have been had she condescended to visit her native regions more frequently: as it happened, her unhappy childhood at Highcross had prejudiced her against the entire county, and she came there as little as possible. But once or twice a year she made her way to the old house, which stood in parkland (but not very ancient parkland) between Cotterhall and Blaxton. Her aweful father was now bedridden, and therefore less threatening than he had been in his patriarchal days: indeed, she now had the upper hand, and could have moved back to South Yorkshire in style with her gay London entourage. But the gloomy old dump, she declared, was a perfect frost. It got her down. It was damp and dirty, and the air—honestly, you could hardly breathe in it, it was thicker even than a London fog. She preferred London, where she moved in a fast Bohemian set. She was said to mix with artists and writers and women-about-town.

Gertrude had really had a rotten time as a girl. She had been sickly and lonely. Rescued from a sadistic governess who had luckily overstepped the mark and been given the sack, she had been sent away to Cheltenham Ladies' College, where she had been slightly less sickly and lonely. Her mother was a hypochondriac who spent most of her time undergoing unnecessary surgery, and it is much to Gertrude Wadsworth's credit that she refused to follow this powerful maternal example. At the age of twenty-one, she had decided to be well, and to tell herself every morning that every day in every way she was getting better and better. It worked. She flourished. She would never overcome some of her natural disadvantages— she took after her father rather than her mother in physique, and she was far too tall, plain-featured, large-boned, large-nosed, heavy and tending to stoutness—but she gallantly decided to ignore these drawbacks. She addressed her innate shyness frontally, charging it as though she were taking a fence, and leaping, on most occasions, boldly and safely to the other side.

Her unnatural advantages were considerable. She was very rich. And she was an only child. She was also far from stupid, though she often seemed stupid. In her social world, it was often safer to seem stupid. And she did not need to pass examinations.

She wanted to be good and to do good. Whether this was an advantage or a disadvantage was not clear.

Her father, Joel Heathcote Wadsworth, owned Bednerby Main and all the coal that came from it. It was on his behalf that the colliers, rope boys, pit boys, stokers, pit sinkers and pony drivers trooped forth each morning at dawn to work all day below the earth. (Some of them worked night shifts: production had to be kept moving.) He was an extraordinarily disagreeable old man, foul of mouth and foul of temper. Nobody liked him. His colliery managers hated him. His estate workers hated him. His wife hated him, and took her revenge on him by paring away bits of her body until there was nothing much left for him to abuse. His daughter Gertrude hated him, because he was cruel and rude to her, and mocked her height and girth and features. Joel Heathcote Wadsworth had no class. He spoke broad Yorkshire, pitilessly, like the farmer's son he was, and he played the tyrant and the bully. But now, in nineteen twenty-something, his wife was dead—an operation too far, on a perfectly healthy organ, had finished her off, to her own weak surprise—and he himself had been semi-paralysed by a stroke. The stroke had served him right, in the view of his servants. He was not intemperate in his drinking habits, but he ate far too much, weighed twenty stone, and was intemperate in all other ways available to him, working himself up into a red-faced apoplectic rage at least twice a day about matters of utter triviality. And now he was confined to a spinal chair, and at their mercy. They were not very kind to him. It was their turn now. They were the masters now.

For Gertrude Wadsworth, this was liberation. She had not been disinherited, as far as she knew, and the rest of her life was before her. She was only thirty-five. She would never marry. But she could enjoy herself, and help others to enjoy themselves. She could try to have some fun.

Highcross House was not designed for fun. It had no tradition of fun. Nevertheless, once or twice a year Gertrude left her bijou little London house in Trevor Square and travelled north to see what was going on amongst the old slag heaps. She tried to import festivity. This was good of her, as her acquaintances acknowledged. Miss Heald was one of these acquaintances.

Sylvia Heald and Gertrude Wadsworth had met at a charity concert given by the Operatic Society at the Breaseborough Hippodrome, in aid of the Miners' Welfare Fund, and had taken to one another through a shared dislike of the principal soprano's striking air of misplaced self-satisfaction. A wincing look of cultured despair had passed between them, involuntarily, and they had fallen into conversation over the ices. Miss Heald had subsequently prevailed upon Miss Wadsworth to present the prizes at the school speech day, a considerable coup, as Miss Wadsworth, through a mixture of guilt and shyness, ignored most local activities. Miss Wadsworth had been impressed by Breaseborough Secondary School, which seemed to compare not unfavourably with Cheltenham Ladies', and the friendship had mildly prospered. Miss Wadsworth had been agreeably surprised to find Miss Heald and her companion Miss Haworth so well read, though she was too polite to show her surprise. She pleased herself and them by sending them books and magazines from London. (It was through Gertrude that Miss Heald had first discovered the poetry of T. S. Eliot and Edith Sitwell.) Of the visual arts, Gertrude noted, the Misses H. knew nothing—but then, how could they, up there in that ugly wilderness? She herself had hardly looked at a painting until she was twenty. There *were* no paintings in South Yorkshire.

Gertrude was now a frequenter of Private Views and the Chelsea Arts Club. She was a member of the Sesame Club, where she liked to entertain. She was renowned for her generosity over drinks and dinners, and was kind, on principle, to many young artists. She was still not very sure of her taste, and relied on others to introduce her to the new, the shocking, the up to the minute. Arnold Bennett took her under his wing, as he took several gauche and serious young men and women, and explained to her the merits of Roderic O'Conor and Modigliani, two painters whom he seemed to think he had invented for himself. He introduced her to Roger Fry, who introduced her in turn to the Omega Workshops, where Gertrude spent a lot of money on furnishings for the house in Trevor Square. Would she, she wondered, when her father died, as he surely soon must, attempt to do over the décor of Highcross House? Get rid of the Victorian drapes, the Scottish baronial plaid, the dark reds, the plush, the meat-colours, the brawn textures, the gravy browning? And fill it with turquoise and lime, with shrimp and apricot and buttercup? Or should she just sell the pile for a song and move away and forget it and what it stood on and stood for?

Such were the benevolent and artistic thoughts of Gertrude Wadsworth as she got herself up for her annual Easter bash. She had invited a hundred guests from all over the county, her highest score yet. Her father was confined to his quarters, and Otley and Bateman understood that they were not to bring him out whatever he said. Miss Wadsworth adjusted her flesh-pink stockings and suspenders, heaving largely inside the supposed liberation of her supple newfangled buskless corset—'light and airy and soft and lissom', its label had declared, and, with its mere seven bonings, it was 'to all intents and purposes non-existent'. So it had promised, but nevertheless Miss Wadsworth found it uncomfortably restricting. Why did one have to wear such things? And why was she such a bloody awful shape, as her father was never tired of remarking? When the fashion, now, was to look boyish? Gertrude Wadsworth might from some angles look mannish, but boyish, never. She groaned, sighed and bit the bullet, pulling on her *eau-de-Nil* low-waisted gown with its silvery beaded fringing. What did it matter if she looked a perfect fright? Nobody would care. She draped herself with long chains of pearl and paste diamond. They seemed to make matters even worse, so she took them off again. Her shoes, at least, were pretty. Her feet were not very large. Large, but not very large.

A hundred guests, from all over the West Riding. A scattering of gentlefolk from farms and halls and manors. The colliery manager and his wife, and Captain Sligo, the moustached owner of Pottles Pit. The nice Methodist minister from Wath. (She had not invited any vicars. She disapproved of the Church of England.) The Misses Heald and Haworth. Mr and Mrs Farnsworth. Some local businessmen and manufacturers, glassmakers, confectioners, a wholesale potato dealer. A few doctors, a racing driver and a pianist. A painter and a poet. Some farmers, and a scion of the Wardale family. A professor from Northam University. An antiquary from Leeds, and a bookseller from Sheffield. And there was a handful of houseguests, her chums from London, who were occupying the damp and disused bedrooms, and who would add a cosmopolitan tone to the occasion. A heterogeneous mix, a crude but brave mingling. And into this tricky gathering, as yet unknown to Gertrude Wadsworth, would enter innocent, inexperienced little Bessie Bawtry, garlanded with academic laurels, yet naked of all other ornament. Bessie Bawtry had not even a string of artificial pearls to dangle round her neck.

But did that matter, for a fresh girl of eighteen? Will not her natural grace and beauty glow and glimmer sweetly? 'Full many a gem of purest ray serene, / The dark unfathomed caves of ocean bear'. 'Whatever you are, be That: Whatever you say, be True'. Bessie Bawtry has many a humble motto to guide her, and she is much prettier than Gertrude Wadsworth has ever been, will ever be.

It is natural, at Bessie's age, that she should be paralysed with fear and apprehension. She has never been to so large a house in her life. Highcross House is far larger even than Breaseborough School, which is a sizeable stone-faced building grandly decorated with four grumpy cherubs. Highcross House is not as large as King's College, or Trinity, or Newnham College, but to Bessie's eye it is getting on that way. It is too large to be a home, and there is nothing homely about it. Above the gatepost in the cold spring evening loom two affronted stone figures, and the drive winds onwards and out of sight towards the Victorian mansion. Bessie, sitting squashed between Miss Heald and Miss Haworth, in Phil Barron's Austin, wishes she could jump out and run away into the night. But she knows she has to go through with this ordeal. She reminds herself that she is a pet, that she is clever, that she has a State and a County Major and a College Exhibition. But her throat is dry, and her hands are cold and damp. She never perspires, but a cold dew seems to have settled on her brow. She is turning into a frog. It is meant to work the other way round. She is supposed to turn into a princess, at this, her first ball. But instead, she is turning into a frog. A frog, in a homemade dress.

Joe Barron will be there, she tells herself. He too has been a beneficiary of Miss Wadsworth's broad benevolence. He will be a welcome and an easy guest. Joe is good with people. The

Barrons, as Bessie knows well, are one of the best families in the neighbourhood. And Joe has always been a good friend to Bessie, kind to her in her hesitations, supportive of her ambitions. She has come to rely on his partiality for her. She knows she can always fall back on Joe's good will. He is a friend, perhaps more than a friend. But Bessie has not seen so much of Joe since her recent triumphs. It was too bad about his not getting a County. She had imagined that they would go up to Cambridge together, that he would be there for her as an escort and an ally amidst the alien youth of southern England. What will happen to him now? He can't spend the rest of his life selling Barron Glass. Can he? Is he jealous of her success? Has he been avoiding her?

Highcross House comes into focus, on its slight eminence, in the fading glimmer of dusk. It is, unusually, ablaze with light, and making an effort to welcome its guests. It stands on the site of what was once Highcross Farm, a building which nobody now remembers. The old farm had been a pleasing and harmonious dwelling, built of a light and delicate limestone of pink and ochre and a weathered orange, with a steep tiled roof, whereas the new Highcross is heavy, red and brutal, well pointed, ostentatious, penitential, and, like its present owner, angry and severe. Bessie Bawtry's home in Slotton Road has six rooms: this house has about forty. It stands uncomfortably upon its land. The Heathcote Wadsworths had been wise to build up here, on magnesian limestone, away from the fault line, rather than on top of their own burrowings, for the clay Coal Measures are riddled with subsidence. They have built wisely, but they have not built with elegance. This is not a house to inspire affection.

Bessie is in no position to make such distinctions, for the sheer size of the thing overwhelms her spirits and blurs her vision, but the London houseguests have made much mock of it—such arch and spiteful mock that poor Gertrude has almost felt within herself an impulse to defend it. It is not its fault that it is so ungainly, so unsmart, so out-of-every-fashion. She has tried to make up for its failings with lights and flowers, with ribbons and candles, and music spills out of the doorway and across the gravel terrace.

Vast polished floorboards, acres of sideboards, huge bulbous banisters, heavy-framed mirrors, false Tartan and some fine Georgian Sheffield plate. Fruit cup, more alcoholic than it tastes, and little sandwiches, and sausage rolls with flaky greasy pastry. Is this a party? What is it for? What *are* parties for? Here are chattering and giggling, and a room where the carpet has been rolled back for dancing. The older folk gather and gossip in corners, the more confidant of the younger ones flap and flirt. It should be easy to escape notice in this mêlée, to mix, to blend in, to vanish. Not many of the guests here are accustomed to this kind of party. Will the locals and the gentry mix, will trade speak to houseguest, will doctor speak to colliery manager? Will they recognize one another for what they are, or will the signals be too confusing? Gertrude Wadsworth hasn't the faintest about how to introduce anyone to anyone, and she doesn't know who half of them are in the first place. She is gauche and graceless and red in the face, despite her layers of bright pink face powder. But there is enough noise going on to cover the gaps, and some people, at least, seem to be having a good time. What more can one hope for?

Bessie Bawtry is lost. She has surrendered her grey cloth coat to a maid in a cloakroom, and is now exposed in her crêpe de Chine frock with its unintentionally uneven hemline. She has lost sight of Miss Heald and Miss Haworth. She cannot see any of the Barrons. Where is Joe, her reliable sixth-form sweetheart? She had been sure she would find him here. She recognizes Mr Spooner from the Laurels, but she has never been introduced to him, so that's not much good. She is lost in a sea of unknown shapes and faces. She dares not take a glass of the fruit cup from the silver tray that is offered to her. A feeling of panic pervades her. She longs to be back home, at her cramped little table, with her Latin grammar, her *Golden Treasury,* her certificates. But she cannot go home. There is no way home. She is stranded. And now this huge woman in pale green bears down upon her, angrily, gruffly, and demands her name.

'I'm Miss Bawtry,' offers Bessie, knowing that she is now one of the grown-ups, no longer little Bessie, but Miss Bawtry, for had not Miss Strachey herself, the principal of Newnham College, so addressed her?

'Miss Bawtry, eh! Miss Bawtry!' parrots the cruel hard-faced big woman, and she laughs, a dismissive, contemptuous laugh. 'Well, *Miss* Bawtry, make yourself at home here, won't you! Have a glass of wine, why don't you!'

Bessie knows she has done something wrong, but what is it, what can it be? She turns away, in confusion. But the big woman pursues her, catches her hand, and says, 'Come along, Miss Bawtry, let me introduce you to—to Freddie Farley. Freddie, come here and speak to Miss Bawtry!'

And Freddie Farley, summoned from another conversation, is forced to speak to Bessie Bawtry. He is gentler with her than Gertrude Wadsworth has been, for unlike Gertrude he is not shy, he is easy and sociable, and he does the best he can with this nice timid little blond girlie: he walks her to another room, asks her questions, and learns from her that she is be-tween school and college, that she has a place at Cambridge, that she lives in Breaseborough, and that she has never before been to Highcross or met her hostess.

'Cambridge, eh!' he echoes admiringly. 'You must be a clever one, then!'

Bessie Bawtry does not know whether this is meant as a compliment, nor, if it were, how she should receive it. She says nothing. Freddie starts to speak to her of all the people he knows at Cambridge, but of course she has never heard of any of them, nor can she respond to any of his inquiries about the town, or the colleges, or the dons. Freddie Farley cannot think of any other topic of conversation. He is getting nowhere with this one. He asks her to dance, but she says she cannot dance. He will have to ditch her, he can't spend the rest of the evening trying to talk to this tongue-tied mousie of a schoolgirl, it is too painful. He has done his best. He tells her to look up his cousin Douglas at St John's when she goes up next autumn. And he hands her on, like a parcel, to Angela and Cedric, and bows his way out.

Bessie is overcome by a sense of unutterable failure. Freddie Farley, good-natured, lightweight, has undone all her bright hopes, all her prospects. He has pushed her back into the mire, just as she was beginning to clamber painfully out of it. She has not understood one word he has said to her, but she has understood its import. It is as she suspected. Cambridge is a place peopled by confident characters like Freddie Farley, in dinner jackets, who will be unspeakably bored by Bessie Bawtry. There will be no place for her there. She is a failure before she even arrives. There is no way forward, she is condemned to Breaseborough for ever.

Angela and Cedric, far less friendly than Freddie, reinforce his message. They quiz her about her schooling, cut her short when she mentions Miss Heald, and walk away from her in midsentence.

Bessie escapes to a cloakroom, and sits in the water closet until someone comes and rattles the door handle.

She finds her lonely way to the library, where she lurks behind a bookcase. The titles of the books swim before her eyes. *The Decline and Fall of the Roman Empire. Punch* and the *Spectator* in bound, unread volumes. Samuel Johnson, Smollett, Richardson. Bessie knows that she is more capable than most of the people in this house of reading those volumes. But what does that matter? Books do not matter. They are the foothills. Beyond them stretch Alpine ranges of unscaleable and giddy horror. There is no happiness to be had on earth.

'So do you think Gertrude is *happy*?' asks the poet of the painter, as they take refuge from their social obligations in the library alcove. They are pursuing a conversation about their hostess, initiated earlier on the dance floor. Bessie Bawtry, perched out of sight on the library steps, tries not to listen, because she knows that eavesdropping is wrong. But she dare not move, and she can't help overhearing.

'Happy as happikins,' says the painter, settling into the window seat and kicking off her tight glacé kid buckled shoes. She rubs her toes, and yawns. It's been a long day, and most of the folk up here are heavy going, and the tunes are old-fashioned. Gertrude has tried hard, but she hasn't quite pulled it off. It's too shaming to retire to bed alone before midnight, but really, she's almost had enough. Not that it's very pleasant in the guest rooms. It's arctic up there.

'No, but seriously,' says the poet.

The painter yawns again, and wrinkles her snub nose in what she believes to be a fetching and playful manner. She reaches into her little beaded reticule for a cigarette, and pushes it into her mother-of-pearl cigarette holder, and lights up.

Bessie thinks that smoking in a library is very wrong, but it's not her place to reveal herself and say so, is it?

'She's a very good sort, is Gertrude,' persists the earnest bearded poet. 'I think she might respond.'

'You want to pack *everyone* off to Vienna,' says the painter. 'I don't think it's the right thing for *everyone*. I think Gertrude is better off being a virgin.'

'How do you know she's a virgin?'

'I think she must be, don't you?'

'What an appalling thing to say,' says the poet, although secretly he agrees with the painter.

'I imagine she's a lesbian. If she's anything,' says the painter. Her cigarette smoke perfumes the dusty air. 'But I don't suppose she's anything.'

'Everybody is something,' says the poet.

'So they say, these days, but I don't believe it. I think lots of people have no sex urge at all. I think a lot of people get on quite well without it. I don't, and you don't, but I bet our Gertrude does. She does quite nicely as she is, if you ask me. And she does very nicely by us too. Quite a place she's got here, isn't it? Have you ever seen anything like it?'

'It's dreary,' says the poet.

'But big,' says the painter, who comes from Bloomsbury via Potters Bar.

'And such sad people,' says the poet.

'What's sad about them?' says the painter, although secretly she agrees with the poet. 'They seem to be having a merry old time of it. In their own dismal kind of way.'

'And what a landscape,' continues the poet, who is not listening to the painter. 'What have they done to it? It's terrible, terrible.'

The poet had been naïvely shocked by what he had seen out of the railway-carriage window. He had never been north before. He had not known it was like this. The pitheads, the quarries, the scars, the mountains of slag, the spoil heaps, the careless, casual filthy dumping. The lack of the most elementary, animal cleanliness. You could not get away from it—the lack of *toilet training*. Not even animals foul their own nest as this northern race had done. Had they lost all sense of dignity and human worth? That they should let their slaves live in such subhuman dirt? Poor Gertrude, heiress of muck. It's wrong, he tells the painter. It's disgusting. Mountains and mountains of shit. You can't do that to the countryside.

The poet comes from the soft green valleys of Somerset, and is just finishing a successful analysis.

'Oh, I think it's quite dramatic,' says the painter, intent on being perverse. 'Sublime, in its way.'

'Sublime?' echoes the poet. 'It's not sublime. It's just a filthy mess and muddle.'

'Oh well, maybe you're right,' yawns the painter. She isn't

interested in landscape. Landscape is old hat. She paints people, in violent shades of orange and pink. She prefers people.

'Anyway,' says the painter, 'it's interesting. For a change.'

She stubs out her cigarette on the parquet. It's lucky Bessie cannot witness this act of vandalism. Things are bad enough for Bessie behind the bookcase. She would not like to be an accomplice in this deed.

'I met a *very* nice young man,' says the painter, starting up again, provocatively. 'A young local. The D. H. Lawrence of Breaseborough. Red-haired, and all. Did you spot him? I made him dance with me. He didn't want to, but I made him.'

'Was he a gamekeeper?' asks the poet.

'No, I'm afraid not. Nothing so romantic. He said he was a travelling salesman. I told him he couldn't be, but he insisted that he was. He was very young and handsome, and he quoted poetry at me.'

'What sort of poetry?'

'How would I know? You know I can't read. Something about soft hands and peerless eyes. It was very pretty.'

'Keats,' says the poet.

'Who?'

'Keats, you ninny.'

The painter pretends that she does not mind being called a ninny, but she does. She does not think it nice of the poet to tease her about her reading habits. It was true that she had been incapable of reading more than half a page of the article on narcissism he'd put under her nose on the train down to Yorkshire, but she bet that not many other of the party-goers at this festivity would have been able to plough through it either. The poet is a beast.

'You're a beast,' says the painter to the poet. 'A beastly beastly beast.'

Bessie cannot make out what happens next, but it sounds improper. A scuffling and a giggling and a short cry of surprise.

The kind of thing you tried not to hear going on in the back row of the cinema.

To Bessie, the whole interchange has been both improper and, mercifully, largely incomprehensible. There have been words in it that Bessie has never heard before. She had got the Keats quote, though, brief though it was. It was from 'Ode on Melancholy'. They'd done it with Miss Heald for Oxbridge entrance.

But what on earth was all that business about Vienna? Bessie sits tight, and hears the conversation strike up again, as the bodily noises quieten down.

'You know,' says the painter reflectively, and solemnly, in a quite different mode, as though the kissing interlude had never taken place: 'You know, I think Gertrude probably is happy. Maybe not happy as happikins, that was a silly thing to say, but happy enough. She's sort of—self-sufficient. She's self-contained. She doesn't need any of us. She can live without us. Don't you think? I think she's not afraid. And most of us are afraid. Most of the time. I think she's got so used to being afraid that now she really isn't afraid any more. She's grown out of it. She's grown up. I think that's why I like her. What do *you* think?'

'I think I love and love and love you,' said the poet, entranced by this brave and uncharacteristic outburst of generosity from Potters Bar and Bloomsbury. 'I love and love you, you beautiful beautiful darling.'

He does not sound as though he means it very seriously, but how can one tell? People don't talk like that when they are serious. Do they?

Hours later, Joe Barron is still looking for Bessie Bawtry, but he cannot find her. Bessie had come to the party with Miss Heald and Miss Haworth and his brother Phil, but he can't see Phil either. Have they all gone home? It is after midnight, a late hour in South Yorkshire. He may as well drive back home to Laburnum House in the tradesman's van in which he'd arrived. He has hidden it way down the drive, outside the gateposts, under a chestnut tree, by the cattle grid. The van has BARRON & SONS GLASS AND FANCYWARE, TELEPHONE COTTERHALL 225 emblazoned upon it. Not quite a pumpkin, but it would not have done as a conveyance for Bessie Bawtry. After all, nothing but the best is good enough for Bessie.

⊙ⱮⱮⱮↄ

After the Easter party at Highcross, Bessie Bawtry took to her bed. Her pretext was a bad cold, which developed into a fever. It was less severe and dramatic than the Spanish flu, but it was hot enough to keep her indoors and under covers for weeks. She was not promoted to the best bed this time, but Dora was demoted from the twin room and sent downstairs to sleep with the cats on the couch in the kitchen. Bessie's mother blamed the festivity and the folly of stepping out at night in a thin dress. It was no wonder that Bessie was ill. It served her right for trying to have fun. Mutely, grudgingly, Ellen Bawtry carried jugs of lemon barley water and bowls of soup up the stairs to Bessie. Mutely, grudgingly, Bessie accepted them, and delicately she sipped. She could not eat. She refused to get better. She lay in bed, with an air of listless indifference, reading until her head ached and her eyes were sore. She began to lose weight, and her mother began to worry about her. Ellen's attentions became less grudging. Dr Marr was called in, diagnosed 'nervous prostration', prescribed tonics.

Bessie's father too became anxious. His little girl was fading and he didn't like it. He tried to entertain her, bringing to her bedside the new wireless set he'd bought for them all last Christmas. He sat by her, breathing heavily and fiddling with the knobs. Her father understood the wireless: he had taken instruction from Mr Ogilvy, B.Sc., from whom he had bought the set, and had assembled it himself on the kitchen table. He

91

was now more expert than his mentor at coaxing sounds from the brown box. Home Service talks, dance tunes, classical music, weather forecasts. Bessie listened patiently. She preferred reading, but she acknowledged the submission with which her father bowed to divert her. He sat on Dora's bed, tapping his big broad feet in time to the incongruous beat of ragtime.

'That's good, Bess, isn't it?' he would say hopefully. 'It's a good clear signal, isn't it?'

Bessie didn't like ragtime, but she managed to smile to please her father.

Sister Dora ran errands and delivered messages, as she had before. She brought library books, writing paper, throat sweets. She hung around, waiting for a kind word, for thanks, for recognition. Gratitude would come in the end, she was almost sure. Bessie accepted Dora's attentions as though they were her due. Dora was lucky to be allowed to wait upon her big sister.

Bessie was depressed. She was sinking. Her body felt limp. Her mind felt limp, yet at the same time curiously overactive, with a detached hot invisible motion of its own, as though it were not really she herself who lay there. It was not Bessie Bawtry, late of Breaseborough Secondary and recently accepted at university, who lay there, in this small bedroom, in this small corner house. It was some simulacrum, some chrysalis, some meaningless waxy body container, in which a new form of life was trying to hatch. Poor Bessie, we have been too hard on her. Our tone has been harsh and pitiless. It is the tone she taught us, it is true, but we must try to unlearn it, we must try to see her as she was, suffering, longing, vulnerable, unformed. How is she to know how to manage these hot flushes of grief, these night sweats and terrors, these humiliations and tribulations? She reads for solace, for enlightenment, for escape, for a sight of the next rung upwards on the ladder, for the next gleam of light ahead that might lead her from the prison of her cavemind. Books have hitherto been her friends and allies, and she had harnessed them to her will, but now they too begin to threaten and oppress her, to show her darknesses too horrid and lights too blinding. They no longer befriend, they mock. She saw through and rejected the Bible long ago, for she has seen that there is no God: God is a stone at the mouth of the tomb. But those other books, books that had seemed to lead her out into the bright air from the darkness of soot and gravecloths, they now confuse and alarm her. How can she cope with this rich world of words and language and light? She is a weak little grub. How could she have thought she could ever take part in the butterfly display of the educated world?

She lay still, in turmoil. A seething, a pregnant brewing, a splitting, a proliferation of particles. Is it a sickness, is it a fermentation, is it a couching, and what will it bring forth? Is it a growing or a dying?

Miss Heald was told of her protégée's sickness, and came round, bearing books. Mrs Bawtry eyed her daughter's visitor with respect and distrust. She blamed her for this malady, for was it not Miss Heald who had procured the invitation to Highcross? Was it not Miss Heald who had overtaxed her daughter's mind? Books were the last thing Bessie needed. Books breed maggots in the brain.

Miss Heald, adding her own small but influential impetus to the nationwide process of cultural diffusion, brought a volume of plays by Bernard Shaw, Lawrence's *The White Peacock,* Hardy's *The Woodlanders* and some little poetry magazines. She brought T. S. Eliot, whose *Waste Land* she had now read: she recommended Bessie to try 'The Love Song of J. Alfred Prufrock', flattering her by telling her she was probably the only young woman in South Yorkshire who would understand it. She told Bessie that she herself was preparing a paper to deliver to the Literary Institute in which she hoped to compare the dramatic monologues of Browning and Eliot.

She brought the poems of Edith Sitwell which had, like so much, been drawn to her attention first by Gertrude Wadsworth. Gertrude knew Edith Sitwell personally. The Sitwell family, for reasons of geographical proximity, had something of a reputation in Breaseborough, though not, it must be said, a very happy reputation. They were, naturally, despised in their own land. Too much coal dust had settled in the lake at Renishaw for the Sitwells to be regarded with favour or admiration. Their eccentricities were relayed round the neighbourhood, and mocked. But they were noticed. And Gertrude Wadsworth, who knew and liked Edith, was loyal to Edith, and therefore Sylvia Heald was loyal to Edith, and tried to pass on her loyalty to Bessie Bawtry. Loyalty fought with class hatred in Bessie, and it was not yet clear which would win.

Gertrude Wadsworth had once merrily described herself as 'a poor man's Edith Sitwell'—identifying with the plainness, the oddness, the lack of conventional sexual charm. 'I wish I could write,' Miss Wadsworth often declared. 'Or paint. Or do *anything*.' And then she would laugh her jolly girl's laugh.

Gertrude Wadsworth, only daughter of a rich mean man, was, in point of fact, a great deal richer than Edith Sitwell, who at this time lived in a shabby flat up four flights of stairs in Bayswater, pouring tea from a cracked brown teapot, and offering her guests iced penny buns. Gertrude Wadsworth lived in a pretty house in Knightsbridge, and could have afforded a staff of chauffeurs, cooks and lady's maids, had she been able to endure the close physical proximity and deference of her own species.

None of this was known to Bessie Bawtry, who rose to Miss Heald's barbed bait as she lay sickly in her bed. Her saucer eyes were painfully hooked by Sitwell and Eliot, by Eliot and Sitwell, by Prufrock and *Façade*. They swam with effort. But no, she was too ill. She closed the pages, closed her eyes.

At night, in the ice-cool metallic spring darkness, as she tried to sleep, she was besieged by temptations. To quiet, surrender, brain fever, despair. Yet something in her was also gestating. If she stayed alive, if she crawled out and kept her appointment with her destiny, she would undergo a metamorphosis. If she stayed here, she and all of her line would rot.

Images of Highcross House and the large threatening figure of Miss Wadsworth swam into her nighttime dreaming. She had been able to make no sense of that evening, of that building, of that woman. It had all been shapeless, noisy, confusing. *Three o'clock in the morning.* The hit tune goes round and round unwanted in her head. Bessie lived again and again through those moments of humiliation—the endless drive leading onwards and upwards, the snarling stone monsters on the gateposts warning her to keep out, the threatening merriment of the lighted threshold, the house too large for the eye to control, the candles, the flowers, the heavy silver, the maid who snatched her coat and left her naked, the drooping and dipping of her hem, the swooping of towering Miss Wadsworth, her shame at the wrong thing said, her helplessness with Freddie Farley, her rejection by those two smart-set shiners, her retreat, her hiding, her crumpled abiding, her cowardice, her smarting eyes, her stinging red nose: and afterwards, looping backwards through the torments of memory, she goes back in the nightwatch to that December visit to Cambridge for her interview, where instead of a kindly welcome she had found humiliation, grief, rawness, her very skin aflame with tenderness, her clothes exposed, her accent exposed, amidst all those confident southern girls from boarding schools, and Miss Strachey, the principal, examining her across her large desk as though she were a discarded morsel, and addressing her, with insulting condescension: *So you have a County Scholarship to support you, I see?* The tone burns. And petted Bessie, who had been so proud of that scholarship, saw it held up for inspection as though it were a damp kitchen rag, a servant's dishcloth, instead of a laurel wreath. Austere Miss Strachey, shapeless and sexless Miss Wadsworth, they had undone her. *I'm pretty, I'm clever, I'm pretty,* whispered Bessie to herself at three in the morning. *I'm eighteen years old, and I have an eighteen-inch waist, and yellow hair, and blue eyes. I'm pretty, I'm clever, I can read* The Waste Land, The Waist Land, *I'm not plain Jane as tall as a crane. I'm petite and I'm pretty, I'm not like Dora, dumb dull dim Dora, stick-in-the-mud Dora. I can escape, I can escape, I can escape.*

But Miss Wadsworth and Miss Strachey, two vast grotesque affronted figures, rose before her like angry angels to bar the way. Downstairs, uncomplaining Dora slept heavily on the lumpy horsehair couch.

Joe Barron came to see Bessie, bearing gifts. He, like Miss Heald, felt implicated in her illness. He had failed to find her at the Highcross party. He had looked for her, but he had not looked very hard. He had assumed she had found her way through the social maze, and he had forgotten about her, and enjoyed himself. He had danced with an outrageous young woman from London, and flirted with her, and talked nonsense with her, as though he were another kind of person altogether. He had enjoyed himself. Then he had driven home alone, in the Fancy Glass van. And he had been happy, driving back through the night. He always liked driving through darkness. A badger had slowly crossed the road in the light of his headlights. He had been pleased to see its old-man's gait. And since the party, he had stepped out once or twice with his old friend Alice Vestrey. They had been to the cinema in Rotherham. In the summer they had played tennis together, mixed doubles with Phil and Rowena. Now they were keen on swimming at Bednerby Pool. Alice was taking diving lessons. Alice was a sport.

There was nothing wrong in all of this, for his friendship with Bessie was only a friendship. She could not expect anything more from him. They were too young and too untried to have an understanding. He had kissed her once when he was playing Lysander to her Hermia—indeed he had kissed her several times, and perhaps more warmly than the performance had demanded. But that was in play, not for real. And Bessie was on her way to Cambridge, which seemed to him still a distant goal. She was outstripping him and leaving him behind. Soon she would be a woman of the world, where she would meet other suitors, other admirers, he assured her, while he would remain a poor perpetual provincial, for ever left behind. (Into his mind fluttered, as he spoke, the memory of that outrageous young woman from London, with her fast talk and her beaded skirt.)

Bessie laughed uneasily at this. She knew that Joe could tell she was afraid. He watched her with tenderness and not a little anxiety as she unwrapped his offering of a nice little leather-bound edition of Keats's sonnets which he had picked up on his travels in a second-hand bookshop in Doncaster. 'For Bessie, Bright Star, from Joe', he had inscribed it.

Bessie, sitting up in her bedjacket of lacy cream wool, thanked him for the Keats, and said she would treasure it. She said she hoped her health would be good enough to let her go to Cambridge. She gazed at him earnestly from innocent eyes.

'Of course it will,' said Joe with conviction. 'Anyway, it's just got to be. You can't waste a big chance like that. I'd give my eyeteeth to get into Cambridge. If I've got any eyeteeth. What *are* eyeteeth?'

And so they chatted, pleasantly, whimsically, with only the mildest edge of flirtation, as Joe attempted to rally her spirits and reinforce her image of herself as a successful person, as he tried to weaken her clinging to weakness. Joe Barron was an observant and generous young man, and he could sense in Bessie a yearning towards inertia, failure, self-pity, collapse. She needed careful nurture. Would she, with strength, with support, grow straight and strong? He was sure she would. He cajoled, he flattered, he encouraged. She could get up and walk, if she chose.

It was kind of Joe Barron to take such trouble to encourage Bessie to be brave about her future, for his own future at this time was opaque. His father continued to refuse to contemplate financing any more education, and expected him, it seemed, to spend the rest of his life in the family business. It was not an appealing prospect. Joe Barron was ambitious, and hoped for more from life. Joe Barron's life as a travelling salesman made him ache with boredom. He was easily bored. He could not take any interest in glass or Bakelite. But it was hard to know where to turn. His mother sympathized with his aspirations, and maybe she would wear his father down in time. But how much time was there? How late could one wait to apply for a university place? Joe Barron did not know how the system worked. He had stumbled and missed a step, and could not see where the road should lead next. Maybe this was all there was. The road to nowhere.

His father Ben was an irascible, crabby old chap, at the best of times, and hard to please. Ben was annoyed with Joe's reluctance to commit himself to Cotterhall, but he was not wholly pleased by Bennett's enthusiasm for the family business. He didn't want him to get a hold on the firm. He was a patriarch, and he wanted submission, obedience. He stymied Bennett's attempts at innovation and experiment. Trouble was brewing in Barron Glass, and in Laburnum House. Joe wanted to get away from all of this, into a world where—well, he knew not what. The world he wanted took no clear shape. A world of ideas, and talk, and good works, and public service, and progress. The kind of world he read about in books. Culture. Civilization. Was it wrong to dream of these things? Was it presumptuous?

He did not at this stage speak of these ill-formed desires to Bessie Bawtry, though in time to come he may. He did not speak of tensions at home, nor did he reveal to her the rebuffs he endured on the road. (Not everybody wanted Barron Glassware, and Joe was not a natural salesman.) To Bessie, he put on a good front. He was biding his time, he would work it through, all would be well—that was the line he took, though at this period he found it hard to believe it himself. And Bessie must get better. The Breaseborough air was bad for her lungs. No wonder she was off-colour. She would pick up like a primrose, as soon as she got away.

Bessie drank all this in gratefully. She liked the attention. A nice-looking, eligible young man, sitting by her bedside, devoting himself to cheering her up. It was well worth being ill, to get this kind of attention. She thought she could do better with her life than marry a local boy like Joe Barron, handsome and clever though he was. But meanwhile, his attentions were acceptable to her.

Joe patted her hand in a brotherly way, as he looked at his watch, thinking to himself that it was time he set off to keep his appointment with Alice Vestrey. He had done his bit. He thought he could do better with his life than marry a local girl like Bessie Bawtry, pretty and clever though she was. Bessie could tell that he was beginning to strain to leave the sickroom. But she would wheedle him back. He would come again. Oh yes, he would come again. He promised. Of course he would come soon.

Did Joe Barron suspect, as he walked away, that in that little room he might have embarked on a lifetime of tragic appeasement?

Bessie Bawtry thought that on balance she would get better and go to college. She would get better, and show them all what she was made of. She was made of stronger stuff than they thought.

Or then again, perhaps she would lie here for ever, like the Dairyman's Daughter.

Energy and inertia struggled for possession of her. They exhausted her. She was so very very tired. The nights were so long. They were given over to the thorn and the wilderness.

She lay and suffocated, she put her head under the bedclothes and tried to choke herself to death in safety. This was a small, mean town, full of small, mean people. Out there was a world. Politics, jazz, science, stars, aeroplanes. This was a small valley. A worldwide depression was driving towards Hammervale, bringing news of the mass revolts, the crazed ideologies, the conflagrations and massacres and emigrations of the violent twentieth century. Even sheltered Bessie knew something of troubles in the Soviet Union and China, of troubles in Europe, of Hitler and Mussolini, of strikes and lockouts, of stock-market crashes, of fortunes lost, of the economic consequences of the peace. She read the *Manchester Guardian*. She knew of Class Warfare. The miners' employers were demanding lower wages and longer hours. The General Strike was on its way. The Depression was on its way. Depressed, Bessie hid her head under the pillow. Her own life was so small, so pitiable, so precious. It was hardly worth the effort to stay alive, in all this shapeless and indifferent turmoil. It would be easier to give in and let herself die. She could not face the struggles and the humiliations that lay ahead of her, in that place that was meant to be so pleasant. Better to die here, with her life still before her.

But she breathed deeply, pulled herself together, and in the second week of May, she got up.

It was a bad pattern. Slump, recovery, slump. Not healthy. A poor economy of effort. It could hardly end well.

She got up, got herself back on her feet, stiffened her resolve, ratcheted up her sagging will, and started to put together her Cambridge virgin's trousseau. She was the elected bride of scholarship. She had been wooed and won, and she would embrace her destiny.

By the time she was ready to catch the cross-country train from Breaseborough to Cambridge (changing at March) she had managed to regain some pleasure in the prospect that lay ahead. She had received support from Ada Marr, who told her how lucky she was, and from Ethel Gledhill, who was about to go to study at the Royal Academy of Music in London and who seemed unafraid of the prospect. If they could do it, so could she. Her classmate Reggie Oldroyd from Wath was going up to Cambridge to read Law at Downing and he promised to ask her out to tea. It would not be so bad. ·

✺

She maintained a kind of optimism through the first months of her new life. She ate her meals in hall, she was invited out to tea parties by several women and some men, she attended lectures in the old lecture hall in Mill Lane, she sat on the bridge and looked at the punts on the Cam, she went for walks along the Backs, and found her way round various libraries. In the first week she was befriended by a friendless girl from the north, but Bessie quickly saw through that ploy, and shook her off. She was then taken up by a more acceptable young woman called Frances, a doctor's daughter from Suffolk, whose room was in the same hall and on the same corridor. Bessie suffered the attentions of Frances more graciously, and they became friends, forming a threesome with Molly, the daughter of a well-to-do farmer from Somerset.

Bessie was shy, but shyness was not considered a fault in a young woman. She attracted no adverse comment. Her dress, though inexpensive and plain, was unexceptionable, indeed 'appropriate'. Her manners, also, were unobtrusive. When she did not understand what Frances and Molly were talking about, she remained silent. She listened and learned. Her voice and accent remained identifiably northern, as they were to do for the rest of her life, but nobody teased her about them. The college did not much indulge in teasing. It was high-minded, hardworking and earnestly aware of its secular mission. (It was a nondenominational foundation, chapel free.) There were some 'characters', some eccentrics, some intense artistic souls, some giddy husband-seeking socialites, but the majority of the undergraduates were serious and eager to justify their selected status. They knew that they were the chosen few, and that their college and their university expected much of them. They represented their sex. They were pioneers. They owed it to their college to do well.

This atmosphere of cloistered commitment suited Bessie Bawtry. It helped to distance and to neutralize the painful memory of the misconceived fun of Highcross House, fun which she had found so unfunny and so exclusive. She was not left out of things here. She was not besieged here by the threat of the strain of do-wacka-doo, oogie-oogie-wah-wah, hello Swanee, Ukulele Lady, and such rubbish. She did not have to try to shimmy like her sister Kate, or get to know Susie like we knew Susie, or imitate the vamp of Savannah, hard-hearted Hannah. Some of the young women knew some of the songs of the day, but their familiarity with them did not bring them much cachet. You could get by without a gramophone or a wireless set. Frivolous noise was discouraged. Nor was Bessie pressed to play hockey, though many did, and she was only mildly and it seemed to her affectionately mocked by Frances and Molly for her failure to learn to ride a bicycle. (Frances and Molly gave up on her, after pushing her down a green slope a few times: Bessie simply had no sense of balance, and was of little faith.) The sober tea and coffee and cocoa parties were well within her social range, and she enjoyed the mild competition over the quality of coffee sets, for she had been presented with a very pretty set of her own as a leaving gift by Miss Heald: it was a smart modern Deco design of black and orange, which Bessie had doubted a little until she saw how much others admired it. A coffee set of your own, at that date, marked a rite of passage, and Bessie loved hers accordingly. She had a set of six little silver coffee spoons too, which her parents had bought for her, much to her surprise. She would stare at them with wonder. They were her very own.

They had thin, delicate little handles, marked with her monogram of EB, in elaborate, intertwined, curling script.

Sometimes Bessie even found herself wondering if some of the other young women were not a little dull. She exempted Frances and Molly, whose indulgence towards herself placed them beyond such reproach. But some of the others—were they not predictable, even timid in their views? She missed the intense intellectual sixth-form discussions back in Breaseborough. There was something cosy, girlish and coy in the atmosphere even of an aspiring and austere women's college. Most of the undergraduates had been to highly regimented singlesex schools, and hardly knew any men apart from their brothers. (Bessie was not tempted by intense female friendships—'raves', as they were vulgarly called by some—though one or two were offered to her.) Yes, she found she could safely despise some of these well-qualified young women, from schools more famed than her own. She knew more of the world than they. She had led a less sheltered life than they. She was more accustomed to mixed company. Had she not talked of Keats and Browning and the dramatic monologue, of Shaw and socialism, of Ruskin and Robert Owen and Miners' Welfare, with Joe Barron, with Ada Marr, with Ivy Barron and George Bellew and Jimmie Otley and Ethel Gledhill and Leila Das? A girl from Cheltenham Ladies' College would not know a mine if she saw one.

Bessie had even been for a ride on the back of Phil Barron's motorbike. (It had been terrifying.)

And Miss Heald, as Bessie increasingly realized, had been a rarity amongst schoolmistresses. Few of her contemporaries had been encouraged to read as widely as Bessie, and some of these Cambridge dons knew less of T. S. Eliot and Edith Sitwell, I. A. Richards and Virginia Woolf than Miss Heald in South Yorkshire. Bessie Bawtry had been well prepared. Intellectually, Bessie, in these early months, felt secure.

The college buildings, with their warm red brick, their

large sunny windows, their handsome bronze gates, their turrets and oriels, were everything that Breaseborough was not. They were built in harmony, to please. They were the heavenly city. Acanthus and sunflower adorned them. And the college routine was comforting and dignified. Bessie had her own room, and there was no slavish little spaniel Dora tagging at her heels. Bessie was treated like a lady. She was provided with clean laundry. Maids in uniform waited in hall, maids cleaned her room and brought her a scuttle full of coal each day to make up her fire in its efficient little grate. She took to her newly refined status as though made for it. Had she not always known she was born to be a lady? She enjoyed her six hours of daily reading, she enjoyed her supervisions, she enjoyed attending lectures and making notes in her clear, free, even, open hand. Nobody threatened her. The air was clean. Even the coal seemed cleaner than the coal up north. She sat by her hearth and toasted her legs, her fair hair falling forward, her head bent over Chaucer and Dryden and her notes on I. A. Richards. The room was all her own. She felt the safety of the space about her. She seemed to be in control.

There were some anxieties and hesitations. She worried about money. Although she took care of every penny, she had at once realized—indeed, from the time of her first interview had foreknown—that she would be on a smaller allowance than most of her fellow students. Most of them were the daughters of barristers, of headmasters, of civil servants and farmers, of local government officers, of archdeacons and doctors and architects. Bessie did not discover any other daughters of electricians, though she might, had she tried, have encountered the daughter of a carpenter, a builder, a soldier-mechanic. Some of the acts of careless spending which she witnessed astonished her, though pride concealed her surprise. Frances from Suffolk, a kind and generous girl, noticed Bessie's moments of embarrassment, and was tactful in her little gifts of tea and scones and biscuits—'Try this, Bess, it's delicious, it's a shortbread, my mother sent it, do you like it?' Frances and Molly bought the cake from Fitzbillie's on Silver Street when the trio gave a party. All this was done so thoughtfully that Bessie was able to accept with silent gratitude. She was their little pet—they even called her 'Pet'—and it was natural that they should treat her.

Nevertheless, there was always a residual anxiety about her rail ticket home, about the cost of sending her trunk on ahead, about repairs to shoes, and extras for jam or sweets or laundry or firelighters. She kept a little notebook, for petty-cash entries. And petty they were—a shilling here, a sixpence there. Some of these women—Bessie was not the only one—lived like mice. Bessie did not mind living like a mouse, for she knew it was in a good cause, and, as we have seen, she had not been brought up to indulgence. But one did need shoes, laundry, paper, envelopes, cough mixture and the train fare home. The scholarship money had to be measured out with care.

To Bessie, the college food was a pleasure. She did not notice that the soup was a thin, semi-transparent gravy, that the vegetables were wet, and the beef overcooked and tough. She did not care that the rhubarb and custard lacked élan. She did not expect claret, and sole and partridge would have terrified her. The food came, and her mother had not cooked it, and that was good enough, at this stage in her life, for Bessie Bawtry. She was in receipt of regular, nourishing meals. What more could one want? She listened to the Latin grace before Hall with primly bowed head, and was glad that she was not one of the scholars designated to read it aloud. She blessed the Lord, although she did not believe in him. She blessed the West Yorkshire Education Authority, whose form the Lord, for her benefit, had taken.

She was happy. She reported her happiness to Miss Heald, to her parents, to the girls back home engaged to shop assistants or garage mechanics, to those on vacation from other forms of higher education. She boasted to Dora of her room, her friends, her coffee set, her conquests, her excursions. In her first Cambridge summer she took tea at the Orchard in Grantchester (though Dr Leavis, whose supervisions she attended, had already reinforced Miss Heald's suspicions and taught her not to admire Rupert Brooke). She bought books— a Hogarth Press copy of T. S. Eliot's *Homage to John Dryden* and secondhand copies of the works of George Gissing and Mark Rutherford. She was to read and admire Virginia Woolf's *Mrs Dalloway,* which was too new to have captured Dr Leavis's attention. She was taken punting, and drank cider sitting in deep grass. Once in a while she smoked a cigarette, delicately, to 'keep away the midges'.

See her, as she sits reading on a rug in the spacious college garden, amidst the glow of red brick and fresh white paint, amidst delphinium and lavender, by a sunken pond of water lilies. See her as she walks along the bank of the Cam, in her button-bar shoes, in her wide-collared, low-waisted, above-the-knee cotton frock. Her shingled hair, neatly cut and shampooed in Newnham Village, shines in the sun, and her legs are slim and brown. She is petite and slight, her skin is clear and fair, and her breasts are firm and small and shapely. She has escaped. Surely she has escaped. She has left the smuts and the clinker behind her. Pale blue and gold is she, with her cotton dress and her huge periwinkle eyes and her neat little ankles. She has cotton gloves for the daytime, and, folded in a drawer in tissue, she treasures the glacé kid gloves she wore at her first ball. She cannot dance, but she has been to a May Week Ball, invited by a polite young man from Pembroke who is reading Modern Languages. (They tried to teach her to dance, back in Breaseborough, but she could not get the hang of it. She could never hear the beat.) It does not matter that she cannot dance. Young women are in short supply at Cambridge, and Bessie is a pretty little thing, a decorative escort, full of shy admiring glances and sweet smiles. The sweetness of her nature is taken for granted by the young men who walk her out. Bessie will never ever snarl or snap or scorn.

She walks on, from her first summer into her second autumn, into her second year, budding, expectant, breathing in the clean and smokeless air, shaping her sentences, shaping her life, expanding her acquaintance.

The cinema she attends, and the theatre. She sees pioneering productions at the Festival Theatre by Tyrone Guthrie and Ninette de Valois, though she has to leave early to rush back to college before the gates close: she rarely sees the last acts of plays. She sees, unknowingly, the early efforts of undergraduate Michael Redgrave. She is much taken by college performances of plays by Ibsen and Pirandello, and a Marlowe Society production of *Coriolanus* directed (though she does not know this) by a colourful and sexually ambiguous character called Frank Birch, who will double careers in the theatre and the wartime Secret Service. (Volumnia is played by the charming pink-faced young George 'Dadie' Rylands, friend and protégé of Virginia Woolf: at this period, in the university dramatic societies, female roles were played by young men, as they were in the days of Shakespeare, a convention deplored by some and much relished by others.) She sees *The Bacchae,* all-male, performed in Greek. She sees *Elektra,* also in Greek, performed at Girton, with a thrilling performance of the deadly Clytemnestra by a hook-nosed Girton girl. Her life is full of discoveries. She sticks a Medici print of Van Gogh's sunflowers on her wall. She reads of the mysteries of Tutankhamen, and buys a poster with Egyptian figures on it. Egypt, for a brief while, is all the rage, and the Egyptian dead are in fashion. She has an impassioned conversation with Reggie Oldroyd about evolution. If Darwin is right, why haven't human beings evolved more *visibly* since the time of the Pharaohs? Surely six thousand years is a longish time? And what, challenged Reggie, are we supposed to have evolved into, since the Pharaohs? Are we supposed to have shed a toe, or a finger, or gained an extra eye or a different number of choppers? Don't be an ass, Reggie! laughs Bessie—though that is, in fact, sort of what she had meant.

Will Bessie Bawtry grow a third eye, or an extra toe? Watch and see if she sprouts. She may mutate at any moment. Dr Hawthorn is in the wings, waiting to spot a mutation.

See her turn the corner into Petty Cury, a street of which the very name enchants—Bessie Bawtry, undergraduate and scholar, in the very heart of Cambridge, where once walked Milton, Wordsworth, and those brave early women who strode ahead and made smooth the path for such fortunate followers as Bessie from the north. Autumn is ripening, and so is she. Is she not every inch a success? How proud they are of her back home! Her little feet are light upon the pavement. She dawdles, looking in shop windows. She is on her way to Downing College, to talk about D. H. Lawrence, the miner's son from Nottingham. She is shy, but can hold her own in debate.

Watch her now as she walks up Sidgwick Avenue, amidst the rich rotting smell of autumn leaves. The glossy chestnuts split, the five-fingered fronds are trodden into leafmeal, the winged seeds drift, the brickwork glows red. She is off to discuss Andrew Marvell, that aristocratic Yorkshire poet of the northern dales. She will speak of him with the diminutive and kindly dwarf, the learned Miss Wellesford, who has a soft spot for our Bessie. Oh happiness! She is in her place, and all is well.

Christmas comes, and she catches a mild chill, and is fortified with Virol.

Where is Joe Barron, all this while? Please God that he has escaped too. If he has escaped Bessie, then all can be undone. Let it be undone. Let it all never have happened. Let it be unwound, unstitched, unwounded. An extra toe would surely deter Joe Barron? Quickly, quickly. It seems slow, this process, but now is the moment to prevent all the pain. If Bessie mutates now, then Joe will be saved, and all that may come to be will be cancelled, and posterity will be spared. Faro Gaulden will not have to sit and stare at that screen, nor will Faro's mother be condemned to grief and pain, for neither of them will be born. They will be spared. Not to be born is best, as the ancients said. Can't somebody tell that, now, to Bessie Bawtry and Joe Barron, before they inflict their shortcomings and their misgivings and their indecisions upon their suffering gene pool and bloodline? Can't somebody warn them, before it is too late?

Bessie did not mutate. She seemed to thrive and prosper, according to her own lights and her own plans. But, gradually, almost inevitably, something seemed to begin to go wrong. Her first year in Cambridge passed pleasantly and without incident, but in the middle of her second year she began to show vague signs of distress, signs that intensified as the last term of the year approached. There were telltale signals that anyone familiar with her medical track record would have noted with alarm. There were retirings to bed, and missings of lectures, and unfinished essays, and visits to the sick bay and the college nurse. The college nurse could not find much wrong with her, and suspected a case of examination nerves. Clearly Bessie had not got influenza, though there were flu panics and epidemics throughout the twenties, but Bessie's temperature was if anything subnormal. The nurse listened with interest to the story of the Spanish flu in Breaseborough, then gave her charge a prescription for a placebo tonic, and sent her cheerily away. Bessie meekly drank up the bottle of mixture, and, two weeks into the summer term of her second year, she took, decisively, to her bed.

She seemed determined to stay there. If she were not allowed into the sick bay, she would stay in her room and die.

Her friend Frances, the doctor's daughter, sympathetic about money and food, proved less sympathetic about illness. If Bessie wanted to stay in bed, let her. What could be wrong with her? Was she upset about that young man at Pembroke who had stood her up over an evening at the Festival Theatre? Bessie had certainly set her cap at him. She would have to pay the price of failure. Frances, who had herself no intention of marrying, and no interest in men, had taken against the young man from Pembroke. He had laughed too much, and had too many teeth in too square a jaw. Others thought him handsome, but Frances did not.

Molly, the farmer's daughter, showed more concern, and kept calling in with jugs of lemonade and mugs of hot milk. She too wondered if there were a man in the case. Bessie had sometimes claimed to have an admirer back home in Breaseborough, an old schoolfriend called Joe, who, belatedly, was to sit his Cambridge entrance that autumn. Did this Joe really exist, or was he a defensive invention, a strategic ploy? Many girls invented boyfriends back home, in order to avoid sexual overtures in Cambridge, or to explain a lack of sexual overtures. If this Joe did exist, had he broken off with Bessie? Did Bessie dread Joe's arrival? Or his failure to arrive? Molly did not like the look of Bessie, as she lay pale, hot and miserable on her spinsterly couch, propped up on patchwork-covered pillows in a darkened room, complaining her head ached. Molly, a motherly young woman, who had cared for sucking calves and puppies and kittens, felt she ought to do something about Bessie. If she continued to lie around like this she would fail part one of her Tripos, and then where would she be? Molly knew what heroic efforts had brought Bessie from Breaseborough to Cambridge. She did not want to see them wasted. For herself, it would not matter much if she did not do well. She would marry, one day, she felt sure. And she was not delicate like Bessie. Perhaps Bessie was ill, really ill? Was it meningitis, rheumatic fever, heart disease? She felt hot to the touch, but her temperature remained normal. What did that mean? Was Bessie letting down the cause of Higher Education for Women?

Molly took the liberty of writing to Mrs Bawtry about her daughter. She had no conception of the scale of this transgression. She had missed her own mother a good deal in her first year, and certainly, had she been off-colour (which she never was), she would have wished to see her arrive at college with hampers and motherly kisses and good will. So Molly wrote to Mrs Bawtry, a nice note saying Bessie was a little poorly, expecting this to elicit a comforting message in return. She was not to know how she had miscalculated, nor how seriously her letter would be read in Breaseborough. Surely only a fatal illness could justify a letter from a stranger?

Mrs Bawtry, imagining the worst, determined that it was her duty to go and rescue her daughter from whatever it was that had laid her low. The thought of the train journey alarmed her, and she did not know what she would do for the fare. Ellen Cudworth had made a little money before her marriage as a pattern-maker, but as Ellen Bawtry she had never had a penny of her own. Every penny that she spent was taken from the housekeeping that Bert gave her from his pay packet each Friday night. Where would she find the five pounds she would need for a visit to Cambridge? She hardly knew where to turn. She did not dare to ask her own husband, her daughter's father, because she feared his criticism of her budget. Being a 'bad manager' was the worst fear she had. So she asked young Dora.

Dora, by now, was working for Auntie Florrie as a dressmaker's assistant. She cut out patterns, stitched and machined seams on the handsome Singer treadle of polished brown wood and gleaming black and gold metal. She was a lot better at dressmaking than her mother had ever been. (The blouse she had made for Bessie's Cambridge trousseau, of pale blue flowered artificial silk with a soft necktie and contrasting white binding, had been quite professional.) And she seemed to have a knack of getting the shapes together very thriftily. Wartime exigencies had schooled her well. Auntie Florrie was very pleased with her. She paid her by the hour, and the shillings mounted up. Dora liked the days she spent at Auntie Florrie's, cutting out on the floor of the front room, or trying on and pinning. Florrie had a little dog called Trigger, and Dora loved Trigger. She knelt in the coal dust and dog hair, on a peg rug, cutting out children's dresses and ladies' wear, watched by a wire-haired fox terrier that was her friend. It was not very hygienic at Auntie Florrie's, but nobody seemed to mind.

Yes, Dora told her mother, she did have five pounds saved up, and of course her mother could 'borrow' it to go and see Bessie in Cambridge.

And Ellen Bawtry would have braved the unknown and gone to Cambridge, had not a telegram arrived, forbidding her. Bessie had rallied, and risen from her couch, and cranked herself back into gear. The image of her discordant, uneasy mother, lost in mannerly Cambridge, had filled Bessie with such pitiful anxiety (on whose behalf she could not have said, but perhaps not wholly on her own?) that she pulled herself together, and started to revise for part one of her Tripos, which she was to sit at the end of May.

Mrs Bawtry, stout, ill-dressed and clumsy: respectable, proud, plain and cleanly: willing to enter the realms of the enemy in search of her lost daughter, whom, despite all love-lessness, she loved. She would have knocked at the tomb door and said, come forth. But it was not asked of her. The summons was cancelled. Her daughter sealed the tomb from within.

The shade of Ellen Bawtry shuffles along the long corridor in her best purple paisley dress and her flat best shoes, a little cracked and creaking under her combined Cudworth-Bawtry weight. Past the portraits, past the busts of antique matrons, beneath the Greek key frieze that tops the high wall, Ellen Bawtry pads along, on the polished, clinically disinfected wood-block floor. She is a substantial shade, an obese York-shire shade. She looks neither to right nor to left. Her face is set with a grim fix of disapproving fear. But she approves the high shine on the wood blocks.

Or so it might have been, had the call been answered.

The ghosts of classical scholars and wrangling mathematicians also walk these corridors and haunt these gardens. You may see them marching, heads held high, gaunt, caped, high-browed, shabby, eccentric, with touches of lace, with cameos at the throat, with big noses and haughty expressions and confident steps. They pace the lawns beneath the trees, of a summer evening. They perambulate the sundial and the sunken fishpond. Gallant old women, pioneers and protestors and adventurers. Quaint phrases linger after them, snatches and tags of Greek and of Latin, a faint odour of learning and of courage. Sherry, biscuits, peppermint, cocoa, violet.

What have they to say, these learned ladies, to the shade of Ellen Bawtry? They do not speak the same language. They do not inhabit the same realm. A faint dying snigger of recessive laughter hangs in the air. Ellen Bawtry hears it, turns, listens, wounded, suspicious, shakes her head.

The slut scrubs the steps. The damp souls of housemaids sprout despondently in little cupboards and kitchens, in dark corners and cold attics.

Mrs Bawtry shuffles on, in search of her lost daughter. The wide corridors seem infinite, and, like the corridors of a maze, they lead her nowhere. She will never find her daughter here. It is as well that she does not come here to try.

The black beetles scuttle. Surely somebody should sweep them up.

Had Bessie Bawtry, somewhere in these corridors, over-heard the phrase 'They let the scum of the earth in here now'?

So Bessie Bawtry recovered, and bravely faced the possibility of failure, and sat for part one of her Tripos. She sat down, on the afternoon of Monday, 23 May, and confronted her first paper of what was then known as English B. Three hours of it, and a warm day; the sun shone outside, and indoors pens scratched on paper. Three hours of questions on La Tène fire-dogs, the Beaker people, bronze shields and the Mildenhall burials: to be followed by other papers on other hot days on the Vikings, on Teutonic brooches, on socketed axes, on the Plymstock and Arreton Down hoards, on trade routes and runes and ruins. Was it for this that Miss Heald had encouraged Bessie Bawtry to read J. Alfred Prufrock and Edith Sitwell? What had all this to do with English Literature? What was she doing here?

Bessie was all at sea, and knew it, for it had taken her a year or so of her time at Cambridge to realize that these remote topics were part of her syllabus, not merely interesting background information, which she could take or leave as she chose. It had never occurred to her that she would be examined on them. She had sat with wandering and wondering mind through lectures on trade routes, dutifully taking notes, but taking little in, and mishearing 'roots' for 'routes'—the sense was the same as the sound to her. Tree roots, trade routes, flies trapped in Baltic amber, coral necklaces, skulls in potholes, skulls split by axe heads. What had all these to do with the Word? She had been utterly confused. These subjects seemed as remote from the English literature which she had thought she was studying as the discoveries then being made by Newnham scholar Gertrude Caton-Thompson in the pre-dynastic settlement sites and Neolithic cultures of the Nile. It was the shock of discovering that she had to sit papers on trade routes that had precipitated her collapse. She did not dare to reveal her folly to anyone. She did not want to make herself out to be a slack, stupid, dumb girl from the north, who did not even know what course she was supposed to be studying. Had not Miss Heald insisted that it was of the ut-most importance to READ THE QUESTIONS CAREFULLY and AN-

SWER THE CORRECT NUMBER IN THE TIME GIVEN? (It was Joe Barron's failure to do this, in Miss Heald's view, that had cost him his County.) And now she had done far far worse than Joe Barron! She had prepared for the wrong papers. Miss Heald would never forgive her.

No wonder Bessie had taken to her bed.

However, Bessie thought she might manage to scrape by, for during her convalescence she had managed to swot up secretly on some of the areas she had neglected. And now, sitting in front of her first paper, she was able to find, even in this archaeological waste land, a theme or two on which she could discourse intelligently—the conception of Fate amongst the Scandinavian peoples and its influence upon the form of the saga, a short essay on 'The wo of these women that woneth in cotes'. And she was safe with her *Beowulf,* for she had her *Beowulf* by heart, as she had had her Virgil two years earlier for her Higher Certificate examination. She knew her *Beowulf* through and throughly. What could be conquered late by industry, she had conquered. And so she scraped by, though for the rest of her life those teasing terrible objects and subjects would rise up before her to torment her in her dreams—the Jellinge stone, the Oseberg Viking Ship, the Halton Cross, the funerary rites of the Romans in Britain. She would never be free of them, until death came to free her. They were scorched and scarred into her. They would be incinerated with her upon her funeral pyre.

As soon as Bessie had completed her last paper, she collapsed again, and this time she managed to run a high fever and was briefly admitted to the college sick bay. If she were to fail utterly, would she be eligible for a sick note and an *ae-grotat*? She did not want to go home until she had established either failure or success. But she could not languish in the sick bay for ever. She had to go home. She had nowhere else to go. She would have to wait in Slotton Road for the news, good or bad. So home she went, with her box and her railway ticket.

(In fact, she need not have gone straight home. She could have gone to stay for a couple of weeks with Molly in Somerset. Molly's mother had warmly invited her. But Bessie had declined. She wanted to *feel* as though she had nowhere else to go. She felt safer with fewer options. She preferred a sense of mild grievance over the risk of new scenes and new pleasures. She would have liked to see the farm, but she had not the spirit for it. So she perversely cherished her sense of exclusion.)

And maybe she had other reasons for going home.

She waited, anxiously, in Slotton Road, for her results. Did her parents realize how worried she was? She hoped not. Fortunately for her, they were distracted by an event of larger portent. They had become interested in the forthcoming total eclipse of the sun, predicted for Wednesday, 29 June of that year. You wouldn't have thought, Bessie said to Ethel Gledhill, that they'd be interested in that kind of thing, would you?

Bert and Ellen's interest was not astronomical. The eclipse happened to coincide with their wedding anniversary, and it happened to reach totality in their own county of Yorkshire, which made it seem special. The eclipse had been made for the Bawtrys, and they intended to see it at its best. Bert negotiated two days off work, days owed to him from previous unclaimed holidays, and willingly granted in recognition of his public-spirited and voluntary efforts at the cinema. The eclipse was due to occur at 6.23 a.m., well to the northwest of Breaseborough, and Bert and Ellen were off on their motorbike and sidecar to spend a night with cousins in Darlington. The Great North Road would be crowded with eclipse spectators, travelling towards the sensational morning darkness. It would be a spree.

Bessie could not decide what line to take about the eclipse. Was it proper to find it exciting? On balance, she thought it was not. She would ignore it, and think of higher things. She thought of Women's Suffrage, and almost attended a rally in Barnsley in favour of its extension to all women over twenty-one. (Married women and property-owning women over thirty had won the vote in 1918, when Bessie was still a child.) Bessie was to call herself a feminist for the rest of her life, though it is not clear how she herself contributed to the feminist cause. She was to read, on publication, Shaw's *The Intelligent Woman's Guide to Socialism,* the first of the Penguin Pelicans, and always claimed that it had affected her profoundly. And maybe it did. The reading of a book can be a contribution to a cause.

The days of waiting seemed long. It was an anxious time. Would the examination results be published in *The Times,* as some but not all Tripos results were? (Women's were published in a separate column, demarcated from the men's, indicating that they were not recognized as full members of the university.) Would they be published in the *Breaseborough Times,* which, though chiefly concerned with advertisements and sporting and social fixtures, did, as we have seen, take a sporadic interest in the intellectual successes of the children of its town? Did humiliation await her? Well, we have all been through this. There is nothing special about this. So Bessie told herself, each morning, as she got up to see if there was an envelope for her.

The *Breaseborough Times* published aerial views of collieries and reports of accidents. A seventy-five-year-old man, injured in a fall on a night shift at Bednerby Main, had died in Wardale Hospital. He had fallen into a four-foot-two-inch manhole while walking down Wardale Plain, miles underground. (The hospital, in June, was briefly closed because of an outbreak of smallpox, as the paper reported.) Did Bessie think it odd that a man of seventy-five should be working underground in the middle of the night? Yes, to be fair to her, she did. This life seemed horrible to her. There must be a better world than this. Had she any idea what Wardale Plain might look like? She had read her Virgil, and could guess. The smoky vale of Acheron, the highway of the dead.

Even women died at the pit. On 25 June, a Mrs S. A. Harrison was killed while working at Denvers Main. What was her job there? We do not know. The *Breaseborough Times* does not say. Presumably she was not working underground. By the 1920s the days of Zola's *Germinal* were over, surely.

The coal fire at college had flickered so cheerily in its little grate. If she failed, would she be allowed back to Cambridge to try again? Or would she be obliged to descend into obscurity? No, she would never descend. She would keep her head above the closing fissures. She would keep a clean house.

Beneath your feet they tramp and dig and hack and choke.

The insulted earth smoulders, heaves and splits. The toxic gases cluster, leak and spill.

The envelope arrived ten days before the sun went out, nine days before her parents set off on their outing. Bessie did not fail. She passed. She did not pass with good grades, with scholarship-justifying grades, as she had earlier hoped and expected, as others had hoped and expected. She, who had always been top of the class, had to be satisfied with what was colloquially known as a 'Two Two'—a Class Two, Division Two pass. But she had passed, and she was relieved. Her parents were not familiar with the niceties of grades. Bessie made sure they did not take too much interest in them now.

Bert and Ellen Bawtry congratulate their daughter. Is she a graduate yet? It seems she is only halfway there, but so far, so good. They will never understand the Cambridge jargon. They are happy, as they take to the open highway. Ellen puts on her goggles and her weird horned and ear-flapped wool hat, Bert dons his motorbike gear, they wave, and off they go. The Great North Road, with its famous staging posts, its new AA signs, its sprouting of bed and breakfast accommodations, its teas with Hovis, its beauty spots, allures them with its promise of displacement and romance. They rattle along in fine spirits. Cousins Ada and George Cudworth have boldly embraced the new Motoring Age, and have opened a B and B with Homemade Teas just this side of Darlington. They take in travellers from Edinburgh on their way south, from London on their way north. They brew tea and burn toast and fry bacon and bake rock cakes, and they dry sheets in their backyard on a clothesline with a wooden prop. Eggs, boiled, 4d each, poached or scrambled 5d each, with bread and butter for your tea. Dora would have loved to go to Auntie Ada's for the eclipse, but there is not room for her in the sidecar. She will have to stay in Breaseborough with Bessie. But, as she admires and believes she loves Bessie, she does not feel left out. Well, not much, anyway.

The people of the coalfields love the dales and the moors and the open roads. The people of Yorkshire love the Great North Road, the highway to adventure, and will complain when it is renamed the A1. Dora has done an original school project on the Great North Road, for which she got good marks. She would like to have gone too.

Does a workforce gather on coal, like insects on a wound? Sheep graze the short sweet turf of the dales. Nobody herds them underground.

Back in Breaseborough, Bessie was visited by Joe Barron. Were Joe Barron and Bessie Bawtry courting? Dora, who was deputed to chaperone them as they sat on the couch in the front room, thought that they were, though she was not quite sure what courting involved. This was an age of sexual innocence, and Dora was to remain an innocent all her life. Bessie and Joe sat close to one another, and whispered. Had Bert and Ellen gone to Darlington partly in order to give Joe Barron a sporting chance? They approved of Joe. He was a polite young man, of good family. They would be delighted if Joe made an offer for Bessie. It would be a step up in the world for Bessie. Bert and Ellen didn't care much about such things, but they were not wholly indifferent to them either.

Bessie and Joe Barron spoke of many matters. They were young, and they were idealistic and hopeful, and they agreed with Bernard Shaw that there must be a better world than this. They went together to a lecture at the Settlement in Sheffield on Anglo-Soviet relations, which took a mildly pro-Soviet line. They went together to see Greta Garbo in a movie at the Rialto, and they went to see a production of *Dr Faustus* by the Northam Players.

Joe Barron, she had been informed by Reggie Oldroyd, would be joining her in Cambridge next October, to read Law at Downing. She now, on home ground, discovered this to be true. Joe had wasted two years of his life selling glass, but his father had relented, and he had been coached, and had worked through long evenings, and had sat his entrance examinations and obtained a place. His mother and his sisters had supported him. His long wait was over, and his real free life was about to begin. So it's a pity, you might think, to find him still hanging around his hometown sweetheart, just when he could have made a break for it, and got away from it all.

Bessie was very pretty, in those days. She wasn't as handsome as Garbo, but she was much prettier than the young woman who played Helen in Marlowe's *Faustus* in Northam. Her extra toe remained well hidden.

Sexual attraction and pity do not mix well. They are a dangerous combination, as granddaughter Faro, whose conception begins to seem more and more unavoidable, will one day discover.

ᏫᎤᎲᎤ

So Bessie Bawtry took her degree, and she got a Two One in part two of the English Tripos (Part Two, Section A, held under the Old Regulations). She appears to have written, amongst other topics, on Greek Tragedy, Donne, *Paradise Lost*, Swift and Samuel Butler, and to have addressed Samuel Richardson's sneer 'that had he not known who Fielding was, he should have believed he was an ostler'. One wonders what she had to say about this. She left Cambridge, armed with references from Miss Wellesford and the great F. R. Leavis himself, but jobs were hard to come by in those days of slump, and she found herself, to her dismay, back in Breaseborough, teaching at her own old school, and living at home again with Ellen and Bert. She had not travelled far. Her Yorkshire accent had perhaps prejudiced interviewers against her. This was not her opinion, for she did not believe herself to have a Yorkshire accent, but this is what others suspected. Miss Heald felt obliged to take her back into the fold. Her protégée, her prodigal, had come home, to the town she had sworn she would leave for ever. It was a defeat, though nobody dared to say so. She came home, as one less favoured member of staff brutally whispered, 'with her tail between her legs'.

Dora once risked a remark about Breaseborough not being so bad after all, but Bessie ignored it. She did not want to reconcile herself to Breaseborough.

In later years, she was never to speak of this period. She did not speak of it to her children or to her granddaughter. But it was there, on record. Also on record was a prize-winning review she had written for the *Yorkshire Post* of the Sheffield Settlement's production of *Journey's End*. The *Breaseborough Times* had reproduced it in full, with the headline 'High Literary Quality: Breaseborough Teacher Wins Award', and a photograph of pretty twenty-three-year-old Miss Bawtry. Her father was quoted as saying, 'I thought she would stand a good chance, so I had a little bet with my daughter, and now we have both won something.'

Joe was still at Downing, making up for the two years he had lost, and enjoying himself: he played tennis (quite well), went boating and, unlike Bessie, drank claret (though not much). He escorted young ladies to tea dances at the Dorothy Café, in the approved manner, and to May Balls. He was charming, good-looking and good-hearted. Too good-hearted, perhaps, for he considered himself by now to be morally bound to Bessie Bawtry, despite the fact that she had almost become engaged to a young man from Pembroke. That commitment had been broken off for reasons that were never to become clear, but Joe could have used it as an excuse, had he wished to. He too got an upper second degree and liked to tell the tale of how, bracing himself to read the class lists pinned up at the Senate House, he began at the bottom and, not finding his name in either the thirds or lower seconds, at first concluded he had failed.

Joe embarked on a precarious and initially penurious life as a barrister in Northam, and taught at the WEA in the evenings, partly for the money (though the work was ill paid) and partly through a sense of social duty. He and Bessie were married a couple of years later in Breaseborough Church, which was odd, as they both came from chapel families. This part of the story is full of oddities and lacunae. It is not clear why they married at all. But they did.

If this story were merely a fiction, it would be possible to fill in these gaps with plausible incidents, but the narrator here has to admit to considerable difficulty, indeed to failure. I have tried—and I apologize for that intrusive authorial 'I', which I have done my best to avoid—I have tried to understand why Joe and Bessie married, and I have tried to invent some plausible dialogue for them that might explain it. They must have had a lot to say to one another while they were courting in the front room, while Dora made herself scarce and made herself a cup of tea out the back. There must have been pleasantness, once, surely. There must, surely, have been a pleasant beginning, before the bitter end. Molly used to say that there was a strong sexual attraction between Joe and Bessie when they were young—and certainly Bessie seems to have had no difficulty in conceiving, although she had other gynaecological difficulties. But perhaps Molly said that to please or appease Bessie's children, over whom the storm clouds of discontent were to gather. It was not their fault, motherly Molly wanted to say. The children were not to be blamed for the misery of the parents.

Maybe there was love, once. But later bitterness has utterly obscured it. The water is dark with resentment and contempt. Bessie had always been strong on contempt, even as a child, but who could have foreseen that it would have thickened and spread until it stained and darkened and poisoned all things? Joe did not foresee it, or he would not have married her. Nobody warned him.

We are left with the facts, and they are sparse. Joe Barron and Bessie Bawtry married, in St Andrews Church in Breaseborough, with Dora and Ivy as bridesmaids. They set up house in a nice suburb in Northam in a semi-detached purchased for them by Joe's father. The Barron parents had been neither pleased nor displeased by the match: socially, Bessie was not much of a catch, but she was a polite, well-educated and thoroughly respectable young woman, so she would do. The Barrons were not ambitious. Bessie, of course, gave up her teaching career, as married women were obliged to do in those days. She said she regretted this, but she did not say it with much conviction. She was certainly glad to get out of Breaseborough at last. Perhaps she married Joe to get out of Breaseborough.

Did Joe marry her because he felt he had to play the knight in shining armour and rescue her from the humiliation of her return home, from the shock of being jilted by that cool large-toothed young man from Pembroke? Did he pity her? Or did he love her, had he always loved her? He had no need to marry her. He could have looked elsewhere and married out. He had no need to marry into Hammervale.

We would not be asking these questions had all turned out well for Joe and Bessie. But all did not turn out well. We do not know the details of what went wrong.

Joe and Bessie married, and moved to Northam. Bessie had two miscarriages before being delivered of a healthy son, Robert. Three years later, war broke out.

Bessie's second child, Christine Flora Barron, was born in the Montagu Maternity Hospital in Northam, at two thirty in the afternoon, towards the end of the phoney war, before the bombs began to fall in earnest upon London and the industrial cities of the north of England. Christine Flora Barron is of more interest to us and to geneticist Dr Hawthorn than her brother Robert, for she is in the direct matrilineal line of descent. Robert is consigned (or will consign himself) to a minor role: almost to a non-speaking part. We shall come back to Chrissie and her childhood shortly, but meanwhile let us return—or rather let us leap forward in time—to Chrissie's daughter and Bessie's granddaughter Faro, whom we left, if you remember, in a Nonconformist chapel in Bessie's birthplace, Breaseborough, in the company of Bessie's sister, her Great-Aunt Dora.

᠙᠎ᠣ

Faro, as we are reunited with her, is still to be found in Breaseborough, but she and Auntie Dora have left the chapel and the assembled Cudworths, and are now sitting together in Dora's little house on Swinton Road. This is the house where Dora has lived alone for many decades, so close to the house on Slotton Road where she was born. Faro has driven Dora home, and now they are sitting together over cups of instant coffee: Faro's coffee is black, and Dora's is made with old-fashioned full-cream silver-top milk and a dash of hot water. (Faro, who had prepared these beverages to their respective tastes, had not at all liked the look of the contents of Dora's fridge-freezer.) Dora's house is small, cramped and stuffed, and it smells of old woman, of Minton the cat and his predecessors, of geranium, of paraffin and of the soot of centuries. The pits are dead, and the air in Breaseborough is purer now, cleansed by the Clean Air Acts of the late 1950s, but the smell of the past lingers and loiters in cushions and soft furnishings, in curtains and cupboards. Faro sniffs, inquisitively, diagnostically. It is an interesting smell, but not to be endured for long. Faro has made it clear that she cannot stay long, as she has to hit the road to London. This is a lie, but it is a white lie. Faro intends to spend the night in the Phoenix Hotel on the Northam bypass. Faro suspects that Dora knows she is lying. Dora is no fool, although she has often been treated as one.

Faro stays for an hour, chatting, hearing the same old stories, and some new ones. Faro is interested in the past, and is intrigued by Dora's many-layered décor. Dora enjoys talking about what she calls her 'treasures'. A strange mixture of styles and substances and periods presents itself in Dora's small front room: its furnishings include a Victorian dresser covered in knickknacks, cross-stitched antimacassars, brass fire-irons in front of a bricked-up fireplace, flooring of patterned linoleum covered by peg rugs and a Turkey carpet runner, and a three-piece suite clothed in worn dark green chintzy loosecovers that had been handed on many years ago from sister Bessie. The scorched plastic lampshades, pleated, fluted and heavily stitched down their ribs, defy all categorization: they are, claims Dora, original Barron pieces, dating back to the twenties or thirties. And that range of table napkin rings displayed on the mantelpiece—rings representing bunny rabbits, pussy cats, doggies and chucky hen—those too, Dora says, are Barron designs. This is news to Faro, and she gets up to inspect them more closely. There is, she finds, something unpleasing in their texture, in the streak and mix of their browns and greens. (Faro, it is to be recalled, is her grandmother's daughter's daughter, by directly traceable mitochondrial descent.) The table lamp, in contrast, is a dated futuristic 1951 piece inspired by the Festival of Britain, and nothing to do with Barron design at all: Dora had purchased it on one of her jaunts to Sheffield.

The wallpaper is flowered in autumn tints of orange and brown and yellow, and a frieze of leaves runs below the picture rail. (Do people still have picture rails? Faro thinks not. Seb's pad has a picture rail, but Seb is not people.) From Dora's picture rail depend various items—a framed embroidery picture of a bluebell wood, a watercolour of an estuary which Dora says her Grandma Bawtry won at a whist drive, a green Wedgwood plate with a pattern of ivy and a leaning plastic container from which a spider plant, in every stage of death, rebirth and pupping, dangles dreadfully, at an uncomfortable angle, sprouting feebly but as it were perpetually, in papery stripes of yellows and whites and browns and greens. A row of pots, filled with geranium, begonia, cactus, African violet and shrimp plant, stands upon the windowsill: they thrive more pleasantly than the spider plant, despite the fact that Auntie Dora claims they like to be watered from time to time with hot tea. And all this accumulated clutter is dominated by an enormous television set of the very latest model, which has every possible new device attached to it. Dora cannot work them all, but she likes, as she puts it, to be up to the minute. Who knows, she may need Sky or subtitles or digital or sign language any day? She's not sure what they are, but she wants the option.

'So Bennett Barron went bankrupt?' prompted Faro, trying to steer the conversation away from price differentials at Morrison's, Kwiksave and Mrs Maggs on the corner, and the weight of tins of cat food.

'More or less,' said Dora, with the satisfaction that Yorkshire people so often take in the sorrows of others. 'He ruined the business. He wasn't declared bankrupt, but he ruined the business. Dragged his brother Alfred into it too. And it didn't affect your father' (*my grandfather,* silently emended Faro— Dora was always muddling up her generations), 'no, it didn't affect your father, he'd got away by then, it was hard on the girls. Mind you, they asked for it. Man-mad, Rowena was. And Ivy was worse, she wasn't interested in men at all. Yes, a lot of what went wrong with the firm was Bennett's fault. He was too newfangled. He wasn't satisfied with glass. He wanted to invest in that stuff made of milk.'

'What?'

'That stuff made of milk. You know the stuff—what was it called? They used to make picnic sets of it. And clocks and things. And buttons. What *was* it called? It began with a C. Anyway, Bennett went in for it, but it didn't work out. Well, it wouldn't, would it? Bennett wanted to use it for lamp-shades. But it didn't work out. Casein, that's what it was called. Bennett wanted to go in for casein. Nearly ruined the business over casein.'

'What *is* casein?' asked Faro nervously, for she was be-ginning to think that Auntie Dora's narrow-tracked but hith-erto reliable mind was at last wandering. 'I've never even heard of it.'

'You wouldn't have, would you? It's out of fashion now, isn't it? I don't know if they still make it. It's a sort of—product. It's a product, made of dried milk. They used to make cups and saucers of it. Picnic sets and cigarette boxes and suchlike.'

She *has* gone mad, said Faro to herself. Picnic sets made of milk? And the moon is made of cream cheese.

'It was all the rage,' repeated Dora, with retrospective be-wilderment at the vagaries of modes. 'It was all the rage, but it didn't catch on.'

Faro vowed to herself that she would try to remember this classic Auntie Dora sequence, but knew already that she would forget its wording. Auntie Dora's speech, although dis-tinctive, was almost impossible to reproduce. Whenever Faro tried to report it, in an attempt to amuse her friends or her mother, she found herself at a loss. It was too idiosyncratic, its patterns too deep to repeat. Even Dora's accent defied mim-icry and mockery. Faro was a good mimic, but she couldn't 'do' Dora, just as she had never been able to 'do' her Grandma Barron. They were inimitable. They could not be captured.

They should, in theory, have been sitting targets. But no, they always escaped. They escape now, still on the wing, or hiding, protected, in the obscuring undergrowth.

Breaseborough, to young Faro Gaulden from London, was disquieting. Breaseborough jerked one from the banal to the surreal, from the ancient to the postmodern, without warning. A visit to Breaseborough could blow the mind. And this visit, with its Stone Age skulls, its DNA, its iced buns, its casein and Auntie Dora, had been almost too rich. (Can one extract the DNA from the casein of a mock-tortoiseshell cigarette box? And reconstruct from it the South Yorkshire 1920s cow?) Faro had had enough of these teasers. She needed to take cover in the real world of the recognizable.

The Phoenix Hotel, on the ring road round Northam, was comfortingly recognizable. An ordinary, modern, two-storey, moderately priced 1980s business motel, built in red brick, in a postmodern style that belonged to all periods and to none, in a jumbled compromise between château and chalet and dungeon and supermarket. Just the place in which to recover from the too-pressing, high-smelling past. The Phoenix stood on a featureless stretch of dual carriageway that would, if one let it, whisk one straight past Breaseborough and Cotterhall and Wath and Rawmarsh and Pontefract and all those small-time, small-town eccentric subplaces, with their strangely lingering indigenous populations: it would whisk one painlessly on, from motorway to motorway, from ring road to ring road, to north, to south, to east and to west, along the length and breadth of Britain. (Auntie Dora has a friend called Dorothy who lives in Wath. She often speaks of her to Faro and to Faro's mother.)

What a relief, after the chapel, after the bridge rolls, after Auntie Dora and the undying malingering spider plant, to check in somewhere so anonymous, so utterly ahistorical!

Faro collected her plastic electronic key from the receptionist, and took a lift to the first floor: she would have preferred to walk, after all that sitting about, but where were the stairs? She would settle herself in for a comfortable evening, in the timelessness that she recognized as real time. She would dine in the restaurant: room service was fun but it so often arrived cold and congealed these days, and anyway it would be more fun to have a snoop about and to stare at all the other real-unreal unknown transit people, people whom one need never see again. Motorway people, without history, without provenance. But first, she would change gear with a stiff drink from her plastic half-bottle from her United Airways flight back from JFK.

Singing to herself, Faro poured herself three fingers of whisky, and splashed in some water from the tap. Then she inspected her terrain. How many bedrooms had she slept in this year? Twenty? Thirty? Faro liked to be on the move. Her job took her about a bit. *There's you and me and the bottle makes three tonight,* sang Faro Gaulden to herself: an old fifties lyric picked up from a new movie she'd just seen. Faro had a good voice. Her father had been musical, and so was she. She loved this song. It seemed paradoxically appropriate to her comfortable solitude. She was so happy to be alone.

The room wasn't at all bad. A queen-sized bed, bedside lights that worked, a red winking clock, a minibar, curtains covered with pale pink and grey zigzags and a poster print of a moorland scene with sheep. Very nice, very meaningless. Faro had had enough of meaning. She drew the curtains, swigged her drink, went into the bathroom and was promptly hit on the head by the shower-curtain rail. It fell on her from on high, as she was wondering whether to wash her feet under the cold tap. She tried to stick it back up again, but it didn't seem to fit anymore. Should she complain? It seemed a bit rich, to be hit on the head at the price of a hundred quid a night, but why bother? She bunged it in the bath. The mag was paying.

It was a whole lot cleaner and brighter here in room 122 of the Phoenix than it had been in the chapel or at Auntie

Dora's, but the cleanness had a curious smell to it. A disinfectant perfume. Faro sniffed, sniffed again, inhaled. A horrible, fruity smell. A *pink* smell. It seemed a pervasive smell these days in cheaper toilet facilities—perhaps some people actually liked it? She was surprised to encounter it here. Faro preferred green smells to pink smells. Pine and mint. Or fern. Not that real ferns smell of anything much, do they? What on earth, wondered Faro, can casein have smelled of? Sourness, surely? Perhaps that was why it hadn't caught on?

The drink was rising to Faro's head in little spurts and spasms of temporary happiness. She was beginning to feel light and cheerful, cheerful enough to ring Seb as she had promised she would. Ringing Seb these days was almost always an ordeal, but she was feeling strong enough to take him on. Seb Jones was a leech, a bloodsucker. She dialled, he answered, as though he had been waiting to pounce. He needed her energy. As she spoke, she could feel it coursing from herself to him through the telephone wire. His gaunt and cavernous features would be softening, warming, filling out a little as she spoke, and his hair would cease to recede from his bony temples for the twenty minutes of this mercy call. Seb was younger than she was, he was only twenty-nine, but he was beginning to look like an old man. Once she had thought his grim pallor romantic. Now she had come to see it as something quite other. Nevertheless, she chatted lightly on. She told him about the manic Dr Hawthorn, about Steve the skeleton, and about the room full of stout Cudworths. 'I'm too fat,' she cried to him, in what she hoped was entertainingly mock despair, 'I'm too fat, and soon I'll look like Auntie Dora and weigh fourteen stone! She's even fatter than my grandma used to be! And that's saying something! I've got fat genes, and there's the end of it! They've got control of me!'

Faro looked admiringly at herself in the mirror, as she let out this volley of cries. She was looking just fine. The summer weather suited her.

Seb wanted to know what she was having for her supper. She must eat up, drink up. He liked a fleshly Faro to feed upon. And he was looking forward to hearing more about the Cudworths. He took a malicious interest in the Cudworths, none of whom he had ever met. Seb wanted to know if the real Steve had been there, along with his skeleton? No, said Faro, Steve Nieman hadn't showed up. Rumour had it that he was a bit embarrassed about his fortuitous fame and his unrelated bone-find. Had Dr Hawthorn stolen a sample of her DNA, Seb inquired, and had she been to see the cave where the skeleton was discovered? Seb was quite interested in DNA, but he was even more interested in caverns and potholes and sewerage and subterranean workings. He had even tried potholing himself. Faro disapproved of his underground obsessions, and did not want to talk about caverns: she was in fact feeling slightly guilty that she hadn't found time to visit the site and interview Steve Nieman. The site wasn't open to the public, but she could easily have wangled it, as a science journalist. They'd have been pleased to see her, probably. She knew she'd been lazy. She hadn't bothered. She might have to come back another day. She diverted Seb back to DNA, and told him about the darling little toothbrush swab-thing with which she had scraped her inner cheek for Dr Hawthorn. Dr Hawthorn had a nice fresh sample of her DNA, newly filed away and labelled, along with the swabs from Auntie Dora, Bill Cudworth and all the other Breaseborough folk.

'Were you wise to let him have it?' asked Seb. 'It isn't a good idea to give away your body parts. And suppose you find you've got some incurable disease? Suppose you find you're a changeling? There might be worse things than fatness back there in the gene bank. It's dangerous, digging around in there. You don't know what you might find.'

Seb was beginning to turn nasty: he always did. Twenty minutes of him was enough.

'I can't be a changeling,' said Faro, more robustly than she

131

intended. 'Anyway, what if I were? I might find I'm the living missing link with Neanderthal woman. That would be fun, wouldn't it?'

(Faro had felt a superstitious flicker of fear as she had handed back her swab, and she had watched carefully as Dr Hawthorn had sealed it up in its little plastic wallet. What indeed if it held bad news? If it did, would Dr Hawthorn tell her? He didn't look like the kind of chap who spent much time worrying about medical ethics. But she didn't want to talk to Seb about this. Seb was always taking advantage of her weaknesses, her sillinesses. He was cruel, was Seb. Why, oh why did she listen to him?)

'Neanderthal woman? Nonsense. There wasn't any interbreeding. They've proved it,' said Seb, the edge of pleading menace sharper in his voice.

'No, they haven't *proved* it,' said Faro, who knew more about this than he did, although her mind was not as organized as his. 'They can't *prove* it. They've found a chap in Portugal who might be a cross-breed. Lagar Velho boy, that's his name. It would only take one positive result for them to have to rethink the whole of prehistory.'

Faro uttered this with confidence. Faro did not mention that Lagar Velho boy was almost twenty-five thousand years old, but she felt she had scored a point. Clearly Seb had never heard of Lagar Velho boy, with his coloured shroud of red ochre, his pierced snail-shell necklet, his little toys of rabbit bone. Seb was momentarily silenced, and Faro took advantage of the pause to ask him what he had been up to.

'Working, working,' was all he would admit. And in Seb's case, that could mean anything or nothing. Seb's career, if such it was, remained a puzzle to Faro. He wrote a film column, and he made films, sometimes, and he wrote short stories, sometimes, and in his spare time, of which he had much, he lectured on horror movies at Holborn.

Faro did not live with Seb, though she had once tried to. Seb lived in a room of his own in Bloomsbury, in a squalor even Faro found extreme. Seb was becoming more and more of a worry to Faro. He was demanding and haggard and neurotic, and she wished she'd never gone to bed with him in the first place. He seemed to think he had staked her. He'd stuck his prick in her, and staked her, and then he had become dependent. He needed her, though at first he'd pretended not to, and Faro found need hard to resist. She hadn't realized he was so helpless when she took him on. Now she didn't seem to be able to wriggle free. She was resigned to sticking with him, in a low-key kind of way, for the next stretch. Until something else happened.

'You'd better go and get some supper yourself,' said Faro, in a terminally cheerful tone. 'I'm too fat, and you're too thin. You'd better go and eat some chips.'

Seb didn't seem to mind this bossy nanny tone, which Faro herself found false and shaming. He liked it.

Seb said he was meeting Raoul and Rona in the Red Lion and would probably have Today's Special. Today's Special was always the same. It was always lasagne. 'Rather you than me,' said Faro. She was sick to death of lasagne.

As Faro Gaulden tidied herself up for dinner, unbidden memories of Seb's style of fucking came to revisit her. At first she had found it quite exciting, and a welcome change from the limpness of her previous long-term lover. Seb had not been at all limp, despite his unhealthy appearance. He had a cock as hard as a lump of wood, which was almost permanently, in her company, erect. He liked games of bondage, and so, at first, did she. It was quite fun, letting herself be tied to the table leg, while he went at her. But after a while she began to realize that although he was as hard as a lump of wood, he was about as insensitive. He could do it, for hours, monotonously, and that had its advantages, from a woman's point of view, but it did get tedious. Also, it was dirty on the floor. Faro didn't much mind mess, but the smell of carpet and cigarette ends began to get her down. It got dull, being thumped at, in and out, in and out. Faro began to long for something a little more varied, a little more soft and sensuous. And when she did manage to connect up with an orgasm of her own, she had a sense that he sneered at her for it. So she'd taken to faking. It wasn't as hurtful to be sneered at for a fake. But then she'd realized that the whole business was a waste of time. Why bother? So she'd refused to sleep with him anymore, but did that get rid of him? Oh no. He claimed other rights in her. And she was sorry for him, so she'd let him. He'd got her where he wanted her. She was still tied to the table leg.

This conclusion to this sequence of thoughts made her smile at herself, as she gargled with minted mouthwash, as she curved her lips to the lipstick. What nonsense! She was a free woman, alone in the Heartfree Motel. Round any corner waited a new future. She primped up her halo of curls for the last time, smiled in a more come-hither manner and took herself down to the restaurant, where she confidently requested a table for one.

There was a special promotional menu of prawns. Prawns were in or with everything, and if you filled in the form on the back of your menu you could win a couple of free seats for the Bother Boys next month at the Rialto. A heavenly happiness took possession of Faro Gaulden, as she joked with the waiter about the Bother Boys. She tucked into her prawns and noodles (Indonesian style) and looked around her. Young businessmen, a few older businessmen, a scattering of businesswomen. At the table next to hers sat a mixed-sex party of eight, all, she guessed, in their late thirties, early forties. She eavesdropped as she sipped her lager. At first the men, wearing ties but in their shirt sleeves, made the running, commanding, assertive, in joking joshing public Yorkshire voices, but gradually the women began to strike up their own orchestra, as they steered the conversation towards less rowdy topics, as they brought it back to the matters of the day. They were all delegates at some sort of conference. They were talking about fuel emissions, methane and waste management. One dark-suited black man, the most solemnly dressed of the group, sat quietly at the far end of the table; he kept his jacket on throughout the meal. He was treated with deference. Was he the boss, a flown-in American? She thought she had detected an American accent. The women careered along. Catalytic converters, government regulations, the Kyoto agreement, electric trams. They knew their stuff. Women did, these days, didn't they? It was a good time to be alive, for a woman like Faro, reflected Faro. Perhaps she should ask them what they were all up to? There might be a story in it for her section. Women and transport, women and motoring, women and lead-free petrol, women and waste.

Faro didn't notice Mr Iowa Cudworth until she'd finished her coffee, signed her bill and started to make her way towards the foyer. She'd been sitting with her back to him. He too had been eating alone, and he saluted her, waving his prawn-embossed menu at her as she passed. She waved, hesitated, crossed over to him.

'Hello, cousin,' she said.

'I thought it was you,' he said with admiration. And Faro knew she looked great, in her pretty cotton heliotrope mail-order frock. She was full of bounce and bubble. The beer bubbled. She bubbled. Her hair bubbled. She agreed to join Mr Iowa for a drink in the bar.

Faro is a beauty. She catches the eye. She caught Peter Cudworth's eye. She had caught the eye of the black American at the next table, though he had not attempted to catch hers.

The Cudworth cousins ordered a malt each, and Faro succeeded in signing for them. 'You're my guest in my country,' she said broadly. He liked that.

They settled, happy amidst the executive egalitarian décor, and exchanged the stories of their lives. Consanguinity had brought them together in this random staging post, but how close a degree of consanguinity could they establish? How much did their DNA overlap? And how had they both come to hear of the Hawthorn project? There was much to discuss, and no danger in discussing it, for both Faro and Mr Iowa were in rapid transit, and would not clog or cling. They were settled, with a smoky glass of Laphroaig, but they were settled only for a nightwatch. They were not settlers. They were hunter-gatherers. They were on the move, like most of the moneyed millennial masses, and in the morning they would move on.

Professor Peter Cudworth of Iowa, as he revealed himself to be, was an economist, born in New Jersey and educated at MIT in Boston (yes, nodded Faro, she did know what that was). He now taught a branch of business studies in the Midwest. Booms and slumps were his passion, and he knew a great deal about stock-market cycles, though he admitted that he had not proved very good at profiting from his knowledge. He had his theories and his hunches, and sometimes they were proved right on the Dow Jones, but not often enough for him to take any big risks with his moderate income. He wasn't seriously interested in money. He was interested only in the theory of money. His professorial salary was quite enough for him. He liked his students. He liked most of his colleagues. He liked Iowa. He wasn't complaining. And what about Faro? What was her field?

Faro liked Peter Cudworth. She was usually affable and disposed to like people at this time of night. Peter Cudworth was of medium height, and stocky, as were most of the Cudworths, but he was attractive. He had pleasing short curly brown hair, so tightly curled that she longed to run her fingers through it, and a small darling Dutch beard. He looked like a little Cavalier, a curled cavalier of the West. A pleasant, friendly, cousinly sort of chap. With, as he had almost immediately made clear, a wife and two children back home.

Faro's field, she declared, was the history of science, which she had studied at the University of Waterford. She now worked for a scientific magazine called *Prometheus*, once a weekly periodical of distinction, but recently transformed, she had to own, into a popular rag. A new and pushy editor had taken its eminent title successfully down-market and was thriving on a mixture of mildly sensationalized stories and serious reportage. It had a lot of brightly coloured pictures and very large headlines. It was doing very well. The public was into science, which was lucky for Faro, and she was well in with its editor, which was also lucky for Faro. He gave her a free hand with her section, a women's section called, with a marked lack of originality, 'Pandora's Box.' Most of this, Faro volunteered, Faro could write standing on her head, but her editor also sent her off to cover conferences or to interview eminent persons for the main body of the mag. She got some good trips out of it. She liked travelling. She was also supposed to be writing a popular book on changing concepts of evolutionary determinism, based on her own rapidly dating thesis, but she wasn't getting on so well with that. She kept getting distracted. But it was a good topic, didn't he think?

Was it the magazine or the book that had taken her to Breaseborough? he wanted to know. Well, both and neither, she said. She'd been browsing through new gene-map theories and stories about mitochondrial DNA on the Internet when suddenly the name Cudworth had leaped up at her, and she'd got on to Dr Hawthorn's project. She was herself a Cudworth, by direct matrilineal descent. Her great-grandmother Ellen had been born a Cudworth. So that makes an eighth of me a Cudworth, doesn't it? But the magazine had been keen for her to cover the story anyway. It was too big for 'Pandora's Box,' so she thought she'd try to write a proper feature on it. The magazine had agreed to pay her expenses, anyway. And yes, she would like another. The same again, thank you.

She herself was, she explained, when Peter came back from the bar, by way of being a neo-Lamarckian. Or a Bergsonian. She didn't hold with Darwinian or genetic determinism. Of course she knew that that *was* how things were, but she didn't *like* the way things were. She didn't approve of it. And that was no doubt why she'd been attracted to tackle the subject in the first place. As an act of pointless but heroic resistance. A forlorn hope. She'd like to think one could rediscover an argument that would reinstate the freedom of the will and the adaptability of the species. Otherwise everything was too damn depressing, wasn't it? (Here, she breathed deeply, her large eyes shone, and her broad and gentle bosom lifted and sank with the tide of her feeling.) How could one, asked Faro, believe that everything was genetically or environmentally determined, and at the same time that all mutation was random? Hadn't Peter himself just been speaking about the randomness and unpredictability of cycles in the stock market? Did he really *believe* they were random? Where does the random meet the determined? What is the name of their meeting place?

Faro's brain tended to race, late at night. Great swathes of ideas associated themselves freely in her head, and their colours merged and swirled. She knew she was the least disciplined, the least logical of thinkers, but she also knew that there was something in what she was thinking. Some thought was happening to her or in her or round about her. These psychedelic patternings might not be described as thought by more rigorous minds, but they were something. She could see them, she could feel them. They were not nothing.

'I mean,' she said, 'there must have been something, some *mental* process, that shifted some of the Cudworths and the Bawtrys out of this dump. Something that made for migration. I don't believe it was just the melting of the ice, or the changing climate, or the discovery of coal, or the end of the coal industry. They didn't just flow about, like water flowing downhill. Some stayed, some moved. It was a movement of the mind. My lot stayed around here a lot longer than yours. How did yours get away?'

A memory, just beyond retrieval, like a shadow of an unremembered dream, is nagging at Faro. But it is not her memory, so she cannot remember it. It is not in reach. It hovers and flickers, with a faint colouring, a rustling, an inarticulate appeal.

Peter Cudworth said that his grandparents had emigrated from Leeds in the 1920s, in the slump years. They had gone initially to Canada, and then on to the States. His grandfather had been a civil engineer. His father was a lawyer, now retired, and his mother an all-American-Swedish dietician. They had done well, the emigrant Cudworths, had attained a respectable, comfortable middle-class life. The next generation had done well too. Peter had a brother who designed computer software in Chicago, a sister who ran a catering company in Cincinnati. His grandparents had been right to leave when they did. What was it that had made them get up and go? she insisted. It was hard for him to say. It was all too long ago. They'd been proud of their English roots, of course, but they'd never shown any signs of wanting to come back. His grandmother had kept in touch with her side of the family, with the Coles of Headingley, but his Cudworth grandfather hadn't bothered. He'd lost touch. Peter couldn't even remember any Cudworth Christmas cards, certainly no family newsletters. He'd made a new life, and that was all there was to it. Not very exciting, not very romantic. Quite a dull story.

So why had he come over? Faro wanted to know. Why had he been to the meeting? What had he hoped to find? Why had he bothered?

Why is she pressing him? Peter is equable, and does not mind being pressed.

He'd become curious, he said. He'd been coming over to England anyway on business, his first visit to the old country, and he'd decided, while he was here, to try to find out where the Cudworths came from. Family trees were all the fashion in the States, she must know that? Everybody seemed to be trying to trace origins. The origins of families and of species. So he'd thought, why not? He too, like Faro, had found the details of the Hawthorn meeting on the Internet. The dull name of Cudworth glimmered up at him as soon as he started to look for it. He'd joined the One-Name Society, contacted Bill Cudworth, and here he was. And it had all been quite interesting, hadn't it?

'Quite interesting and quite boring,' said Faro, fixing him with her vast dark eyes. She was not wholly satisfied with his mundane explanation.

He laughed it off. Yes, he agreed, they didn't seem the most dynamic group in the world. They weren't exactly the cutting edge, were they, the Breaseborough Cudworths?

'You don't know this part of the world,' accused Faro. 'I do.'

'So you still have family living around here?'

Faro described her Great-Aunt Dora, her grandmother's only sister. Dora Bawtry, daughter of Ellen Cudworth Bawtry, born before the First World War.

'Never budged,' concluded Faro. 'Been here all her lifelong life. All her one and only life.'

'So your grandmother must have married out?' probed Peter Cudworth from Iowa, staring at the exotic Faro, whose appearance suggested something far from the Anglo-Saxon, far from the pre-Anglo-Saxon, far from Cotterhall. There was something dark and luxuriant in Faro that surely came from over the hills and far away.

'No, not really,' said Faro. 'In fact, not at all. She married the boy next door. Her childhood sweetheart. But she did get away. They moved to another world. A million light-years away, all the way to Surrey. That's in the south of England, you know. That's where my grandparents ended up. I don't know how they managed it. I'm not sure if they did manage it. My mother goes on about how they didn't manage it. I used to take it for granted that they lived in Surrey. But now it seems a mystery. And as for *my* parents—how they got together, God alone knows.'

Faro Gaulden, suspected Peter Cudworth from Iowa, had not liked the Cudworth reunion. Something about it had disturbed her. He'd found it a bit disturbing himself, but he was used to keeping his unease under cover. He didn't tell stories to strangers. He wasn't sure if it would be wise to listen to any more confidences from Faro. Was she dangerous, was she compromising, was she trouble? He didn't need trouble: he had trouble enough at home. Her mood, which had at first seemed so sweet and high, was wavering now, like a needle attracted to some invisible force, plunging and dipping, then soaring up again. She was a stranger to him and he could not read her. Was she always like this? There was nothing sexual in her manner: he was accustomed to the almost routine, juvenile and to him unattractive sexiness of some of his female students, and there was none of that in Faro. But then, she was English, and maybe they did things differently here? She was, he guessed, a little older than most of his postgraduates. He had been warned incessantly about the dangers of sexual harassment, and knew well the litigation that could arise from a shut door, an open door, a friendly hand, a harsh word, a kind word, a late-night drink, a low grade, a high grade. But Faro Gaulden's behaviour, though animated, was neither sexy nor provocative. It was intense, pleading, poignant. And this was a motel in Yorkshire, not a campus in the Midwest. And she was his cousin. He would not flee. He would not play the coward. He stayed, trapped by her violet, violent dark eyes.

He stayed, and Faro Gaulden recited her history to Peter Cudworth. She had not intended to do this, but it broke from her, and flowed.

She told him of her father's death. She galloped through the dreadful story. Nine months dead, her father was, and he had died of the drink. Cirrhosis of the liver. He had been a desperate, wild, mad, drinking man. A useless man, a squalid, sordid, wasted man. A glamorous, handsome man. Oh, the waste of it, groaned Faro. And oh, the wretched conjunction of her mother and her father! How could such an improbable union ever have come to be? Her mother, niece of Dora

Bawtry, daughter of Bessie Bawtry—her mother, wretched, suffering, miserable, betrayed, abandoned, undone! What a sad life she had led! What freakish current of history had swirled her mother and her father together? And her father's life—how it had been wasted and blasted, blasted and wasted. And now he was dead.

'My father,' said Faro, with an attempt at mock and comic dignity, regaining composure, 'was not even English. He was a stick of driftwood from the Second World War. He was a tragic accident. He was the son of refugees. He wasn't English, but he wasn't properly Jewish either. You'd have known where you were if he'd been Jewish. I'd have known who *I* was if he'd been Jewish. He was *partly* Jewish, of course, but part of him was Polish, part German, part Slovakian. I don't know who he was. He was a Central European disaster. Actually' (here she changes tone and tack), 'actually, he was *born* in England. He had a British passport. So I suppose he was English, really. What does it matter what he was? He was a disaster. He drank himself to death. You can't imagine the unspeakable funeral. All those women. It was ludicrous. It wasn't tragic, it was ridiculous. The waste of it all, the terrible waste.'

'I'm very sorry,' said Peter Cudworth inadequately. It was clear that this young woman had been, still was, obsessed by her father.

'I suppose you could blame my *mother,*' said Faro wildly, 'for letting all this happen. You can blame her for conniving, for collaboration. But I don't blame my mother. I blame *him.* Though she ought to have had more sense.'

Peter Cudworth, who felt himself in no position to take sides or to blame anybody, and who had lost the thread of her impassioned diatribe, said mildly, 'I suppose we all blame our parents for a lot of things that can't really be helped.'

Faro did not hear him. She was melting and glittering and glowing with violet electric light, in her heliotrope dress, as she turned towards an invisible subterranean sun.

'They called me Faro after the Faeroe Islands!' she suddenly cried. 'Can you imagine the stupidity, the mockery! How dared they? They said I was conceived on the Faeroes! The Dry Islands! Puffins and whale blubber! What a joke!'

Peter Cudworth murmured that Faro seemed quite a nice name to him. How did she spell it? When she'd first introduced herself he'd seen it more as an Egyptian sort of Pharaoh, but he must have got that wrong?

'It's all very well for you,' said Faro. 'You're called a nice sensible name. Peter's a good name, a good rocklike name. *My whole life,*' said Faro loudly and earnestly, 'has been ruined by my name. And they didn't even spell it right. They spelt it like some damn stupid tourist airport in Portugal. F-A-R-O, that's how I spell it. They said it looked nicer like that on the birth certificate. I ask you. Who wants to be called after an airport?'

The barman coughed, and ostentatiously wiped the bar once more. The clock struck one.

Faro and Peter made their way to their respective beds. They shook hands in the featureless corridor, and Faro said she was sorry if she'd gone on a bit about her dad. It had all been a bit upsetting. And it had been a long day, hadn't it? Peter said it had been a real pleasure to meet her, he'd enjoyed talking to her. And so, politely, subdued, they parted.

Faro, in the safety of her bedroom, poured herself a glass of carbonated water from the minibar and sat down on her bed. Her mind was curdling and churning as violently clashing images washed around in it. Was it her mind, was it her spirit, was it her soul, or was it merely a processing machine? What was it that contained these pictures, these memories? Would the vessel burst and break? Sometimes she thought she could not stand it anymore. Talking about her father had set in motion the terrible turbulence which was always waiting to engulf her and sweep her away. Was it from him that it came?

She sees Auntie Dora's little house, that grim warm ark

stranded on the shelf of time. She sees Golders Green Cemetery, and her father's many mourners. She sees her mother,
hard-faced, proud, stoic, ceremonially dressed in melodramatic black. She sees her grandfather, a sweet and patient
man, and her grandmother, a scolding shrew. She sees her
Gaulden grandparents, washed up back in the 1930s on the
Finchley Road, and hanging on there through her sixties
childhood. She tries not to see her father, Nick Gaulden, but
he is there, unbidden. He is everywhere. He will not lie quietly.

Faro had loved her father. Her father had been much
loved, and he himself had loved many. He had been a Don
Juan, a seducer. First, he had seduced her mother, and ruined
her life for ever. (That is not how Faro's mother sees it, but it
is how Faro, in this stage of her life, chooses to see it.) Then
he had moved on, and loved and ruined others. Faro had suffered a disturbed childhood, reared in a succession of households of grossly unorthodox complexity—*ménages à trois, à
quatres, à six,* households without a single responsible adult
apart from her nobly enduring mother, households where no
meals appeared on time. There had been quiet flats where Faro
and her mother were alone, and noisy houses where they had
taken in battered refugees from Nick Gaulden's other pas-
sions. Nick Gaulden, unlike Don Juan, had found it hard to
abandon his mistresses. He had let them pile up behind him
and around him, in heaps of twisted wreckage, smouldering,
impacted. As though he feared to be left alone on a dark night.
As though he feared to lose them all.

In her turbulent childhood, Faro had oscillated from extreme to extreme, from happiness to despair, from neglect and
alcoholic excesses to gleams of joy and elation. Had it been
heroic, squalid, creative, experimental, desperate, or all these
things? Had her history been a blueprint for a future of the
extended family, or an unrelieved, irredeemable mess? She had
tried to hate her father, but had failed. Her mother had tried
to hate her father, and seemed to have succeeded, for her

mother had survived, had made sense of her life, had prospered. But what had been the price of that survival? Faro's mother Chrissie has paid too high a price. You can tell that from the sharp set of her lips, from the wrinkles round her eyes, from the sharp edge of her tongue.

Faro cannot reconcile herself to her father's death, or to his life. She bleeds inwardly for her mother, to whom she has been too close, too close, for her poor mother who has turned cold and stiff. Her mother, a grim and sensible woman, a Yorkshire woman of Yorkshire grit. Chrissie had put the Gaulden wreckage behind her, had against heavy odds made herself a career, had in the end remarried. But Faro knew her mother, and knew that her mother had a broken heart.

Sitting on her bed, drinking fizzy water fortified with the dregs of JFK—well, why save it, better to empty the bottle—Faro recalls that long-ago evening when her mother Chrissie had tried to cheer up her little girl by telling her about the Faeroe Islands. Her father had gone upstairs to visit his second (or was it perhaps by then his third?) family, and Faro had seemed so peaky and sad and bereft downstairs in the Chief Wife's apartment. And Chrissie, perhaps unwisely, had assured Faro that not all had always been sadness and deprivation and humiliation and fear. There had been happier times in earlier days, out there, at the top of the world, out on a rock in the middle of the Atlantic, with the white sailing clouds above and the grassy turf below, and the westward view to Ultima Thule, where the great whales sailed. And Chrissie and Nick Gaulden had been happy there, promised Chrissie. They had eaten the dark meat of fish-flavoured puffin, and the Camembert-ripe flesh of rotted shark, and little white fresh mushrooms that sprang like manna from the hilltops. They had watched the little fawn and golden Faeroe ponies graze. They had loved one another, and all had been well for a while. Not all of life had been broken crockery and bruises and bailiffs.

'And he has always adored you,' said Chrissie Gaulden, as she pegged patiently away at a scarlet bedside rug made of pre-cut Anchor wool. 'He adored you from the moment he saw you. He loved babies.'

'He *still* loves babies,' the young Faro had said, as the wailing of the youngest Gaulden bastard drifted down the uncarpeted wooden stairs. And both women had laughed, the comradely laughter of women on their own.

Ah well, thinks Faro, as she polishes off the contents of her beaker, perhaps it really hasn't been too bad. She yawns, vigorously. All those conglomerations of people, all those Barrons and Bawtrys, all those Goldsteins and Goldbergs and Gauldens, back in the bombed waste land of Europe. Jews, Czechs, Slovaks, Poles, Gypsies—God knows what. God and Dr Hawthorn. And she was the end-product. A miracle, really.

She hadn't meant it when she'd told Peter Cudworth that she hated her own name. In fact, most of the time, she loved it. Faro was a good name, an original name, and it had served her well at her London comprehensive school. It amused, it was memorable, and now it made a good journalist's byline. It was a lucky name, taken not only from the isles of the north and a Portuguese resort, but also from a Regency card game. It designated Faro herself as a winner in luck's lottery. And Gaulden was a good name too. Nick's parents had done well so wittily to anglicize whatever it had once been. Nick said they'd stolen the name from a manor house in Somerset, but she'd never bothered to check. If so, good on them. Oh yes, it was all OK really. She forgave them all. And, in a mood of forgiveness, she went into the bathroom, brushed her teeth rather forcefully and clumsily, slapped some moisturizer on her moist and resilient skin, and flopped into bed. She was too tired to have a bath, and it was too late, and anyway the pole from the shower curtain was still lying in the tub. She'd fix it in the morning. She lay down, and fell instantly asleep.

She fell instantly asleep, as was her way, and, as was her way, she woke at three in the morning consumed and feverish with panic, terror and remorse. What could she have been thinking of the night before, to have told her life story to a stranger? She was always telling secrets to strangers. A couple of drinks, and she couldn't keep her mouth shut. Why did she do it? What did Peter Cudworth care that her father was dead? There were so many dead. Dead without hope, dead without purpose, dead without reprieve. Living without hope, dying without hope, dying young, dying in caves, dying of self-inflicted wounds, dying from axe blows to the head, dying of the drink, dying in death camps, dying of history, dying reluctant, dying angry. All, all, dragged to death as at the horse's tail? What was the point of all the dead? Faro moaned and rocked and put the pillow over her head for comfort. She was going mad. For comfort she bashed her head back and forth under the pillow. Was redemption waiting, now, on the horizon, for the human race? Was death at last to die? Yes, so they claimed. Immortal life was within reach. Cloning, genetic engineering, spare-part surgery, xenografts, then immortality. Nobody shall die needlessly. All shall be saved, and all manner of people shall be saved. Man, at last, has conquered and outwitted death. It's taken a long time, but he's done it.

But what, howled Faro, silently, uselessly, into the synthetic foam of her motel pillow, what of the dead themselves? What of the *already dead*? Shall there be a resurrection for them? Shall there be a Harrowing of Hell? Shall they be redeemed, all of them? What of the virtuous heathen? What of those born before the genome? What of those who never had a moment's happiness? What about the forgotten bits of prehistory? All the hominid mandibles, all the forelimbs and hindlimbs, all the fossils and partial face and cranial fragments of the past? They had suffered pain. Shall Cotterhall Man be redeemed of his pain?

Steve the skeleton lay very quietly through the night in his air-conditioned temperature-controlled casket. His neighbours were Egyptians, a few millennia younger, better preserved, and of a better social class. Whatever they had endured in life was long over. It could never be revived. Not even Dr Hawthorn could reach it with his swab or his needle. Or could he? Is there to be a new hell? And if so, who will come to harrow it?

Faro Gaulden woke the following morning with a bounce and without a trace of hangover or fatigue. This capacity for instant recovery might be seen, perhaps, as one of the more dangerous legacies of her alcoholic father. But one could take a more optimistic view. She was young, she was in excellent health, and she had access yet to hope. She uncrumpled and unfurled herself like a revived flower. Her sap rose quickly. She ran her fingers through her glossy black hair, and it stood on end round her head in a faro-halo like the stiff fronds of a chrysanthemum. She conquered the shower rail, thrusting it back into its bracket amidst a scattering of falling plaster, and bathed in a lavish green gel that fought with and overpowered the pinkish sickly odour of synthetic fruits. She towelled herself energetically with the large white bath sheet, then tackled the coffee equipment. The brew basket and the thermal platter and the reinforced decanter held no terrors for Faro, although she'd never seen anything quite like them in all her travels: she tore with her fluoride-strong white teeth at the impenetrable vacuum sachet of ground Colombian, stoked up what she took to be the machine's engine, and got it all bubbling in no time. Its red eye blinked, its steel tubes hissed, its hot brown liquid spurted forth at her command. She drank it down, dressed, signed her bill, marched out, leaped into her car, remembered she had forgotten to get the car-park barrier combination exit pin number from the reception desk, parked at the barrier while she went back for it, was hooted at angrily by various early-morning travelling salesmen, waved at them cheerily as though responding to admiring salutations, and was on her way.

What was her way? Back to London, back down the M1, and back to work. But beyond that, whither? Who cared? She fiddled with her car radio, looking for the beat. She found it, and turned up the volume. A good, clear signal. Knowing her luck, she bet she'd find she'd won those tickets to the Rialto to see the Bother Boys. She put her foot down, and the car in front of her gave way in terror. She put her dark glasses on, and sang along in the fast lane.

Peter Cudworth, rising at eight thirty, looked in the breakfast room for his cousin Faro, but could not see her. Nor was she visible in the foyer, nor waiting in line for the cashier. She was nowhere to be seen. In bed still, he supposed, sleeping it off. He loitered, regretful. He would have liked to say goodbye. But there was no sign or sense of her. As he paid his bill, he asked, boldly, for Miss Faro Gaulden, and got what his Yorkshire kin would have called a funny look. He was told that Miss Gaulden had left an hour ago. This reply made him feel old, and he made his way, soberly, to his hired car.

Miss Gaulden, by this time, was on her mobile talking to her mother Chrissie in Oxfordshire from a petrol station. Faro and her mother speak nearly every day, sometimes several times a day. Faro has forgotten that last night she thought her mother was a heartbroken tragedy queen, and has connected up with the real daytime Chrissie, who wants to know all about the Cudworths. 'You should have come, Mum,' yells Faro, over the racket of the garage forecourt. 'It was hilarious! What? Yes, Auntie Dora's fine. And I met this lovely cousin from Iowa. What? I can't *hear* you! No, he's a Cudworth. Iowa, not Argentina. The Argentine one didn't show. You should have seen the skeleton. What? Yes, in a cave. Peter Cudworth, his name was. He's a professor. I can't hear you! Are you still there? Shit! Can you hear me? Can you hear me? Shit!'

Faro switches off her flat-batteried handset and gets back on the road to London, thinking, as she drives south, of the migration of the grandparents of Peter Cudworth. He had told

149

her that it was an everyday story, a dull story, but nevertheless she finds it full of mystery. How had they managed it? What had made them want to manage it? How had they got their passports and visa papers? How had they known how to get them? Why had they gone, and others not? Why hadn't depressed Yorkshire emptied itself into Canada? Had they gone to Canada first because it was easier to get into part of the British Empire than into the U.S.? All the way from Leeds to Toronto to New Jersey! She simply could not begin to fill in the links of the chain. Human beings were opaque, amazing, in their leaps, their motivations. And yet there *were* links, reaching backwards into the cavernous recesses of time itself, into the limestone, into the potholes, into the caverns. How could one begin to follow the leaps? Did families remain static for centuries, then suddenly, in an instant, in a generation, mutate? Did whole cultures leap and surge? How many jumped and fatally missed their footing? How many brave attempts were hit on the head by a spade?

Faro's grandfather Joe Barron, speaking to her one evening as they strolled round the Surrey garden, had mentioned his sisters Ivy and Rowena. 'You can say what you like,' he said, 'but they had pluck.' Faro is trying to remember this, but she cannot. It hovers, out of reach.

Her father's family had suffered a different fate. They had been driven, forced, expelled. Not pluck but wisdom had distinguished their emigration. Back in Berlin they had read the signs and storm clouds correctly. They had not waited for the shattering of crystals and for the nights of long knives. They had packed up and quit. They had survived. But they could not be said to have prospered.

Which does Faro favour, the Breaseborough branch, or the Berlin branch? Who can predict which genes will triumph, or whether her mitochondrial DNA (which has no Berlin component) will ever be passed on?

Faro continues to ponder the mysteries of DNA as she

drives south down the motorway. Is Faro pleased, as a feminist, that it is the female line that has provided these new clues to genealogy, these new aids to research? Is she pleased that the uses of mitochondrial DNA have provoked Dr Hawthorn and his colleagues to comment that it would have been easier to trace family ancestries in the distant past if naming had followed the mother line, as in Iceland, instead of the father line, as in most of what we call the developed world? Yes, she is pleased, though only on a frivolous, point-scoring level. Faro is a feminist, as women of her class and education are these days. She is not a sentimental feminist, and does not hold the view that all women are good, all men bad, all mothers good, all fathers bad—though in her particular domestic circumstances she might well have been expected to adopt this ideological fallacy. (We have not seen much of Chrissie Gaulden née Barron yet, but the serious shortcomings of Nick Gaulden have been touched upon.) But yes, Faro is a feminist, and she is pleased by the irony of the power of the new magic of mitochondrial DNA. She is amused by the way in which men cannot conceal their irritation when she tries to describe the scientific basis of the new research. She has learned to conceal the fact that the reason why female mitochondrial DNA is easier to trace and detect is because it is less 'pure' than unisex nuclear DNA, and therefore more conspicuous under the microscope. We'd better not lay claim to impurity as a virtue, even when it is one. Words like that can lead to grave misunderstandings. History is riddled with such misunderstandings.

Peter Cudworth drives quietly to Loughborough, through middle England. It is a complicated, cross-country route. The roads are not straight, as they are in Iowa, and he could have done with a companion to read the map. His wife Anna was good at map-reading, but she had not wished to accompany him on this trip. England attracted her not at all, and she was afraid to set foot in Europe.

Peter Cudworth had not spoken much of his wife Anna to his cousin Faro. He had established her existence, from reflexive self-protection, but had not evoked her. Nor had Faro enquired after her. Anna was foreign, non-germane, and had no part in the Cudworth story. For Anna, like Faro's father Nick Gaulden, was a second-generation refugee from Old Europe. She too had been newly infected by a curiosity about her homeland. But Anna, unlike Peter, did not dare to go. She was afraid of what she might find. Anna's parents and grandparents came from a village in Saxony in east Germany, newly accessible since the fall of the Berlin Wall. And Anna knew what she might find amidst the wooden chalets and the high sloping pastures. Hatred and guilt might lie in wait for her there. Her family had been the blond oppressors. They had become economic refugees, not moral refugees. They had got out in time, through a mixture of luck and foresight, and Anna had been born an *echt* American. But nothing pleasant could await Anna in that pastoral Saxon landscape amidst the tinkling cowbells.

Anna does not know if she ought or ought not to go back to her homeland. It used to be inaccessible, but it is easy to go there now. Everywhere is opening up. New problems, new challenges have arisen in the last decade. Jews who forced themselves to tour the concentration camps are compelled to retrace their steps yet further, to revisit once-impenetrable domains, to seek the sparse kin who lingered on and lived through the Holocaust, to haunt synagogues and cemeteries behind the Wall and the Curtain. Should Anna also face the unacceptable past? Anna is neurotic, and she torments herself. How innocent, how dull the Cudworth past, said Anna, as she urged her husband to attend Dr Hawthorn's séance. What can Peter find to fear in Breaseborough?

Tourists do not go to Breaseborough, though the Hammervale Millennium Earth Recovery Project is trying to attract them. Hitherto politics have prevented tourists from visiting the innocent beauty spots of Anna's parents' youth. As yet they remain undiscovered, timeless, undeveloped. All that will change, as the glutting scum of money flows on, as operators send out their scuttling coaches. Now would be the time to go to this lost Arcady. Now, if ever. Before the scum mounts and drowns the mountaintops. Bautzen and Spreewald are said to be crowded already, and Weimar is overrun.

Anna, thinks Peter, has become unhealthily obsessed by the past. He is worried about her. Maybe he shouldn't have left her for so long.

Peter Cudworth drives onwards, leaving spoiled industrial England behind him. He finds himself, after one or two wrong turnings, on a straight road through wolds, with long blue views falling gently and spaciously and as it were infinitely to his right, glittering with distant sunlight. The trees are heavy with fresh new leaf, majestic, sculpted. The nearer fields are green and gold. This is a Roman road, and it drives straight. Church spires and church towers rise from time to time from the landscape, and beckon, and recede, and vanish. They are calling to Peter Cudworth to stay, but in one morning he traverses parishes, manors, estates, whole counties. Where the legions slowly tramped, where great carts and lighter carriages followed, Peter Cudworth drives on in his hired capsule, at fifty miles an hour, towards Loughborough, that clean and pleasant town. He drives more slowly and more carefully than his cousin Faro, who is a dashing motorist. He is older and has more, or so he thinks, to lose.

⋙⋘

Bessie Bawtry, like her granddaughter Faro, also called herself a feminist, though the word meant something a little different in the twenties and thirties. There had not been much evidence of feminism in her decision to marry Joe Barron. Perhaps she was biding her time and waiting for the right moment to express herself fully as a feminist.

Faro's mother and Bessie's second child, Christine Barron, as we have seen, was born soon after the beginning of the war, in the Montagu Maternity Hospital in Northam, at two thirty in the afternoon. Christine, like her brother Robert, was a healthy child, though a little yellow from baby jaundice, and weighed a conventional seven pounds one ounce. Bessie was to recall this uneventful birth in embarrassing detail and speak about it to people who could not, in the infant Chrissie's view, have been at all interested in it. Bessie, despite or because of those earlier miscarriages, prided herself on being exceptionally gifted at maternity. Baby Christine had appeared after twelve hours of labour, no forceps, and a little gas and air. (*Who cares? Who cares?* the dumb and infant Chrissie would silently howl, inside her shamed beleaguered head, as she heard this intimate birth saga repeated to total strangers for the hundredth time.) Dr Fox and a midwife had been in attendance. Joe Barron had not been there: in those days husbands were not expected to hang around the delivery room, and Joe Barron would not have been able to do so, even had he wished, as he was in an army camp in Essex at the time.

Baby Christine, Bessie and Robert did not stay long in Northam, for that city of steel was now threatened by the bombs that had already scored in London. The threat of aerial bombardment, which had hung over England through years of appeasement, was at last being realized. Joe thought at first of sending his little family to the safety of America, and even wrote to one of Bessie's college friends, a Quaker in Philadelphia, inquiring about the possibility of evacuation. But Bessie had no intention of being sent to America by herself, nor had the Quaker in Philadelphia any intention of receiving her. So that scheme came to nothing, and Bessie, Robert and the baby found themselves in a small town in the Peak District, which they reached by one of those chains of coincidences that scattered bits of population somewhat randomly around the country at that period. There they took temporary possession of a small newish suburban terraced council house, on the edge of town, and Bessie Barron took up a temporary post teaching at the King's Grammar School, Boys Only. Married women were allowed back to work, at this period. They were all to be sacked as soon as the war was over, when the men came home, but this was not as yet clear to them, and for the time being they were in demand. Bessie enjoyed being in demand, though she did not say so: she abided by the conventions of subdued complaint about the well-recognized inconveniences of war. People complained noticeably less in Pennington than in Breaseborough. There was less of a culture of complaint in Derbyshire. The air was cleaner in Pennington than it had been in Breaseborough. People had less to complain about.

(Had Pennington people migrated to Breaseborough, looking for work, during the Industrial Revolution? Had they liked what they found there? Had they adapted well? Will Dr Hawthorn track them back through their wanderings to the clear source?)

Bessie fought her way through privation and rationing as best she could, which was quite well. She was thrifty, and, like her mother, she prided herself on being a good manager. The enforced reduction of choice calmed her. The egalitarian sufferings of wartime did not displease her. She could do without bananas and tomatoes. She grew her own beans and potatoes in the back garden. She made rhubarb jam and gooseberry pie.

Her sister Dora sometimes came to stay. Auntie Dora was good with the children. Dora, unlike Bessie, liked children, and enjoyed playing board games and card games and doing jigsaws with them. She taught them how to do French knitting with a cotton bobbin and nails, and how to make fluffy pompoms from cardboard milk-bottle tops and the wool of unravelled jerseys. She helped them to make Christmas decorations out of silver paper, and dye an Easter egg with onion skin. Eggs were priceless: Robert and Chrissie would share one as a treat. (Faro, when told this story of the halved egg, would not believe it. She thought it was a bit of World War Two folklore. But Faro would be wrong.)

Dora taught Robert and Chrissie to play patience, and bought them a delightful card game called Belisha, based on collecting road signs and the staging posts of the Great North Road. She was a good auntie, and she smelled sweetly, of baby powder, perspiration and yellowy butter.

Bessie welcomed Dora's practical help and her company, but she simultaneously despised them. She was always relieved when Dora caught the bus back to Breaseborough and left her to her own devices. She could not think properly when Dora was around.

Picture Bessie, alone of an evening, towards the end of the war, in the drab front room of that little rented house in Pennington. There she sat, marking the exercise books of the King's Grammar School boys. She had been teaching them about dependent clauses and the use of the semi-colon. She preferred grammar to Dora. She ticked and crossed and added comments with her red pencil. In Europe, terrible events were taking place. Bessie kept in touch: she read the *Manchester Guardian* and Joe's censored letters and she listened to the Home Service. Bessie was no fool, unlike the women she heard gossiping in the greengrocer as they queued for carrots. Upstairs, Robert slept quietly in his bed, and Chrissie whimpered restlessly. Chrissie was a poor sleeper, and suffered frequently from earache, but Bessie did not believe in pampering babies, and she let her cry. Chrissie would soon snuffle herself to sleep.

Joe was out there in Italy, and she sat here in Derbyshire.

Bessie enjoyed teaching the boys. She had hated teaching in Breaseborough. It had been too sad. She had felt like an understudy, a second best. But here she had independence and authority. Nobody knew she had been Bessie Bawtry. Here, she was Mrs Barron, with a husband at the front. She mimicked the mannerisms of Miss Heald, and held the attention of the class. The headmaster was grateful to her and treated her with respect. The biology teacher was her friend, and had set up an aquarium for Robert and Chrissie. It held two newts. They sat on their miniature stony terraces like ageless little dinosaurs, and watched Bessie quizzically with their jewelled eyes.

What was she thinking of? What were her prospects? Was she eager for her husband's return? Was she lonely in her double bed? Was she wondering, as Dr Hawthorn was to wonder on her behalf, how on earth she had got to *here* from *there*? Was she wondering where the next staging post of her journey would be?

Robert missed his father but was too proud to show his feelings to his mother, who did not encourage emotions. Bessie rarely spoke of Joe, though whether this was because she thought of him too much or too little was not clear to Robert, and never would be. Chrissie did not miss her father, for she was too small to have any recollection of him. In some ways, she later decided, life had been simpler without him. He was a stranger to her when he returned. She was at first suspicious of him, and cried angrily when he tried to make her acquaintance. But he was a gentle father, and he did not pinch her cheeks or force his kisses upon her. He bided his time, and he won her round. He had brought her from Italy a little shell brooch, which she cherished, and a colouring book with outlines of moths and butterflies. She had never had such treasures. She cried when the colours of her paints ran and turned the pages into a smeared and murky brown. She wanted the swallowtails and the red admirals and the brimstones to be clear and brilliant and perfect, as they were in the picture on the book's jacket. 'Don't cry, pet,' Joe said, touched by her intense distress. 'It's lovely. You've done it beautifully.' But she knew it wasn't lovely. She was her mother's daughter, and she knew.

It was 1945 when Joe Barron came back with his gifts, and he had been promoted to the rank of major. He had been mentioned in dispatches and had met the Pope. He was eager to stand for Parliament as a Labour candidate. Radical already, he had been further radicalized by the war. He found himself swept along on the tide of left-wing reforming enthusiasm that took some of the nation, though not much of Yorkshire, so much by surprise. He was adopted by the West Yorkshire constituency of Holderfield Hartley, in the old industrial textile city of Holderfield. It was thought to have a safe Tory majority, but to everyone's astonishment, including his own, Joe won the seat. He found himself, in his thirties, a young lawyer with a Cambridge degree and a respectable war record, and an elected Member of Parliament. The world was all before him. He had won through.

Bessie promptly, or fairly promptly, went to bed. It would be more dramatic to say that she went to bed as soon as Joe Barron came home alive and in minor triumph, but it wasn't quite as simple as that. She seemed, at first, pleased to see him, and to hear his soldier's tales. She assured him that she would stand by his high-risk decision to stand for Parliament. She too was a Labour voter, and she agreed with his political position. They had been through all of this together, in earlier days. She did not feel she could go canvassing with or for him— the prospect of knocking on the doors of potentially hostile strangers filled her with understandable alarm—but she composed a 'Message to Women' for the Hartley Divisional Labour Party, in which, as the Labour candidate's wife, she declared that she would like to be with her husband in his election campaign, but that the cares of a young family kept her at home. 'This election,' she wrote, 'gives us women a great opportunity of realizing some of our dreams of a better way of living. Many women fail to see the connection between politics and everyday life, and they have paid dearly for their blindness in the last few years. There is no aspect of everyday life which is not influenced for good or ill by the nature of the government in power. The topics on which women are particularly interested—home, family, freedom from worry, hatred of war—are all affected by party politics. Every woman must decide which party serves those interests best. Good homes need good houses, and the housing policy of the Labour Party is the most far-reaching and the most practical. Happy family life requires steady employment, good wages, healthy and well-educated children. The industrial and financial policy of the Labour Party ensures employment and security at work...' And so on. It ended USE YOUR VOTE AND ENSURE THE SUCCESS OF MAJOR J. BARRON...

This leaflet, printed by Woollons & Sons at 42, Cemetery Road, Holderfield, showed a softly smiling head-and-shoulders oval studio photograph of Mrs J. Barron. She is wearing a V-necked paisley-patterned dress. Bessie was fond of paisley.

Bessie went to bed straight after the celebrations of the election. What was it to be this time? Shingles, neuralgia, lumbago, neuritis, peritonitis, a hiatus hernia? Whatever it was, she kept to her bed long enough for Joe to feel he had wronged her. He had hoped and expected that she would be proud of him and his survival and his success. And so, in a sense, she was, and so, in a very reduced sense, she was to remain. But she was also bitter with him. He had left her, all those years, to cope on hard rations, to dig for victory, to bring up two young children with the help of only one ill-trained teenage maid (and the maid had been called up, towards the end of the war)—and now he came home, just like that, and expected her to rejoice. He had been having a fine time of it overseas, in North Africa, in Greece, and Italy, and now he thought he could come home like a hero. Whereas she had been given the sack.

Women up and down the country were responding like this, though nobody was allowed to admit it.

She had not wanted to leave Pennington, and her council house, and her newts, and the King's School, and the biology teacher, and the boys of 5B, who had been coming on so well under her expert tuition. But of course she could not admit that, even to herself. She knew she had to rejoice. She knew it was beneath her dignity to dig her own garden and sit down to macaroni cheese or fried Spam with the maid while they both listened to the wireless. She knew she had to prefer the prospect of being an MP's wife.

Joe was not surprised by Bessie's withdrawal. He understood that she had been through trying times without him, and he was sorry to see her take to her bed. But he was not surprised. He had seen Bessie's retreats before now. He had hoped she would grow out of them. Now, he began to wonder what the future held. Where would they go from here?

Was it at this period that Bessie's voice began to take on that bitter, caustic, nagging tone that was to be hers until death? This was the tone that rang in Chrissie's ears throughout her girlhood and her adult life. She was never able to remember what Bessie sounded like before Joe came back from the wars. Maybe a sweeter, more affectionate, more maternal voice had spoken then? Maybe, in those early postwar years, Bessie was exacting some indirect and protracted revenge for the disappointments of her own life. Maybe she meant to call hostilities to an end when she had made her point, but forgot to do so. Chrissie could never unwind the scroll of time to the point where Bessie had been sweet. Though sweet she must surely, once, have been, or Joe would not have married her. Would he?

Chrissie was brought up against a background of warfare. The alarums of domestic warfare succeeded the distant bombardments of World War Two. Like Neville Chamberlain, Joe Barron went in for appeasement. He had had pacifist tendencies, as a young man, which had been fortified by a brief membership of the Peace Pledge Union, and although he had, like many others, abandoned them at the time of Munich, he had had enough of war by 1946. He wanted peace in his time. And anyway, much of what Bessie said he acknowledged to be true. She had indeed had a hard war, on the domestic front. A single mother, alone, in a strange town. An educated woman, with a Cambridge degree, living lonely in a council house, teaching three days a week, turning the mangle two days a week, and reading Victorian novels and country-house detective stories and Arthur Ransome tales by night, night after night after night, in the long blackout. Bessie had reason to feel she had been neglected and abandoned, though she cannot have thought it was his fault.

Joe did his best to make amends for this hard time. He suppressed his suspicion that she had enjoyed her teaching, because she so bitterly resisted any interpretation that allowed her past pleasure—or any pleasure ever. She wanted the martyr's crown of gold. And anyway, there was no way back to the classroom and the common room. It was better, now, to believe, with her, that she had been a wartime martyr. He tried to improve her lot as fast as he could. He moved her out of the cosy little council house, where little Chrissie had been mysteriously happy, and into a fair-sized, comfortable, semi-detached home in a good leafy quarter of the Hartley district of Holderfield, a district which remained Tory at heart, despite Joe's freak electoral return. He bought her one of the earliest electrical washing machines, so that she would not have to turn the mangle. He bought her a refrigerator, and a vast and heavy ironing machine, and an electrical airing cabinet with heated rails, and a Kenwood mixer, and an electrical dishwasher of primitive design which never really worked very well. He paid for a full-time daily help and a gardener, and he never even thought of querying the grocery bills. He tried, poor chap, he tried. And the harder he tried, the angrier she became.

Pretty Bessie Bawtry had lost her figure during the war. Who had stolen it, where had it gone? She was heard to blame macaroni cheese. Macaroni cheese was the villain. Her muscles had become unnaturally and weirdly slack, and her breasts and belly sagged, shapelessly. She was not yet as fat as Ellen, but she was getting on that way. The Cudworth gene had linked up with macaroni cheese to disastrous effect. Her face remained youthful and unlined, but her body was the body of an old woman. Dora had a tendency to stoutness too, but Dora at this period was still energetic and walked miles with her dog, and ran around Breaseborough busily. Dora learned to drive a car, but it did not make her lazy. She would drive out to the moors with her girlfriends, for picnics, and they would go for long rambles at weekends. Spinster Dora's body thickened, but it did not droop and sag. It was childbirth that ruined Bessie. Robert and Chrissie were responsible for Bessie's deformed and dangling bosom, for the folds of white tripe flesh above her thighs.

Joe was faithful to her, as far as we can tell. People were faithful to their wives in those days. He was away a good deal, in London, in the constituency, in chambers. He had plenty of time off.

Robert and Chrissie, those small criminals, those suckling succubi, were brought up in an atmosphere of low-key tension and low-key dissatisfaction, which would occasionally heighten into arias of loud and angry distress. Bessie would complain daily about 'all the flopping housework' that burdened her, and for years Robert and Chrissie did not even notice that in practice she did hardly any housework at all. The housework was done by Mrs Macaulay, or Mrs Todd, or Mrs Stephens, or their various successors. Bessie, they were later to agree, was an agoraphobic as well as a hypochondriac: she hated going out. No wonder she grew slack. She felt safe only in her own nice thirties suburban home, with its pale polished wood, its cream paint, its nice broad shallow stairs and its polished banisters. When invited out, she would respond with irrational panic. After her initial spasm of loyalty, she could not have been described as a supportive constituency wife. She felt out of place amongst the lower and lower-middle classes from which she had risen, and frightened by the middle classes into which she had moved, and appalled by the working classes with whom she had sympathized, and whose cause she had espoused. So she had nowhere to go. She sat at home, and polished the silver, and listened to *Woman's Hour* on the wireless, and read books. She was full of opinions. She knew it all. She knew it better than anyone. She criticized, sourly, the government, the opposition, the Americans, the communists, the Catholics, the Church of England. She criticized men. It was men who had ruined the world. 'The wo of these women that woneth in cotes'. She knew that woe.

You would not have guessed, from the attitudes of bleak Bessie Barron, that there were those in Britain in the late 1940s who felt a mood of optimism—a cramped, ill-nourished optimism, but an optimism, nevertheless.

Robert and Chrissie reacted differently to this pervasive and corrosive family spirit. Both, naturally, were expected to be hardworking, achieving, upwardly mobile little brats, for they had taken in ambition with their mother's breast-destroying milk. But they had also imbibed despair.

Robert, being a boy, decided early in his career, at about the age of four, that the best thing to do was to grit one's teeth, bite the tit or bite the bullet. Slog away, learn one's letters, get on with it, and get out of it. He was the son of both his parents, after all. Chrissie too saw the advantages of the hard-work escape route, but she did not take it. There was a perverse, wicked, rebellious streak in Chrissie, which was to lead her to a kind of liberation. She was a shrewd little thing, and she had seen what was happening. What good did it do you to work so hard, to pass your exams, to go to university like a good girl? You ended up miserable, cooped up, trapped, just the same. With all your education, you ended up washing dishes, baking tarts, moaning on about the mangle or the airing cupboard or the butcher's bill or the laziness of Mrs Todd. You might as well have some fun now, as you were going to pay later anyway. And there was fun to be had, in Holderfield, in the 1950s, when Chrissie was a girl.

Did Chrissie take after her Barron aunts? Was she more Barron than Bawtry? Joe, watching her progress with admiration and concerned alarm, could see something of his sisters in her. She had the Barron red hair, and she would toss it from time to time with flamboyant and passionate fury. She was a passionate child, bold, reckless, restless and the reverse of agoraphobic. As a small child, she was forever rushing and leaping and falling and racing. She fell out of trees and slid down rocks and crashed her tricycle. She broke off her two front teeth diving from the top board into the swimming pool. She was a tomboy. She had none of Bessie's physical timidity. She was combative, rebellious. She would lose her temper with her mother, and shout, and be scolded, and be banished to her bedroom in fits of noisy weeping. Once she was so rude to Bessie that Joe felt compelled to beat her bottom with the back of a hairbrush, an act which he regretted until his death, and indeed he apologized for it upon his deathbed. For Chrissie had responded with such howls of anguish and despair, had wept so bitterly for so many hours, had tormented him with such gazes of resentful hatred, that he had never dared lift a finger to her again. She was a wild and stubborn little creature, with a strong will. He did not want to break it or to see it broken.

Nor did he want to see her go the way of his sisters. The Barron girls had fled far from Cotterhall, but their flight had partaken of desperation, and in Rowena's case had ended in tragedy. He did not speak of them much to Robert and Chrissie, who had to piece the story together for themselves, as best they could.

Rowena Barron had at last gone on her cruise. She had saved her pennies, not for Jesus, but for herself, working for her father and her brother in that little wooden cubbyhole that was called her 'office'. After years of plans and dreams she had booked herself and her friend Gertie Thomson on to their voyage to the Orient. But it had not worked out quite as expected. Somehow, mysteriously, the moment for departure to Cythera was already past. Rowena had been good-looking, in her early and late teens, but she had been endowed with that healthy, sudden passing beauty which blossoms and dies before it has time to mature. Rowena had grown thin and beaky, and her spirits and bounce had flattened. She had always, according to Ivy, been 'man-mad', and she proved this by embarking on a shipboard romance with a rotter from Cape Town, whom she was obliged to marry. She settled in Cape Town, bore a child and died of some illness or other—nobody could quite say what. None of the Barrons ever met the rotter. The rotter had thought Rowena had money, and Rowena had hoped the rotter had money, and as neither of them had much they ended up in a short marriage of mutual recrimination, culminating in early death. Rowena had not set a good example for Chrissie to follow.

Ivy, in contrast, had made a more successful job of emigrating. Her life in Cotterhall had been constricted, though she had tried to make the best of it: she had, for a while, joined 'the fast set' with speed-loving brother Phil, and had ridden a motorbike round the Yorkshire moors, but had given this up after a nasty accident. (One of her best friends was found dead in a ditch at the bottom of Stanage Edge.) Unlike Rowena, Ivy decided to avoid sex, and had set up house with a clever piano-playing young woman from Sheffield who gave piano lessons and, more rarely, concerts. Ivy worked in a tearoom as a waitress, and then took over as manageress of a small health-food shop which sold date slices, dried apricots, dried bananas, Fru-grains, rice crackers, Horlicks tablets and other delicacies. It did well during and immediately after the war, during the period of sweet rationing and sugar shortage.

Ivy, who had been shocked by the news of her sister Rowena's death, had wanted to sail out to see her South African brother-in-law and her orphaned niece. She had a notion of rescuing the niece, of bringing her back to England. She was dissuaded. But the idea of escape increasingly attracted her. At this period, many were planning emigration to the colonies. With victory, many voted Labour, and then left the country, as did Ivy. (She was very proud to have a brother in Parliament, but felt she could not wait for the improvements he was sure to introduce.) She was able to emigrate more easily because she inherited a small legacy from her parents, both of whom had died in 1945, in Cotterhall, in their early seventies, within a few months of one another.

Pa Barron left the business to his son Bennett, and he left small legacies to Alfred and Ivy. He left nothing to Joe or Phil. (This caused trouble, though he had had his reasons.) Ivy decided to spend her windfall on a one-way passage to Australia. She would sail off for ever with her friend Pat, and make a new life for herself. All the Barrons apart from Joe—including Bessie Barron, who was not even a real Barron—were outraged by what they saw as alienation and appropriation of Barron money. Why should Pat Parker from Sheffield, whose friendship with Ivy had given rise to unpleasant gossip, be able to sail round the world on the hard-won profits of Barron Glass? (In fact, though none of the Barrons of that generation were ever to know this, Pat Parker from Sheffield had done nothing of the sort: she had a little nest egg of her own, and was happy to spend it on her shared cabin with Ivy, and to invest what was left of it, when they arrived, in a small market garden.)

Pat and Ivy sailed away in the spring of 1947, after one of the hardest and longest winters in living memory, to the warmth of the Antipodes. What did they talk about in their cabin, as they sailed southwards? We shall never know. They never came back. In England, that winter, snow lay banked up and grimed for months, and Chrissie, a school-trotting satchelled schoolgirl, forgot the natural contours of her hometown, and rediscovered them with surprise when at last the thaw came.

No wonder Pat and Ivy had fled this grim cold dirty rationed land. Joe Barron was to fly out to visit them, many years later, in the 1970s, much to the jealous disapproval of Bessie, and he found them happily settled and apparently content with their lot. They had good friends, and belonged to musical and literary societies. Pat played the piano, and Ivy wrote poems, which she published in the local press. They had not done badly. But he was not sure that he wanted his daughter Chrissie to sail away with a strange woman. And he certainly did not want her to waste herself on a gold-digging remittance man, as Rowena had done. Joe wanted his daughter to live at peace in her own land. He wanted a land fit for heroes, with council housing fit for heroes, but he also wanted a land fit for women. Fit for women such as his wife might have been, such as his daughter might yet be.

The discontent of women was festering and the smell of it spread.

Joe's mother had not seemed discontented. A shy and kindly woman, a martyr to what would one day be labelled 'adaptive preference formation', she had never questioned the patriarchal authority and manners of her husband, nor his occasional outbursts of temper, nor his gloomy silences. Patiently she had stitched her glowing silks, and planted bulbs in her shrubbery, and made bland white sauces, and declared her delight in the meanest portion of chicken wing, and thought herself fortunate. Whereas Bessie, who had so much more, was full of bitterness and complaint. Times were changing. Where would it all end?

Bessie's sister Dora did not seem discontented either. She had not proved as upwardly mobile as Bessie, nor had she acquired the status symbol of a husband, but in her own way she had done well for herself. She and Auntie Florrie had worked away at their dressmaking business both before and during the war, and had proved very adept at making a little rationed cloth go a long way. They unstitched and restitched, they remade and made over. Their services were always in demand. Auntie Florrie rented a little corner shop, and branched out into fancy goods. Before the war Auntie Florrie's nephew Sam from the garage had taught Dora to drive, and she got her licence in 1935: when petrol rationing eased, Dora bought a little Morris car and travelled around the neighbourhood buying and selling. In a small way, but profitably. She even went as far as Rotherham and Sheffield and Doncaster and Northam. She became the agent for an insurance company, and sold policies through the haberdashery and fancy goods network. She bought National Savings Certificates, and put her money in a building society, and bought herself a little house in Swinton Road in Breaseborough, two streets away from her parents' house in Slotton Road. This was considered odd of her, but not very odd. It was understood that Dora wanted her independence. It was also understood that she didn't want to go too far way, in case she was needed. And anyway, Dora liked Breaseborough. It was her home. But then, she had low expectations, and low tastes. Dora was not refined. She was a simple, undemanding soul. A little workhorse, that's how she described herself.

It seemed as natural for Dora to stay as it had seemed natural that Bessie should leave. She had plenty of friends there, when she was young, chiefly amongst the young unmarrieds—a couple of primary-school teachers, a gentleman's tailor, a shop assistant from the department store, Sam the garage mechanic, Len the bicycle repairman and racing cyclist. It was a classless, unpretending little group. Why didn't Dora marry, when she was so fond of babies? Nobody knew. She just didn't. She wasn't the marrying type. She didn't dislike men—Sam and Len and the gentleman's tailor were regular visitors—but she didn't like the marrying *type* of man.

It never occurred to Robert and Chrissie that their parents might have stayed on in Cotterhall or Breaseborough, and that Joe Barron, given less determination, might still have been working with his brother in his father's glassworks. This scenario had never crossed their minds. The exodus from Breaseborough was the premise of their birth and being. Joe-and-Bessie were inconceivable, to them, as a married couple in Cotterhall or Breaseborough. Chrissie and Robert had been brought up to regard Breaseborough as a foreign country. Bessie herself never went there. She spoke of it with loathing. She despised her birthplace. She declared, to anyone who would listen, that she hated it and everything about it. It gave her the shudders. Breaseborough, for Bessie, was off the map. She had cut herself off from it for ever. She vowed she would never return.

Her parents, however, were allowed to come out of Breaseborough to visit her. Bert and Ellen were invited to come to stay for Christmas in the spacious Barron house in Hartley, where she boasted two spare bedrooms, and a downstairs cloakroom with a washbowl and a WC. And sister Dora was allowed to come too. Dora came more frequently to Hartley than the grandparents, and when they were little Robert and Chrissie were, as we have seen, very fond of her. It was Dora who took Chrissie to the dental hospital in Leeds when Chrissie broke off both her front teeth, and it was Dora who watched the nerve extraction and the drilling, and it was Dora who took Chrissie on follow-up visits for the fitting of the crowns. Bessie enjoyed her own illnesses, after her fashion, but she was squeamish about the illnesses of others: Dora didn't like hospitals either, but she braced herself for the ordeal, as a good auntie should.

Bessie bossed Dora, and condescended to her, and told her off, and put her down, and criticized her, but she did not cast her off. Dora was useful.

Bessie had not quarrelled with her parents or her sister, as the second-generation Barrons had all quarrelled with one another. But she made the demarcations plain. They were kin, but they were different.

Bessie, it is clear, had serious problems with her attitude towards her origins. Bessie had suffered a good education and had risen in the world. Breaseborough Secondary School had taught her to despise Breaseborough town and Breaseborough people, and by extension she was obliged to despise her parents and her sister. This was a commonplace social problem in postwar England, where the English class system was at unacknowledged odds with the new welfare state, the Labour Party, and the egalitarian social optimism which Joe and Bessie Barron in principle represented. Many upwardly mobile families found themselves caught in similar contradictions. But Bessie, we suspect, suffered from an extreme form of contradiction. For Breaseborough Secondary School and Miss Heald had taught Bessie an exceptionally high opinion of herself. She was not just one of many bright young girls marching along the radiant way into the socialist future. She belonged to no cohort. She was singled out, elect.

Bessie had clung to this sense of election through illness, crisis, misgiving, the threat of failure. She believed in it. She believed in her own superiority. And on one level, her confidence in her own self-worth was so great that she believed that everything that belonged to her or was associated with her was special and remarkable. Her parents, her sister, even her despised birthplace must be remarkable, because they were hers. She shed on them a reflected glory.

This mind-set created an uneasy and unresolved conflict in her which may, we assume, have accounted for many of her apparent inconsistencies. (For an educated woman, proud of her rationality, she was stacked with inconsistencies.)

Auntie Dora thought that it would be nice if the children came to stay with her from time to time for a day or two, in her little house in Breaseborough, now they were getting to be a little older. Would Bessie let them come? Would the children like to come?

The children said they would like to go to stay, though nobody would have listened to them if they'd said they didn't. They liked their auntie, and were eager to get away from home.

Bessie was torn by the proposal. Part of her longed to be rid of her children, who were a constant worry to her, even though she paid them little attention. But part of her feared that the shame and dirt of Breaseborough would infect them, and that Dora would enchant them and alienate them and turn them into the wrong kind of children.

It is a curious fact that Bessie, who prided herself on being exceptionally gifted at maternity, did not really like children. She quite liked babies, but she didn't like children. Children were noisy, and quarrelsome, and mobile, and demanding. Her mother Ellen hadn't liked children either, as both Bessie and Dora would testify. She preferred rattling along in the sidecar. Ellen, according to Bessie and Dora, hadn't even liked babies. But maybe Bessie and Dora were bad witnesses. They wanted a conviction and they may have distorted the evidence. Ellen has never been called upon to answer the charge.

Bessie did indeed consider herself to be 'exceptionally gifted at maternity', but then she had a way of considering herself exceptionally gifted at everything she undertook. It was impossible even for those who knew her intimately to tell whether this high estimation of herself sprang from vanity, or insecurity, or from the high opinion of Miss Heald, or from her success in the educational system. For she was a success, and that should not be forgotten. The fact that she did nothing with that success may explain why she prided herself so much on maternity. Yet even that pride was deeply ambivalent. Granddaughter Faro, years later, was to recall her grandmother's frequently reiterated lament that she had spent all the years of her prime 'wiping babies' bottoms'. This would have seemed merely a pardonable exaggeration had it not been for the venomous disgust with which those words 'babies' bottoms' were always spat forth. Faro detected in this a deep dislike of her children and of bodily functions, but when Faro mentioned this interpretation to her own mother Chrissie, Chrissie looked at her blankly. She'd forgotten that particular phrase of complaint. Unlike so many others, it had failed to wound. It hadn't struck home.

What else but maternity had Bessie Barron left to pride herself upon? The conditions of her life seemed to offer no other opportunities for pride. So she conquered the language and the technology of child-rearing, as she had conquered the language of Chaucer and of Marvell and the techniques of I. A. Richards's *Practical Criticism*. She taught herself all about Truby King, and sterilizing bottles, and formula feeds, and nappy rash, and birth weights, and Harrington squares, and terry towelling, and vaccinations. There was more to maternity in those days. You didn't just go and buy the new brand-name disposable nappies in a supermarket. You spent your time at the tub. You spent your time wiping babies' bottoms. Oh yes. But that didn't mean you liked it. Did it? Bessie didn't seem to like it. And her two children, the fruits of her maternal gift, felt themselves to be a useless and unwanted by-product of it, rather than its fulfillment.

Nevertheless, she was not entirely happy about letting them go, for they were her justification and her raison d'être. When they were gone, she was nobody. Perhaps she was afraid that her children would like Breaseborough? Would they like it *too much*? Would they try to hook her back into it, to drag her back?

One thing was clear: whatever suspicions and apprehensions she may have had about her sister, she couldn't have been jealous of Dora's single state, could she? A married woman had far, far higher status than a single one. Everyone knew that.

So the children do go and stay with Dora, from time to

time. They keep in touch with Breaseborough through Dora. It is more than an ancestral memory for them. It is a real place. They know her house, and their Bawtry grandparents' house. They are allowed to climb into Auntie Dora's high bed with Trixie in the mornings, where she tells them stories. They do not visit the Barrons in Cotterhall, for the Barron grandparents are dead, and some kind of family feud has divided the rest of the Barrons. Auntie Dora never goes to Cotterhall. (Many years later, Dora will say to her great-niece Faro, 'We never had much to do with Cotterhall people. We didn't get involved with them.')

Joe is pleased that Robert and Chrissie visit the old place from time to time, though, like Bessie, he rarely goes there himself. And he likes to see little Chrissie kiss her fat old grandma, her whiskery old grandpa. Perhaps she will grow up to be a normal, healthy, happy, affectionate little girl, after all. Joe is beginning to dread the genetic trap.

ꙮ

Joe watched both his children with concern, when he was at home, and would from time to time attempt to defend them from the fallout of their mother's erratically darkening temperament. (That beating, undertaken on Bessie's behalf, had been highly uncharacteristic.) Robert gave less obvious cause for anxiety: he was serious, scholarly, a little introverted. He was sent to a conventional prep school, then to a minor Yorkshire public school, well out of his mother's way. His progress reports were good. He plodded on, sharpening his critical faculties. His point hardened. Wastepaper baskets filled. He discarded, discarded. He was to become picky, pedantic. Even as a boy, he picked and pierced. He defended himself carefully, and protected his own core. Nobody could get near Robert.

Chrissie, in contrast, was emotional, female, flibbertigibbet. She veered and tacked and turned with the wind. She liked

173

the wind. Like her uncle Phil Barron, she liked speed. She adored it. Yes, she took after the Barrons, not after the Cudworths and the Bawtrys, in her sporting skills. She could wack a rounders ball, serve an ace, dive off the top board and jump the long jump. She nearly killed herself when she was given her first two-wheel bicycle, a dashing little red Raleigh: she couldn't resist freewheeling down from Sowerbrigg Tops at thirty miles an hour, and ended up in hospital with a concussion and a split knee. This taught her no lesson: as soon as she could get back on again, she did. She discovered riding, as middle-class suburban girls did in those days, and she loved it disproportionately: the wind in your face, the thunder of hooves, the rush, the lack of control. And she longed to ski. How she longed to ski! But here, her parents put their feet down. Skiing was expensive. In the fifties, when Chrissie was a girl, foreign travel was still rationed. Only the rich went off to ski. No, Chrissie could not join the school ski party.

Chrissie also was sent to private schools, despite Joe's Labour principles, despite the excellence of the state education he himself had received at Breaseborough. He spent as much money on her as he spent on Robert. Not for her the second-rate female role. She was to get nothing but the best. But she was not sent away to boarding school. In her case, the best was considered to be a single-sex day school with high academic standards and a socially superior intake. And perhaps, at the back of his mind, Joe thought that if Chrissie wasn't sent away to school, she could keep an eye on Bessie, who was becoming increasingly neurotic and withdrawn. Let the daughter watch over the mother.

(Joe Barron, we should tell you, is no longer a Member of Parliament. He failed to be returned in the next general election: although he had been a popular constituency man, the swing went against him, and he resumed his life as a barrister, with a fair amount of success.)

Joe had no idea of what Chrissie really got up to, during

her girlhood and adolescence. Nor had Bessie. Bessie's agoraphobia had led to an increasing lack of supervision. When the children were very small, she was able and willing to keep them under her eye and under her thumb, but as they grew larger they found that it was easier and easier to escape from her. Bessie never learned to drive—many women didn't drive, in those days, and two-car families were rare—and she soon abandoned any pretence of walking them to school. The friendly chats at the school gate were an ordeal to her, and the other mothers filled her with dismay, even with terror. She pretended to despise the other mothers, but in practice she feared them, or so Chrissie suspected. Bessie convinced herself that it was quite safe for Robert and Chrissie to walk or take the bus or tram alone. She even sent Chrissie, aged seven, down to the shops for her. And it is fair to say that the streets were safer, then. Robert and Chrissie grew independent early. Independent, and secretive. In the house, they continued to behave in a subdued and respectful manner for most of the time, though Chrissie, as we have seen, punctuated her respect with wild outbursts of indignation. Out of the house, they did more or less what they pleased. And it pleased Chrissie, as she grew into her teens, to join the fast set at Holderfield High. Robert, at that age, was more interested in fighter pilots and model aeroplanes. Chrissie was interested in sex.

Her friends were not the kind of friends that Bessie and Joe would have approved, though as she never brought them home they were not to know this.

There are more ways than one of going to the bad.

Rotters from Cape Town were not available in Holderfield. Rotters were out of date. Chrissie amused herself with the Tory youth of the county. They were the brothers of her schoolfriends, and they were shallow and smoothly callow, and they had more money than was good for them, and they drank more than they could hold, and they groped Chrissie with enthusiasm when they found she seemed willing. Heavy petting, it was called. They could not have been more different from those high-minded, hardworking, highly motivated between-the-wars fifth- and sixth-formers of Breaseborough Secondary School—Reggie Oldroyd, Philip Walters, George Bellew. Chrissie liked them because they were so awful, and so unlike anything her mother could have dreamed of. If she went out with boys like this, she could surely never turn into her mother? Turning into her mother was (and was long to remain) Chrissie's darkest fear. These dreadful, unacceptable boys, with good manners and bad morals, would inoculate her against Bessie and her fate.

Chrissie's father was a sweet and serious man of high principles, and look what had happened to him. Already, by the age of fifteen, Chrissie could see that his virtues had made him unhappy. So she preferred these frightful frivolous lads, who copied out her essays to use when they got back to school, who never read a book, who flunked their exams, who stole from their parents when their money ran out, who nicked drinks from their parents' drink trolleys, who liked to sit in the back row of the cinema with a hand in her pants or her bra. You didn't have to fall in love with them. They didn't have to fall in love with you. But you could have fun with them. And fun, at fifteen, was what Chrissie thought she wanted. She thought she'd have some while she could.

These bad boys lived a subversive, underhand, underground life, well hidden from their parents, most of whom were respectable, middle-class churchgoing folk. The age of open rebellion had not yet dawned. This was an era of cheating and hiding and lying. Sexual relations, for teenagers, were rarely penetrative. The hand in the bra, the dirty handkerchief, the spilt seed. Terror of pregnancy haunted both girls and boys, and with good reason. So they stopped, just short of the limit, again and again. Even fast girls like Chrissie Barron knew when to stop. That was the code. These were the last years of restraint, if this licentious fumbling could be called restraint.

Many of the contradictions of the nineteenth century were still in place in the 1950s. A provincial manufacturing town like Holderfield was layered backwards into its prosperous Victorian past. Large houses built of large blocks of granite had not yet been refashioned into flats, or demolished to make way for estates, or sold up to institutions: some were still inhabited by a single spinster, the last of a line, or a lonely widower, living in one room and eating off a tray. Old-fashioned servants had all but disappeared, with the war, as young women found the freedom of munitions and biscuit factories, though most middle-class women with families, including Bessie, had a daily help. An era was passing, but it had not yet departed. Vast gardens surrounded by gloomy conifers and high hedges went to seed, for gardeners, like maids, were in short supply. Small ornamental ponds, neglected for decades, grew deep with Canadian pond weed, and swarmed with silvery minnow and purple-and-orange stickleback. Sundials tried to keep their heads clear and record the passing of their reign, but they gave in to the ivy, one by one, and went under. The ivy tugged at them and pried at them and cracked them and weighed them down, and they fell into the burgeoning wilderness.

These large, neglected gardens were invaded by children. Chrissie and her gang, aged ten, crept through many a hedge to play secretly in clearings, to make themselves dens in the undergrowth, to fish for minnows with nets and jam jars in the abandoned pools. Occasionally a witchlike figure would scream from a window, or an old man with a stick would totter down cracked steps towards them, but the children were quick and knew their escape routes.

On one of these forays, Chrissie lost the little oval brooch that her father had brought back to her from the wars. It was neither a very beautiful nor an expensive little brooch. It was made of painted shells, stuck on plaster, with a circlet of pearls and a fragment of reflecting glass in its centre—a trumpery trinket, Italian, cheap, picked up from a roadside stall by Joe as he moved north through Perugia with the army. He had bought it for the little girl he had hardly seen, who had been growing up in his absence. Chrissie loved this brooch. It was her treasure. It was pointless, functionless, decorative, and her own. And now it was gone. She could not think what had happened to it, and wept for days as she mournfully searched the house, the garden, the schoolyard, the playing fields, the road to the bus stop, and all the secret truant places she could think of. Obsessively she sobbed and searched, telling herself madly, as children will, that the brooch was the key to her father's love, and that if she did not find it he would cease to love her, and would leave her for London, or for another war. An intense guilt and grief shook her, though she told nobody its cause. She almost fell ill. But she looked at her mother, and recovered. She pulled herself together, and tried to forget.

Five years later, when she was fifteen, she found the brooch, under the copper beech tree at the bottom of Miss Haversham's garden. (Miss Haversham was not the proprietor's real name. Her real name was unknown to her intruders.) Chrissie found it as she was picking beech leaves off herself, after an energetic and frustrating tussle with Dave Appleton at the beginning of the summer hols. The discovery struck her as profoundly significant. 'That which was lost shall be found,' she declared to Dave Appleton as he wiped off his trousers and zipped himself up. 'And all things that were lost shall be found.'

'What?' said Dave Appleton.

And Chrissie showed him her shell brooch, which had lain quietly waiting for her for these last five years. There could not be another like it in the whole of Yorkshire, in the whole of England, in the whole of recorded time. It had been lost, and it had come back to her. Her father's love was once more secured. 'Amazing, isn't it?' said Chrissie, as she polished it up on the hem of her cotton skirt.

Dave was not a poetic lad, and he was suffering from post-ejaculation sadness and embarrassment, but he managed to agree that it was a bit of a coincidence.

'You'd better put it somewhere safe this time,' he said.

And so she did, but she forgot where the safe place was, and so lost it once more. But this time she did not grieve for it, for she knew that it would be restored once more.

She did not tell her father that she had found it. But then she had never told him that she had lost it. Some things are better not said.

The growing Chrissie Barron was not a conscientious scholar, though she did well enough at Holderfield High. She got reasonably good grades, without much effort, but she did not strive to be top of the class, as her mother had striven. She was happy enough to be in the top ten. She appeared to have less ambition than her parents had expected. What was she going to do with her life? Robert at this point seemed set to be a lawyer, in his father's footsteps. But Chrissie, though frequently argumentative, said she did not want to be a lawyer. She was not even sure at this stage that she wanted to go to university. At times she thought she might be an archaeologist, and recover lost things. At other times she thought she might be a surgeon, or an air stewardess, or a ski instructor, or a barmaid. She did not want anything to do with words. The House of her mother was heavy with the Word. Chrissie did not like words. She had had enough of words.

Joe Barron urged her to stick at her studies, to do her homework, to defer pleasure, as Miss Heald had instructed the class at Breaseborough. He liked to see her enjoy herself, but he did not want to see her lose ground. It was hard to get your foot back on the ladder, if you slipped. As he had slipped, when he had failed to get the County Major so confidently predicted by Miss Heald. Sometimes he thought Chrissie took her advantages for granted. He had worked hard for those advantages. Were Chrissie and Robert aware of the sacrifices that had been made for their future? Of the expense of bringing them up as a professional man's children?

He need not have worried. Of course they were aware. In their view, the cost of their education, of their school uniforms, of their hockey sticks and tennis rackets and bicycles was being drummed into them day and night. They were always being told what they cost their parents. And of course they were not grateful. Why should they be? They hadn't chosen to be brought up like this, had they? They hadn't asked to be born.

◊∭◊

Bessie nearly kept her vow not to set foot in South Yorkshire again. In the fifties, she had managed to escape Yorkshire altogether, for when Robert was eighteen and Chrissie fifteen Joe Barron took silk, and as a Queen's Counsel he was no longer expected to live near his old circuit. He moved south, to London chambers, and the family moved south, to Surrey. To placate Bessie he bought a bigger, cleaner and broader house than the one in Holderfield. Bessie liked it very much. It had two bathrooms, and a conservatory, and two acres of garden to screen her from her uninquisitive neighbours. Bessie's isolation was complete and triumphant, her metamorphosis achieved. She was delighted, she said, to have left Yorkshire for good. She liked the mild Surrey countryside, the big leisurely houses, the clean air, the quiet, the milder spring. She had always preferred rational Jane Austen to the self-pitying and hysterical Brontës. Frances and Molly, with whom she still kept in touch, would prefer to make their annual visit to Farnleigh, she was sure. They could never have liked Holderfield.

Chrissie was puzzled by the violence of Bessie's rejection of Yorkshire, by her praise of tame and suburban Surrey, by her need for a useless surrounding space into which she never ventured.

180

How could Bessie explain to Chrissie that it would take her the rest of her life to decontaminate herself? That she needed an unoccupied and neutral zone around her to protect her from the frightening world's intrusions and assaults?

Bessie's loneliness, to Chrissie, seemed deadly. Chrissie, at sixteen, yearned for action. The big house in Farnleigh, to Chrissie, was a living tomb, though she was rapidly discovering the possibilities of Farnleigh's co-educational grammar school, to which she had been transferred, and where she was to take her A-levels.

Bessie settled into the anonymity of the south. She avoided messages and memories from Holderfield and Breaseborough. She cut herself off and transplanted herself. She did not try to put down new roots, for she did not seem to want connections. She settled into solitude.

She never went back to Holderfield. There was nobody there that she ever wished to see again. She had made no friends there. Mrs Macaulay, Mrs Todd, Mrs Stephens—these had been her companions. These had been those who took the place of friends. Her correspondence with the biology teacher in Pennington lapsed.

Bessie Barron now sank into depression with an almost voluptuous abandon. In Holderfield, she had been forced from time to time to struggle towards an appearance of activity and normality. In Surrey, she gave in to despair. She lay in bed late and slept in the afternoons and began to watch television from time to time, a medium she had formerly derided. Inside her airy house, she wove her own dark cave and hid in it, surrounded by strangely lowbrow magazines and detective stories and soap operas. And Joe, also despairing, would have let her hide away there undisturbed, had it not been for Robert and Chrissie. Robert was almost free now of the family doom, and it was Chrissie who seemed to Joe to bear the brunt of her mother's mental state. For Bessie was not consistently subdued and inert: she could rouse herself to spasms of violent and angry rhetoric.

One weekend evening, Chrissie, charged to pick lettuce from the garden and wash it for supper, had failed to give satisfaction. The leaves, said Bessie, were *dirty*. 'They're not dirty,' said Chrissie mildly, 'they're a bit bruised, that's all.' '*Dirty,*' yelled Bessie. 'Wash them, wash them,' yelled Bessie. 'I've tried,' said Chrissie less mildly, staring at the crinkled foliage. 'Really, Chrissie, you are useless, quite useless,' bawled Bessie. 'You can't even make a salad properly. You stupid, stupid girl. Can't you do anything properly?'

Joe, overhearing but not witnessing this interchange, heard the kitchen door bang, and saw Chrissie flounce out into the garden angrily. A quarter of an hour later he followed her and found her lying on the grass sobbing by the raspberries. 'Come on, pet,' he said gently.

'She's mad,' said Chrissie, as she struggled to her feet. 'The lettuce was fine. I did my best. She's mad. The lettuce grows that way. I did my best.'

'Come on in, child,' said Joe. 'Come on in.'

And they sat down together to the poached salmon and the boiled new potatoes and the despised green leaves, crushed and wilted by a battery of cleanliness.

It was a nice meal. Bessie was a good cook.

It was soon after this episode that Bessie agreed to see a specialist, and started to take the tablets. They didn't seem to have much effect, though Robert and Chrissie agreed that perhaps she lost her temper less often and less irrationally. She didn't seem to be any happier, though she took a certain grim and monotonous satisfaction in talking about the specialist's diagnosis of 'endogenous depression'. The specialist, of course, like anyone connected with Bessie, was always described as 'eminent'. Chrissie, at this period, found a slightly shaming relief in being able to say, to schoolfriends, 'My mother's rather ill, I'm afraid.'

In later years, Chrissie decided that the eminent specialist had been a bloody fool.

Would a better doctor have come up with better advice? Would a worse husband have achieved better results? Can one blame Bessie Barron for handling her own unhappiness in this unproductive way? Can one blame anyone for anything ever? There's no point in feeling sorry for Bessie. It's far, far too late for that. There's still hope for Chrissie, but it's far too late for Bessie and far too late for Joe.

Bessie settled for endogenous depression in the alien land of Surrey, and she returned once more, and once only, to Breaseborough. She went in order to bury her mother, though she did not achieve that purpose.

Bert Bawtry, whose real name was George, had died well before the Barrons moved south to Surrey. He died in 1950, of a set of complications following an attack of pneumonia. He was sixty-nine years old, and he was buried in the Breaseborough Cemetery, on the windy plateau, where Bessie had once learned by heart the sad inscriptions. Bessie attended the service with her mother and Dora and a straggle of neighbours and cousins and colleagues from the days of the electrical works and the Destructor. Joe did not go, though he would have done had he been able. The children were not invited. Children were not expected to attend funerals, not even the funerals of grandparents. The pious days of little Henry and his bearer were long over. It is to be doubted whether anybody who said good-bye to Bert had any faith or interest whatsoever in the life everlasting. This life had, some of them thought, been quite bad enough.

It was Ellen's last illness that summoned Bessie home for the last time. Ellen had been failing for some time, as Dora had faithfully and fully reported. She had developed chest pains, first diagnosed as heart disease, then as lung cancer. This diagnosis was not considered very surprising by either of her daughters. True, Ellen had never smoked a cigarette in her life, as far as they knew, but in Breaseborough you didn't have to be a smoker to inhale smoke. And you didn't have to go down the pits to ruin your lungs. Just living, breathing and walking in the streets would do it. So Dora and Bessie were not indignant or astonished. This kind of death happened all the time. Ellen had well outlived her husband, as women did, and do. It was time for her to go.

The link between cigarettes and lung cancer was well known, even at this period, however much this pre-knowledge was to be disputed and denied. The links between lung cancer, passive smoking and other kinds of pollution were less well established. But Dora and Bessie were not interested in cause and effect. They were fatalistic about death. It came, and that was that. (As far as other people were concerned, that was that. It was always a bit different when it seemed to be coming for you.)

Dora, as was expected, had done all the hard work during Ellen's illness. She had popped round to Slotton Road every morning and every evening, poaching eggs, frying up bacon, making Welsh rarebit, burning the occasional pork chop. From January to July she had been on the run, back and forth, changing the sheets, emptying the chamber pot, listening to the laboured breathing, the spitting in the handkerchief. There was pain, but Dr Marr's successor gave her what he could to alleviate it. Ellen did not want to go into hospital. She wanted to die where she had given birth, in the Tudor-style bed from Leeds with its half-tester.

In July, Dora moved back into the house in Slotton Road. The time was near. She slept again in the bed of her childhood, from which she had so often been evicted by the health crises of delicate Bessie. She smelled the smell of the old house, and dreamed of her father. Was it her fancy, or did the smell of pear drops from the amyl acetate from his accumulator boxes linger yet? He had always liked to have a child around, when he messed about with his soldering and tinkering. Dora remembered sitting on a little wooden buffet by him and hand-ing him screws and bolts and bits of wire. Those had been happy times.

Dora dreamed of Bert, and woke to tend to her mother. Her mother remained grim and unpleased and unpleasing. Time and old age had not improved her character. What Dora was doing for her was no more than her duty.

Ellen Bawtry had never taken Dora into her arms and cuddled her and rocked her and comforted her. She had not been a tender mother. And Dora was not a tender nurse. But she was conscientious. She did her best. She would have liked to be able to hug her mother, and to kiss her, and to hold her hand through the nightwatches. But when she tried, once, to touch that gnarled hand with its embedded wedding ring, Ellen had snatched it away angrily. Ellen didn't like fuss.

Dora was hurt by this rejection. But she tried not to show it.

Ellen grew worse, and Dora knew she would have to summon Bessie, the First Daughter, the First Lady of Breaseborough. Dora did not look forward to this task. She did not like using the telephone. Although she was in other ways a competent person, who could even change a car tyre, to her the telephone remained a newfangled instrument, to be used with thrift and caution. She would become more familiar with it as the years passed, and had one of her own installed before the end of the decade (for emergencies only), but she always tended to shout down it and never learned the art of hanging up. Now she had to brace herself to go round to Auntie Florrie's, and her armpits grew clammy as she yelled the bad news down the line at six o'clock on a Sunday evening.

Bessie did not receive the message well. Ellen had decided to die at a most inconvenient time. As Bessie loudly reminded Dora, she and Joe and the children were about to go off the next week to Lyme Regis for their annual seaside summer holiday. The cottage was already booked and paid for and could not be cancelled. She would come when they got back at the end of August. She'll never last that long, said Dora. If you want to see her, you'll have to come now, before you go to Lyme. Bessie, whose domestic life lacked all appointments and employment, conceded that she could come up on the Wednesday, in two days' time. She couldn't leave on a Monday, because that was the day the gardener came, nor on a Tuesday, for on Tuesday mornings she and Mrs Baker cleaned the silver, and on Tuesday afternoons the grocery order was delivered. She would come by train on Wednesday. Wednesday was library day, but she supposed she could send Chrissie, now term was over.

'You can sleep in my house,' said Dora. 'It's empty. I'm staying with Mother.'

No reproach entered Dora's tone. Had she not been using her unnatural telephone pitch she would have sounded deferential and placatory.

Bessie greeted this offer with a temporary silence. Dora panicked. Had the instrument seized up? Had she pressed the wrong bit? She shook the heavy receiver, miserably. Had she been cut off?

She had not been cut off. When she put her ear back to the earpiece she heard Bessie say, 'We'll see about that.'

One cannot blame Bessie for hesitating as she flinched from the thought of spending a night under Dora's roof at Breaseborough. Bessie, since her schooldays, had become more and more fastidious in her habits—obsessively so, in Chrissie's opinion. She liked to wake in a room where sunlight streamed in through spotless windowpanes. Dora had travelled in the opposite direction. She had grown messier and messier as the years had gone by. She had a hatred of waste, and she could not bear to throw away anything that might come in handy in the next war. She collected paper bags, old jars, rubber bands, bits of string, old magazines, broken clothes-pegs. Her little house filled up rapidly. Dora did not like space and air. She liked a good fug.

Chrissie as a child had enjoyed this relaxed and unhygienic

regime—the cosy teas of buttered toast, the puddings of tinned fruit and whipped evaporated milk, the fish and chips wrapped in newspaper, the jumble of pot plants and tea cosies and egg timers and biscuit tins that occupied the small, square wooden kitchen table. But even Chrissie was to register that the nature of the clutter grew more unattractive year by post-war year. The kitchen table, once a plain wood, was covered with an unappealing pink-check stick-on badly fitting plastic coating, which began to peel round the edges, but stuck there, barely wiped, for decades. Biscuit tins gave way to—or rather, alas, were joined by—plastic boxes, tupperware, melaware, polythene. Cancerous growths of polymer branched and spread. Drawers burst and shelves buckled with hoardings. The new postwar rubbish was more durable than the old. It did not perish. Dora picked, saved, purchased, built up her nest.

Bessie found Dora's nest disgusting. She could hardly breathe its fetid air. Would she really be obliged to spend a night or two in it, in the good cause of paying her last respects to her mother? She had had her mother and Dora to stay with her in Surrey for a whole week over Christmas. Hadn't that been enough?

No, it had not been enough. Duty was duty. Bessie Barron sat on the train from St Pancras to Northam in a state of sub-dued anxiety. She rarely went anywhere alone. She began to calm down as the train made its way through the unattractive northern suburbs of London, and settled back into her seat. She could cope with the confines of a railway carriage, and she smiled graciously at the ticket inspector. The rhythm of the train soothed her, and she opened a book. She had brought three books with her, for she was still a greedy and rapid reader: two were detective stories, a Dorothy Sayers and a Margery Allingham, for Bessie enjoyed detective fiction, par-ticularly novels with well-educated, upper-class, but apparently gormless heroes. They made her feel quite safe and superior. And she knew that it was acceptable to read such works. Even professors of English Literature read such works. And wrote them too, come to that. The third book was from Farnleigh Library, selected for her by Miss Ashley, and collected for her by Chrissie. It was about travel and wildlife in India and was somewhat luridly entitled *Man-eaters of Kumaon*. Perhaps Miss Ashley had slipped up this time, though her taste could usually be trusted. Bessie liked travel books. She always said that she wanted to travel, and that she hoped to do so when the children were off her hands, when Joe had more time, when Joe retired. She would like to see more of Abroad, which in those days meant Europe.

Bessie engrossed herself in a story of eccentric but charming Bohemians, village witchcraft, and murders masterminded from vested interests overseas. Bessie solved the ancient runic riddle engraved on the old wellhead in no time. She was good at crossword puzzles.

Up in Breaseborough, Ellen Cudworth Bawtry was gasping for breath. She was about to have what Dora called 'a do'. Dora, watching helplessly, could only say, 'Bessie's coming, Mother. Bessie's on her way. She'll be here soon, Mother. Hang on for Bessie.'

Bessie was miles away, her eyes on the page, her drugged imagination in a Suffolk village drinking vintage port with a satanic vicar, as the dull Midlands flowed past her streaked window.

Ellen hung on for Bessie.

Bessie put away her book, and got off the train at Northam Station, and changed for the branch line. She began to feel worse as she drew nearer home. The familiar ugliness which she had tried so hard to forget closed in again upon her—the dark weeping slabs of railway cuttings, the pitheads, the cooling stations, the terraced houses marching in formation up the hillsides, the dirty washing hanging on dirty lines. It was dangerous to come back. Bad things awaited her. Bessie Barron got out at Breaseborough and looked for a taxi. There was no taxi. She decided to walk. It was not far to Slotton Road, and her overnight case was not heavy.

She walked carefully, upon the uneven pavements, up the hill, to Slotton Road. She too was now breathing heavily, from emotion and unaccustomed exertion. The hill was longer than it had been when she was a girl. She wished not to be here. She felt that at any moment a hand could rise from the cracks in the paving stones and grab her by the ankle and pull her under, into the hollowness beneath. It had waited for her to come back. It had been futile to try to get away.

She tried to walk quicker, but her ankles were swelling under her own weight. She was no longer the willowy blond girl who had trodden lightly on the asphalt. She was a Surrey matron, and the mother of two. They could not force her to come back, they could not entomb her here. But if they did get her now, she'd be too slow to run away.

Bessie made it to Slotton Road, and rang the bell. Dora, long-suffering Dora, shook her head, looking solid and grim. It couldn't be much longer now, whispered Dora, with glum importance. It was clear that she was willing to yield authority to Bessie at once. Bessie would know what to do.

Slowly Bessie mounted the mean and narrow staircase. It seemed shorter but steeper than it used to be. She paused for breath on the seventh step. The walk from the station had knocked her out. Joe was always trying to persuade her to take more exercise, but she paid no attention to his advice, and made no connection with it now as she puffed, waited, then lugged herself onwards and upwards.

Ellen lay in the bed in which Bessie had been born, in which Bessie had nearly died of influenza. Now Ellen was dying in it. She had never had a good complexion, and had turned a sullen yellow. She had lost much of her considerable weight, and her heavy jowls sagged loosely. She was wearing a bedjacket over her nightdress. At least it looked clean. Bessie noted that Dora had made an effort.

Bessie did not kiss her mother in greeting, The Bawtrys did not hold with kissing. She sat down, heavily, on the chair by the bed, and said, 'Well, I've come, Mother.'

Ellen ceded nothing. 'Yes,' was all she said.

And there they sat, mother and daughter, looking at one another. There was nothing to be said. The silence was stiff and solid. Thousands of years of silence lay banked up behind them, lay coldly between them. There were no words. It was as though language had not been invented. Neither would cede, neither would give. What would happen? Ellen did the one thing left to her. She began to cough.

Dora, listening from the bottom of the stairs, was relieved to hear this familiar, ghastly, wrenching sound. At least Bessie would know now she hadn't wasted her journey. And Bessie, staring at her mother, was thinking the same thing. At least she hadn't wasted her train fare. This was the end.

Mother and daughters found nothing to say to one another, but sisters Bessie and Dora on that portentous evening recovered some of the old intimacy of childhood. Bessie decided to stay the night with Dora in the old twin room. Slotton Road was slightly to be preferred to Swinton Road. And they both thought Ellen would die in the night.

They sat up late, the pair of them, listening for sounds from upstairs, listening to the ticking of the grandfather clock. Ellen's thin old tortoiseshell cat, Tibby, sat on Bessie's knee and purred. Tibby was the last of a dynasty of Bawtry cats. Her great-great-grandmother's grandmother had been rescued from the Destructor long ago, and cat after cat had slept on the couch, and eaten scraps from the same earthenware dish, and kept the mice away. Tibby would find a good home in Swinton Road with Dora. Tibby, like her mistress, would not live long. Bessie stroked Tibby, and Dora worked at her crochet, and in low voices the sisters spoke of their childhood, of earlier cats, of the motorbike and sidecar, of their pet rabbits Nancy and Peter who had ended up in a pie. Bert and Ellen had not been forgiven for that treachery. Childish grievances were rehearsed. No, she had not been very gentle with them, that old woman upstairs. She had not been a motherly mother.

Towards midnight, Bessie asked Dora if she knew what kind of contraception their parents might have used. Dora was shocked and flattered by this question. She didn't know the answer. It was hard to associate Ellen Bawtry with Marie Stopes. They must have used something, said Bessie.

At one in the morning, the fat middle-aged daughters took themselves to bed. Bessie settled herself in first, and was reading her Margery Allingham when Dora, in her pyjamas, came to join her. They lay there, companionably. Bessie read for a while, then turned off her light and grunted good night. Dora lay awake for a long time, listening.

Ellen did not die that night, or the next night. On Thursday she seemed, if anything, slightly better, and had managed to have a brief conversation with Bessie about her family and the inferiority of Bessie's fishmonger's cod. Surrey cod was not as good as Yorkshire cod, and the price was shocking.

Ellen gave no sign that she knew her end was approaching, or that Bessie's presence was unusual.

On Friday, Ellen was still, stubbornly, alive, and over her morning toast Bessie announced to Dora that she would go home that afternoon. Her family needed her. On Saturday they were to drive westward from Surrey to Lyme Regis. Everything was settled. It could not be altered now. Everything was planned. They had an AA route map. Joe, Robert and Chrissie must not be disappointed. They could not go without her. They would not understand about towels and bed linen.

(Robert and Chrissie, now nineteen and sixteen, had mixed feelings about this family holiday. But tradition was tradition, and it was still the 1950s.)

Dora accepted Bessie's decision meekly. Of course Bessie's plans must have priority. Family life took precedence over single-daughter life, middle-class Surrey life over Breaseborough life. If Dora had hoped to have company to see her through the last spasm of death, she did not show it. It was good of Bessie to have come all this way. It wasn't anyone's fault that Ellen had missed her cue. It couldn't be helped.

We must not give the impression that Bessie valued a family holiday above her mother's life. She did not prefer the seaside to a deathbed, or pleasure to pain. That was not the kind of person she was. But she had made plans, and she would stick to them. Rigidity, not selfishness, by now ruled her life. Dora understood this, and knew she could not argue with it. Ellen, had she been in a fit condition, would have understood it too. Ellen would have approved of Bessie's decision. She would have done the same herself. Maybe she had done the same herself.

So Bessie said good-bye to her mother, and promised to come again soon. Her mother glared at her from rheumy bloodshot eyes. She was heard by both daughters to mutter, 'That's a likely story,' though neither of them ever admitted that they had heard these words, so they lack confirmation. Maybe they misheard? But those were what Ellen's last words to her elder daughter were thought to have been.

On the train on the way down, Bessie could not settle to her novels, or to the stories of the man-eating tigers of Kumaon. The binding of the tiger book was in very poor condition: it looked as though somebody had dropped it in the bath. She must get Chrissie to make it clear, when she took it back, that it hadn't been her.

Bessie gazed out of the window and felt a slurry of misery rising in her. The self-pity of childhood possessed her. It had all been too difficult, the odds against her had been too high, she had been defeated.

She couldn't afford to think like this. She started to count her assets as the train approached Derby. One husband, a loyal, successful, patient professional man. Two children, one of either sex, and in the right order. A large detached house with grounds. A good summer coat, in one of the new cotton blends, a decent pair of well-polished shoes and a tidy hat. She wasn't sure about the hat, but she was even less sure about her short-cropped, unpermed hair, although Monsieur Claude assured her each month that the cut suited her and that she looked delightful. The hat had a good label, so it couldn't be very wrong, could it? A decent handbag, neither new nor old. And back at the big house in Surrey, at the house called Wood-lawn, she had a fine pedigree cat called Smollett, a much finer cat than poor plebeian old Tibby.

The thought of her Smollett asset amused Bessie, and she was almost smiling to herself as the train pulled in at Derby. There she was joined in her hitherto empty compartment by an elderly female traveller. This person endeared herself to Bessie by getting into a muddle about her ticket, her luggage and her destination. Bessie was able to put her right on all points, and over the next hour or so proceeded to tell her all about her prospective holiday, about Lyme Regis, about the cottage the Barrons had rented, about the sea view, the bed-room and bathroom facilities, the brand name of the electric oven. Bessie preferred gas, but she could manage with the electric, she assured her grey-haired companion. Dutifully, the person asked about Bessie's family, and received rather more information than most people would have wanted. She heard a good deal about my husband the barrister, who had taken silk last year, and about my son who was off to do his National Service, and my daughter who was doing her A-levels at Farnleigh Grammar School. She was subjected to a long analysis of the differences between Holderfield High and Farnleigh Grammar, and of daughter Christine's ability to do well under either regime. No allusion at all was made to the fact that Bessie's mother Ellen was in her deathbed in Breaseborough. There was no place for Ellen in this discourse. The stone was rolled against the door of the tomb, and she would not be allowed out anymore.

Leicester passed, and Luton. No other passenger entered the compartment to disrupt this flow of self-protecting self-congratulatory family description. Bessie had mastered the art of the uninterrupted monologue. She did not like talking to those she considered her equals, but she was very good at addressing the butcher, the baker or the woman in haberdashery in John Lewis's. She would talk to people at bus stops and on buses. She would talk for hours to strangers. The person in the railway compartment listened, politely, as though mesmerized, and at first made no effort to offer any information of her own. Bessie often had this effect on strangers. They tended to accept her at her own valuation. It was less trouble that way.

South of Luton, Bessie at last faltered, and the person from Derby tentatively murmured that she herself was going to Bexhill, to see her sister. Bessie nodded, rather severely. She clearly did not think much of Bexhill. The person, perhaps discouraged, fell silent.

'Of course Lyme Regis,' continued Bessie, as though the Bexhill card had never been played, 'was where Jane Austen set part of *Persuasion*.' It was in some indefinable way clear from her tone that she did not expect the person to recognize this literary allusion, but that she nevertheless could not resist making it. 'And,' Bessie went on, importantly, with that rising inflection that prevents interjection, 'there are many fossils.'

'Yes,' said the harmless old lady from Derby, goaded into response. 'Yes, I know. Isn't that where that young woman found that ichthyosaurus? What was her name? Mary Anning, if I remember rightly.'

Chrissie and Robert, who had sat with embarrassment through many such monologues, would have congratulated the person from Derby, had they ever learned of this interchange. Not many scored so well. And yet Chrissie and Robert were, in general, sorry for their mother. They recognized that it was her insecurity and her unhappiness that made her talk so much. They were old enough to know this, but not old enough to know what to do about it. They could not make things easier for Bessie. They had to watch and suffer for her and for themselves in silence. They worried about her, in their way.

Walking together along the Cobb at Lyme on a clear calm

evening, they discussed their mother, as Bessie and Dora had discussed theirs. They had endured the increasingly neurotic and overorganized ordeal of holiday departure (never again, resolved Robert, never again, swore Chrissie), and now were after all quite pleased to find themselves in this beautiful curving town by the curving bay of the southern sea. Lyme was romantic. Lyme was in good taste, and had not in those days taken on the powerful British seaside odour of onion, vinegar, ketchup and fried foodstuffs. It still smelled of sand, salt, sea and fish. They liked Lyme Regis. They were young, and they were still hopeful.

'She says she's depressed,' said Chrissie.

'Depressed? What's she got to be depressed about?' said Robert.

'It doesn't work like that,' said Chrissie. 'She says it's something called endogenous depression. It's an illness, she says. Like mumps or measles. That's what she says Dr Hancox says.'

Robert didn't bother to reply. He knew it didn't work like that.

'But I don't believe in it,' continued Chrissie. 'It's her own fault. She never goes out, she never sees anyone. No wonder she's depressed. She ought to make more of an effort. It's not natural, never to see anyone.'

'Isn't it?' said Robert. He was not very sociable himself, though he did not admire himself for this. He admired Chrissie's reaction more, but found he could not replicate it. He sometimes tried, but something always seemed to stop him.

'No, it isn't,' said Chrissie firmly. 'She ought to try a bit harder. She ought to get out and see people.'

'She doesn't know anybody to see.'

'She doesn't know anybody because she never goes out.'

They had reached the end of the pier, and stood there, gazing down into the sucking, slapping water. Beneath their feet the large hewn stones of the Cobb were starred and studded with small fossil life, with shell and frond millennia old.

'She says it's his fault, because he won't take her out.'

'There's some truth in that,' said Robert.

'Yes,' said Chrissie. 'But when he does offer, she makes such a fuss. Gets ill, or makes a scene. You know what I mean.'

He did know what she meant. Retreat, hysteria, shouting, sulking, abuse. There'd been less of that since the tablets, but it could still happen, unpredictably, at any time.

Poor Robert and Chrissie, trying to retrace the progress of the disease which was eating up their mother and punishing their father. It stretched back too far for them to know its origins. It stretched back beyond old Ellen Bawtry, who hadn't quite died yet after all. The infection of habit, from generation to generation. Do these two think they can escape? They have been twice transplanted, and more moves are soon to come. Will they be able to take on the colouring of a new environment? Will they succeed where Bessie has failed?

Chrissie and Robert turned, and began the stroll back, through the mild evening air. Promenading, watching, being watched. Chrissie, sweet sixteen and many times kissed, in the first full bloom of youth, attracted admiring and licentious glances. She stepped out proudly, wasp-waist pinched by a broad elasticated yellow belt with a big snake buckle, swishing a full flaring blue-and-white-striped cotton skirt, strutting along with neat brown ankles on open-toed white plastic sandals with a raised cork wedge heel. A tarty tight white V-necked cotton top showed off her full Cudworth breasts, and round her neck was a double string of plastic pearl-simulation popper beads. She flicked from time to time her long bright full red Barron hair. She was a head-turner. Would her unknown admirers recognize that Robert was her brother and not her boyfriend? She did not care. It was attention she wanted, not assignations, as she and Robert performed the evening *passeggiata*. She had plenty of assignations back home in Surrey. Here, she just wanted to make people stare at her, and stare they obligingly did.

The holiday is turning out better than anyone had hoped.

Bessie seems almost relaxed, now she has got her linen sorted and her kitchen organized. Her terrible dissatisfaction is temporarily assuaged. She enjoys sitting in a deck chair with a book, listening to the band. She enjoys watching other people's children build sand castles and run screaming into the tiny waves. She enjoys looking in the antique-shop windows, and lunching in the Lobster Pot. Playing cards of an evening, she becomes quite skittish. They never play cards at home, but on holiday, in a rented lodging, they can become a Happy Family. Bessie and Robert are quite good at cards. Chrissie is hopeless. Joe lets other people win whenever he can.

Joe has sometimes wished that Bessie would learn bridge, for the idle ladies of Hartley had played bridge, and so no doubt do the idle ladies of Farnleigh, were one ever to find out who and where they are. But Bessie, although herself idle, despises idleness, and despises the bridge set as vehemently as she despises the bingo set. And, on balance, Joe sees her point. He himself does not have much respect for the opium of bridge or bingo. Better serious misery than shallow happiness.

The little dark yellow oblong telegram came on the morning of the first Tuesday. It announced in ugly black lettering that Ellen Bawtry had died in the night. MOTHER DIED ONE AM PLEASE RING AUNTIE FLORRIE, it read.

None of them could predict how Bessie would react to this news. They sat there, over breakfast, waiting for some sign from her. But there was no sign. After breakfast, Bessie went out with a purse full of coins to the red telephone box on the corner, but when she came back she did not report what she had said or what was said to her. As far as Chrissie and Robert could later recall, nothing was ever said about Ellen Bawtry's death. It was as though it had never happened. The holiday was to continue, without interruption, as though Ellen Bawtry had never lived and never died. Chrissie remembered feeling that this was carrying stoic reticence, thrift or indifference to an extreme, but as neither Joe nor Robert seemed surprised or otherwise by Bessie's silence, she also kept her mouth shut. Perhaps there was some funerary code at work that she was too young to understand. She felt somebody should have said something, but nobody said anything.

Bessie did not attend her mother's funeral. She stayed in Lyme Regis and completed the full term of her annual seaside holiday.

Dora, Auntie Florrie, and a handful of elderly neighbours and cousins saw Ellen off. She was buried in Breaseborough Cemetery in the same grave as Bert, where it might be expected that they could both lie undisturbed, only slightly more inert and silent in death than they had been in the later years of their lives. It is hard to imagine what will next disturb them, or what will be the end of Breaseborough Cemetery. Subsidence, a methane explosion, a new housing estate, tectonic plate disturbance, another ice age. Or will it be Dracula Hawthorn with his needle?

On the night of the day of the funeral, Joe, Bessie, Robert and Chrissie went to the cinema and saw a torrid Technicolor Hollywood drama set in the South Seas, featuring heavy rain, palm trees, breasts, lust, adultery and alcohol. It was a great deal more lively and colourful than the funeral of Ellen Bawtry, so perhaps the Barrons were wise to prefer it as an entertainment. It was said that Dora had provided nothing for the post-interment refreshment but ham sandwiches, without mustard, and tea. Not much of a feast. She hadn't even bothered to get out the Crown Derby.

The Bawtrys had always been against mustard. To hear them speak of mustard, you would think mustard and its manufacturers had committed some kind of criminal offence.

⚬⚬⚬

What are we to do about these dreadful people? Is there any point in trying to make any sense of their affectless, unnatural, subnormal behaviour? Shall we just forget they ever existed, bury them, and get as far away from them as possible? Put our foot down on the accelerator, jab our finger onto fast forward, and scroll on to join Dr Hawthorn in the electronic age? The next generation can surely bury this lot, and forget all about them. There is no need to grieve for them. They could not help their stony lives. If you think too hard of them and the waste of it all, your heart might break. And what *would* be the point of *that*?

Let's get back to Chrissie. Things may yet turn out well for her.

Chrissie, contemplating the choice between mustard-free ham sandwiches and lust, adultery and alcohol, was drawn strongly towards the latter package. Getting away fast and far was her plan. But she couldn't get away in one move. She had to map her course, and that wasn't easy. You couldn't just say, I'll have lust, adultery and alcohol, please. You had to work out a strategy, and conceal your real objective. That much Chrissie appreciated. She was a clear-headed young woman, quite capable of trying deliberately to plot a course of irrational, lateral and therefore liberating behaviour. But she had obstacles to contend with, including her own ignorance. The future for her was as shapeless and uncertain as it had been to Joe Barron while he was driving around in the Fancy Glass van. Her will was strong, but she was not sure on what, in the immediate future, to exert it. Some decisions would have to be made, and soon.

She knew she would have to get herself some kind of higher education. That was the best way out. She no longer wanted to be an air stewardess or a ski instructor or a barmaid. Of her earlier fantasies, that left only surgery or archaeology, either of which could presumably be combined with parallel careers in lust, adultery and alcohol. The world, which two years earlier had seemed to lie before her like a land of dreams, had narrowed down rather rapidly. It was already too late to be a surgeon, as she had found herself taking the wrong A-levels. She should have started planning even earlier.

That left archaeology.

Fossils, prehistory, bird-fishes, dawn stones, lost cities, torcs and necklets of buried gold.

Perhaps she would settle for archaeology, and the recovery of lost things.

And so it was that Chrissie Barron, the passionate little child, the red-haired rebel, the tearaway, the fast girl who had sworn she would never settle for safety, found herself applying to the University of Cambridge to read a degree in Archaeology and Anthropology. Exactly as though nothing had moved on at all in the postwar world. Exactly as though she were still under the thumb of the spirit of Miss Heald.

Don't laugh at her. Chrissie thought she was rebelling. She thought she was exercising the freedom of the will. She thought she was breaking with the past by choosing the past. After all, nobody in the family had ever been interested in Archaeology and Anthropology, had they? It was a new departure, a new beginning. Wasn't it?

She would have applied to Oxford, not Cambridge, out of bravado. But Oxford didn't offer an undergraduate course in archaeology, and was not to do so for another forty years, so there was no point in her waiting for that. Things moved slowly, in our ancient universities. It took decades to introduce a new degree or to change a syllabus.

Why did she have to go to an ancient university? you may ask. She went to an ancient university because that's what she was programmed to do. She didn't yet know it, but she was programmed to follow in her parents' footsteps. Most people are. It takes a lot of effort to break the pattern. It costs a lot. A hundred pages back, Chrissie's future, like her past, had been utterly unformulated. Anything had been possible. But the nearer she got to the future, the more her past filled in with inherited and acquired characteristics, and the further that freedom fled.

Chrissie thought she was breaking the pattern by refusing to study matrilineal English Literature or patrilineal Law. She knew that there must be some more decisive, some more dramatic way of expressing herself, but she couldn't yet work out what it was. She could always try to get herself pregnant, by losing her virginity either to one of the Farnleigh sixth-formers or to Mr Stuart (Latin and Greek), who seemed willing. But a step like that would create a lot more new problems, for which she wasn't yet ready. Though, if worst came to worst, pregnancy would answer. It remained an option.

She will make a wild leap, and she will make it quite soon, but it will depend on accidental outside agency, on a factor not yet part of the plan. She cannot manage it alone. And it will be a desperate measure, in the eyes of her parents, her teachers, her peers. It will carry her a long way, but not in the directions she had expected.

Chrissie saw archaeology as a revenge on Bessie's hatred of shields and shards and firedogs. Chrissie had grown tired of hearing these dumb things abused. Even as a child, Chrissie had been attracted by a kind of pity to the drab and dismal stone artefacts that were so dully displayed in the museums of the day—to flints and hand axes and notched antlers. She would devote herself to them.

Bessie and Joe considered Chrissie's decision mature and respectable.

So now we can picture Chrissie, at the age of eighteen, about to set off to university, as her mother had before her. Thousands of years of uneducated and minimally educated Bawtrys and Cudworths lie behind these two, this mother and this daughter, and they exert a strong backward pull. But you can't go back, you have to go on. Is there an emergent pattern, and are Bessie and Chrissie the two who created it?

The story could, in theory, have gone in many different directions. But in practice the options are as limited as they are in computerized, apparently open-ended works of interactive fiction. The imagination fails to supply the necessary freedom. It loops back on itself, it repeats itself, it returns to its own obsessions, it provides dull solutions, for it too is a creature of habit, it cannot really initiate, its routes are determined. It needs the Other. But it cannot create the Other. Whether it will meet the Other is a matter of chance.

Chrissie Barron met the Other during her first Cambridge year, in the unpredictable form of Nicolas Gaulden. And from then on, everything was changed. The past, present and future were all changed. New blood entered the bloodstream. A new pattern began to emerge. New births, new beginnings. Conception, marriage, lust, infidelity, adultery, alcohol, death. Surely Nicolas Gaulden's shocking power could do the trick. He could overwhelm any respectability. He could even prevent Chrissie from taking her college degree. He could liberate her from the tyranny of the examination and the grade. Let us celebrate Nick Gaulden. Let us meet him at his funeral, and play the scroll backwards.

⌒⟋⟋⟍⟍⌒

Ellen Bawtry's funeral had been thinly attended, and the ceremony plain. Nicolas Gaulden, in contrast, in death commanded a full house and many tributes: though that, reflected the woman who had been Chrissie Gaulden, as she sat in Golders Green Crematorium, was not entirely to his credit. Nick Gaulden would have been Ellen's grandson-in-law, had she lived long enough to witness her granddaughter's marriage. This relationship seemed improbable, and it was just as well that it never took place in real time. Those two would not have got on at all. So thought Chrissie, as Ellen for some reason swam into her mind. One funeral reminds one of another. Chrissie Gaulden Sinclair sat in the front pew, thinking of Ellen's funeral, which neither she nor her mother had attended, and of those of her own parents, which she had. And now here she was, saying good-bye to her onetime husband Nick. This was only the third funeral of her life. This was one she had not been able to fail. It seemed likely to prompt a replay of the whole of her brief courtship, her brief marriage, and their long fall-out. But she also had to concentrate on the present. She had to be on guard. The story was not over yet. Her memories could wait. There would be a long reckoning.

Chrissie, in sombre, stylish black, had staked her position in the front pew as First, Finest, Most Suffering and Most Enduring Widow. Nick lay there in his coffin, covered in rubbishy wreaths from grieving castoffs, and she could see the rest of the motley congregation through the red eyes in the back of her proud head. She reached for her daughter Faro's hand, and clutched it, as the music stopped. She knew that somebody was about to stand up and say something unutterably silly, unforgivably stupid. She felt it in her bones. Faro squeezed her mother's hand in return. We two against the world.

The ranks were full. There were Gaulden brothers and sisters, a rackety, impossible, Circean, good-looking, foreign, dissolute crew; none of them had come to much good. Nick hadn't been the one black sheep of the flock. They had been prodigals all. How ever had Chrissie Barron got herself mixed up with this lot? Nick's father Gyorgy Gaulden had died a decade earlier, but Nick's mother Eva was still alive, and present, and sharply surveying the chaos she had engendered. Was it for this that Eva and Gyorgy had escaped from the death throes of Europe to the safety of Finchley Road? To bring forth this feckless, wastrel, decadent Bohemian host? This ragged army, this forlorn hope?

Unfair, unkind, said Chrissie to herself, as she tried to block out the valedictory words of Eric Mendelsson, old schoolmate, old drinking partner and poker player, failed poet, failed scrounger, failed failure. Balliol scholar, chess player, charmer, wit. One of the cleverest men of his generation. Could have been a chess grandmaster, could have been a poet, could have been a man. One of the cleverest, but certainly not one of the best-looking: he had always been a big-nosed freak, and now, in his early sixties, he was a scarecrow. His lazy, lopsided, voluptuous, terrible smile illuminated his carrion face, as he spoke from the pulpit of his old friend Nick's schooldays, of the happy hospitable home of Gyorgy and Eva, of the culture and the music and the poetry of the Gauldens...please God let him not start going on about me, thought Chrissie, but how could he avoid her? She had been Nick's first conquest, and how desperately they had loved one another, in those long-ago innocent days. Chrissie and Nick had dropped out together, eloped together, and disappeared together from the face of the known earth. They had fallen down a volcanic fissure into the molten underworld. Would that they had at that instant been transformed together into a fountain, into a reed, into a tree with interwoven boughs, into a breeze or a bird! They had believed that the violence of their love would burn away mortality, would purify and transfix them into an attitude of everlasting devotion. Chrissie, who had preserved her chastity through so many assaults in the suburban undergrowth and on the late train back to Farnleigh from Charing Cross, had abandoned herself without restraint to the embraces and assurances of Nicolas Gaulden, and had run away with him in the fullness of her heart and her youth. And now he lay in a narrow box, waiting to be incinerated. What was left of that bright boy, apart from a trail of devastation?

His children, his grandchildren. He had been prolific. Seven known children and two grandchildren could have attended his funeral, had the roll-call been complete, and who knows how many unacknowledged offspring lurked in the wings, or had never known their parentage? Chrissie, even as she listened to Eric praising (and quite wittily, she had to concede) her own early attempts at soup-making, at running a soup-kitchen, in the flat in Barlby Road, could not resist trying to do a headcount of the numbers of Nick's women whom she had already greeted or spotted that day. There was Moira, downtrodden First Mistress, whom he had never married, and who bore him two children; then Serafina, mother of Aurelius;

then Fiona, who had, after Chrissie's divorce, for a brief spell become a legal Mrs Gaulden; then Stella, mother of Tiger; and finally Jessica, who was rumoured to have been on the verge of a deathbed shotgun wedding, but who was thought not to have made it. Jessica had drawn the short straw, by common consent. Hers had been the hospitalization, the rejected transplant, the catheters, the plastic bags, the death rattle. Jessica had never known Nick in his golden days.

But Jessica had probably been convinced that Nick had loved her only, her only and her ever. That was his trick. That was how he pulled it. And no doubt he'd still been able to manage it, a sick man in his sixties, in need of a new liver. Still the most handsome man in London, in the eyes of far too many.

Whom had she missed? Furtively, Chrissie counted again, on the fingers of the hand that Faro was not clutching. The children: there was Faro, his firstborn; Moira's daughters, Iona and Arethusa, who for a long time had lived upstairs; then the boys—Serafina's Aurelius and Stella's Tiger. There were supposed to be two more boys, somewhere, and another woman—where was Jenny, with her boys, Sam and Derwent? Or was it Derwent and Sam? Chrissie had never met Jenny Pargiter and her sons, and had been unable to locate her earlier in the proceedings, as the funeral party had loitered in the academic-ecclesiastical red-brick cloisters, making uneasy conversation and trying furtively to read the messages on the bouquets that perspired inelegantly in cellophane wraps. Chrissie had been assured, by Stella, that Jenny Pargiter was there, but she looked in vain for a young mother emblematically accompanied, like a martyr, by two identifying Gaulden sons. Perhaps Jenny Pargiter had come without them? Perhaps she had thought them too young or too ill-disciplined for such an outing? Warning notices advised that the spacious cemetery lawns, where mourners from other unknown funerals strayed in the middle distance, were out of bounds to noisy children. Perhaps Jenny Pargiter had decided not to risk it?

But, in that case, which was the unattended Jenny Pargiter, the penultimate mistress? Chrissie had formed no very clear picture of her, but had assumed, as an outdated ex-wife will, that this latter rival must be possessed of grace, style, beauty and probably (though not necessarily) youth. Brooding on a possible Jenny Pargiter, Chrissie now realized that she had managed to summon up little more than a vague assembly of floating attributes, most of them detached from one or another of Nick's death-convened harem—the slenderness of Moira when young, the stateliness of Serafina, the sharpness of Fiona, the blond fey English countryside calm of Stella, the unblemished skin and bright white all-American teeth of young Jessica. These incompatible features had not begun to form a coherent whole, an Identikit Gaulden bride, for none of these women much resembled one another, and had no evident common denominator. Jenny Pargiter might be, indeed almost certainly was, somebody quite other, who would, when correctly identified, add some quite shocking or revealing new ingredient to the retrospective assessment of Nick Gaulden's amorous tastes. Jenny Pargiter was no chimera, no harpy, no composite ghost: she was a solid and unique woman, and somewhere in this chapel she stood, waiting to identify herself as the object of Chrissie's envy and contempt. Or would she, like Stella, prove in the long run, a true friend? Unlikely, now. Chrissie no longer had need of such friends. She could suffer no more, as she had once suffered, the torments of obscure and unallocated resentment and suspicion. Let Jenny Pargiter reveal herself as Helen of Troy, Chrissie need suffer no more. It was all one to her now. Curiosity was all that remained to her.

And yet she was curious about this congregation, this extended family, some of whom she had not seen for years.

Moira, who had lived upstairs, had not visibly improved with the passage of time—a pallid, whining, spiritless creature, a broken reed, a lower-middle-class misery, thin then and scrawny now, her face lined with endurance and forgiveness.

She was wearing a prim dark-striped mannish suit, and her hair had turned a curious ancient tarnished yellow-green-grey, not unlike Auntie Dora's; it was tied back with a large black velvet bow which suggested a bisexual character from a historical costume drama. Moira's daughters, Iona and Arethusa, had grown up handsomely, however, and inherited something of their father's beauty—a noble, high-prowed, clear-cut face, with chiselled lips, and a blue intensity of eye. They were fetchingly dressed, in a similar style: both wore long skirts, dark buttoned jackets, pearl necklaces, wide-brimmed hats. A classic couple. And each was provided with a baby and a husband—Nick Gaulden's only known (though not legitimate) grandchildren. Chrissie had forgotten the names of these infants, had she ever known them, but gathered there was one of each sex.

So the Gaulden line continued. Chrissie, with a conscious act of generosity, chose to be pleased about this. She had never had anything against those poor girls: it was not their fault if they and their mother had been instrumental in the ruin of her life. If it hadn't been them, it would have been others. It was good to see them looking so smug, so well groomed, so well provided. A husband each—unlike their mother, they had not gone in for sharing or a communal home.

Serafina had come next in the catalogue, and there she was, still as large and glossy as ever, in full bloom. She was of West Indian descent, and had robed herself for this occasion in some kind of full-length orange and purple toga: her head she had bound up in a tall and elaborate turban, intricately and lavishly swathed. She looked like an African empress, and this no doubt was her intention. Her son Aurelius stood proudly by her side, sixteen years and already well over six feet tall, wearing the traditional costume of his age and class—trainers, jeans and a black leather bomber jacket decorated with many metal runes and hieroglyphs. A fine, well-made, tawny-golden lad, an excellent proof of the wisdom of crossing one's genes with those of dark strangers. Impossible, any longer, to be jealous of Serafina and Aurelius: they did not recognize possession, jealousy, marriage, divorce, alimony and other such domestic trivia. They were outside the system. Chrissie saw now how petty it had been even to think of resenting Serafina. Although she had, bitterly, jealously, resented. Serafina had been harder to take than Moira. But Serafina had been as inevitable an event in Nick's sexual odyssey as she believed Nick to have been in her own. Serafina had appeared, held court and moved on, massively unscathed.

Fiona, the only other legal wife, was more of a mystery. She had been married for her money, or so Chrissie had always supposed, for, unlike Serafina, she offered no other visible attractions. And Nick must have taken her to the cleaners, after that spell of marital cohabitation in the big house in Frognal, for she now looked more downtrodden than Moira ever had, and twice as old. Her hair was quite white, and she kept fumbling noisily in her handbag for throat sweets to stop herself coughing. She seemed to have a perpetual cough. Perhaps she too was dying, and eager to join Nick in perpetuity. Would she commit suttee by leaping into the furnace? Had anyone ever tried that, at Golders Green? Chrissie had never cared for Fiona. She had never seen the point of her.

Whereas Stella Wakefield, Tiger's mother, Chrissie had come to love. Stella was her only true friend in this gallery, and she hoped she would remain her friend even now Nick was gone. Stella was a brave, blond, Bohemian dissident, who had kept a wise distance between herself and the dangerous Nick; she had never moved in with him and had never allowed him to move in with her, she had seen him when she wanted, on her own terms, and had taken, flatteringly, to ringing Chrissie for advice about how to handle him. Tiger was a delightful, affectionate little lad, whose haphazard barefoot upbringing in a rambling house in Wimbledon had done him no harm at all. He sat, alertly, intelligently to attention, by his mother's

side. He was only about half the size of his half-brother Aurelius, whom he revered, but he was equally smartly if less
conventionally dressed in a red and white jacket with brass
buttons which appeared to have been purchased from an army
surplus store for midget military musicians. He was following
the proceedings with an expression of intense interest on his
eager face. Death had no dominion over him, that was plain
to see, nor over Stella, who believed (and why not?) in the
transmigration of souls, and who had come to Golders Green
dressed in a beautiful many-coloured tapestry wool coat embroidered with the symbols of the zodiac. (Chrissie eyed it en-
viously, and was waiting for an appropriate moment after the
ceremony to ask Stella where she had bought it. But Stella
would probably cast her down by telling her she had made it
herself. Stella, unlike Chrissie, was very creative.)

Moira, Serafina, Stella, the unknown Jenny Pargiter and
Jessica. Poor little Jessica—she had been picked up in the off-
licence. Or so rumour had it.

So there they were, all Nick's women. What a lot of messed-
up, wasted lives. But there were, at least, a lot of them—maybe
there was something to celebrate in that? Fecundity, prodi-
gality, the life force? And yes, anticipating her very thought,
old Eric was moving on to this theme—well, you could see
that in the circumstances Eric kind of had to. Bachelor, celi-
bate, unreproductive Eric Mendelsson began to sing the praises
of babies, and to declare what a fine father old Nick had
been. The jokes were a bit risky, but nobody leaps up to stop
the proceedings during a funeral oration—it's only at wed-
dings that witnesses are asked to raise objections. And it was
all a bit late in the day for that. Eric told funny stories about
Augustus John and Sabine Baring-Gould and other prolific
parents, who had had difficulties in recognizing all the members of their own vast brood, and who had taken to saluting
all small children with a vague paternal benevolence. 'And
whose little girl are you?' 'Why, *yours,* Papa, *yours!*' Nick,

dispatched to the primary school gates on a rare occasion to collect one of his own, had identified the wrong infant, and had dragged it struggling down the road until overtaken by an angry Arethusa.

Polite laughter. Faro grinds the nails of her spare hand into her palm. It's not all that funny, is it?

Chrissie is wondering how all this lot ever got paid for. Had anybody in that gathering ever earned an honest living? How shocked her own thrifty Yorkshire-bred parents would have been had they ever known the full extent of the fecklessness and recklessness of the Gauldens. She had done her best to conceal it from them. She had become a mistress of deception and misrepresentation. But they must have guessed at some of it. They weren't stupid.

Perhaps it wasn't fair to say that nobody in that chapel had ever had a proper job. Some of them had tried. It is true that the first generation of the Gaulden family, once uprooted from Berlin and its homeland, had found it difficult to settle and to find appropriate employment. But it had not come to England to make its fortune. It had come here to survive. Like many thousands of others it had left most of its possessions behind, and it was not easy to make a fresh start in a foreign country on the brink of war. They were lucky to have been allowed to settle in Finchley, and not to have been interned as enemy aliens on the Isle of Man.

Gyorgy had been traumatized by the events of Europe. His own parents had been interned as political dissidents, and died in a camp. Most of his family disappeared. Gyorgy never recovered, physically or mentally, from the shock of his sudden forced exodus. His health had suffered; and he developed chronic asthma, though he found it difficult to give up smoking. And he lacked the resilience and the élan of some of the new refugees, who were to found publishing houses, start businesses, retrain for professions, re-enter academe or join the BBC. Gyorgy could not make a new start. Gyorgy haunted the Reading Room of the British Museum, that refuge of the refugee, where he claimed to be writing a history of his native province, but no person ever saw a word of his manuscript. He dwindled into invalidism, while his wife went out to work.

Eva Gaulden, despite bearing several children, managed to earn enough money to keep her family going. She worked first as matron in a hostel for refugee children, then as translator of black propaganda for the BBC, and finally as subeditor and typist for a respected literary monthly financed with American money. Maybe she could have founded a publishing house, had she been less preoccupied with children and survival, with Gyorgy and the news from Europe. But she kept going. She kept a roof over their heads.

Eva Gaulden, unlike Bessie Bawtry, had been faced with hard and potentially deadly choices, and had worked hard all her life, and now the most gifted and beautiful of all her sons had gone before her. Tributes were paid to Eva that day, and rightly. It is not good to lose a child, even when one is in one's eighties, even when he has invited his own death. Chrissie squeezed Faro's hand again, as Eric began to round off his eulogy. Maybe Eric was right. With so many dead people behind him, maybe Nick had done well to try to spread his seed and his genes and to repopulate North London. And it was wrong to think harshly of Eric. Eric might have wasted his talents in the eyes of the world, and blown his mind with many substances, but who was to blame him? He had done no harm in his mild life. He had merely wasted it. There were worse things.

The only Gaulden relative who had ever made serious money was said to have made it somewhat dishonourably. Gyorgy's nephew, Victor Rose, was said to have made a small fortune. (Chrissie sneaked a glance around the room and back up at the gallery, to see if she could see him, but if he was there, she didn't recognize him. But she hadn't set eyes on him for years, had she? She had lost touch with most of this lot.) Victor Rose had made his fortune out of scrap, then landfill. The images that this *métier* evoked were not fortunate. Smoke, bulldozers, incinerators, mountains of rubbish, noxious gas and scavenging birds of prey. Seagulls, the rats of the sky.

Now was the time for the coffin to slip forward to its destruction. A waste of good wood, Bessie might have remarked: Bessie had often declared that she would be happy to be buried in a bin bag. But she hadn't been allowed that choice. Her dispatch had proved quite expensive. Joe and Bessie Barron had been cremated in Surrey, and both had slid away, like liners down the last runway into the ocean of fire. Joe had escaped first, for he had died in his early seventies, after some years of ill health and a few months of painful illness. Until the onset of that last illness, and for a few weeks after its onset, he took Bessie an early-morning cup of tea in bed. She never said thank you. She lay there like a white worm and took it from him. When he was too ill to perform this ministration, she complained to Chrissie that he was faking. Shortly after this he died. Bessie had survived some years of widowhood, during which she had complained bitterly about the size of her pension. Then she too had departed, in a surprising, mysterious and wholly uncharacteristic manner. We shall return to that story.

Nick Gaulden, whose boxed remains were even now gliding smoothly down the polished track, had not, in his early years, given much thought to pensions. Had he left anything at all to anyone? He had been a long time dying, and had had plenty of time to think of these things. Had he died as he had lived, in debt? Had he made a will? Chrissie had no cause to worry for herself, for her days of want were over, but she could see the possibility of feuds and factions, heirs and claimants, amongst the other Gaulden branches. He ought to have left at least some token for Faro, his firstborn. Who had owned the house in Kentish Town, where he had shacked up with young Jessica?

The curtains parted, electronically, and the coffin slid out of sight. There was a fair amount of stifled and not-so-stifled

212

sobbing and sniffling, and Chrissie, glancing covertly sideways, could see tears pouring down Faro's cheeks. Poor girl, what a father, what a history. Chrissie's own eyes felt dried up at the source. He should have died earlier, had he wished her to weep for him. There had been a time when had he died, she would have followed him. But now the time for tears was over. So the woman who had been Chrissie Gaulden told herself, as she stood erect, to attention, like royalty.

And now Nick Gaulden was bursting into incandescence, and rising in smoke through the crematorium chimney, and drifting into the upper reaches of the thickly peopled autumn air. The skies above this place were dense with the souls of the departed. Conveyor-belt cremation, five in a day, and the other four today all Asian, if one could judge by the names on the wreaths and cards and markers. The old European diaspora was dying out, and members of the new diaspora were already leaving their subcontinental signatures on the walls of memory: *'Love Always Dad'*, exhorted Shanti Ramesh Patel, claimed by the new wave of death. The generation of traumas and death-camp tattoos, of Finchley Road accents, of chicken soup and Viennese pastries and pickled cucumber, would soon be completely extinguished, leaving a heritage of semi-assimilated survivor guilt. The old tearooms and cafés had been converted into Thai restaurants, pizzerias, Chinese takeaways and sushi bars. The Jewish landmark of Bloom's with its chopped fish still survived, outliving its more famous East End ancestor— but for how long, she wondered. These children of the Holocaust, these friends of yesterday, these second-generation settlers—Eric Mendelsson, Anna Hayman, Michael Rudetski, Rachel Rosenthal, Edith Woolfson, Dieter Kahn, Hannah Roditi—why, they were all old now, and their hair was grey. We are all old, thought Chrissie with astonishment, as she wandered out with the crowd to the cloisters, to the 'designated dispersal areas', to the green lawns where delicate clumps of pale mauve-pink autumn crocus reared their softly tissued little horns and trumpets in pretty clusters. It seems like yesterday, but we are all old.

Such unexpected, such pretty little flowers, so hidden for so long, and then so startling, appearing from nowhere, from the cropped smooth flattened grass, putting up their tender heads like snails from their shells, unfolding like the fronds of the anemones of the sea. Brave little flowers, to risk the trampling of the booted foot. For, unlike anemones and snails, they could not retract. They could not shrink back to safety. If you trod on them, they would bruise and bleed and die.

Tears for the poor crocus rose in Chrissie's eyes. She wept for them.

It was a mild and pleasant day, a global-warming, *fin de siècle,* autumnal day, a gracious day for a funeral, a better day than Nick Gaulden had deserved. But why invoke desert when the ash was yet hot? The sun shone down upon the nondenominational red arches, upon the ranks of standard rose with their votive tags, upon the rectangular pond where goldfish rose to bask and warm their plump backs, upon the sundial, upon the plaques and tablets of stone and ceramic, upon the guests and mourners, and upon Jenny Pargiter, to whom Chrissie now found herself being introduced by Stella Wakefield.

'Jenny,' said Stella, pulling by the elbow towards Chrissie an immensely tall, red-faced, stoutish woman in her mid-forties, clad, like Chrissie herself, in widow's black. She towered over Stella like a pillar, and Stella was not small. Jenny Pargiter's hair was a frazzled brownish grey, the veins in her cheeks and nose were broken, her face was unpowdered, and her eyes were Saxon-blue. She did not seem at all eager to be introduced to Chrissie. She stood in her own orbit, unmoved.

'Jenny,' said Stella, with what, from her, was almost a plea. 'Jenny, let me introduce you to Chrissie. Chrissie Sinclair, I should say. Chrissie, this is Jenny Pargiter.'

Chrissie looked round for Faro, for moral support, but Faro had deserted her, had gone off to suck up to her half-

214

sisters Arethusa and Iona, and to pet their babies: so Chrissie had to stare Jenny Pargiter out on her own. She went through the defensive routine that life with Nick Gaulden had taught her: straighten the shoulders, rear the head, pull in the chin, raise the back of the neck, square the body, tuck in the elbows, stare, confront.

'Hello,' said Chrissie Gaulden, now Lady Sinclair, to Jenny Pargiter.

'Hello,' said Jenny Pargiter, with massive indifference. 'Nice to meet you. At last.'

Chrissie did not think that it was at all nice to meet Jenny Pargiter, and could not think why her friend and ally Stella had been so malicious as to force this awkward and unnecessary introduction. Jenny was not at all what she had expected. She bore no resemblance to any of Nick's other women. She was far, far too big. Serafina was big, but not in this ungainly English way. The sight of Jenny filled Chrissie with a panic which she could not at first analyse. Perhaps it was the sheer unexpectedness of this bulk? No, it cannot have been that. It was what the bulk implied. Jenny had clearly not attached Nick Gaulden to her through her appearance, so she must have had some other more dangerous, invisible attraction which had kept him in her thrall for four long years. Perhaps, like a gross Wagnerian soprano, she hid within herself a voice of superlative purity and power? The voice of sex itself? What siren songs had Jenny sung to deceive poor Nicolas and to lure him to her bed? Jenny Pargiter was a heavyweight rival, a mattress crusher, and now Nick was dead, and neither of them, none of them, could ever win him back.

Nevertheless, 'Nice to meet *you*,' responded Chrissie, that gracious Lady. 'A nice service, didn't you think?'

And niceties they had exchanged, for a few minutes, until the drift towards the cars seemed to be about to begin. There was to be a wake, at Fiona's in Frognal. Fiona had volunteered. Money had spoken. All were invited. Chrissie and Faro had not yet decided whether they would attend.

Faro had been keeping half an eye on her mother, during the drifting introductions and greetings and formings of little groups and clutches of Gauldens and honorary Gauldens, of old schoolmates and fellow drinkers from the Three Horseshoes, the Freemason's Arms, the Wells, the Magdala. A thick, incestuous congregation, in which Faro knew far too many familiar faces, though she did not recognize that very tall person to whom Chrissie and Stella were now speaking: was she some kind of interloper, or some skeleton from a hitherto locked cupboard? Faro was not sure how much more of this scene she could take.

She had managed, so far, to avoid a conversation with Eric Mendelsson, whose very existence seemed to reproach her, and she had survived her ritual exchange with Iona and Arethusa—a mixture of affection, effrontery, attitude and regret. She had waved at Paul Noble, been embraced by Dieter Kahn, sidestepped her uncle Rudi, kissed her grandmother Eva, and been lobbied by Joachim Barker, who always wanted her to get him a job. Even at her father's funeral he tried it on. Who did he think she was? She was lucky to have a job herself. Nobody had a job these days. His reproachful eyes followed her as she advanced upon the diminutive Tiger Wakefield (surely he was very undersized for his age, whatever his age was?), who had been beckoning at her eagerly for some time. Joachim was all washed up. Like her father, like Eric, he had been a man of promise, but all he did now was to walk the Heath in all weathers, like a tramp. He wanted to write an article for her mag, but she was sure he couldn't put two words together anymore, poor old sod.

Tiger Wakefield wanted to point out to Faro that the top of the sundial was missing. Its brass plate, its roman numerals and its gnomon had been removed. Tiger thought this was a disgrace. 'In a cemetery, of all places,' he said, as he patted the empty round flat surface, cratered like a pancake, pitted like the moon. An absence, where time should have been.

'Do you think it's been vandalized? Do you think it was stolen? Should we report it? Do you think they know?'

'You're a very *busy* little chap,' sighed Faro, in response to this barrage. 'What does it matter? Let it be.'

'And is that Nick's smoke?' he wanted to know next, as he pointed to the thick black billows ascending, straight and undispersed, into the still air.

'I don't know,' said Faro. 'I don't know how it works. I don't know if they do them straightaway, or if they stockpile them. Do them in batches.'

'I wonder who's going to get the ashes,' said Tiger, scanning the gathering knowingly. 'A lot of claimants, aren't there?'

'Don't,' said Faro.

'Sorry,' said Tiger.

'That's all right,' said Faro, as she blew her nose.

That word 'stockpile' had been unfortunate. But Tiger shouldn't have encouraged her. He had led her on into treachery. Unlike her, he had hardly known his father. He owed him little. But Faro owed Nick much. She should not have made a joke at his expense.

Nick Gaulden had dreamed of harmony and had created discord. He had wished to gather his family into his ark and to protect it. He had failed.

Yet, had he looked down from that column of smoke, from those black dispersing particles, he might have felt some pleasure and some pride. For they were all there, his women and his children and his grandchildren, a good-looking, striking, disparate brood, chatting quietly and civilly in small groups in the mild autumn air, making their way towards the cars in the parking bays, towards the cars strung bumper to bumper for him along Hoop Lane. From a height, all was peace, fruition, forgiveness, ripeness. Forgotten the quarrels both trivial and tragic, the rows over borrowed books and stolen matches, over bank balances and babies, over precedences and priorities, over infidelities and betrayals: forgotten the violence, the screams, the tears and the bruises, the shaming revelations, the recriminations. All shall be saved, all shall be transfigured.

The warm air was static, breezeless. A winged seed detached itself effortlessly from a tree and spiralled slowly, slowly downwards, so slowly that it seemed to hover and suspend itself as it pondered, arrested, and languidly readopted its downward course. High over Finchley a bird-plane caught the sinking afternoon light and it too seemed to remain stationary, motionless, suspended above the mourners, before curving round and gliding smoothly to the south. An acorn, audibly, fell to the pavement, accentuating the quiet and the hush. Struggle was struck into stillness. So may it be.

Chrissie and Faro decided they would go to the wake after all. 'Come on, Mum,' urged Faro, as she fastened her seat belt and switched on the engine of her speedy dark blue Toyota, 'we might as well give it a whirl. We may never see some of this crowd again.'

'Just as well,' said Chrissie, shortly but indecisively.

'Oh, come on, Christine,' persisted Faro. 'They're not so bad, some of them. And I want to see what Fiona's house is like, don't you?'

As Chrissie now owned half of a very handsome house in Oxfordshire, she conceded that she might take the risk. She had already wasted too many years of her life resenting the house in Frognal and the woman in the house in Frognal. All that was over now. She had almost forgotten what it was like: to feel, as she had felt, that she was being flayed alive in public, her skin peeled away, inch by inch, before a mocking crowd. She had survived those humiliating torments of jealousy, and she knew that now she looked not only presentable but also impregnable. She could never attract pity now. She looked like what she was: a semi-retired, well-to-do, happily married professional woman, with an income of her own and a husband with a life of his own. The red of her hair was a deeper shade than nature had given her, her complexion was maintained and skilfully tinted, her hat was well judged, and her expensive well-cut Italian dress was becoming. She had nothing to be ashamed of here. The female Barrons did not age well, but she had at least looked after herself, and, unlike her mother, she had not grown obese. She had never been a beauty, like Serafina, like Stella, but at least she did not look as uncompromisingly strange as Jenny Pargiter or as aged as Fiona McKnight. Whatever had happened to Fiona? Could it be that she too had, simply, grown old?

Chrissie, during the course of the afternoon's events, had adjusted her first defensive, hostile dismissal of Fiona: Fiona did not look shabby, she merely gave the impression of looking shabby. Fiona looked as though she did not care. Unlike Chrissie, she had let herself go. This was, in itself, interesting, and Chrissie found herself sharing Faro's curiosity about the house in Frognal that she had never entered. Once, on one dark night, she had stood on the pavement outside, at midnight, weeping noisily and uncontrollably and drunkenly, and gazing upwards at the lighted windows behind which the faithless Nick and the thief Fiona sat. She had nourished fantasies of committing a vengeful suicide on Fiona McKnight's front steps. She had dreamed of swallowing spirits of salts, right there, and expiring in public agony. Her twisted corpse would have met them in the morning when they came out for the milk. She might have made the local headlines. FIRST WIFE OF 'FACE OF THE SIXTIES' NICOLAS GAULDEN, FOUND DEAD ON DOORSTEP OF SECOND WIFE'S FIFTY-THOUSAND-POUND HAMP-STEAD HOUSE.

Chrissie remembered, dimly, these embarrassing day-dreams. What would the house be worth now? Well over a million, no doubt. Yes, Faro was right, it was time to abandon these indulgent revenge fancies, and to go in. She might as well inspect Fiona's soft furnishings, while the offer was open. She would never have to invite her back.

'I can't stay late,' said Chrissie to Faro, hoping her daughter had not been able to follow this undignified sequence of memory flashes. 'I told Don I'd be back tonight. He'll worry if I'm late.'

'Don won't mind,' said Faro, as she rather too pushily negotiated the traffic round the White Stone Pond. Faro was not sure that she approved of her mother's second marriage, and of her submissive postures in the company of Donald Sinclair. Was it for this that the battle had been fought, those long lonely nights been endured, those risks been taken? For a convenient, conventional second marriage to a rich, clever, institutional old bore?

Actually, Faro liked Donald Sinclair. But she liked to toy with the idea that she didn't. She didn't *have* to, did she? She was free to dissent.

'No, Don won't mind,' said Chrissie. 'He never minds anything. He's very good at getting his own supper.'

The banality of this response made Faro yelp with contempt. 'I should bloody well think he is! If he can't get his own supper by now it's a pity.'

'Well, you know, that generation . . .' said Chrissie vaguely. She had left a packet of mushroom tortellini in the fridge, and a carton of microwaveable Gorgonzola and walnut and Parmesan sauce. Don was fond of pasta.

'After all,' continued Faro remorselessly, 'it's not as though you bury your first husband every day of the week. And he was my *father*.'

'Yes, darling, I know,' said Chrissie meekly. She knew she must not repeat the mistake Bessie had made, of forbidding Chrissie to mourn her father. So overcome with self-pity and anger had Bessie been, on Joe's inconveniently sudden departure, that neither Robert nor Chrissie had been allowed in her presence to show any sorrow for his loss. Bessie had continued to revile him dead, as she had reviled him alive. It had been intolerable.

And yet Chrissie knew she was at times in danger of forgetting that Nick had been Faro's father. He hadn't been an ideal father, but nevertheless, Chrissie had said bad things about him, things that should never have been said. A child ought to be allowed to respect its parent, even if, like Nick, he was not respectable. And sometimes she forgot that she herself was Faro's mother. Faro seemed such a triumphant, confident, careless creature. As though she had come from nowhere.

Bessie, reflected Chrissie, as she and Faro sat in a traffic jam in Heath Street outside the shop window of yet another expensive new boutique, Bessie had been a real bloodsucker as well as a shrew. Women weren't supposed to think this kind of thing about other women these days, Chrissie knew. Everything had changed since she was a girl. Women good, men bad. That's how the bleating went nowadays. And in the case of Nick Gaulden you could see there was something in it. He had been a bit of a traitor. On the other hand, none of his women could say they hadn't been free to choose to say no to Nick. He hadn't forced anybody. They'd been free to choose, and they'd all chosen him, one after another. Some of them had thrown themselves at him. They'd all wanted a bit of the action. They'd all wanted a slice of pinup boy Nick. They couldn't take out a retrospective claim for damages, could they? And anyway, they wouldn't have got anything out of him if they'd tried. You can't get blood out of a rolling stone. You don't sue a man in debt. Or if you do, you deserve the nothing that you get.

Lucky for Nick that the Child Support Agency hadn't been thought up earlier. Lucky for Nick that his women hadn't been litigious. Lucky for him that they had all loved him so much. The women who had chosen Nick had known what they were choosing, and they had got what they wanted. For a time, at least.

Whereas with Bessie—there had been no end to her demands, her needs. She had never been satisfied.

Chrissie had a long history with Nick Gaulden. She had met him when she was still a girl, before she was twenty. She had her memories. For decades, she had been afraid to look at them, afraid they could still cause her pain. Now that he was gone, now that the story was over, perhaps she would be able to dare to look at them again. They could not be taken away from her now. They were hers. No more pain, no more deceit could corrode or heap earth upon them. What would they look like now, if she tried to excavate them? Would they be worm-eaten, ashen, corrupt? Or would they gleam like buried gold? In the new age after Nick's death, would she be able to recover him? For her memories of him now were equivalent to all other memories of him. All had lost him. He was equally dead to all.

The wake was a riot. Wine, spirits and reminiscences flowed, as a great red harvest sun swam low in the cream-layered pink and violet sky: monstrous, swollen, presaging a disaster that had already happened. It lit Fiona McKnight's drawing room with a last lurid glow, then suddenly gave up and sank from sight.

Fiona's house had a view. It looked out over London. On a clear day, you could see the Crystal Palace on the Surrey shore. Here Nick Gaulden and Fiona McKnight Gaulden had sat, night after night, listening to music on her expensive sound system, watching the sun set, pretending to be a proper middle-aged married couple. For three or four years they had kept it up. Whereas, as Serafina now loudly recalled, most of us lived in basements. Staring at brick walls, into dank areas, into other people's kitchens.

'Once I threw a mug at him,' boasted Serafina, 'and it went right through the window and across the alley and into the kitchen window next door. Think of that! Those were the days!'

'You get what you pay for,' said Joachim Barker, helping himself to a couple of smoked-salmon sandwiches.

Eva Gaulden, who had long lost count of the number and names of her legitimate and illegitimate grandchildren, was listening patiently to Arethusa, who was talking about amniocentesis and prenatal scans. The new technology of childbirth. Arethusa seemed indignant about something or other, but Eva couldn't work out what it was. 'Yes, my dear,' she said, from time to time, as her mind flitted from decade to decade, from migration to migration, from image to image, from face to face. Vienna, Berlin, Dover, London, the Taunton Children's Home, London, the Finchley Road, Golders Green. It ended at Golders Green. Nick had been born in the sick bay of the Taunton orphanage where she'd been working, and she'd been too busy to pay him much attention. Times had been hard, in the late thirties. But Nick seemed to have found plenty of attention later on in life, so that was all right. 'Yes, my dear, you're quite right,' Eva said, and patted Arethusa's hand, and left her in midsentence to look for Rudi, to make sure Rudi was still alive.

Stella, ever gracious, was being pleasant to Moira. But Moira did not seem to need her pleasantness. The downtrodden Moira, it emerged, had turned into a psychoanalyst, and now worked at the Tavistock. Stella was astonished. 'However did you manage that?' she asked. 'Didn't you have to pass exams?'

Tiger was tormenting Aurelius. He wanted to hear about cricket. Aurelius was mad about cricket. Why? What was the point of it? Could Tiger go and see a match with him one day? What was cricket *for*? Was Aurelius a batter or a bowler? Did he play for his school? Why was Lord's called Lord's? Who was the fastest bowler in the world? Tiger adored Aurelius.

Faro had been trapped by Eric Mendelsson. Like the Ancient Mariner he had accosted her and forced her to hear his tale. Back he went, over his ancient friendship with Nick, over their rivalries at school, their wartime looting of bomb sites, their truancies, their delinquencies, their failed ambitions. They had been going to do such things, the pair of them. Nick the painter, Eric the poet. (They had published a few pamphlets together, back in the sixties.) Eric was already very drunk, although the night was young: Faro was surprised that somebody who drank so habitually could still get so drunk. And you'd have thought that at a liver-transplant funeral he might have taken things a bit steadier. But no, like the mariner, he was condemned to endless repetition. He was stuck in his groove, in his three-mile-island of North London, in his own personal Spandau, which he paced hopelessly, day in, day out, year in, year out. Nick Gaulden had always been willing to offer him a drink, a joint, a seat by the fire. Eric Mendelsson had hung on, through the changing panorama of Nick's women: faithful, unrejected, like a black dog, like a familiar devil. While Eric continued to drink more, why should Nick Gaulden try to drink less? Eric droned on, stumbling, slurring, repeating himself. Eric's speech was slurred even when he was sober. Listening to his drawlings, Faro felt her own youth and health rising irresistibly within her like a fountain: it was hard to keep the lid on all the bubbling within her. She could feel it springing, spurting, its pressure gathering and rising like a jet. She felt herself taking strength even from Eric's rheumy eye, his crooked teeth, his crooked smile. Clear water, welling upwards, the nub of its crystal surface throbbing and pulsing. Youth, hope, *jouissance*! Alas, poor Eric. How good her Dad had been to him. Good old Dad. She could never have endured the boredom.

Stella Wakefield had moved on from the subject of Moira's new career, and was now discussing green funerals with a young man called Dennis Rose. Stella wanted to be buried in a shroud of bracken and a coffin of willow beneath an oak tree in Horner Woods. She would rise again in a great clump of golden honey fungus. Dennis Rose did not seem to get the hang of this. He said that there wasn't room on the planet for that kind of thing. Stella pointed out that it was because the planet was so overcrowded that green funerals were a good idea. They didn't pollute, they didn't interfere with the nitrogen cycle. Dennis Rose said that his father was doing his bit for the planet, he was in landfill, he owned a lot of sites up north. Stella said that she believed landfill wasn't always a good thing—didn't it create a lot of methane gas? Dennis said all that had changed, that was the bad old days, landfill was ecologically very sound now, and his father's firm was working in partnership with a land reclamation scheme in South Yorkshire. It was reclaiming and landscaping Hammervale and the Lower Ham Valley, and turning them into a leisure centre, an earth park, a golf course and a field studies centre. Stella said that sounded ghastly to her, could he be serious? Dennis said, had she ever seen Hammervale? Nothing could be more ghastly than Hammervale. Whatever his dad Victor did to Hammervale would be an improvement. Anything would be an improvement. Stella conceded that she had never seen Hammervale. You just go and have a look, before you start talking about greenery, said young Dennis, squarely standing his ground.

Serafina, at Tiger's request, was unwinding her turban. She uncoiled it, length after length, to reveal a neat head capped by close-fitting tight black curls. The contrast was startling. Tiger was impressed. 'Put it back on again,' he urged, and Serafina obligingly twisted, wound, coiled and tucked, and behold, the wonderful erection was back in place. She didn't even have to look. Her fingers knew. It was almost as good as the Indian rope trick, said Tiger.

And where was Jenny Pargiter, the disconcerting giant? She was looming, alone, gazing out over the city, garbed in her blacks. She was keeping her secrets.

Chrissie, the other black widow, found herself talking about plastic coffins to Fiona McKnight. It was Fiona who had raised the subject. Fiona was as sharp as a kitchen knife, as unsentimental as a lemon. Chrissie had always been afraid of Fiona. Because Fiona was cruel and rich and had class. But now, in this Hampstead eyrie, Chrissie felt her fear evaporate:

for Fiona was nothing more nor less than a beady-eyed, clever, dried-up little old woman, with a cackle of a laugh, and a fine collection of bric-à-brac. Fiona had given up the Fine Arts, in which she and Nick had not very profitably dabbled together, and had taken up Bakelite. Did Chrissie know anything about Bakelite? It was fascinating stuff, fascinating. Did Chrissie know that in 1938 someone had invented and designed the Bakelite coffin? Bizarre, what? Fiona had just been up to Doncaster to see an exhibition of the stuff. She was thinking, herself, of opening a new gallery. Plastic, shellac, Bakelite, casein. She was tired of trying to be modern. She was sick of the cutting edge. She thought she'd turn kitsch in her old age. What? Might be fun, what?

'I had an uncle once who was fond of Bakelite,' said Chrissie helpfully. 'He used to manufacture it.'

Fiona found this fascinating, fascinating. Did Chrissie know the trademark? Did Chrissie have any pieces? No, Chrissie didn't. She didn't really know anything much about that side of the family at all. But she'd try to find out, if Fiona really wanted her to.

'You're married to an archaeologist, aren't you?' accused Fiona McKnight. 'Burial sites, funerary rites, all that kind of thing?'

Fiona was taken with a fit of coughing, which she quenched with neat vodka.

Yes, agreed Chrissie, that was his kind of thing.

'I met your husband,' said Fiona. 'Met him at the Academy. Agreeable chap. Good for you. Never felt like taking the risk again myself. Lost interest in that kind of thing. Not that you could describe Nick as that kind of thing. Bit of a one-off, Nick, wasn't he?'

'I don't know,' said Chrissie thoughtfully. 'Maybe he was a type, after all. Quite a rare one. But a type.'

Fiona spluttered, coughed into her handkerchief, reached into her bag, lit up a cigarette.

'Can't give it up,' she said. 'It was hell, sitting and standing through all that chat and all that guitar music. Without a fag. I thought Eric would never get to the end. Have one?'

'No thanks,' said Chrissie. 'I stopped.'

'Good for you. Good for you. How did you manage it? You used to be heavy on the draw, like me, didn't you?'

'I made myself sick,' said Chrissie.

Fiona thought that very funny, or so her excessive laughter might have suggested.

'Rum do, eh?' she said, when her mirth died down. 'Poor old Nick. Shall I tell you a secret? I thought I'd rescue him, I thought I'd save him from himself. Go on, laugh, do. And look what happened. Here I am, an old hag, smoking like a chimney and drinking like a fish. Serves me right, what? Did you think you'd save him? Did we all think we could save him?'

'When I knew him first,' said Chrissie, slowly and carefully, 'there was nothing to save him *from*. Or there didn't seem to be. When I knew Nick he was young, remember. And none of these bad things had happened.'

Fiona's eyes glittered, too bright in the withering of her too-small pinched white face.

'And not so many of the good ones, either,' she said, with companionable malice. 'We had some fun up here, Nick and I. On our good days.'

And Jenny Pargiter stared out lonely over the city, like the figurehead of a great ship about to slip its anchor.

⁂

Christine Flora Barron Gaulden Sinclair sat back in her seat on the last slow train from Paddington and shut her eyes. It had been a long day. The train was taking her back to Oxfordshire, and it was taking her through the stations of Nick's past. Paddington, Radley, Appleford, Slough, Didcot, Cholsey, Goring,

Pangbourne, Reading, Ashton-under-Wychwood, Queen's Norton. Nick Gaulden and Don Sinclair had both been Oxford men, though Don Sinclair had done more to deserve the title. And now Chrissie lived in a pleasant seventeeth-century house of yellow stone with latticed windows standing just off a village green in the Cotswolds. A pretty, rustic, charming building of character, with many original features, as the estate agents had accurately described it to the Sinclairs. A picture-postcard house. A second home for a second marriage. Bessie Barron had liked it a great deal and had been to stay in it as often as she was invited. More often, in fact.

Bessie Barron had also approved of Donald Sinclair. Nick Gaulden had not been her kind of person at all.

Chrissie shut her eyes, amidst the smell of old upholstery, newsprint, stale coffee and plastic beaker, as the train rattled through Radley. It rattled her backwards, to her first strange and fatal meeting with Nick Gaulden. Watch her as the years peel away from her, as her skin lifts and tightens, her hair re-burnishes, her waist dwindles, her hard mouth softens, her eyes widen, her lashes lengthen. There is Chrissie Barron, nineteen years old and a virgin, waiting for everything to happen to her. Nick Gaulden walks into the room, and it begins to happen. He walks up to her, and offers her a cigarette. She accepts. She already has a glass of wine. It is a party, not a funeral, a summer party in a narrow little terraced house in a Cambridge side street. Nick is visiting from Oxford, he tells her. He is reading Greats. She tells him she is at the end of her first year, reading what is known as Arc and Anth. They cannot hear one another very well, for the room is crowded and everyone is shouting. The ash on her cigarette lengthens. He takes it from her, gently, as though it were precious, reaches behind him to a saucer on the mantelpiece, shakes off the ash, and gently, as though it were precious, restores the cigarette to her hand. Their hands touch in the transaction. It is done. That is it. A violent current passes from Nick Gaulden to

Chrissie Barron, and both begin to tremble. It is as simple, as irreversible as that. That is how life is engendered.

Transformed into a fountain, a tree, a breeze, a bird? Forget the poetry, forget the dignity of mythology. Chrissie at times has wished that she had been fried to a cinder at that first contact, that she had been frazzled and scorched to death. The adult Chrissie winces in her ageing body as the train grinds into Didcot.

Chrissie had to climb back into college that first party night, for by the time she and Nick parted, the gates were locked. They did not sleep with one another that first night, nor the next, nor the next. It was a courtship, and Nick was a romantic. He liked foreplay. He could make it last. He wooed her with words as well as gestures—words, as she was later to discover, not all his own. She remembers them now. Words are like terrible little metallic containers, like capsules. They preserve what should be forgotten. They endure. When punctured, they release their dangerous, poisonous spores, to reinfect the drying, withering flesh.

> For I rather had owner be
> Of thee one hour, than all else ever.

John Donne had been all the rage in those days. A poet of the fifties. A lot of people quoted him.

Nick had wooed her with words his own and not his own, with kisses, with caresses, and with hard liquor. For those had been the drinking years, not the drugged years, and Nick had been a pioneer with the whisky bottle. He had hitched eastwards across the counties of Middle England to visit her, arriving, dramatic, on her threshold, with a bottle in a brown bag.

He had deflowered her in her college bed. Chrissie, who has forgotten much, lost in a blur of pain, alcohol, sorrow, age and sheer relentless weighty brain-numbing overloading time,

229

can remember every moment of this long-ago event, every sensation.

The train draws out of Didcot, hesitates, stops. Something is wrong with its engine. An apology comes over the loud-speaker. There will be a slight delay.

A woman's first sexual experience is frequently disappointing and incomplete. Chrissie Barron's, unfortunately for her, had been ecstatic. She had left the body and soared upwards. Her fleshly body had lain pinioned beneath Nick's warm completed weight, and her spirit body had soared upwards, as her blood soaked the sheets. She had been freed of the body through the body. So many times on the verge of initiation, she had at last crossed the threshold and discovered the mystery.

All had been perfect. Both had been awestruck by the simplicity of it. They had been made for one another, they were two halves of the same body, fused into one. And they could do it again, and again, and again. They could come together and achieve this miracle any time, any place. In a bed, in a ditch, in a field.

That summer they had eloped to France, and on to Italy. With a canvas bag full of clothes, and thirty pounds in their pockets. Chrissie had lied to her parents: she told them she was going on holiday with her college friends Ilse and Barbara. Chrissie and Nick had wandered through Europe, drunkenly, in the innocence of the first youth of their passion. Chrissie had been subdued and given over to it. She had been soaked and saturated with sex. She became more and less than human. She took leave of her senses and was enthralled by her senses. And Nick had sworn he would love her, her only, her for ever, in endless, rapturous, hyperbolic protestation. She had drunk in his vows, through France, through the Alps, and down the Adriatic. He had sworn his love in bus stations, in cheap cafés, in wine cellars, in mountain villages, in classical ruins, and in a bedroom full of mosquitoes, where beneath the slowly turning creaking fan the walls had been spattered with their conjoined, commingled blood. Together, forever, he had said. And she had believed him.

Or had she? How could she have done? Even to this day she did not know if she had believed him or not.

No, of course she could not have believed him.

Chrissie Barron, as the disembodied official voice apologizes once more for the delay, finds herself, forty years on, blushing with shame. Of course she had not believed him. She had known, even then, even at the very beginning, even at Cambridge, that he was faithless, that he was sleeping with other women, that he was transported by his own rhetoric, that he was a collector, that there was no way in which she could be the one and only love of his life. Even then, ignorant though she was, she had recognized that the very intensity of his lovemaking signified its duplicity. Yet she had deceived herself, she had pretended not to notice. She had hidden even from him the fact that she had once found another woman's knickers stuffed down at the bottom of his Oxford bed-sitter bed. Why on earth had she not confronted him, then and there, with those stained purple net pants, and brought the whole thing to an end? She knew the answer. It was because she had not wanted to lose him. She wanted to pretend, even to herself, that they and what they signified did not exist. So she had lied, and lied, and lied. She had stuffed knowledge down to the bottom of the bed and hidden it. And Nick, deceived and deceiving, drunk on words and liquor, had continued to swear undying and exclusive love.

The train had left Didcot and was slowing down again just beyond Goring. It was a very slow train.

And yet, thought Chrissie, she had put up some resistance. She had struggled against his version, his desire for total collusion. The story would have been tidier and more extreme had she succumbed at once, and abandoned all to his dominion. But something in her—some remnant of her sensible, Yorkshire, Bawtry-Barron self—had clung to the idea that she ought to stick it out, to get her degree, and run mad later, when she had some qualifications to fall back on. (Had something in her remembered Joe Barron's two years as a travelling salesman, and Bessie's collapse before her part one English B?)

In her last Cambridge summer, her last long vacation, she had made a bid for freedom. She had told Nick that they must part. Had they quarrelled? Not exactly. But she had told him that she would not spend the summer with him. They must have a trial separation. (Did she tell herself that if their love survived this test, then she would, as he was urging, marry him?)

It was an old-fashioned test, a trial by distance. Chrissie signed herself up to spend her vacation on the Faeroe Islands. He would never follow her there. She would be out of sight and out of reach, working on an archaeological dig. She would take herself off, with respectable, serious, hardworking colleagues, students and professionals, and dig in the damp earth.

Bessie and Joe were relieved and delighted, and Joe offered at once to pay for the cost of the exercise. Chrissie said he need not bother, she had got a grant. At that point, her career was still open. Bessie and Joe had not at this point met Nick Gaulden, but emanations from him had reached them, and they had formed the conclusion that he was not a suitable match for their daughter. They had both sensed, though they never mentioned it to one another or to her, that Chrissie was no longer a virgin. They had both decided that handsome Nick Gaulden from Oxford, the Finchley Road and a Taunton orphanage, was not a marrying man. They still, at the back of their liberated minds, perceived of marriage as a woman's destiny.

Bessie and Joe were wrong. Nick Gaulden pursued Christine Barron to the Faeroe Islands, and claimed her as his bride. Was this what she had intended him to do? Probably.

It had not been easy. The Faeroe Islands are inaccessible. They are not very far away as the gull flies—three hundred and eighty miles from Norway, and only two hundred from

232

Shetland—but they are hard to reach, because not many people want to go there. They were not a popular tourist destination then, and they are not very popular now, even though the world has speeded up so much. They are too cold, too barren, too rocky and too wet, the land of the sheep and the puffin and the whale. Chrissie had liked the idea of them precisely because they were so unwelcoming. Nick Gaulden was a classical scholar, of sorts, and gifted in the Romance languages: he had seduced her in the soft option of the classical Mediterranean. The Nordic scene was not for him, and that was why Chrissie Barron had signed on as a willing hand to attempt an excavation of the supposed tomb and home of Sigmundur, who had expired on a heap of seaweed at the end of the first millennium of Our Lord, in A.D. 1000. If Nick Gaulden's professed passion lasted for a month's absence, so be it, she would believe in it and surrender. If not, let him dally with the second-best lady of the purple knickers.

Chrissie, in those days, had been so sure, poor thing, that she was not second best.

Chrissie had read the sagas and studied the strange, elliptical story of Sigmundur's rise and fall. Sigmundur was credited with having introduced Christianity to the Faeroes, at the behest of King Olaf of Norway. Christianity had not done Sigmundur much good, for he had died in the maelstrom of a long feud of family hatreds and pagan practices, but it had certainly caught on as a creed with a Lutheran vengeance in later centuries in the Faeroes—a wasteland in need of a dark and stark religion. Chrissie had hardly spared a thought for Sigmundur in many a long year, but now, on the night of Nick's funeral, she dredged up from the dark ages of her memory the amusing fact that Sigmundur's wife Turid, a powerful woman in her time, had been known by the title of 'Principal Widow', a title to which Chrissie herself felt she could now also lay claim. How many wives had Sigmundur had? She had forgotten. Not as many as Nick Gaulden, for sure. He hadn't had as much choice. There hadn't been as many people around in those remote and unpeopled parts. There had been a seduction in a birch wood by a Norwegian fjord, or something like that. Sigmundur and Turid, the only man and woman in the wood of the wide world. He had chosen her because there was no one else to choose. A woman like an axe. Had that remote community on the islands of Skuvoy and Sandoy and Streymoy celebrated the coming of the end of the millennium with jollity and fermented shark and stuffed sheep's testicle and sliced blubber and fly agaric soup? Or had they let the moment pass unmarked?

Prehistory was Chrissie's period. The Old Stone Age. The Vikings and the sagas were a colourful diversion, a light relief from that unimaginable dark cold lurch at the beginning, when all the pain in the cave began. And there had been light relief and jollity, in that summer of the sixties, amongst her archaeological comrades, far away from the threat of Nick Gaulden. There had been singing and drinking as well as digging. Chrissie, worn out and rubbed aflame with sex, had retreated to a pre-pubertal Girl Guide and Boy Scout enclave. Group Leader was Professor Arkwright, an affable, bearded, boyish, British troll. Not Nick's type at all. There had been thirteen of them on the dig, twelve workers, and Arkwright the Leader. They had all slept in a disused fish-gutting factory, where Chrissie shared a dormitory with four other young women, all of them vacation volunteers. There was Harriet from St Andrews, Susan from Edinburgh, Beth from Chipping Norton and Elinor from Dublin. Their room had smelt of damp, of oil, of gut, of lanolin, of mildewed straw, of herring. First there was fog, and then it rained steadily, for days, and they could never get dry, for the tumble-dryer machine had not yet reached this island: wet wool socks and cable-knit sweaters were hung on improvised washing lines, and turned by hand before a smoky fire. By day they laboured, slicing through the turf and stony earth, measuring, sifting, digging up stones, shards, animal bones, the shells of limpets and of mussels. How had people survived, century after century, in this outpost? Chrissie had wondered then, and wondered now. Holderfield in comparison had glittered like Paris of the *belle époque,* and even Breaseborough had been recast in Chrissie's recollection as a thriving, diverse and cultured community. Life had been primitive through much of Europe in the year 1000, and in Ultima Thule, nine hundred and sixty-odd years later, it remained so still. No videos then, no fax, no e-mail and, for many, still, no electricity. The men had fished and farmed, the women had stitched and knitted. In winter the days were dark and the evenings long, though in summer a pale endless light played on the cliffs and the turf and the seething waters. Professor Arkwright hoped to find the headless body of Sigmundur, or the foundations of his church, or his burial cross, or his deadly gold chain, the source of so much strife. His student vassals would dig for him.

The Faeroes would have changed by now, supposed Chrissie. E-mail and mobile telephone and helicopter would have accessed all the islands. Maybe they were now overrun with tourists. She did not know. She had never dared even to think of going back.

It had rained without much relief on Skuvoy that summer. Shoulder to shoulder, Harriet McGough and Chrissie Barron, in a trench of mud, had scraped and prodded. Harriet, her dark hair dripping rat's tails, her cheeks reddened by the wind, recited her griefs and hopes to Chrissie, well out of earshot of the religious and censorious Susan, who did not care for bedtime stories. Harriet described her boyfriend, Jim McAllister, an aspiring marine biologist at Aberdeen, and the fright they'd had in May when Harriet had thought she was up the spout. Chrissie kept nodding, sympathetically, as she agreed that condoms were necessary but disgusting—though the truth was that Nick Gaulden's objections to condoms were as strong, though less high-minded than Susan Lindsay's, and Chrissie had been obliged to grapple with the Dutch cap. So far it had worked. At least, Chrissie had said to herself, as she picked delicately at a protruding flinty nodule with dirty cracked fingernails, at least I don't have to worry about *that* at the moment, on this faraway Faeroe, with the womb blood seeping out of me right now through a sodden tampon into the gusset of my bottle-green cotton knickers. How the hell, wondered Chrissie, was she going to manage to wash them and get them dry again in this soaking drenching sodding dump?

They scraped and chatted, deep in their trench, in their Wellington boots and their weatherproofed jackets. What a masochistic way to spend the summer! Puffin casserole and potatoes again for supper, and some sheep cheese if lucky. Not much grows on the thin soil of the Faeroes. Oats and rye fail, and the barley does not ripen. The turnip does well, but one can soon have enough of the turnip. The leek, the beet and the cabbage survive, if cherished, and, in the spring, watercress flourishes. But Ceres has not poured her cornucopia freely upon the Faeroes. Fish head and lamb tail and sea fowl eke out her spare bounty, along with cans and tins and jars of baked beans, corned beef, pressed pork and pickled herring. But Harriet and Chrissie had been content, in their manner, as they gently coaxed the past to reveal itself to them, as their conversation moved from contraception and conception to the specialized named fogs of the islands: the high white hilltop fog called *Skadda,* the valley fog called something unpronounceable, and the common, pervasive, sea-blanketing thick, murky fog called *Morkye.* They had seen examples of all these, both in their natural forms, and as illustrated in his slide show by climatologist Crispin Christiansen in the lively Faeroese capital of Tórshavn. He had predicted the weather would lift this very day, and maybe, after all, the rain was slackening, and was not that a glimmer of sunshine making its way towards them across the lightening glistening ocean?

It was a gleam of sunshine, and it brought with it Nick Gaulden. He had come to seek his Christine. Undeterred, nay, inspired by distance and difficulty, he had hitched his way up through England, through Scotland, on a seaplane to Shetland, and across the sea on a trawler, a heroic four-day journey, and now he stood there, outlined against the sunburst, against the steeply rising hillside, gazing down at Chrissie in her subterranean chamber with her little trowel in her dirty hand. 'So *there* you are,' he yelled down at her, as she pushed her red wet hair back from her brow with the back of her hand. He too was wet: water streamed from his head and down the open throat of his shirt.

'Come on up *out* of there,' shouted the irresistible, travel-stained, consciously Byronic Nick Gaulden. 'Come out! Come out!'

And Chrissie Barron had clambered up out of the tomb which she had dug with her own shovel, and staggered, muddy, stinking of wool and fish, into his waiting arms. Out of the cleft of the earth she had climbed, into the watery sunlight.

Well, one could not argue with such persistence.

Her fellow diggers had been impressed by this apparition, though not all had taken it well. Professor Arkwright had been enraged by the distraction, and, when it became clear that Nick had no intention of shouldering a spade, he gave Chrissie the sack. She could clear off to Tórshavn and make her own way back. She was no longer part of the expedition. Hangers-on not welcome. It was clear that the Prof felt Nick had made a mockery of his own elaborate yearlong preparations for this excursion by turning up there, dripping and smiling, as though he had swum like a fish across the straits.

But on his first evening, Nick had been allowed to share the puffin stew, the smoky hearth, and to tell his traveller's tales. Harriet, Elinor, Hamish and Otto had egged him on, as he described the seaplane and the trawler and the Viking captain with his golden rings and the gold chain round his thick neck. And they in turn had told him the story of Sigmundur and his cousins and the blood feud. Nick had brought with him a bottle of Bells 'Afore Ye Go' whisky, and he had passed it round. Then he had reeled meekly off to sleep in the men's longroom, as though obeying some medieval monastic rite. 'Tomorrow,' he had threatened Chrissie, as he kissed her, like a troubadour, a chaste good night. And she had made her way with torch and lantern in her long damp nightdress to her straw mattress.

The next day Chrissie and Nick had been ferried across the shining water to the sunny mainland island. They booked into the Viking Hostel, where they declared themselves to be man and wife, and took a double room the size of a single bed. It had a shelf, a bed, a chair and a hook on the back of the door, and its walls were whitewashed like the walls of a hermit's cell. There, all night, they had made love, though what Nick Gaulden told her, as he reclaimed her, was 'I've come to fuck you, I've come to fuck you so hard you'll never be able to get away again.'

And the forbidden word, so rarely uttered then, so common now, had plunged into Chrissie like a sword, and her flesh had closed around the wound as her blood drenched the bed. They had entered a new age of fucking. This was for real.

In the morning they caught a country bus to the next bay, with a picnic, and had walked along the hilltop on the sweet short green grass. Wildflowers strewed their way—the crowfoot, the eyebright, the gilly flower, the starry saxifrage. Bugloss and self-heal blossomed purple and blue in banks and fissures, and beneath them, in the clear waters of a little cove, they could see great powerful coils of ribbed and ribboned seaweeds ebbing and flowing, inhaling and exhaling, with the sucking breathing waves of the tide. They came across a meadow of mushrooms, of little bubbles of the earth, and they sat down amongst them to eat their rye-bread sandwiches, and Nick had built a tiny toy fire of grass and paper, and lit it with his cigarette lighter, and grilled for her a mushroom skewered on a twig. So kind he had been, so gentle, so dedicated to her body's pleasures. A lover beyond all praise.

The train began to move again, through darkened Oxfordshire, towards Ashton, and her little station stop beyond, where her car was waiting for her. Chrissie had not dared to think about the Faeroes episode for years. She had blotted out the past and brutally repressed it. If Nick had not come for her then, would she have escaped him? And had he persisted only because she had provoked him?

These questions would never be answered.

Her parents had not received the news of her marriage to Nicolas Gaulden well. She had married him on her twenty-first birthday, and they had not been invited to attend. In fact Bessie had once said to Dora that she had no proof that a wedding had ever taken place. Both Bessie and Joe had assumed that the marriage, and Chrissie's failure to take her degree, had been precipitated by the fact that Chrissie had got herself pregnant. They were half right and half wrong. Chrissie had thought herself pregnant, but she had been mistaken. Too much sex had fucked up her menstrual cycle, but the Dutch cap had not betrayed her. Nick said he was delighted when she told him she thought she was pregnant, and insisted on marrying her. She was at that stage more than willing. And, believing herself to be already inseminated, she had given up using the Dutch cap. And thus Faro had been conceived. She was born, to the surprise of many, a decorous ten months after the ceremony in Oxford Register Office. She was a normal-sized baby, and apparently, despite the mixup, neither premature nor late. The perfect, seven-pound, full-term, life-attached baby. Aged all of ten minutes, she had latched on to the nipple like a leech. Nick and Chrissie had adored her. Joe and Bessie had, of course, adored her. Eva and Gyorgy Gaulden had adored her too, though more absentmindedly, for they were already losing count.

What had the young couple lived on, in their Oxford digs, and then in their Barlby Road soup-kitchen? Carrots, beans, potatoes, mince and air. Nick's college grant. Handouts and hand-me-downs and grandparental contributions. Odd jobs, improvisations and minor theft. The Family Allowance. Chrissie ran a play group and charged for it: she discovered necessity had taught her how to keep a good balance sheet. Nick sold his handsome face to a newspaper hoarding and smiled down surreally upon London, ten foot tall, with a cigarette in his mouth. Those were the days. They got by. Nobody starved.

Chrissie felt, during this wild heyday, that she had truly escaped Bessie at last. She had burned her boats. Good-bye, Mother. For how could Nick and Bessie possibly get on? They did meet, occasionally, but their coexistence was not convincing. Nick, who thought he could charm anybody, failed utterly with Bessie. His smiles dashed against the rock of her disapproval in vain. Chrissie had found the experience of sitting in the same room with the pair of them so extreme that she thought she might faint, if one could faint while sitting upright holding a cup of tea in a Parker Knoll upholstered chair in Surrey. Images of Nick in less proper situations were so thickly manifested about him that Chrissie was sure that Bessie could see them too. From her expression as she stared at Nick perhaps she could. She was no fool.

Joe was always civil to his son-in-law, whom he deplored. He could see the point of him, all too clearly. He worried about his little girl, married to a penniless rotter. He did not think it was going to work. And, of course, he was right, for eventually, after surviving or almost surviving several years of Moira and Serafina, Chrissie had asked her father for advice about a divorce, and he had helped to arrange it. He was less worried about her at this stage than he had been earlier, for Chrissie had showed considerable powers of survival. She had even, through Eva Gaulden, found herself a proper job. If she could get rid of Nick, she might be fine. She might remarry. Joe hoped she would.

But Chrissie's divorce had one serious disadvantage. It brought Bessie back into her daughter's life. With the threat of a visitation from the satanic Nick finally and formally re-moved, there was nothing to stop Bessie from seeing a lot more of Chrissie and Faro. Her son Robert was not much use to her, socially: he had turned into a reclusive academic, a historian rather than a lawyer, single, sardonic, locked inhos-pitably away in the University of Waterford. Mothers are ex-pected to favour their sons, but Robert had not allowed her to favour him. So Bessie concentrated on Chrissie. This had not been good for Chrissie. Joe had done his best to protect his daughter from his wife, but it had not been easy.

Bessie would ring Chrissie, and complain to her, for hours on end. She would demand her company. And Chrissie would, as often as she could, oblige. Bessie, by this stage, had become even more grossly and conspicuously unreasonable than she had been during Chrissie's schooldays. She continued to take great pride in her officially depressed status, and liked to re-cite the names and quantities of the many pills she swallowed daily. As far as Chrissie could see, they did not seem to do her much good, but maybe she would have been even worse with-out them, who could say? Bessie, at this period, shocked Chrissie on one occasion by telling her that she had been to see her doctor for some minor ailment, and had managed to read, in his notes on her, upside down, the word 'hypochon-driac'. What had shocked Chrissie most about this was that Bessie had seemed to accept the charge, and to find it very funny. This was bewildering. What did Bessie know or think about herself? It was a mystery. Bessie was a mystery.

Chrissie felt sorry for her mother, now that Bessie was age-ing. She was no longer afraid of her, or shamed by her. But she continued to be puzzled by her. Would she ever be able to make any sense of Bessie's strange and uneventful and disap-pointed life?

Chrissie knew her visits to Woodlawn were a relief to her father, who, after his retirement, would take advantage of Chrissie's sacrificial appearances to disappear himself, on brief excursions—to Buxton and Bayreuth, to Glyndebourne and Salzburg. He set up the fiction that he went away for the music, for Bessie's indifference to music was so well established and so often reiterated that she could hardly renege on it now in order to dog his footsteps. He himself was not at first as ardent a music lover as he claimed. Like many Yorkshiremen, he had always been deeply moved by oratorio, and tears came to his eyes whenever he heard the great choruses from *The Messiah*. He also had a habit of singing to himself the cry from Mendelssohn's *Elijah*: 'If with all your heart ye truly seek me, ye shall ever surely find me.' This too brought tears to the eyes, for he sought, and was not sure that he found. But in these later years, his musical interests widened, and he came intensely to enjoy Mozart, Beethoven, even Wagner, during his weeks of escape. Another example of successful adaptive preference formation.

One of the unkindest things Joe ever said to Chrissie about Bessie was provoked by the subject of music. On the eve of his last trip to Salzburg, Bessie had been holding forth over supper about Mozart. She seemed to disapprove of Mozart. Walking in the garden after supper that evening, Joe had said to Chrissie, 'You know, your mother believes that if she could be bothered to learn to play the violin, she would be the greatest violinist in the world. In fact I think she believes she *is* the greatest violinist in the world. It's just that she never found time to learn to play the violin.' And Chrissie, disloyally, had laughed, while wondering how Joe had managed not to murder Bessie.

Joe was a dutiful husband, and he had taken Bessie on many nonmusical holidays. But he never took her on the world tour he had promised her. She often complained about this. It was clear that Joe could not face her company as he circled the globe. So he fobbed her off with shorter trips to Cyprus, to Malta, to Italy, to France, to the Dalmatian coast—all places that in her Breaseborough days would have seemed dream destinations. But they were not good enough for her now. She complained and nagged and complained. Her war of attrition failed, proved counterproductive. Joe became stubborn. And he held the purse strings. So that was that.

Chrissie thought that towards the end he began to take a pleasure in denying Bessie. His character had been deformed by hers. He held the purse strings, but she had won. This had been sad to see.

Joe had died before he had a chance to meet Donald Sinclair. He never knew that his daughter remarried. He died three months before his sister Ivy died in Australia. It was Chrissie who rang to give her aunt the bad news. As we have seen, Bessie did not like her sister-in-law, and had continued to dislike her, although she had not seen her for more than thirty years. So it was Chrissie who had to tell her of Joe's death.

'I know why you've rung,' said Ivy Barron, in a strong Yorkshire accent almost identical to that of Bessie Barron's, though lower in register. 'I'm sorry. I knew he wasn't well. Thank you, Christine, for letting me know.'

Chrissie wrote to Ivy once a fortnight, after Joe's death, taking over Joe's old routine. But Ivy did not live long. The same illness carried them both away. They died of asbestosis, a killer disease, contracted decades earlier in the playground of Cromwell Place Infants in Cotterhall. Ivy had fled from Cotterhall and Barron Glass and South Yorkshire to the uttermost parts of the earth, but she had fled, as the scriptures prophesied, in vain, for even there the Cotterhall dust claimed her, as it had claimed Joe Barron in Surrey.

Joe's illness had been wrongly diagnosed for years, as angina. Lawyers in Surrey were not expected to die of asbestosis.

They were all dead now. Joe, Bessie, Ivy and Nick Gaulden.

The train was three quarters of an hour late when it arrived at Queen's Norton, but there was her car, waiting for her. She got in, switched on the ignition, switched on the radio, then switched it off again. She wondered if Don would have eaten all the supper, or would he have left some for her? She thought she might be hungry. She'd been too busy talking and listening to eat much at the wake. Little frilled oblongs of ravioli began to materialize like manna in her mind as she drove through the sleeping landscape. She left the main road for her own turning. A badger shuffled slowly into the hedgerow. She drove slowly up her own drive, parked, quietly closed the car door. She stood for a moment in the garden, breathing in the night air. The air on the Oxfordshire-Northamptonshire border was soft and clean and pure, and smelled of grass and apple and newly clipped box. Over her head stretched Cassiopeia, like a great butterfly. This was rural England, pretty England, the England of second homes and donnish retreats. Chrissie loved it. Nick, who had never been to Queen's Norton, had despised it. Orphanage-born Nick had been faithful to his own exiled urban style.

It was after midnight. Quietly, like a thief in the night, she unlocked the front door, and closed it behind her. Her little black cat, Pandora, had heard her, and padded across the stone-flagged hall to greet her with a muted cry, but from her husband Donald there was no sound, for he had gone to bed, as instructed, and would now be sleeping soundly in his separate room.

Had he eaten his supper up, like a good boy? Chrissie eased off her funeral shoes, and made her way in nylon feet along the polished wooden corridor to the kitchen, where she switched on some of its many lighting effects. The daffodil-yellow ceramic tiles glowed at her and the dangling brass-bottomed pans glinted against the marigold paintwork. Pandora rubbed against her legs and purred politely. Chrissie plugged in the kettle. She would make herself a mug of Marmite.

Don had left his dishes in the sink. College-fostered, he feared and distrusted the dishwasher. She loaded them—two plates, a knife, a fork, a wineglass. She looked around for the remains of the pasta, and found them, in a bowl in the refrigerator, neatly covered with cling film. Should she pop them in the microwave, heat them up, eat them? No, she would have them for lunch tomorrow. She was pleased but not surprised to see them so thriftily preserved. She and Don shared many little generational habits. They both disliked waste. Faro would have scraped these ragged grey-white leavings messily into the garbage. Faro seemed to think food grew on trees. Faro threw away loaves of bread. Thrift, jealousy, rage, pain—all seemed to have spared the blessed Faro.

The mushrooms of the Faeroes had sprung from the earth so bravely in their little clumps. 'The earth hath bubbles, as the water hath, and these are of them.' Had they, like Macbeth's witches, made her false promises? In her garden here, at Queen's Norton, she had a fairy ring. Each autumn a circle of low white puffballs sprouted from the grass, raising their small plushy domes from a surround of trimmed grass and clover and illicit rosettes of daisy and plantain. The gardener mowed them down, and back they came, week after week, year after year. Ten years now she had been married to Donald Sinclair. It did not seem very long. Ten months her marriage to Nick Gaulden had lasted, before the arrival of Faro and of Moira. It had seemed a lifetime.

The purple crocus, the fairy ring. But Nick Gaulden would not come again, would he?

Chrissie sat down, sipped at her hot dark brew of Marmite, stirred it, sipped again.

After many desertions, Chrissie had continued, against the odds, against the evidence, to believe that Nick Gaulden would come again to reclaim her. Long after it was reasonable to expect any such reprieve, she had continued to await his return. Surely he would come for her in the end! Even now, now that he was burnt to ash, she half expected him to tap upon the darkened windowpane. Now, more than ever.

He had haunted her for more than half her life. She had seen his shadow disappear around corners, had heard his voice in crowded rooms, had seen his handwriting on messages in hotel lobbies, in airports, on noticeboards in public places. She knew he had not forgotten her. When she ceased to see his ghost, that would be when he had forgotten her.

He had not been very pleased to hear about her marriage to Donald, or so Faro reported. He seemed to think that Chrissie was doing it expressly to annoy him. Like Bluebeard, he did not like escapers or deserters.

Bessie, in contrast, had been very pleased by her family connection with Sir Donald Sinclair, archaeologist, author, academic, onetime head of college and titled gentleman. Chrissie, in middle age, was no longer as embarrassed by Bessie as she had been when young, but nevertheless she still winced occasionally when she heard Bessie boasting to the Surrey housewives and shopkeepers about her son-in-law and his fine attributes. Donald, being a gentleman, put up with it all very well and, with Chrissie's encouragement, kept out of her way as much as he could: he still had a room in college, to which he could retreat during Bessie's Oxfordshire visits.

But there had been bad evenings. As Chrissie brushed her teeth—a task which takes her much longer than it takes her daughter Faro, and which she has to approach with much more delicacy and care—she revisits one of them, and so may we.

An autumn evening, some ten years or so ago, in the eighties, in the first year of Chrissie's second marriage. A mother-daughter scene. Perhaps it is Bessie's first visit to Queen's Norton. Bessie is a widow now, and she and Chrissie are sitting in the Osborne & Little and linen-loose-cover country drawing room pretending to watch the BBC nine o'clock news. (Bessie refuses, in company, to acknowledge the existence of commercial channels, though she has occasionally and inadvertently betrayed her acquaintance with them.) Don is out, at a pub or a club or a dinner, or sitting in his college room, or sitting on the Paddington train. A pleasant wood fire is flickering in the grate. Chrissie thinks it is pleasant, but her mother feigns horror that a daughter of hers should have fallen for such a time-wasting, dirty, polluting and unsatisfactory source of heat. Bessie hates coal and she extends her hatred to logs. Chrissie has given up trying to defend her flames. She likes them, and if she can't have flames at her age, it's a pity. She likes to see the dark wood blossom and the deep light glow.

Bessie, on this remembered evening, has reverted to her obsession with the dead Joe's alleged parsimony. It is an inexhaustible theme. Chrissie fingers the remote control, wondering whether to turn the volume up or down, or whether to let Prime Minister Thatcher and Bessie Barron talk it out with even honours. She lets them both play and tries to listen to neither.

Sometimes Chrissie wonders if Bessie is veering towards senility. Is this endless repetition a sign of dementia? Is this obsession with money a symptom of florid paranoia? But Bessie's brain is still sharp. She does not repeat herself word for word, and she phrases and rephrases her arguments with some skill, as though she were the barrister of the family, and the late Joe were in the dock. Item: that he never took her on the world cruise that he had promised her. Item: that he had refused to convert the second bathroom into a shower room. Item: that he had bought a rhododendron of a sort she particularly disliked and deliberately planted it in full view of the drawing-room window at Woodlawn. (Can Chrissie be right to recall that it was a rhododendron called Judas Maccabaeus? Surely not?) Item: that at school aged thirteen Joe had missed six weeks pretending to have meningitis, though everybody knew he wasn't really ill. Item: that for eight years, during the war and after the war, Bessie had hardly been out of an evening, nor had she in the whole of her life owned more than two evening dresses. (*So fucking what?* yells Chrissie's voice inside her head. *So fucking what? Who wants a fucking evening dress?*) Item: that Bessie had never been out of England until 1954, whereas lucky Joe had been all over Europe with the army. Item: that on their last holiday in Greece the hotel hadn't provided proper puddings, only fruit, and not very good fruit at that. Item: that Joe had always asked her to endorse her state pension of £68 a month and had paid it direct into her housekeeping bank account without letting her touch it. Item: that he had made her cash her Granny Bonds. Item: that she was expected to survive on half of his pension, whereas if he'd outlived her he'd have got the lot. Was she, as a woman, worth only half a man?

These accusations infuriated Chrissie, though occasionally it did cross her mind that Bessie was talking not like an unreconstructed housewife but like an avant-garde feminist. And although Bessie muddled the chronology and gravity of her complaints, they did not qualify as madness. The charges were clear, and real, and some of them may have had substance. Maybe Joe, in later years, had begun to take an oblique revenge. But if he had, who could have blamed him? And how could one feel sympathy for a woman who spoke with such venom of so kind a husband? Better if she had been mad, for one can forgive the mad. *Forbid me not to weep, he was my father.* A line of blank verse from a forgotten play goes through Chrissie's head like a dirge as she listens to her mother's undying rancour. *Forbid me not to weep, he was my father.*

No, the state of widowhood had not brought much grace or relief to Bessie Barron's bitter spirit. Chrissie, staring then at the flickering fire and the flickering screen, and now at the washbowl streaked with the red spittle which indicates the need for yet another trip to the dental hygienist, remembers her father's last remarks to her as he lay dying. 'Now, Chrissie,' he had said, a lifetime's regret in his voice, his pale blue bloodshot eyes watering with the sadness and waste and failure of it all, 'now, my pet, you must watch out for your mother when

248

I'm gone. Don't let her devour you. She'll try to, you know. Don't depend on Robert. He won't help. She'll stick with you. I'm afraid she's not the sweetheart that she used to be.'

Had Bessie ever been sweet, in those long-ago years before she married Joe and bore him two children? Again and again, Chrissie has asked herself this question. 'She's not the sweetheart that she used to be.' Whenever she thinks of these words, Chrissie feels her own eyes fill with tears.

Bessie, by the fire, had talked herself out, and fallen asleep, in the deep armchair, her thickened legs and dropsical ankles stuck out before her like a doll's, her too-short skirt riding up over her protruding belly to reveal petticoat and knicker. She had snored, gently and evenly.

There had been many such evenings.

Had Chrissie married Donald Sinclair to get away from Bessie, as she had married Nick Gaulden? If so, the plan hadn't quite worked.

Chrissie would willingly have undone her very self in order to undo these wrongs, this pain. Better not to be, better never to have been born, as the ancients said. Not to be born is best. Better the rock, the mineral, the cavern. A curse on the bedrock and coalface of Hammervale and all that came out of it. Many and many a time Chrissie has wished herself unborn or dead. The pain of her mother's life and of her own continued living appals her. She is old now, and she should have reached a calm shore. But the tide frets and frets, and the tears do not dry. She perishes in the torment of the rocky saltwater shallows, she scrapes and drifts and bleeds.

It is time for Chrissie to go to bed and to enter the world of nightmare, where Nick Gaulden, ever-loving traitor, burns to death. Let her sleep. She is exhausted. She has made great efforts. But she has not tried hard enough.

Her last night thoughts are of Nick's eldest daughter, Faro. If Chrissie knew how to pray, she would pray for Faro's survival and for Faro's happiness. Although she has no faith, and does not know how to pray, she prays for Faro. Maybe prayer will invent itself and its own future.

⊙πℕ⊙

Faro, ignorant of prayer, is once more dully tethered to the telephone, talking to Seb about Dr Hawthorn, gene pools and the Cook Islands. He is trying to pin her down to another meeting, and she is trying to avoid one. She is straining at the leash, as usual. Seb is her clog and her dependant and she is sick to death of him. He has gone dead, like a spent match, like grey coke, like clinker. He is a dead weight, pulling at her like an old sick dog. And he's only twenty-nine. But Faro is strong enough for two. She'll drag him along a bit longer.

She's always saying this kind of thing to herself.

Faro has seen Sebastian a couple of times since her return from the Cudworth meeting in Breaseborough, and both occasions have been even more draining than usual. She has decided there is something seriously wrong with Seb. He is wasting away. It is true that most people would appear thin in comparison with that solid gathering in the Wesleyan chapel hall, but Seb's thinness is becoming more and more unhealthy. His skin has taken on a pallid, parchment-like, unnatural texture, a mummified dryness, as though he has been living underground. And indeed he does not go out much in daylight. He prefers the dark. Faro turns naturally to the light, but he prefers the dark. It was a big mistake, getting involved with him in the first place. On the first post-Breaseborough evening she'd gone round to his place and tried to jolly him along, with jokes and stories and a Chinese stir-fry and a bottle of Valpolicella. She'd poured out her energy, but he'd hardly flickered. On the second evening, she'd gone for neutral territory, and that frightful gloomy cavernous smoky pub in Holborn that he favoured. She'd had a couple of drinks and a packet of crispy-bacon-flavoured snacklets, and then she'd run

250

away to the Central Line, saying she'd got to write her 'Pandora's Box' entry for the mag. Which was true, so why did he make her sound as though she were lying?

Now, on the phone, she is doing her best to resist his machinations. His technique is serpentine. Every time she is about to ring off, he introduces another issue to which she is forced or sometimes even tempted to respond, for Sebastian is not a man without interest, or she wouldn't be talking to him at all, would she? For the moment, she has the initiative. She is telling him about Dr Hawthorn's mitochondrial-based theories about migrations in the South Seas, which she has just been looking up on the Internet. Dr Hawthorn's web site carries a high-minded protest about the DNA pirates who are colonizing the remoter parts of the world by buying up the gene pools of isolated tribes for the purpose of commercial experiment and exploitation. Dr Hawthorn's web site argues that this is unethical. A man should not be allowed to sell his kidneys or his DNA, whatever the going price. Dr Hawthorn claims his own interests are purely scientific, not commercial. What does Seb think?

Nobody, thinks Faro, though she does not say so, would wish to buy the Cudworth-Bawtry genes. Who would wish to purchase inertia, ill-humour and a tendency to run stout in early middle age? With extra chins and jowls and swollen ankles?

Seb is not interested in the Cook Islands. They are too exotic and too far away for him. He hears her out, and then strikes up his own subject. He too has been on the Internet, and he wants to tell Faro about *Biston betularia*, the Manchester moth, aka the peppered moth. It's the kind of thing that ought to grab her. She can write a piece about it, he says. Seb says there is some new stuff on the net about this famous moth. According to a local Linnaean Society up north, it is behaving in a peculiar manner. Its population, which was thought to have been decreasing as a result of the Clean Air Acts, is showing a sudden and unexplained upsurge. It is fluttering and flourishing all over Hammervale. Yes, Hammervale, Seb assures her. She can look it up for herself if she wants. Hammervale is specifically mentioned. And so is Breaseborough. Not many items on the net mention Breaseborough, but this one does.

Damnit, this is, unfortunately, quite interesting. Seb is a wily chap. Has he made all this up? Has he trapped the moth in his death-jar and stuck it with a pin solely in order to trap her and stifle her and stab her?

Seb does not seem to have grasped the evolutionary point about the Manchester moth. He seems to think it grew visibly darker during the nineteenth century, as the soot of the Industrial Revolution poured from the chimneys and furnaces of Manchester and Preston and Liverpool and Leeds, as filth silted the canals and blackened the vegetation.

'Of course it didn't grow darker,' protests Faro, rising to the bait. After all, this is a subject about which she really does know something. 'It's just that the darker ones survived amidst the muck and the paler ones shone out like beacons and got eaten by pigeons. It's a classic illustration of the survival of the fittest.'

'It grew darker,' insists Seb, with that querulous edge of righteous mocking pedantry which pricks her so sharply. 'It was a Lamarckian moth. It willed its own darkness. It acquired several shades of darkness. It clung on by willing its own darkness.'

The man's barking mad, thinks Faro. She can see a vision of the peppered moth. She had written about it lovingly in her thesis. She sees its dusky wings open against the blackened bark of a city tree. A pollarded, peeling, shabby, robust city tree. Faro can see a plane tree from her own first-floor window. Does a Shepherd's Bush moth nestle invisibly camouflaged in its crevices even now? A W12 moth, right here in her own artisanal terraced overpriced turn-of-the-century jerry-built cul-de-sac? Oh, to get out and stand by a tree, a living tree, instead of standing here trapped on the end of this fucking telephone line talking to a fucking manipulative sadistic leech!

Seb tries to keep the moth-plot going, but Faro knows she will have to break the current now, or she will either go mad or agree to let him come to supper tomorrow.

'Oh Jesus!' cries Faro suddenly, with excessive violence. 'There's the bell! Sorry, Seb, got to go, it must be Tessa, she said she might pop round.'

Seb knows she is lying, but what can he do? 'Speak to you soon,' yells Faro, and rams the phone down hard on its plastic cradle. She is breathing fast. It is hard work, ending a phone call.

She goes to the door, and opens it, as though pretending even to herself that Tessa is about to call. Of course there is no Tessa. Tessa is touring Scandinavia with Opera East, singing in the chorus of *Peter Grimes*. The sight of the empty corridor is reassuring to Faro. She goes back into her flat and pours herself a glass of wine. Shall she boil up some spaghetti? Shall she watch TV? Shall she check her e-mail? Shall she check up on *Biston betularia* on the Internet? Shall she ring Chrissie? Shall she ring her friend Cath? Shall she try yet again to contact Steve Nieman at the Earth Project?

She really needs to speak to Steve Nieman about his skeleton discovery. She ought to be getting on with her *Prometheus* article about Cotterhall Man, but her editor won't like it unless she's got the human angle. Anyway, she's interested in the human angle. She wants to speak to Steve. She's got a Northam number for him, and she's left several messages on his answering machine, but he hasn't responded. Maybe he doesn't want to speak to her. Maybe he thinks she's a meddling journalist. Maybe she is a meddling journalist.

She puts on the spaghetti water and eats a sour grape. Maybe Steve Nieman will know the latest about the peppered moth. Maybe Seb is speaking the truth, and Hammervale is swarming with them. Maybe they are settling even now on Auntie Dora's window ledges and drying their wings on Great-Grandma Bawtry's blackened tombstone. Faro had once visited this tombstone, and had stared at it solemnly for about a minute and a half. It had not yielded up any secrets. How stupid she had been, not to spend more time up there after the Cudworth gene convention. She was too impatient. She hadn't been able to wait to get into her car and drive away, as far as she could, down south, down the motorway, down any old motorway, away from it all.

Faro drains her spaghetti so vigorously that the hot floury water splashes onto her wrist, and snakes of pasta leap out of the colander and into the sink. She puts some butter on the spaghetti, and some Parmesan, and some raw garlic, and sits down to enjoy this modest feast. When she is halfway through it, the phone rings. Will it be Seb again? Shall she let it ring? No, she cannot let it ring. She will have to risk Seb. Her curiosity and her optimism, at this early-evening hour, are too great. It may be something wonderful. She may have won the lottery, or the Nobel Prize, or two free tickets to see the Bother Boys at the Rialto in Northam.

The phone call is from Northam, but it is not offering her the Bother Boys. It is Steve Nieman, returning her call.

Faro, once more, is driving up the M1 to Northam, where she has a date with Steve Nieman. She is looking forward to it. He seems eager to tell her all about his great discovery. Faro and Steve had talked for an hour on the phone, about the cave, about the Earth Project, about English Heritage and lottery money and the millennium, about the Cudworths and the Bawtrys and Dr Hawthorn, about Auntie Dora and Steve Nieman's Grandma Levy and the freakish behaviour of the Hammervale peppered moth. Steve's mind is quick and his jokes engaging. He is full of energy. He makes the spirits rise. They had laughed a lot. Faro knows she will like Steve Nieman.

And Steve Nieman, she can tell at the first glance, is a like-able chap. He is waiting for her in the bar of the city-centre hotel into which she has booked herself. She has checked herself in, overcome the irritation of finding the boasted hotel car park permanently full, found a municipal park, unpacked, and taken herself down in the lift to keep her appointment with the Howard Carter of Hammervale. And there he is. There is no mistaking Steve Nieman in this businessman décor. Nobody else could be he. Like Faro herself, he is endowed with a lot of curly hair. It is lighter in colour than hers, a rich brown with a bronzed reddish tinge, but it is as thickly sprouting. He wears jeans and trainers and an open-necked blue-checked shirt over a washing-machine-bruised T-shirt. He is an outdoor, casual, honest-Injun kind of young man, some-where in his early thirties, and deeply tanned by the South Yorkshire sun. He wears a golden bracelet on one bony wrist and a small earring in one ear.

'Hi!' says Steve, bounding at her with outstretched hand. 'You must be Faro! I'm Steve. Glad to meet you.'

Steve is radiant with good will and welcome. His hand-shake is friendly and firm, and his skin, unlike Sebastian's, is warm and vibrant. His smile is open. Faro smiles back. They stand there, looking at one another. Animal magnetism flick-ers back and forth between them. Faro had known he would look like this, and she knows he is as pleased as she is with what he sees. She is proud of her persistence. She had gone on ringing this man until he rang her back. Good for her.

They settle down to half a pint while they plan their campaign. Steve suggests they go and have a meal—does she like Indian? There's a famous vegetarian Indian up Broom Street, if she likes that kind of thing—and he'll tell her all about it. Then, the next day, they'll go to see Cotterhall Man in his glass coffin—Steve has made an appointment, they will be expected—and later in the morning he'll take her to see the Earth Project and the cave. What about that?

Faro sips her Murphy's and says that it sounds just great.

She is suffused with happiness. What fun, says Faro, wiping a little froth of white foam from her upper lip. Vegetarian curry, Cotterhall Man and a cave. What could be more delightful? This is her summer holiday, and she's being paid for it. She sips her black drink, and Steve drains his amber brew. Faro can't stop smiling. One couldn't possibly come to any harm, with a man like Steve Nieman in an Indian vegetarian restaurant in Northam.

Steve is well known in the Star of Asia, and the waiters are sweetly courteous to his attractive guest. They unfold her napkin for her and offer her pickles. The walls glow pink and the lights are dim. Small fish dart around in a large tank. A yellow candle flickers between Steve and Faro in a thickening shroud of wax. The air is full of spices.

Over spinach and eggplant and okra and rice and keema peas and pints of lager, Steve narrates the story of his historic discovery. Although he must have told it all many times before, he enjoys telling it again, and Faro knows she is hearing an uncensored, privileged version. Steve is telling her how it really was. He is doing her that honour. She has his confidence. They are part of the same plot.

Steve reveals himself as a happy-go-lucky amateur. He'd started to take a degree in geology, way back, but hadn't been much interested in the kind of jobs it seemed to be leading to. So he'd gone off for a year or two to work in a kibbutz in Israel, where he'd learned carpentry. He'd enjoyed it. He'd come home and been attached for a while to a craft commune in Camberwell, then had founded a workshop of his own with his then girlfriend. But he'd found the bookkeeping and the VAT an absolute pain, and when his friend Niall had asked him if he was free to come and work on this Hammervale development he'd jumped at it. There'd been plenty of work going up here, and good-quality, interesting work. Building the exhibition centre, the observatory, the field studies centre, the water house. He'd show her some of it tomorrow. It wasn't big money, but it was steady, and the work was useful. Reclamation. Making the place into something. It had been a tip before—a whole series of tips. But she would know about that, because her people were from round here, weren't they?

Sort of, agreed Faro. Her grandparents were Breaseborough people. She had an auntie still living here.

Anyway, said Steve, he'd got to like the area a lot. He'd been here a couple of years now. He wouldn't say he was settled here, but he liked it. He was a bit of a wanderer, but he liked it here.

And what about the skeleton, prompted Faro.

Steve told her about the skeleton. He'd found it by accident. He hadn't been looking for anything. He'd just been scrambling around one evening. Fascinating, it was, the landscape round here—old canals, locks, disused pitheads, quarries. And the limestone cliffs. Sort of undiscovered terrain. They'd been told to keep out of the development area, partly because a landfill company had started work before the Trust put a stop to it and bought them out, and it was supposed to be unsafe. But Steve hadn't been able to resist getting up there to have a look. There was a particularly interesting area called Coddy Holes, just at the bottom of Cotterhall cliff, which had been partly blasted by the landfill—a shame really. The development money had put a stop to all that. It was where the local youth used to go and hang out. They weren't allowed up there anymore, but Steve hadn't been able to resist going up to have a nose around. It was just up the far side of the railway and the canal, to the west, on the escarpment. Did she know where he meant? No? He'd love to show her. Though a lot of it looked very different now—some of it had been replanted. Then it was all just raw, ploughed mud and earth, at the bottom, and above, all the old secret places. And he'd gone climbing. It was a beautiful summer evening, almost exactly a year ago, and you know how it is, he kept meaning to turn back, but then he'd see something interesting just up above him, so he'd gone on scrambling up, through the rocks and the undergrowth and the thorn trees, and eventually he'd seen this sort of gap ahead of him, in the limestone. It looked kind of newish, as though something had collapsed during the blasting. But of course he'd gone on, and when he got nearer, he could see there was an entrance to what looked like a cave. Boy's Own stuff. He had to investigate.

'Of course you did,' agreed Faro.

'Well,' said Steve, 'there was a cave. I kind of fell into it. I thought I'd just put my nose in, but the ground gave way in a pile of loose dirt and scree and stones and stuff, and I skidded right down in there. For a moment I thought I'd fucking had it. I thought, what if I go down a fucking mineshaft? That whole area is undermined, you know. It would have been my own fault, wouldn't it? But it was OK, it didn't go any further. And there was a cave, a natural cave, quite big enough to stand up in. And there was this chap, lying on a ledge. Pretty well dead, he was. Just bones. But quite a lot of bones. My little landslide had knocked a few bits off him—don't tell anyone I told you that, I think they all know, but we don't mention it. But he still looked pretty well complete. Anyway, there he was, just lying there. Where he'd always been.'

'Wow,' said Faro.

'That's what I thought. Wow. And of course I didn't know who or what he was, did I? He could have been anything. A dead potholer. A murder victim. How on earth was I to know he'd been there for eight thousand years and was about to become a national treasure? Anyway, there he was. Do you know what I did? I said, "Hello." Stupid, wasn't it? But I felt I had to say something.'

Steve grinned, and ran his curry-scented fingers through his thick hair, and appealed to Faro for approval. She granted it.

'Of course you had to say something. Were you frightened?'

'No, I was thrilled. I felt he'd be pleased I'd found him. It was a bit of a miracle, you know. They had been going to blow up the whole ridge. He might have ended up as bone-meal, with all the garbage of South Yorkshire on top of him. Actually, I'm not really sure he likes being in the university either. You'll see what I mean. But perhaps it's better than being mashed up with a lot of old hamburger cartons and pet-food tins. If you had to choose.'

'And how did you get out again?'

'It was easier getting out than in. A bit of a scramble, but nothing too tricky. I'll show you.'

'What an adventure,' said Faro admiringly. 'And how long did it take them to find out who he really was?'

'Oh, months and months. Tests and radiocarbon dating and all that stuff. You know, I'll tell you something. I nearly didn't tell anyone he was there. I thought there might be trouble. I mean, I wasn't meant to be up there at all. And I realized I shouldn't have touched him.'

'*Did* you touch him?'

Steve looked guilty. 'Yes, I did. I—I sort of patted his head. And it sort of fell sideways.'

Faro choked into her lager. Yes, she would have another pint, why not, well perhaps a half-pint.

'Did it fall *off*?' she then wanted to know.

'Not right off,' said Steve, with winning candour.

Faro found Steve's attitude to his discovery admirable in every way. He seemed so thoroughly human. He spoke of his skeleton not as of a trophy, but as of a fellow human being. This was not unknown amongst the scientists with whom she had professional contact, but most of them, like Dr Hawthorn, were more given to making populist jokes in an effort towards a disarming appearance of humanity. They didn't really care about the dead. There seemed to be a tenderness in Steve Nieman. It was a relief. She liked it. She liked him.

'So what did you do next? Did you report him at once?'

'I didn't know what to do. I knew I'd have to own up, fingerprints, disturbing the landscape, and all that. Anyway, I was beginning to think he might be a bit of a coup after all, and I might as well claim the credit as well as the blame. But I didn't know who to report him *to*. The police? The project manager? My mate Niall? In the end I told Niall, and Niall told Charlie Henderson, and Charlie got on to the police, and the police got on to the forensics, and the forensics got on to the university.'

'And you became a hero.'

'In a manner of speaking. I got a bit of a bollocking from Charlie Henderson and from my mum. But it all blew over. Everyone's quite pleased with me now. I'm careful not to give interviews without telling them, because they don't like that much. And I'm careful what I say.'

'You're giving me an interview,' said Faro.

'You're different,' said innocent Steve, without pausing to think.

'How do you know?' asked Faro, but didn't wait for a reply, because the question had been dangerous, premature and impertinent. 'You realize,' said Faro quickly, 'that he might be my ancestor? If Dr Hawthorn can track back the mitochondria, he might be able to prove it. You might have disinterred the bones of my ancestor.'

'I didn't disinter them,' said Steve. 'I just happened upon them. They were disinterred—well, exposed, really—by a blast of TNT set off by those greedy buggers from Rose & Rose. What a name, for a firm of methane-gas peddlers! Rose & Rose and coming up roses. They've even got a slogan about it for their sites. Cotterhall Man wouldn't have stood much of a chance if they'd been allowed to carry on with their plan for the region. I'm telling you, he'd have been hundreds of feet deep under the impacted refuse of South Yorkshire. It wouldn't have been nice for him at all.'

'Who did you say?' asked Faro.

'Who did I say what? Rose & Rose? You know, well-known vandals and mass poisoners. They've got craters of garbage on both sides of the Pennines. Did you read about that disaster in Kirkdale? Fifty homes evacuated, and one subsided and fell down the hole and was never seen again. The cat went with it. There was a terrible stink. Poor cat.'

'Rose & Rose,' said Faro, picking up her next pint, and nibbling a flake of poppadom. 'Rose & Rose. Oh dear. I think I'm related to them too. In fact, I know I am. How odd. How embarrassing.'

'How come?' asked Steve.

Faro tried to explain. Victor Rose, founder of the Rose & Rose family business, was her father's cousin, son of her paternal grandfather's older brother, if she'd got the generations right. She'd never really known him, though she'd met him once or twice at family events—a wedding, an anniversary. And she'd met his son Dennis Rose quite recently, last autumn, at her own father's funeral. Victor hadn't been there, as far as she had been able to see, but she and Dennis had had quite a long talk about something stupid—the superiority of the Honda to the Toyota, Japanese takeover bids, that kind of crap. They hadn't got on to Hammervale and landfill. Though she had known that Rose & Rose were into waste management. Bit of a coincidence, wasn't it, if she was related both to Cotterhall Man and to Rose & Rose? Made her a bit of a missing link, didn't it?

'Not really,' said Steve. 'We're all descended from Eve. Or Lucy, as we now seem to prefer to call her.'

Faro could tell he was trying to make her feel better, and that he didn't think much of Rose & Rose, although he didn't want to offend against kinship by insulting her cousins. She said that she didn't think much of them herself, and that he could be as rude about them as he liked. Had they really got such a bad reputation?

'I don't know,' said Steve. 'They've got a bad name round here, but that's largely because people don't want landfill on their own doorstep, do they? And there are stories. I think they struck some kind of a deal with the council. They've started a new tip over by Denvers Main. There was supposed to be something fishy about the sale of that land, but I didn't follow it.'

'You know,' said Faro, 'they say that there are only three hundred thousand human generations between us and our common ancestor. That if I held hands with my mother, and she with hers, and so on and so on, the line would stretch only from London to Northam before we were linking hands with the common ancestor of ourselves and the chimpanzee.'

'How ever do they prove that?'

'They don't. It's just the sort of illustration that popular science goes in for these days. It may be true. It probably is. It's like that image of crowding all the population of the world onto the Isle of Man. My mag loves that kind of thing. Five million years' time span, or something like that. I'm not very good at figures. And it's only eight thousand years back to your skeleton. You'd be holding hands with him well this side of Potters Bar.'

'Well,' said Steve, 'that means you and I are next of kin.'

Faro smiled. 'That's quite nice, really,' she said.

And she and Steve wandered back together to Faro's hotel, through the rebuilt streets of Northam, streets which had been bombed back to brickwork and earth during World War Two. Faro's grandmother Bessie had been evacuated from Northam to Pennington in rural Derbyshire, but Faro had never been to Pennington, though Grandma had sometimes spoken to her of the clever boys of 5B. Steve and Faro were far too young to remember the craters of war, the flapping wallpaper and suspended fireplaces and the valiant blossoming of buddleia and willowherb and such plants as love the rubble of masonry. They did not see the older archaeology of Northam: they saw only the postwar layers of the bold and brutal sixties, the nervous eclectic seventies, the postmodern eighties, the cottage-châteaux-supermarkets of the nineties.

They were children of the present. They strolled through the warm night.

'Have a drink,' said Faro.

And they sat in the executive bar, and swapped family stories, as Faro had swapped family stories with Peter Cudworth. Faro told Steve of the arrival of the Gauldens in England in the 1930s, and about Eva Gaulden's struggle to adapt and make ends meet. Steve told Faro that his own family had emigrated from Eastern Europe during the 1880s, and were, unlike the Gauldens, 'wholly Jewish'—'whatever that might mean'.

'One thing's for sure,' said Faro, 'it's a damn sight easier to get back to Breaseborough than to work out where all those Gauldens came from. Though there's not much of a record on either side.'

'Everyone seems to be into their ancestors these days,' said Steve. 'Do you think it's a millennial thing? Have you ever been to any of the death camps?'

Faro shook her head.

'No. Have you?'

'No. I wouldn't even go to the Holocaust Museum in Jerusalem. Couldn't face it. It's all on the Internet now, you know. They're trying to retrieve every man, woman and child. Every tooth and every bone and every golden ring.'

'Bit bloody late, isn't it?' said Faro. 'What good will it do anyone? They're all bloody dead, aren't they?'

'People seem to need to know,' said Steve sententiously, and then laughed suddenly. 'You know, I got them in a terrible tizzy one Passover, when Great-Granny Charles from Riga was going on and on about how she didn't know how old she was and had never seen her own birth certificate and blah blah blah till you could die. She was as deaf as a post, one of those little dried-up old granny types, you know, like a fossil, all bony, dressed in black, you know the sort, but as strong as a whippet, and all her own teeth in her head. Imagine that, at ninety-two, and never heard of fluoride. And I said, why didn't she get herself radiocarbon dated. *She* didn't hear what I said, of course, she never heard anything and never listened to anyone, but everyone else did. My ma was furious. Outrage, scandal. And my brother picked up on it and kept yelling it at Granny until she got it too, and then wow was I in the doghouse. I still can't see why they took it so badly. I mean, if you want to know, why don't you find out? But they didn't want to know. And they thought I was being cheeky. Me, cheeky? Like they kept saying, next year in Jerusalem. And when I asked, why didn't they go next year to Jerusalem, they'd got plenty of money, why not just buy a ticket and go, they didn't go for that either. *I* was the only one that went to Jerusalem. They didn't like that either. They didn't approve of the kibbutzim. Too left-wing for them. Too outdoor and too left-wing.'

'And why did you go to Israel?'

'Somebody had to,' said Steve, without flippancy.

Faro stared at him, but he was looking down at the table.

'Your great-granny must be dead now,' volunteered Faro.

'Long dead. And both my grannies too. I'd have more sense now. I wouldn't dare try to stir it up like that. I was only a boy. What about you? You said your father's mother was still alive? What about the other one?'

'Oh, my Breaseborough granny died quite a while ago. About eight or nine years ago. One day I'll tell you about the strange death of Grandma Barron.'

'Tell me now,' said Steve.

'No, I'm too tired, I wouldn't do it justice. I'll tell you another time.'

'OK, that's a deal,' said Steve, and took the hint, and took his leave. They parted, in the hotel foyer, with much good will. There would be another time. They had a joint project. They would meet in the morning. They had enjoyed one another's company, and had left time in which to say unsaid things. It is not often one can feel so pleased with an evening, reflected

Faro, as she brushed her teeth and slapped her face with moisturizer. The dead could sleep quietly in their resting places tonight, and she could sleep quietly in her own weirdly wedge-shaped executive bed after watching a bit of late-night TV. No dreams of hell tonight, no dreams of burials or burnings. Steve Nieman was an aboveground, aboveboard chap. He was a chap who knew when to say hello and when to say good-bye. She liked him. Sweet dreams.

Dora Bawtry does not know that her great-niece Faro is back again in South Yorkshire, fifteen miles along the valley. Dora's dreams have not been good. Dora has not been feeling too well of late. Dora has not been feeling well since the day of the chapel meeting and the DNA swab. Her legs seem more swollen than ever, and she finds it harder and harder to get up the steep, short and narrow staircase. Sometimes she thinks she might spend the night downstairs in the armchair. But she knows that would be the beginning of the end. There is nothing wrong with her chest, she tells herself—she does not wheeze as her mother and father had wheezed. But she is short of breath and her legs don't work too well. She has no unmarried daughter to wait on her, though she has a younger neighbour who will shop for her and get her the heavier items—cat food, bottled drinks, washing powder. Some of her friends have died, some have moved away, some have turned peculiar. Some, though still living near by, are too far to visit easily. She gave up her car years ago, and although public transport is not bad she finds it hard to get on and off the buses. What will happen when she cannot get up that staircase?

As Faro and Steve Nieman are discussing methane gas and landfill, Dora is putting herself to bed. And when she is in bed and sleeping, she dreams a dream. She is a great dreamer, though you might not think it from looking at her stolid inexpressive countenance and her thick ankles. Her days are uneventful, but her nights are not.

Now, in old age, her dreams frequently feature bones, skulls and mortality. Any little incident—and she is a great one for tracking her dreams back to daytime incidents—seems able to set her off. A shining round knuckle bone at the butcher's, silver-blue and gleaming with polished gristle in its socket, can spark a nightmare of bony clubs and truncheons. A television news story about an exhumed Red Indian returned from Brompton graveyard to the Black Hills of Dakota can fill the screen of her sleep with scalps and campfires and herds of bison and memories of silent movies long ago. A trailer for a four-part television series featuring an archaeological dig prompts a conviction that she is being buried alive: she wakes struggling with her forty-year-old scratchy leaking eiderdown.

Dora has never understood why her niece Chrissie and Chrissie's new husband Donald are so keen on old bones, and she thinks little of her elderly neighbour in Ardwick Street who has enrolled in a local-history class and spends happy days on coach trips to visit prehistoric and Roman sites in Doncaster and Rotherham and Northam. Dora has nightmares enough about deaths and burials without, as she puts it, going looking for them.

She is stoic about these nightly visitations. She is getting old, and will die soon. Naturally the prospect worries her. She is bound to have bad dreams.

Her sister Bessie had got off lightly, in death. Sometimes Dora thinks this was not fair. Bessie had had all the luck.

Her dream of the Cotterhall skull is not therefore unexpected, though it is peculiarly distinct and memorable. Nor, though it is profoundly disturbing, is it wholly horrifying.

Dora dreams that she is a little girl again, taking her father his lunch at the works. This she was allowed to do, in the school holidays, as a treat. Down at the works was the flaming fiery furnace known as the Destructor, into which Pa Bawtry would occasionally be asked to chuck unwanted puppies and kittens, the waste product of the animal population of Brease-borough. The Destructor, ceremonially opened in 1902 (Pa Bawtry had attended the dinner), was, Dora had later decided, an early sort of recycling machine, but when she was little she had no idea what it was, and the idea of it frightened her. Not even her unimaginative parents had threatened her with the Destructor if she was a naughty girl, but you couldn't help thinking you might just fall in by mistake. If you got too near. Which you didn't.

In her dream, little Dora trots along down Bank Street and Cliff Street past the Primitive Methodists and the Powder Works towards Bednerby, where she meets her father at the gate, clutching a box of potted-meat sandwiches. And in her dream her father asks her what he never asked her in life. He asks her if she would like to see the Destructor. And she says yes. So he leads her through a maze of corridors, along iron walkways, up gridded steps, until he reaches a great oval metal door clasped with huge metal bolts. He asks her, again, if she is sure she wants to look inside, and she says she does. He un-bolts the metal door with his bare hands—and in her dream, she wonders why his hands do not burn and blister—and to-gether he and she look within at the heart of its incandescent flames. And there, within it, ranged, are tiers upon tiers of glowing skulls, a great bonehouse of them, a bonfire, a bone-fire, a pyramid, all glowing, yellow-red-bright, flowering and blazing with brilliant light. They glow but they are not con-sumed. They are immortal, imperishable, in the refining fire. Dora puts her stubby little hand into her father's big dirty hot one, and they stand there, gazing at all the firefolk who have gone before, in that crematorium cavern. And Pa holds her hand, and she is not afraid.

When she wakes, she thinks, yes, that dream came from that glowing skull that Dr Hawthorn kept showing off on his screen, all red and green and electric. And hadn't there been some nasty pictures in the paper recently of some skull museum out in the Far East? What people want to go to museums for to look at that kind of thing, Dora cannot imagine.

But she can still feel that big warm hand of her father's, squeezing hers. And his tobacco smell on the dawn air.

Faro Gaulden and Steve Nieman stand in silence and gaze at Cotterhall Man in his air-conditioned, humidity-controlled casket. He has been reassembled and laid out as found, but there has as yet been no attempt to reproduce in fibreglass the environment of his deathbed. Small bits of him are missing, as Steve had warned Faro: they are undergoing testing in various laboratories up and down the country. But they are small bits, and Faro is impressed by how complete he looks. No wonder Steve had thought he might be a twentieth-century potholer or a suicide or a murder victim. Instead of a 6000 B.C. murder victim, which is what Dr Hawthorn and the archaeologists believe him to have been. The gash in the back of his skull is clearly visible. Faro can feel it. She can feel the blow fall.

Cotterhall Man is a sombre sight. Faro, like all late-twentieth-century products of the Western educational system, has seen many museum bodies. She has seen Australopithecus and Neanderthal remains. She has seen Egyptian mummies and she has seen Magdalenian Girl and Lindow Man. She has worried about them all, every single one of them, but none has touched her as deeply as Cotterhall Man, with his cleft yellow skull, his helpless, hapless grin, his long shanks and his winged pelvis. He is her kinsman. He cannot move, he cannot speak to her. He must lie there and wait for the next probe.

Their reverent attention is broken by Professor Armitage, who bustles in again to make sure they are behaving themselves, and to give Faro yet more data about Northam University's prominent record in palaeontology and allied fields of research. He wants to make sure his department gets a good write-up. And it would be helpful if Miss Gaulden could mention the generous sponsorship of Rose & Rose.

'Who?' asks Faro quite sharply. Steve's sideways glance tells her to say no more, to let Armitage speak.

Professor Armitage describes the helpful collaboration of Rose & Rose, who have been associated for some time with the Earth Project, and who have paid for some of the costs of transportation and preservation of the skeleton. They have also financed a research post to assist with collating data and publicizing the find. Eventually it is hoped that Cotterhall Man will be displayed as an exhibit for the paying public. All this costs money, as Miss Gaulden will appreciate. Rose & Rose have been most supportive.

Faro wants to ask why, but Steve's expression again warns her to say nothing.

Professor Armitage is keen to usher them out and see them off the premises. She can tell that he feels proprietorial about the bones. Faro indicates that she would like to stay a moment or two longer, she wants to make a few notes on her short-hand pad, to do a quick sketch of the remains. Armitage potters over to the corner to stare out of the window, while Faro sketches. He sucks noisily at his teeth to encourage her to get a move on. Faro and Steve stand side by side, and after a couple of minutes, as Faro closes her pad, Steve puts out his hand and gently touches her upper arm. Her downy arm is bare, for it is summer. His fingers touch her skin. It is a gesture of condolence. A current passes between them, and Faro turns to look at him. She gazes at him, with her large dark eyes. He is standing very close to her. He gazes back, and smiles.

Professor Armitage will not let them stay any longer. He rattles his keys. Meekly, Faro and Steve turn towards him, acknowledge him, and allow themselves to be led away. As they wait for the lift, Professor Armitage speaks dismissively about Dr Hawthorn. Clearly the professor thinks molecular biology and genetics are upstarts in comparison with his own time-hallowed pursuits, and clearly he is jealous of their glamour and their funding. He concedes that it will nevertheless be of interest to map the genes of Hammervale and of Britain and of Neolithic Man. He is from over the Pennines, himself. He is Cheshire Man. But who knows what interbreeding may have occurred? He sniggers. This is meant to be a joke, but Faro doesn't get it. She does not much care for Professor Armitage. He is a silly man.

She is glad to get out into the open air with Steve Nieman. The university authorities have given her a parking ticket, but on inspection it doesn't seem to mean very much. At least it isn't a clamp. She screws the ticket up and shoves it into her tote bag.

'Come on, let's get out of here,' says Faro, opening the passenger door for Steve. 'Give me directions. I can never get out of the centre of this city.'

Steve, a nondriver, is not very good at directions, and they go round a featureless multilane stretch of inner ring-road twice before they hit the right exit, but then Faro puts her foot down and they hum along towards Breaseborough and Cotterhall, flying over the motorway and the supertramway and plunging under walkways, bypassing Breaseborough itself, until they reach the valley and the entrance to the Earth Project. Steve knows his way here. Faro would not have recognized it, for all is changed. Miles of spoil and tip have been cleared, the valley has been landscaped, and modern buildings rise and glitter before her. Green glass, sculpted walls of pink-white limestone, yellow wood. She can tell that Steve is proud of it. He wants to show her round his place. This makes her inexplicably happy. Some of the site is not yet open to the public, but Steve has a pass and can take Faro where she pleases. But they have to start, he apologizes, in the Schools Reception Unit, because at the moment that's the only way in.

That's fine with Faro. She doesn't at all mind becoming a schoolgirl and mingling with the small crowds. She examines the models of the valley then and now, and admires the photographs of wildlife, and listens to button-operated birdsong, and gazes into an aquarium of clean Hammer water filled with humble weed and fish. It is innocent and redeemed.

She is also interested in the displays in the next chamber, which commemorate Our Industrial Heritage. Old machinery is displayed in glass cases, and there are one or two hands-on exhibits. Here a press of a button produces the simulated rumbling explosions of quarry blasting, or the hiss of natural gas escaping from a bore hole made by a drilling rig. Lumps of coal and shale and limestone are mounted and described. (Faro does not spend long on these. She is not very good at minerals: she prefers the organic.) The walls are covered with photographs of old Breaseborough, Rotherham, Doncaster, Wath. Charts list the numbers of the dead in various industrial accidents over the past century. Four had died in 1906 during the construction of the Cotterhall viaduct, and seventy-five in the Cadeby Colliery disaster of July 1912. Eight were killed by the powder works explosion in 1924, twenty-one in the fire at the cooling tower in Spotforth in 1928, three in the coal washery plant in 1934. One surface worker was hit by a train at Silverwood in 1956. These are not sum totals. They are merely illustrations. Non-industrial fatalities include the drowning of a wood-turner in the great flood of 1880, and the death of a miner after injuries sustained during the violent confrontations between troops and workers at the Burtin Main pit lockout in 1893.

Faro stares at these grim records, and peers into the sepia past of her great-grandparents, at boys in caps and men in waistcoats with watch chains, at women in aprons and headscarves and girls in Sunday bonnets. Where had all these people come from? They had come in, from the farms, from the villages, from the countryside around. And now it was all over. Production had ceased. The Industrial Revolution had ground to a standstill, here as elsewhere, and the unemployment figures, however massaged, were alarmingly high. For the work had gone, but the people had stayed. Young men, Steve had told her, were hired not even by the day, but by the hour. The girls did better. They worked in supermarkets, in packaging goods for the supermarkets, in homes for the elderly whose greatest pleasure in life had been shopping in those supermarkets.

Faro pauses in front of a controversial panel giving information about deaths in the past from industrial diseases, and the state of litigation in various current claims for compensation for vibration white finger, asbestosis, nystagmus, silicosis, mesothelioma and other occupational hazards. Steve said this panel was not popular with local employers, who thought it put ideas into people's heads, but the council, almost as left-wing as it had been in the days of Old Labour, had stood solid and refused to have it removed. So there the panel stood, recording, as information filtered in, long-delayed deaths both in the neighbourhood and far afield. (The deaths of Joe Barron in Surrey and Ivy Barron in Australia are not yet added to the list, but who knows, one day they may be, for no secrets now are safe from the genealogist and the microbiologist.)

Rose & Rose, says Steve at Faro's elbow, do not like this panel at all.

Faro is getting impatient. She moves quickly through descriptions of coal processing, steel-making and pop bottling, and looks in vain for any sign of Barron Glass or any mention of the mysteries of casein. This may be her heritage, but it seems a long way back to her. She is beginning to think it is time to get out into the open air, and Steve seems to read her mind, though as he leads her out he makes her pause before what he says is his favourite photograph.

'Do look at this one,' he says. 'What about that for a caption?'

Faro stares at a vast enlargement firmly dated 1962. It shows a huge and complicated plant, consisting of cylinders, wheels, boxes, generators, tubing, screws, pipes and hoppers, standing in a warehouse beneath a skylight in a sloping roof. It is a serious outfit on a fairly large scale, though it has an element of Heath Robinson fantasy. To the left of the picture stands a middle-aged man in an overall, with an important wallet in his breast pocket. He is staring intently through his thick serious glasses at a metallic object which he is holding in both hands. This appears to consist of two shield-shaped studded plates with scalloped edges, joined by a thin metal belt, resembling a brassiere fit for a Valkyrie. The gentleman's expression of judicious pride is delightful. The caption reads 'This photograph shows the workshop at Peat Handworth Ltd on Common Road, Breaseborough. What this firm used to manufacture is unknown. Does anyone recognize this gentleman or what he is holding?'

So quickly, says Steve, do we vanish from history. And the automated doors open for them and let them out of the controlled lighting into the sunshine, where they blink like owls at the brightness.

Oh, it is lovely out there, in the fresh air. They wander along the riverbank through the Wild Nature Park, past meadows planted with poppies and cornflowers and daisies, past willow wigwams and water sculptures. Bednerby Main effluent and old landfill had been leaking into canal and river for decades, but it has all been cleaned up now, and the water is clear again, for the first time for more than a century. Reed mace grows in the lagoons of slurry. Fish and heron and a kingfisher have returned, and there is rumour of an otter, though Steve has not seen it. But he has seen daring boys jump thirty feet down off the bridge into the water and come up smiling.

Steve shows her the pond, and the water house that he built with his own hands. She pats its smooth warm yellow wood, and smiles at him. He is right to be proud of it. It is charming. He is proud of the whole project. He is hurt that the national press has been at best indifferent, at worst contemptuous.

They have organic sandwiches in their pockets, for their midday picnic, purchased from the organic restaurant. Steve is a vegetarian.

They wander up the valley, then turn uphill, along a cinder track, towards the escarpment and the cave. Faro asks Steve about the costs of the whole project. They must be colossal. How can it all be financed? Heritage money, lottery money, and some deal with Rose & Rose and the council. And the Wadsworth Trust had put in a million or two. Who were the Wadsworths? They were pit-owners, they used to own a lot of land round here until they were bought out by the National Coal Board when the mines were nationalized. There was a Miss Gertrude Wadsworth, who lived to be a hundred and who left most of her fortune to local environmental causes. They'd been in a bit of a legal battle with other claimants, but the Earth Project had qualified. Neat, really. Full circle. Polluter pays.

Yes, neat, says Faro, who cannot imagine possessing a million pounds, and could not care less. Easy come, easy go, that's Faro. They pass various danger signals decorated with skulls and crossbones, indicating buried cables and high voltages, and climb over a stretch of orange-red plastic netting, and note a dumped armchair, a rusted chassis and nubbles of old coal amongst the cinders. From time to time strange coiling metal snakeheads of wire and cable protrude from the blackened earth and reddened shale, groping upwards from the deserted Nibelung caverns below. They are now in no-man's-land, between the Wild Nature Park and the natural ridge, where as yet there is no new imported topsoil, and nothing much can grow. But they climb, they will soon be through it, and up on the wilderness of the escarpment. The sun beats gently down on Faro, as they ascend the slope, and a lark sings above them. She gropes in her bag for sunglasses, and wishes she had a hat. Grasshoppers chirp, and butterflies flit about them, as they climb towards Coddy Holes and the scrubby white glimmer of the ridge of limestone, towards a low scattering of silver birch and bracken and gorse and hawthorn.

There are wild roses in the hedgerow. The air is clear. As they ascend, the view extends, across the valley, towards the white limestone castle and the town. Along this track Faro's grandfather Joe Barron walked a hundred times and more, with his sisters, with Alice Vestrey, with Reggie Oldroyd, with Bessie Bawtry. If land and air may be reclaimed, may the dead live again?

They have to climb over a stone wall, and scramble up a steep bank towards the fissure of the cave. It is hard going and Faro's sandals are slippery. Steve goes first, and reaches an arm down towards her. She shakes her head: she's afraid of pulling him down with her. She clings to a thorn tree, finds a footing on a limestone ledge, and is up there with him. But the last stretch, leading up to the cave itself, looks impossible. It is almost vertical, and the scree is loose. Faro stands, shades her eyes, looks doubtful.

'Let's have our sandwiches,' suggests Steve.

Faro nods, gratefully. It's not that she's not game, she knows she'd do it on her own, but she doesn't want to get in a mess while Steve is watching. Perhaps she'll feel better after the sandwiches.

They are delicious. Tomato and mozzarella, cheddar and pickle, wholemeal bread. They sit on a ledge, dangling their feet, and munch. They are much favoured by their habitat, for even as they sit there a jewelled lizard suns itself upon a stone below them, and a marbled white butterfly perches upon a tough thistle-like purple hawkweed. A three-spot mutant ladybug settles on Steve's freckled arm, and he lets it wander along through the thicket of his brown hairs. They gaze out over the valley towards the town with its roofs and treetops, and the bowl of land beyond, some of it a dry summery yellow-green, some still rawly raked. Distant Breaseborough no longer announces itself, as it once did from this vantage point, by its spreading pall of smoke. The river glints below them. To their left, where Great-Grandpa Bawtry's Destructor once stood, is the new generator, fuelled, Steve claims, by chicken shit and chicken litter. Some think this is the last word in recycling, some think it is potentially dangerous. Beyond it, but beyond their vision, lie the little landscaped hillocks of Rose & Rose waste, where seagulls hover and squawk. These too generate electricity from municipal solid waste and landfill gas. Coal is no more, and miners mine no more, but this is still a power belt. There is talk of an anaerobic digester, but it hasn't been built yet.

Through his binoculars, Steve identifies a small row of houses, an end of an old terrace, perched perilously on the edge of a bit of property between Rose & Rose's Greendump Site and the beginning of the Earth Project. This, he tells her, is Goosebutt Terrace, and it is coveted and disputed ground. It has a sitting tenant, in the form of a stubborn old woman who won't budge. She can't be bought out, and enjoys making herself difficult. Resistance has given her a new sense of purpose. She's determined to outlive them all.

Steve tells Faro about the survival of the marbled white and the grizzled skipper. She responds with a reprise of the tale of the peppered moth, which she and Steve have already discussed on the phone. Faro by now has made time to check it out on the Internet. It is true, as Seb had said (though she does not mention death's-head Seb Jones to Steve Nieman), that there is a web site claiming that the peppered moth is on the increase in Hammervale. But then there is an awful lot of rubbish on the Internet, and this one may be just a hoax. (Perhaps Seb put it on there himself, just to annoy and entrap her?) Creationists, she tells Steve, hate the peppered moth and all it signifies. They will go to any extremes of denial to reject its humble story. Faro thinks this is short-sighted of the Creationists, for she feels that its humble story may have some hidden hope in it, instead of the ungodly and determinist de-

276

spair which they believe it portends. She keeps meaning to try to write something about this one day, but perhaps it's too big a subject for her.

Steve says he doesn't know much about the peppered moth, and wouldn't know one if he saw one, so she fills him in on its evolutionary importance. He listens more intelligently, less obstructively, than Sebastian.

She is surprised to find how well she remembers the stuff. She tells him about the history of industrial melanism, first suspected in the late nineteenth century when lepidopterists began to observe that the population of the black *carbonaria* form of the moth was on the increase in the north, whereas the paler *typica* form continued to dominate the southern woodland. Faro cannot rise to the eloquence of J. W. Tutt, who in 1896 wrote with such feeling of the vast quantities of noxious smokes, gases, fumes and impurities in the air of our manufacturing cities, of the continual deposit on fences, trees, walls, washing lines full of washing and freshly painted greenhouses. But she gives the gist of it. It is, after all, in her bones. She is her grandmother's granddaughter. And she manages to give a good account of the self-defeating experiment of one eminent lepidopterist, attempting to test the success of the camouflage of the paler *typica* variety in Dorset woodland. He had released several hundred carefully bred specimens of both *carbonaria* and *typica,* and had lost nearly all of the *typica.* Had they been eaten or were they hiding from him? How would he know the difference? How could he tell? He wandered through the trees calling to them, but none of them answered. He retrieved or accounted for nearly one hundred percent of the *carbonaria,* but the pale ones—well, let's not exaggerate, nearly all the pale ones—had simply vanished. Had they been eaten or not? Were they hiding from him in the thick lichens, were they pretending to be the pale mottled bark of the unpolluted oak and birch? The experiment had to be abandoned for lack of verifiable documentation. The moths had escaped from the laboratory, from the experiment, and from man and from bird. Good luck to them. They had flown free from the evolutionary trap. Surely there is some hope there?

Steve likes this story. He wants to know about current theories about habitat preference. Does the white moth sit on white bark by accident or choice? Does the peppered moth seek the dusky shade?

Nobody knows.

Faro Gaulden and Steve Nieman are not well camouflaged, as they perch on their limestone ledge amidst the bracken and hawthorns and small holly bushes, sharing a date-and-walnut slice. Swallows swoop around them, devouring the plankton of the air. Faro and Steve would easily be spotted by an airborne or a terrestrial predator. Steve is wearing jeans and a bright red shirt, she is wearing baggy off-white cotton trousers and a periwinkle-blue tank top. They are visible from afar, as figures in a landscape. But there are no predators. They are safe. Nobody is trying to eat them. Nobody is trying to kill them but death itself. But death is greedy, and death is persistent. Death is not vanquished yet.

A hawk flutters over them, as, fortified, they climb the last stretch to the cave mouth. Shall they dare to enter? Faro had barked her knee on a stone and it is bleeding slightly. Also her legs are nettled. Does she want to turn back? No, she has got this far, and now she wants to see the ancestral ledge. This time Steve has to help her. He pulls her up and together they slither down again over the brink into the darker cavern. Will there be a landslide, will they be entombed together? No, of course not. The cave is not deep, and the sliding pebbles settle. They sit together, on the subterranean shelf where Cotterhall Man had lain unobserved and alone for so long. Faro licks her finger and wipes away the drying blood from her knee wound. Steve takes her hand and gently and solemnly licks the blood from her finger. He kisses her fingers, one by one. He holds her hand in his. Steve is not the simple man he seems. He kneels down, and he kisses her wounded knee.

⊙

Faro has so far forgotten to tell Steve the story of the strange death of Grandma Barron, as she had promised. She has been in no hurry to tell it, for she and Steve have time before them, all the time in the world. She will remember it as they climb back down the hill to her car, and treat him to a version of it. Faro is at best an unreliable narrator, so it might be wiser to follow Chrissie's account. After all, Chrissie was there at the end.

Time had run out for Bessie Barron in an unexpected manner. Her bitter widowhood, which had been a sore trial to her daughter Chrissie as well as to herself, had seemed set to prolong itself into an unendurable and lengthy afterlife. Bessie would ring her daughter of an evening and say, 'I wish I were dead, but what's going to kill me?' These were not happy conversations for Chrissie. Hypochondria had not served Bessie well. She had cried wolf all her life, but when she needed the wolf, the wolf would not come for her. She was suffering from various new but nowhere near fatal symptoms, which she described with relish. A cataract was forming, and she had developed old person's diabetes, but there were pills and pellets and capsules for everything these days. Anti-depressants, sleeping pills, diuretics, beta-blockers. She lived on a cocktail of drugs. But, unlike a cocktail-cocktail, it didn't seem to cheer her up. Chrissie would think of Nick Gaulden, who at that point was still alive, though seriously committed to drinking himself to death before the age of sixty, and wonder if he had not chosen the better path. At least Nick had known joy.

In the end, Chrissie had cracked, and had offered to take her mother on a cruise. She didn't offer to take her round the world, as Joe Barron was repeatedly said to have repeatedly and falsely promised to do, but she offered to take her across the Atlantic on the *QE2*. And Bessie had been pleased to accept.

Chrissie regretted the offer as soon as she made it, nay before she made it. She felt she had been coerced and worn down. It had been an act of appeasement. Would Bessie's aggressions and invasions be halted by this treat? Chrissie did not for one moment believe that they would be. All would go on as it had done. The enterprise was doomed from the start.

It was not Donald's money that she intended to lavish on her mother. By this stage, she had money of her own. Despite or because of her reckless early marriage and lack of qualifications, Chrissie Gaulden had managed to build up, over the years, a successful career and, eventually, her own business. When Faro started school, Eva Gaulden had found Chrissie a part-time job in the library of a privately owned research institute, a job with flexible hours, well suited to a single mother. The institute had been founded in the 1930s by a rich Middle European immigrant, and Chrissie had spent her first few years cataloguing books and correspondences in languages she did not understand and devising new systems to deal with an eccentric and valuable collection. She had taught herself librarianship and bibliography, and although she had occasionally winced at the irony of finding herself so surrounded by words, she had been grateful for the work and the money. And she was a success. Sir Henry, founding father and well-known philanderer, liked her, and tried to seduce her, but Chrissie had had enough of philanderers and declined to be seduced. Sir Henry did not hold this against her, and continued to take her to the opera when he had a spare ticket. She was promoted, and became assistant director. Her greatest coup was to foresee the electronic age, and to force Sir Henry and his staff into an early familiarity with the word processor, the personal computer and the floppy disk. Chrissie might not have acquired the right A-levels to become a surgeon, and had failed in the last ditch to become an archaeologist, but she worked out for herself the implications of the digital revolution and she made sure the institute was properly wired up. So well had she managed this transition that she was able to smile at the struggles of greater institutions—the British Library, the university presses, even the Home Office—as they made expensive mistakes.

The institute had introduced her to eligible widower Donald Sinclair. She had tried to explain the modern world to him, as he attempted, disastrously and ineptly, to communicate by modern technology with colleagues in Greece, Turkey and Bulgaria. She failed: he was too old to learn new tricks, and could not even send a fax. So she married him.

Marriage had enabled her to retire from the institute, but she retired with a pension, and went off to found a bibliographical consultancy. She retired from this too, but it still made her an income. So Chrissie had plenty of money in the bank with which to finance a transatlantic trip for herself and her widowed mother. In theory, from afar, this seemed such a nice thing to do, and Chrissie managed to feel nice about it at times, as she made the bookings, discussed arrangements with Cunard and her travel agent, and told her neighbours about her plans. It all sounded so pleasant. 'My mother and I are going over to New York—she's always wanted to take a sea voyage, and I thought this would be just right for us.' Yes, they nodded, the travel agent, the newsagent, the butcher, the baker, the gardener, and Mrs Fraser at the Hall. Yes, it would be very nice, they all said. But they didn't know Bessie Bawtry, did they?

Donald, of course, knew better. Gallantly he offered to accompany his wife and his mother-in-law, but Chrissie forbade him. Bessie, she knew, would drive him mad. It was too much to expect of him. So they compromised. Donald would fly out to New York, and spend a day or two with them there, and then they would all fly back together. Donald also insisted on paying for a single-room supplement for Chrissie. At her age, she could not be expected to sleep in the same cabin as her mother. It would not be seemly. Chrissie said she could pay for it herself, but Donald pleaded, and she consented. Donald, whatever Faro said, was not a mean Scot. He was a kind and generous man.

So, all was set for the great adventure. Bessie and Chrissie were to cross in August, sailing from Southampton in calm summer weather. That was the plan. Bessie had been much given to seasickness as a child, on fishing-boat outings at Bridlington or Scarborough, and had managed to vomit hero-ically all the way across the Channel on the Dover-to-Calais ferry on her first trip to France in 1954. Chrissie did not want to hear Bessie boasting about feeling ill for five whole days across the Atlantic, even though Bessie had assured Chrissie that she would not mind being sick at all. It would be well worth the trouble. It would all be part of the fun.

For you, maybe, but what about me? Chrissie had thought grimly.

But even Chrissie's forebodings had lifted a little when she saw the great liner in her Southampton dock. There she was, that great cliff of red, white and black, with her sharply curved ocean-slicing throat-cutting prow, her banked ziggurat of white decks, her triumphant funnel. She was a city of the sea, built to accommodate thousands. Big enough for the pair of them, surely. And Bessie was visibly pleased and excited. Even if everything were to go wrong from now on, at least she was enjoying the moment of embarkation. Her cheeks were un-characteristically pink with pleasure as she handed over her passport for inspection and received information about dining arrangements. The Crystal Bar, the Britannia Grill, the Queen's Grill. This was the life. This was what she had been born for: the Best. She was wearing a pretty, loose and not-too-short Liberty-patterned silk dress and jacket of greens and blues, and her feet looked tolerably comfortable in their beige plastic low-heeled sandals. Chrissie had warned her mother that there might be a lot of standing around. Would Bessie, so sedentary and so inert for so long, be able to take the strain? She *must* wear flat shoes, Chrissie had bossily insisted. Bessie liked being bossed by her daughter in this proper caring manner. She was happy to obey.

Chrissie had had nightmares for weeks and weeks about her mother wandering with swollen feet, lost along endless corridors. About her mother locked in the bathroom, stuck in a lift, stuck in her bath.

But so far all seemed to be going well and according to plan. Donald, the perfect gentleman, saw them on board. He spoke to pursers and bursars and made sure the right baggage arrived in the right rooms. He joked that he might stow away. He admitted to being responsible for the bouquets of flowers that greeted them in each adjoining room. Chrissie felt tearful with gratitude. He was a champion. She did not deserve him, when her mean heart was so full of wrath and fear.

Chrissie went up to the boat deck to wave Donald good-bye, and Bessie insisted on coming too. (Chrissie had hoped that Bessie might tactfully have a sit-down and do some un-packing, but she seemed full of an unnatural energy.) So they stood side by side, mother and daughter, up aloft, as they watched Donald dwindle, diminished, below them. They all waved a lot, and Don disappeared into the Cunard building. A steward with a tray offered them glasses of champagne, and a silver band struck up, plaintively playing 'Keep the Home Fires Burning'. Chrissie sipped at her champagne, and Bessie gulped hers down. (Was that wise?) They stood there together, in the late-afternoon sun, and listened to the band, and the screaming of the gulls, and the ship's blast announcing depar-ture, and they stayed above to watch the shore recede. Dozens of little yachts and dinghies and scooters and hoppers and buzzers filled the Solent and accompanied the great ship as she drew slowly away to sea. There were cheers and waves from strangers. Bessie Barron smiled as though she owned the whole world, as though she were the Queen of the *Queen*. She looked happy, at last.

So far so good, thought Chrissie Sinclair.

But Bessie's benign mood, like the weather, seemed set fair. She was determined to be pleased by everything, even by the monotonous television channel that showed nothing but the bridge of the liner cleaving its way through the unresisting water. Bessie was to find this channel particularly enchanting, and would sit to watch it for ten minutes at a time. Her behaviour, on that first evening at sea, was impeccable. She unpacked, and hung all her new clothes tidily in her closet, and praised the bathroom facilities, and inspected her life-saving vest, and locked her passport and dollar bills and traveller's cheques in the combination-lock safe. She popped round to Chrissie's only once during this procedure, to ask if Chrissie had worked out how to switch off the wardrobe light. She arranged her books and her many varieties of tablets on her bedside table, and played with her television set, and read instructions about mealtimes and formal dress and swimming pools and roulette and guest lecturers in the various brochures and folders scattered around for her perusal. Then she sat on her bed, in happy anticipation, waiting to see what would happen next. Or so Chrissie assumed, for there Chrissie found her, when she tapped on her door and suggested that in half an hour they should go up to the Crystal Bar for a drink.

Bessie thought this was a fine idea. Yes, that would be very nice indeed. Should she change for dinner, she wanted to know, and if so, what should she wear? Chrissie said there was no need to change, and Bessie looked very nice as she was. But if she wanted to, well, of course she could. Chrissie was going to wear her Maxine Quirk dress, but she was changing only because she thought it wasn't quite right to go up to dinner in her travelling trousers.

What a pleasant conversation between mother and daughter.

In Bessie Barron's wardrobe hung one new long never-worn evening dress, and one new short never-worn cocktail dress. Each was waiting eagerly for its first outing.

Bessie decided not to change on that first evening. She deferred the pleasure. But she put on her necklace of heavy gold links, and a little pink lipstick. She looked a most agreeable and presentable old lady as she walked by her daughter's side along the corridor towards the lofty lifts. The size of the lifts and the height of the stairwell pleased her, though she was critical of the portrait of Her Majesty. There was nothing claustrophobic about this vessel. It was as spacious as the *Titanic* and almost as luxurious. On the other hand, there was nothing agoraphobic about it either. You could not get lost here, or stray off course. Your course was set. Bessie knew all about port and starboard, naturally, and could feel superior to those who persisted in muddling them up. The décor, apart from Her Majesty, pleased her, and she caught her own reflection in the many mirrors with satisfaction.

Seated in the Crystal Bar on the upper deck, and nibbling at shiny brown and white and pink nuggets, Bessie surprised Chrissie by ordering a champagne cocktail. Chrissie had been expecting to steer her attention towards the quaintly christened selection of alcohol-free or low-alcohol cocktails—perhaps a Lucky Driver, or a Shirley Temple, or a Virgin Mary? But Bessie went straight for the best. Chrissie, who had already fortified herself in her cabin with a few fingers of whisky, decided to join her, and you could not imagine a more agreeable sight than the two of them sipping their sparkling beverages from dainty sparkling glasses as they sailed along the coast of Cornwall and out towards the open ocean.

Dinner also was a success. Bessie basked in the deference paid towards herself and her daughter, for although she was a republican, she was also a naïve and irredeemable snob, and her daughter's unearned title by her second marriage gave her as much pleasure as her daughter's first marriage to a disrespectful layabout had given her pain. She nodded graciously as the smartly dressed maître d'hôtel led them to their table and at the elegant little Irish waitress who smoothed their napkins for them and offered them varieties of bread and water. She smiled at the suave and conspiratorial wine waiter, adorned with silver chains and spoons and badges of office, and at the supernumerary young Dutchman who seemed to be called upon to fill any unlikely gaps in the flow of attentive service. Bessie settled herself down, and inspected the handsome menu with undisguised anticipation, and wondered, aloud, if she should select the caviar.

Chrissie, whose chair commanded a good view of the dining room, gazed around her with interest and began to relax. Perhaps it was all going to be all right. Even the placing of their table seemed to be in their favour. To Chrissie's left sat a chilly threesome, consisting of a formidably handsome couple in their late thirties, and the squat and elderly mother of one or the other of them: this trio spoke in German, when it spoke at all, and was not likely to attempt to set up any potentially embarrassing relationship. To her right sat an American couple of unassuming and vaguely scholarly aspect, in late middle age, who nodded and smiled in a friendly but noninvasive manner. There was nobody here to cause alarm or to distress. All was orderly, all in its place. Bessie could relax, and so could her anxious and protective daughter. Chrissie, who had once so loved disorder, had come to appreciate the virtues of calm. The accents of Breaseborough would mingle sweetly and unobtrusively here, in this placeless place, in this floating island of the people and the voices of the world.

Over their dinner, Bessie and Chrissie conversed harmlessly about Henry James. Bessie was rereading *The Bostonians,* which she had chosen as a good book to accompany her from the Old World to the New. She was enjoying it, but was not sure if she approved of its sexual politics. (She did not use that phrase, but would have done had she been Faro's age, and that is what she meant.) Chrissie was reading, for the first time, *Manhattan Transfer* by Dos Passos. Mother and daughter spoke of the social penetration of Henry James, and of his ambivalent attitude towards women in the professions—the portrait of the young woman doctor was very good, said Bessie. Bessie said that she had attended a supervision at Downing College in Cambridge in which Dr Leavis had spoken of *The Portrait of a Lady,* and had invited Bessie to give an opinion on the significance of James's use of proper names. Bessie had not read this novel for years. Chrissie said she had never read it, and wasn't it about marrying for money? If you've never read it, you have a treat in store, said Bessie, as she polished off her elaborately constructed little tower of strips of tender green and orange vegetables surmounted by thin warm white slices of delicate breast of fowl.

Were they not a credit to their education, this mother and this daughter, as they sailed across the Atlantic speaking of Henry James?

This good behaviour could not last. But the next day, luckily, Bessie managed to find a harmless outlet for her temperamental need for indignation. She was filled with mild and self-gratifying contempt by the inefficiency of some minor aspects of the lifeboat drill. A confusing message was sent out over the Tannoy, which had to be countermanded and then clarified, and when she and Chrissie reached their designated station on the boat deck, the loudspeaker serving their cluster of life-jacketed and self-consciously giggling passengers did not work at all, and instructions had to be yelled out by the unenhanced human voice, and relayed from group to group amidst the gaming tables and the fruit machines. The fruit machines themselves also attracted a certain censoriousness: how could people waste their time on such pointless activity when so many finer delights were on offer? Bessie had never seen so many gambling devices, nor such a variety of them, in her life. Surely the QE2 had not always pandered to such low instincts? She had expected something more refined. And she gathered that bingo was played, in the afternoons, in one of the inferior lounges.

Oh dear, here we go, thought Chrissie. It wasn't going to be plain sailing after all. Things weren't going to be good enough.

Chrissie had already wondered if she might be able to sneak off one evening and have a flutter at the roulette table. Nick Gaulden, at this point in the chronology shacked up with an unknown woman called Jenny Pargiter, had once been a gambler, and she'd learned the spin of the wheel with him, back in the spinning sixties. Her mother wouldn't approve. Maybe she'd be able to sneak out at night when she was asleep?

But Bessie soon forgot her mood of passing irritation with the declining standards of luxury liners. Shortly after the lifeboat exercise, she discovered the library, with which she pronounced herself well pleased. When she had finished her Henry James, there would be plenty here to feed her reading habit. She made friends with the librarian on duty, and settled into a chair with a pile of new hardback novels. Chrissie took a turn by herself on the sun deck. It was safe to leave her mother in an environment of books, and the librarian must be well accustomed to passengers like Bessie Barron. She would probably be pleased to have such an eager consumer on board. Bessie would certainly boost turnover and productivity. Chrissie, pacing briskly along in the comfortable pink-and-white trainers that her mother deplored, remembered all those library books she had carried back and forth for housebound Bessie in Farnleigh. There had been a trauma about a book which Chrissie herself had dropped while reading surreptitiously in the bath. The red binding had run into the pages and stained them. Chrissie had been feeling guilty about this book for thirty years. She had never owned up to the misdemeanour. For some reason she associated it with the death of her grandmother. Was it associative guilt? Was she guilty of the death of her grandmother? She hadn't liked her all that much, but she hadn't wished her dead, had she? They must buy a postcard to send to Auntie Dora, said Chrissie to herself, as she clocked up her second mile.

The horizon stretched in all directions, empty, glittering, blue. She passed joggers and strollers and idlers, all enjoying the sea air. How could one, why should one be sad or guilty, in such a space? Her spirits sang. Seagulls swooped and screeched. She saw a sparrow sitting boldly in the rigging. Was it an English sparrow? Had it embarked at Southampton, and would it go all the way with them to New York? Its little wings would never carry it home now. It was a freeloader, a migrant, a stateless mid-Atlantic sparrow.

And so the first day passed, in mild and passive pleasure. Chrissie was relieved when her mother declined the opportunity of listening to an afternoon lecture by a retired politician who had latterly made a living by making inflammatory and apocalyptic utterances on television and in the tabloids. Bessie chose instead to sit in a deck chair with her feet up, wrapped in a blanket, snoozing over Henry James. Chrissie had no criticism of that: she snoozed herself for half an hour before leaping up restlessly to pad once more up and down the deck. All this was just fine. She could escape from her mother, yet be back to base in a matter of minutes. It was a hundred times better than sitting cooped up by the fire in Queen's Norton, or yawning to death by the television in Surrey. Why hadn't she been brave enough or generous enough to do this before? Vague fantasies of future cruises arose in Chrissie's imagination: if it really was as easy as this, maybe Don could accept one of those invitations to lecture his way round the isles of Greece, and Mother could go along with them for free as part of the package? Or she could offer herself as a travelling computer consultant in the Computer Learning Centre? She could do just as good a job as the professional on board the QE2. And in this way the recurrent Holiday Problem would be solved, and Mother would have something to look forward to all the year round, for as long as she lived. Chrissie thought she saw a clear blue sky opening in the future, as clear as the sky above her.

There was plenty to do on board. Chrissie read her Dos Passos, and wandered around the boutiques deciding not to buy anything, and wondering whether to have a facial in the Steiner Beauty and Fitness Salon. She watched a game of deck quoits, and inspected an appalling photograph of herself and Bessie, taken at the moment of embarkation. Both of them looked quite mad, grinning falsely, eyes red and manic in the flash, a parody of fun. At least she could trust Bessie not to want one of those. Bessie thought commercial photographs were vulgar.

Chrissie watched her fellow passengers, and eavesdropped with interest. Many were elderly, but there were some young families, and one or two honeymoon couples, and one or two who needed to cross the Atlantic and were too neurotic to fly. There were schoolmistresses on a spree and sixty-year-old wives on wedding anniversary or birthday outings and bridge-playing widows and solitary gentlemen. For some this was a trip of a lifetime, but others, she learned, spent much of their lives afloat. They did the Caribbean, the Pacific, the South China Seas. They even did Alaska and the Arctic. Chrissie was amazed by the manifestation of global restlessness. Why were so many people on the run? And where did all the money come from? From shrewd investments, from retirement income and personal pension plans, from golden handshakes and property sales? Did people sell their homes and take to the high seas, like perpetual pilgrims, forever adrift? Did they know what they were seeking, and would they ever find it? Were they happy on the ocean, or did they carry with them their own deep discontent?

The German-speaking trio at the next table seemed discontented. Their demeanour was strange and unnatural. Over dinner on the second night, Chrissie discreetly studied them. Mother, short, iron-grey-haired, unsmiling, dressed in a low-cut solidly manufactured stiff brocade, and adorned with what looked like a string of antique emeralds, ate her way silently through the lavish menu, and drank her way through several glasses of carefully selected wine. Daughter was slim and golden brown, and her skin had the unreal Technicolor gloss of a model or a film star. She wore a white dress and a good deal of what Chrissie hoped was yellow metal costume jewellery. This blond beauty, with her unnaturally flawless complexion and carefully styled hair and elegant figure, also ate her way through the menu, and paid fastidious attention to her choices. So she too one day might be a fat old woman. It seemed unlikely, but it might be so.

The son-in-law looked like a Viking pirate. His dinner jacket confined a broad and straining chest and giant shoulders. His hair was reddish gold, and he had a short gold beard. Despite his girth, he ate less than his womenfolk. Chrissie could not help watching him. She guessed that he was Scandinavian, and he could have stood in for Sigmundur of the Faeroe Islands, after whose thousand-year-old bones Chrissie had once scrabbled in the driving rain. Was he paying for all these langoustines and cheeses and ices, or was it Mother? They were a silent trio. No small talk was exchanged over the dainties. They spoke more to the obsequious, neat-bummed, olive-skinned, plum-waistcoated wine waiter than they spoke to one another. Chrissie, watching them from the corner of her eye, felt indulgent towards her own blue-gowned, chattering mother, who was so visibly enjoying herself and her lamb cutlets and the spectacle of the other diners and the opportunity to wear a long dress. Bessie was chattering about all the things that she wanted to see in New York. Should she go to the lecture on architecture in the Grand Lounge the following morning? She had heard there were good guided tours of the city. She didn't want to miss anything.

Chrissie was already worried about what to do with her mother when they arrived. How would she manage to entertain her for four days without exhausting both of them in the effort? Chrissie was a good walker, but she wasn't as young as she had been, and Bessie did not walk. She had not walked in years. The QE2, with its fourteen lifts and its many decks and corridors, was the perfect answer to Bessie's mobility problem. New York would be a challenge.

The QE2 could cross the Atlantic much quicker than it does. She has deliberately decided to add an extra day and an extra night to her voyage time. Many prefer to travel peacefully rather than to arrive. Many dread their destinations. Cunard has been advised of this, and has slowed her down accordingly.

Bessie's days at sea succeeded one another in agreeable languor. She finished *The Bostonians* and made her way rapidly through a Ruth Rendell and a P. D. James before sinking back into the past with Anthony Trollope. She did not much like the look of *Manhattan Transfer,* and said she would save it up to read on arrival. She made the acquaintance of a retired headmistress, with whom she discussed the comprehensive system, of which neither approved, and the West Riding Education Authority, of which Bessie loyally spoke highly. They also spoke, with restrained competition, of gardening. Bessie established that her garden was the larger, and was content. Bessie also exchanged friendly words with people in passing, and as far as Chrissie could see she did not manage to bore, annoy or embarrass anyone. And she went out of her way to mention from time to time that she was grateful to Chrissie for arranging this treat.

All this was ominously out of character. Chrissie could not help recalling Auntie Dora's description of Grandma Bawtry's death, the death which Bessie had managed to avoid by escaping to Lyme Regis. According to Auntie Dora, the night that Grandma died, she had said to her daughter Dora, 'Thank you, Dora, for all you've done.' Chrissie never knew whether these words had really been spoken, or whether Auntie Dora had invented them on Grandma's behalf. It was impossible to tell, from Dora's narrative style, and there had been no witnesses.

Chrissie Sinclair need not have worried about how to amuse her mother in New York. For Bessie Barron refused to set foot in the New World. On the penultimate night of the crossing, she undressed, and took a bath, and brushed her teeth, and brushed her hair, and applied face cream to the soft folds of her face. She put herself to bed, and sat herself up against a heap of pillows, and reached for her remote control. She switched the television to the channel of grey and white night water that showed the progress of the liner through the ocean. She followed the view of the bridge as it heaved slowly forwards through the sea. New York was within reach, but the *Queen Elizabeth* was in no hurry to arrive there. She was dawdling and losing speed. And Bessie too was beginning to lose speed. She too had no wish to arrive. Ahead lay effort, exhaustion, challenge, confrontation. Here was a quiet, smooth and everlastingly forward motion, into the gunboat greyness of eternity. Bessie Barron did not believe in eternity, but despite her lack of faith in it, it was moving slowly towards her.

She turned down the volume of the repeating track of classical music which accompanied the moving image, and took up her volume of *Washington Square*. She read a few paragraphs of James's slow and stately prose. There had been times when she would have liked to accompany Daisy Miller to Rome, to walk in the Champs Élysées with a refined and admiring American gentleman, to visit Boston, or to see Washington Square. But now that Washington Square was sailing towards her, she no longer wished to go there. The time for wishing was over.

She laid down her book, and gazed once more at the dull grey screen of night. A spatter of raindrops filmed over the glassy lens. Bessie's eyes filmed over into unseeing. The digital minutes and the sea miles clicked silently away, smooth, regular, evenly paced, as they closed in on their destination. What was the point of arrival? Arrival was nothing but disappointment and diminution. Arrival would mean trying to please her daughter by trying to look grateful and trying to be good. The time for all of that was past. Arrival was an unnecessary triviality.

Bessie gazed and gazed at the slow and stately image of movement. The heavy vessel cleaved through the dense and heavy water, and she lay in it, warm in her single bed, as in a capsule, as in a chrysalis, a white grub in her girlish white nightdress. She was content. With or without her knowledge, with or without her consent, with or without her effort, she would sail onwards, away from Breaseborough, away from the smoke and the grime and the slag and the crozzle, away from stifling Dora, away from the hot fevered hours of study, away from the condescension of Gertrude Wadsworth and the rationed contempt of Miss Strachey, away from that snub about Mary Anning and the fossil bones. The long-tried patience of Joe Barron, the courtesy of the tradesmen of Surrey, and the lonely evenings with her supper tray fell away in her wake. No more hesitations in the grocery store, no more waiting for the telephone to ring through an empty house. No more surrender to the drug of ringing her poor long-suffering daughter. There would be no more testing and no more failure. She could lie here forever, suspended, waiting for the next phase. It would come to her. Out there, slowly, it would come to be. The pattern would emerge, if only she could cease from all effort. Watchman, what of the night? Joy cometh in the morning.

It was Chrissie who came in the morning, tapping on the door at nine, surprised that her mother had not yet tapped on hers. For in their soothing shipboard routine, each day, Bessie had woken, rung for the early-morning tea on which she had insisted, then had taken her shower, dressed and knocked on Chrissie's door at a quarter to nine to accompany her to breakfast. But this morning, no knock had summoned Chrissie, nor was there any response when Chrissie went to bang on Bessie's door. Bessie being dead, there was no answer. Five minutes later, Chrissie tried again. As Bessie was still dead, there was still no answer. Chrissie, alarmed by now, went back to her own cabin and rang her mother's telephone number and, failing to get a reply, rang for the floor steward, who came round with a key. He unlocked the door, with Chrissie at his elbow, and, as he was later to tell his colleagues, he realized at once that the old lady was dead, though he couldn't have said why he was so sure. For Bessie Barron was lying quite restfully, on her back, her eyes politely shut, her head centred on the pillow, for all the world as though she were sleeping. Her book lay open, face down, on the bed, with her reading glasses by it. The television silently played on.

The steward put out a warning hand to forestall Chrissie, to give him time to inspect the corpse more closely. But Chrissie was close behind and not to be forestalled. They both stood there together and looked down at the body of Bessie Barron.

Bessie's skin was pale and dry. Otherwise, there was no change in her. There had been no struggle, no fighting for breath. She looked unworn, unused and younger than in life. How could anybody, let alone Bessie Barron, have slipped away with so little fuss?

Chrissie was never able to remember what she and the steward said to one another. She remembered that she had sat down on the bed, and that the steward had rung the number of the ship's hospital. Then he had offered to go and fetch her a cup of tea and she had said she would rather have coffee. Bessie had died without her last cup of early-morning tea. And the doctor and a paramedic had arrived, and Bessie had been pronounced officially dead. The doctor was very calming, for he was used to this kind of thing, but Chrissie felt that she did not need calming. She was already calm. Soon, she knew, there would be a flurry of activity and anxiety—there would be talk of coffins, certificates, insurance, repatriation of remains. But for the moment everything was very still, as though time had stopped. And Chrissie felt a strange weightlessness, as though the Old Woman of the Sea had been lifted from her shoulders. She breathed the air, and her lungs seemed to fill more deeply. Bessie looked now like a light husk. How could she have weighed so much?

The doctor and the nurse were debating whether to use a stretcher or a wheelchair to take Bessie to the morgue. Would Chrissie like to stay a little while alone with her mother? Chrissie reached out a hand and gently touched Bessie's hand and said no, she would not.

A stretcher, a wheelchair? What did it matter? A wheelchair would be simpler. No, Chrissie didn't mind. Bessie wouldn't have minded, so why should she? Bessie had often said she would be happy to be buried in a bin bag, so she would certainly not have thought a wheelchair irreverent. Telephone calls were made. Coffee was brought. It was understood by all that there was to be no fuss. No wailing, no lying in state. A discreet and veiled departure along the corridor to a service elevator, and so down to the hospital on Six Deck, and into the cooler. These things happened all the time. Sea voyages are the pastime of the elderly, and in the natural way of things the elderly die. There was a well-tried procedure, a fast track for the deceased. Routine took over.

Mrs Barron was to be congratulated, posthumously, on the style of her departure. She had shown excellent manners. She had not choked to death noisily in the restaurant, or suffered a stroke by the fruit machines, or fallen down a stairwell and broken a limb. She had not thrown herself overboard, or drowned in her bath. Such things had happened. Mrs Barron had ceased upon the midnight with no pain. Her passing was to be envied.

Bessie was wheeled away, propped up to look as though she was still alive, and Chrissie was escorted to the telecommunications room to ring home. She rang Donald, who said all the right things and asked all the right questions and said he would fly out at once to meet her at the dock if she wanted him. Was Chrissie all right? Yes, of course she was, she said. She wasn't even shocked. It had all happened too smoothly for shock. Maybe she would feel shocked soon. But so far, no. So far, so good. They would speak again the next day.

Then she rang Robert in Waterford, where it was by now early afternoon. Bessie had managed to choose a good hour as well as a good death. Robert said dryly, 'Good God, what a dirty trick to play on you.' These were his very words. Was Chrissie all right, he also wanted to know. Yes, of course she was, she replied. 'Well, who would have thought it?' was Robert's epitaph upon his mother.

Chrissie was more than all right. She was suffused with an extraordinary sensation of lightness. She sat in her cabin for a while, simply breathing. She had rejected offers of sedatives and tranquillizers. She had no need of pills.

Should she ring Faro? No, she would defer that dangerous pleasure.

Her mother's heavy body, weightless and shrunken in death, vanished from sight as though it had never been, and Chrissie spent the rest of the day in a dream. It was her last day on board on this voyage of deliverance. She inspected the travel-insurance documents, as she had promised Donald that she would, and noted that the cost of repatriation of remains was covered for a sum of up to six thousand dollars. The doctor had said that would be more than adequate. She paced the sun deck and the boat deck. The sparrow was still perched in the rigging. What had Bessie died of? Chrissie did not really want to know. Her heart had stopped, and that was that. After so many illnesses, feigned and real, she had decided to die. No more would she be able to torment others by saying she wished she was dead. She had her wish.

Chrissie packed her mother's clothes and possessions neatly into their suitcases. Her outsize underwear, her tights, her slippers, her blouses, her talcum powder, and a thin paisley dressing-gown which Chrissie had known for more than twenty years. She folded the newly purchased evening dress and the newly purchased cocktail dress back into their shrouds of white tissue paper and laid them to rest. She parcelled up the string of cultured pearls from John Lewis on Oxford Street, the amber brooch which Chrissie had given her one Christmas, the golden chain which had been Grandma Bawtry's, and the large opal ring which Joe had bought her on his visit to Ivy in Australia. The lace-edged handkerchiefs smelled of lavender and eau de Cologne. Chrissie sighed, but not with grief. It was the waste of it and the pity of it. The pity and the waste.

Chrissie thought it would be unseemly to take lunch in the restaurant, so she ate a tuna-and-cucumber sandwich in her cabin. In the afternoon, she slept, and woke from her sleep with a sense of levitation. Her body rose from thinly remembered dreams of childhood and seemed to hover over her bed. She lay there for a while, suspended, staring at the ceiling, wondering how to spend her last evening at sea. She was free, now, to go where she willed. She could drink a Manhattan or a White Lady, she could eat a rare steak or a plateful of fritters, she could visit the Casino or go in search of a gigolo. She could gamble away all her holiday money, or strike up conversations with strangers. She could ring Faro, and tell her the whole story. She could ring Nick Gaulden, and tell him his first mother-in-law was dead. Would this be the right moment to reopen the old wounds?

No, she would not ring Nick Gaulden. Only once more would she ring Nick Gaulden, and this was not to be the occasion. And she decided not to ring Faro. Or not yet. Ringing Faro seemed too easy an option. It had begun to occur to her that Faro might, when the time came, greet her own death with a similar light-headed relief. The dawning notion was a shock to her. Was she already a burden to Faro? How could she tell? Were all mothers a burden to their daughters, as fathers were to their sons? She had made Faro's girlhood a muddle and at times a torment, and would one day soon be blamed for those maternal crimes. Chrissie thought about Faro every day and always. Should she have had more children, to disperse the love and the guilt?

As she disrobed herself from the towelling toga of her siesta, and selected a sober outfit of charcoal grey for her evening's entertainments, Chrissie conjured up her daughter Faro. Faro, Chrissie considered, was doing well. Faro had written a thesis on evolutionary determinism. Faro was young and beautiful. Faro would go far. Faro had no clogs on her feet, no chains round her ankles. She would not stick fast. Would she? The Bawtrys would not claim her. Would they?

Chrissie clasped around her throat a silver necklet, and looked at herself in the mirror. Not bad, for a woman rapidly approaching fifty. Not all that good, but not all that bad.

She wondered whether news of her mother's death had reached the whole of the crew, and whether watchful eyes would follow her. Should she brave a solitary meal at the table at which she and her mother had dined together, or should she chicken out and lie low? Pride drove her on, but discretion held her back. She was undecided. She had in the past boldly and with panache confronted so many embarrassments, so many humiliations. And a dead mother was surely neither an embarrassment nor a humiliation. But what would their waiter and their waitress think if she were to turn up alone at their table? Would they inquire about her mother's absence? Bessie had held forth at them and chatted them up, as was her way, and they had responded politely, as was their job. They would be sure to inquire after her. Chrissie decided she could not face it, and in the next instant despised herself for the decision. She stood, irresolute, appalled by the triviality of her hesitation.

She wandered out, still undecided, and walked. She marched along corridors and up stairwells and down stairwells, discovering quarters she had not known existed—a noisy cafeteria, a bar got up to look like an English pub, a night club threatening a show band. She stopped in one of the unfamiliar bars and ordered herself a drink. It went straight to her head. She ordered another. She paid in dollar bills instead of signing the chit with her cabin number, and took herself, defiantly, to the dining room. Gaulden pride and Yorkshire thrift had conquered. She would not waste a meal she had paid for. Her mother couldn't eat hers, but she wouldn't want Chrissie to miss hers, would she?

So, while Bessie Barron spent her first night on ice, Chrissie Sinclair drank pale pink iced soup from an iced goblet, followed by a large rare steak and a glass of burgundy. Emotion had rendered her ravenous. She needed meat. The waiters did not ask after her mother, so she assumed that they already knew that her mother was dead. The diners at the other tables did not know. None of them spoke to her, though they nodded a polite good evening to her, as usual. It was as well that they had all kept at a discreet distance: receiving condolences over steak and burgundy would have been awkward and inelegant.

Chrissie, loitering over her coffee, read her book. She had finished *Manhattan Transfer,* and was reading or pretending to read a bilingual edition of the poems and translations of Yves Bonnefoy which had unaccountably been presented to or perhaps off-loaded upon the *QE2* library. She had picked the volume up out of curiosity, but clearly providence had placed it there. The French poet, of whom Chrissie had never heard, spoke of the deep light leaping from the dark wood and the cracked earth, and of the lifeless shore beyond all singing. This was the shore that Bessie Barron had reached. *Un inerte rivage au-delà de tout chant.*

Chrissie gazed at the words on the page, and part of her mind read them.

Cracked earth and deep light. Chrissie ate a truffle, and thought of Nick Gaulden. She thought of her mother, sitting by the fire at Queen's Norton, rehearsing her everlasting litany of complaint.

Her father, on his deathbed, had taken to reading poetry. Chrissie had seen the volume of Keats on his bedside table in the hospital. He had gone back, at the end, to the old Breaseborough School favourites he had studied with Miss Heald, and had boasted to Chrissie that he was rereading Conrad's *Heart of Darkness* and *Jane Eyre*—a cheery duet, he had drily observed. But he had long given up his old chant of 'If with all your heart ye truly seek me, ye shall ever surely find me.' Had he found God? Had God found him? Or had he despaired of God?

Chrissie sat long over her coffee, thinking of these things.

At last she stirred herself, as the Irish waitress began to hover. She suffered and survived a small crisis about the tipping of the excessively attentive wine waiter, and then she set out again to prowl the floating but by now almost immobile island. She put her head through the door of the cinema, but rejected the infantile sex comedy on offer. The harp-playing in the Crystal Bar was too refined for her mood, but she sat for a few minutes in the Yacht Club sipping a brandy and soda and watching an unfortunate cabaret vocalist trying to arouse some response from an apathetic audience. She then moved on to the Queen's Grill, where there was dancing, and, as she had rightly guessed, a complement of gigolos of both sexes.

The ageing dancers were a little more lively than the cabaret audience, and willing to be organized into one or two group routines by a fresh-faced young man with a microphone. Grey-haired women linked arms and raised their Pop-Sox-clad knees and put themselves through their paces, old men tripped and turned. Legs bulged over elastic garters, knickers and petticoats flashed, bald heads glittered beneath the coloured lights. This was the dance of death. Chrissie smiled vaguely at the macabre scene and had another brandy, tapped time with her foot and sped them on. When the next quickstep began, a kilted professional approached her solitary table, but she shook her head, and kept her station, and gazed on in admiration as a six-foot dyed-blond Valkyrie in stiletto heels swooped down upon a small, silver-haired, moustached and dapper chap in a tuxedo, and swept him onto the dance floor. She pushed him and shoved him and swung him and pummelled him round. She could have picked him up and thrown him over her shoulder, but she didn't. Chrissie almost fancied taking a turn with this giantess, but did not think she would get the offer.

She was not interested in sex comedies or gigolos. It would have been brave to celebrate her mother's death by bedding down with a stranger in a kilt, but she wasn't up to it. She had lost interest in sex decades ago, when she had lost Nick Gaulden. She had once tried to explain this to a therapist, who had greeted her assertion with disbelief. But the therapist hadn't been to bed with Nick Gaulden, had he? So how could he know what he was talking about?

Midnight found Chrissie Sinclair by the roulette wheel in the Casino, with a pile of five-dollar plastic chips on the green baize in front of her. In the old days, in Italy, she and Nick had bet on their own ages, and had won. They had scooped in their spoils and departed from the table in triumph. Luck had been with them, for they had believed themselves lucky. They had needed the money, and it had come to them. Now she needed it no more, and the numbers of her years were well off the board. What should she bet on? She followed the play. The red and the black, the *pair* and the *impair*. She ventured a chip on a *carré*, and lost it, then ventured another on the red, and won. This was cautious play for reckless Chrissie Barron. Should she risk all on the age of her daughter? Now was the time, for even Faro would soon be too old for the roulette table, and off the map of chance.

Chrissie did not want to bring bad luck to her daughter by losing on her number. Chrissie was filled with superstitious fear about Faro. Would Faro marry, have children? Begin again with the little birthdays at the bottom of the table? Faro had proved cautious so far, with lovers whom Chrissie could not approve. Faro was too cautious, too kind. So far she had wasted a couple of years of her young life on a drunken Irish student, and another three on a temperamental married bookseller old enough to be her father, and nearly as unreliable. Faro, like her father, suffered from the delusion—or was it a delusion?—of thinking herself indispensable and irreplaceable. She found it hard to get rid of spongers and admirers. Faro ought to be more ruthless. Was it Chrissie's fault that Faro played the game she played?

The wheel spun, and Chrissie watched it, and did not venture.

The last time Chrissie had slept with Nick Gaulden had been in New York. They had been divorced for some years, and he had already left Fiona McKnight for Stella Wakefield. Chrissie had encountered him there by chance, as she walked along the south side of Central Park. They had met beneath the great golden angel who leads William Tecumseh Sherman to victory on his golden horse. Nick had materialized like a phantom before her eyes in the neon-lit New York twilight. She had so often seen Nick's double appear and fade and alter before her that she had doubted this apparition, but instead of shedding Nick's gait and features as he approached, this figure had continued intensively to acquire them, and he it was, and there he was, before her on the gravel path. What had he been doing in New York? She could not remember. Why had she herself been there? She could not remember. They had greeted one another and spent the evening drinking disgracefully together, as in the old days of their youth. They had ended up in bed together in the Hotel St Moritz.

She could not remember what had happened during the night. Had he made love to her? He had probably tried and failed. He had been very drunk. And so, to be fair, had she.

Not much of an ending to her grand passion, to her one-and-only passion.

Nick had probably forgotten the whole dreamlike and improbable episode. Had it ever occurred, or had she invented it? Should she ring him, ship-to-shore, and ask him? She hadn't spoken to him for a year. Had she got a number for him? Where was he living, with that woman called Jenny Pargiter, and their two brats? Was he still in Kentish Town? Faro would know. Faro was still in touch with her father.

The wheel spun, and defiant Chrissie placed a pile of five-dollar chips on Faro's number. Lucky Faro, let her win. The ball rattled, and settled, and fell neatly into Faro's slot. Of course it did. She had known it would. She should have gambled her all on Faro.

Chrissie took herself and her winnings to bed at two in the morning. She kept one of the plastic counters, and cashed in the rest. The sin ship had now entered territorial waters, and the tables had closed, but the television was still playing. Had Bessie been watching the image of the ocean even as she crossed the straits between this world and the next? If so, hers had been an easy and a blessed passage. Joe had died fighting for breath.

Chrissie lay in bed and watched the bridge and the water and listened to Schubert, and then flicked channels until she found the channel of the perpetually playing Shakespeare cycle. The Shakespeare lottery, the *Sortes Shakespeareanae*. Would there be some riddling equivocation for her at this dark hour, some joyful or fearful prophecy?

Shakespeare's Antony held the screen, in extremis, at the gates of death, calling upon Eros and the night sky.

> Sometimes we see a cloud that's dragonish,
> A vapour sometimes, like a bear, or lion,
> A towered citadel, a pendent rock,
> A forked mountain or blue promontory
> With trees upon't, that nod unto the world
> And mock our eyes with air. Thou hast seen these signs;
> They are black vesper's pageants.

Chrissie lay on her bed in the luxury of unnatural survival. Her head was spinning as the wheel had spun. Unlike her poor father, she had managed to outlive her mother. Time and space stretched before her. She was free to go where she would, and do what she would, and nothing she did would ever hurt Bessie anymore. She no longer needed to protect her mother from the insults and derision of the world, from hostile strangers, from herself. Her suffering mother could suffer no more. It was over. She could never harm her mother more, in thought, in word or in deed.

> Unarm, Eros; the long day's task is done
> And we must sleep.

Chrissie listened, entranced. It was enough that such words had once been written and had come down through time to her. Her mother had appropriated and imprisoned words and language, and now they were freed for Chrissie. At last she could acknowledge their dominion. Chrissie had for many years been a secret reader. She had resented Bessie's approval of this activity. She could make her peace, now, with the Word.

Chrissie shut her eyes, and listened. Bessie had, in her peculiar way, despised Shakespeare. She had been heard to say that she never wanted to see *King Lear* or *Macbeth* again, thank you, she had had enough worries in her own life without going looking for them. And as for *The Winter's Tale*, why, she could write a better play herself.

Remembering this, Chrissie smiled. And Chrissie fell asleep to Shakespeare, as the liner sailed slowly onwards to the Verrazano Bridge and the Statue of Liberty and the St Moritz Hotel, into which, for old times' sake, she had booked herself and her mother.

⚭

Faro told a spirited version of this story to her new blood-sealed friend Steve Nieman. She related it as she clambered down with him from Coddy Holes towards her blue Toyota.

Faro had heard her mother's version of this tale many times, and this time, as usual, she had not avoided the often reiterated cliché that always accompanied the telling of it. How lucky Grandma Barron had been, to die so peacefully, in her bed, in her sleep, in expectation of a nice holiday! Not many people have it so good. Nothing in her life became her like the leaving of it, said Faro to Steve Nieman, tritely, over a cappuccino in the organic restaurant. Though poor Ma had had a nightmare with the New York immigration authorities and the customs formalities and the coroner and the chapel of rest. One of Grandma Barron's suitcases was never seen again, though luckily it hadn't been the one with the Cudworth jewels in it. Grandma had been flown home at great expense and cremated back in Farnleigh, and scattered under the beech tree at Woodlawn. That's where her Cudworth-Bawtry DNA ended up. Good-bye, Grandma. Faro had been there and had helped to dig her in.

And thus, once more, that complex, unfinished, difficult and unhappy woman was dispatched to her last resting place, simplified beyond recognition. Faro told the story well. She told it better than her mother did. She was able to make it more amusing than her mother could. Faro had been quite fond of her poor old grandma.

The mitochondrial DNA of Bessie Barron lives on in her granddaughter, although Bessie's had cheated the worm and the maggot and the prying needle of Dr Hawthorn.

Faro's DNA swab lies with many other Cudworth swabs in a laboratory. It is simple extract of Faro. But Faro is not a simple person, and she too has been simplified by narration. We do not know much about Faro. Why, at her age, and with her beauty, is she living alone in a flat in Shepherd's Bush? Why, at her age, is she so obsessed by death? Why does she collect lame ducks? Why is she attached to the deadly Sebastian in his dreary Holborn flat? Why is she allowing him to devour her with his sticky secretions?

Faro, driving south, away from Steve Nieman and Steve the Skeleton, is asking herself these very questions, and is not coming up with many answers. It must be her dead father's fault, but she can't work out quite why. She is hoping that Steve will help her to change all that. It is early days yet with Steve, but they have exchanged vows—not lovers' vows, but vows of a sort, vows to speak soon, to meet again, to keep in touch, to touch one another again.

If Faro does not have a daughter, her mitochondrial DNA will perish with her and the chain will be broken. It is already getting late in the biological day. She is in her thirties, and the hours hasten. Does Sebastian's DNA call to her? Is it trying to intertwine its helix with hers? What can it be that he wants of her? He does not seem to want to marry her or even to live with her. He does not want to make an honest woman of her, but he seems to expect her to spend her energy making some kind of an honest or at least a viable man of him. Nothing like a marriage has taken place, and yet, at times, thinking of Seb, Faro feels like a drearily married woman, committed to making do and making the best of a bad lot.

The thought of having a baby with Seb is repulsive to her. His DNA is cold and unperpetuating. And yet he clings and clambers up her as she turns towards the light.

Sebastian Jones is the son of a defrocked clergyman. 'Defrocked' is perhaps too strong a word for the once reverend Jones, but it is the punitive epithet that Sebastian himself favours. Sebastian's father had been seduced by one of his middle-aged widowed parishioners and the resulting scandal had enforced his retirement from his pastoral duties. Sebastian affects to find this story bitterly entertaining and can be witty in the telling of it, but anyone can see that he has been damaged by it. Seb has long been an unbeliever—he can hardly recall the distant tracts of his hymn-singing childhood—but he does not like the treachery implicit in his father's behaviour nor the mockery that it has elicited in the press. The once reverend

Jones had betrayed his wife and his God and his Redeemer for the bosomy twelve-stone henna-haired manageress of a dry-cleaning shop in a small town in Somerset. He had forsaken Mrs Jones and his flock for the plump settee and then for the double bed of a woman with dark red talons of nails with which she had rattled tunes upon the till as he collected his clerical garb. The episode was more ridiculous than heroic. It had turned Sebastian and his brothers very queer.

Sebastian, thinks Faro, could easily have been a clergyman himself. Not a modern, healthy, broad-minded, Thought-for-the-Day clergyman, but a dusty old-fashioned one, haunting damp cloisters and parish registers and dark graveyards. The robes would have suited him well. She is sure that it is his family history that has attracted him to the genre of the Gothic, to cadavers and body parts and body piercing. He is an expert in Horror. Faro knows it is fashionable to be interested in that kind of rubbish, but she hates it, and she thinks that Sebastian's interest oversteps the mark. He takes it all too seriously and does not seem to realize that even for its practitioners it is only a game. Nothing real is real for Sebastian. He lives in a maze of corridors and echoes and reflections. She is the only real thing in his life. Faro doesn't suppose that Seb practises necrophilia, and she wishes he wouldn't write stories about it. Some of his stories have been published in horror magazines, of which there seem to be many. Does Sebastian want to murder Faro and copulate with her corpse? The DNA of a necrophiliac is not promising material. Who would want the black-bat baby of such a creature?

And Sebastian has had the audacity to accuse Faro herself of perverse and morbid longings, of an interest in transplants and cloning and spare body parts. Well, she has to be interested in that kind of thing, it's her job, isn't it? It's science, isn't it? How dare he tell her that her problem is that she wants to live for ever? Faro breathes deeply and indignantly, and expels angry air, as she puts her foot sharply down on the brake to avoid piling into the slowing London-bound motorway traffic ahead. KEEP TWO CHEVRONS APART, instructs the M1, just in time to prevent carnage and crumpled bumpers. No, says Faro to herself, she must be firm. She must peel off his white fingers and prise out his little bindweed roots.

The traffic lurches forward again, and as it does so Faro's mind lurches, and bumps into a recognition. Suddenly, she knows that Seb is ill. He has always looked unhealthy, but over the last two months it has turned into something else. Seb is dying. Faro squeezes her foot down gently, eases forward a few inches, then another few yards, then is brought to a halt again. She had sometimes wondered, but now she thinks she knows. She must have been in denial. She must have known for months.

What is it? Cancer? Consumption? He looks consumptive, but people don't have consumption these days, except in the Third World or inner Manchester. He smokes and has a smoker's cough. It could be his lungs. Or is it his liver? He drinks, though not as much as some of his friends, and not as much as the older Gauldens. Or has he got AIDS? The thought of an HIV-positive Sebastian makes Faro's skin prickle. Surely he would have been gentleman enough to tell her if he were? She starts to try to work out how long it is since she had any kind of risky sex with Sebastian, and realizes that despite the miles of newsprint she has read and indeed written upon the topic she is not quite clear about what constitutes risk. Will semen do it, or does there have to be blood and abrasion, blood and punctures? Anyway, it's irrelevant. The virus can lurk in the body for years, like CJD.

Perhaps Sebastian has got CJD? And if so, is that communicable? Faro hates herself for this selfish train of thought, and tries to keep her eyes on the slow-moving car ahead of her, in which a small spotted dog is bouncing about in frenzied excitement on the back seat. In rabid excitement. Shit, says Faro to herself. Shut up, says Faro to herself. And as she slows

down once more to a standstill, she feels a sickening crunch-
ing shattering thud as the vehicle behind her slams into her
back bumper with considerable force. Faro is thrown forward
and then back again. Shit, shit, shit, says Faro aloud. She shuts
her eyes. She does not want to look into the driving mirror to
see the idiot that has driven into her backside. Is she all right?
Yes, she thinks she's all right, but what about her poor car?

Everything behind her has come to a halt. Pitying glances
are cast towards her from cars creeping slowly past her on the
off-side and the near-side lanes. Faro is in the middle lane, the
worst possible place to break down, or so it seems to her in
the moment of stasis before she pulls herself together to see
what is to be done. Slightly dazed, she starts to unbuckle her
seat belt, but as she does so a face appears at her open car
window, a face distorted with fury, yelling obscenities. 'You
fucking cunt! You fucking woman driver cunt of a cunt!' is
what she hears. 'What the fucking hell do you think you're
doing? When did you pass your fucking test, you prat?'

Keep calm, Faro says to herself. You have witnesses. But
the spotted dog has driven away, still leaping.

A youngish man with short fair hair and a red face made
redder by rage is yelling at her. Faro switches off her car engine and says nothing. She knows this incident is not her fault,
for she had been stationary when this idiot slammed into her,
and although distracted by night thoughts she had been driving with daytime caution. It is his fault. Shall she say so? Shall
she shout back? He is trying to wrench open her car door. She
pushes down the lock button. He seems to be beside himself.
Will nobody come to her rescue? Cars behind are hooting and
honking. Shall she just drive on? Faro looks in her driving mirror and sees a long pile-up behind her. Other cars have
crunched into one another in her wake.

So far she has said nothing to the young man, who goes
on yelling at her like a fiend possessed, his face distorted with
wrath. His language is appalling, and he is accusing her of

crimes unrelated to a driving misdemeanour. Faro is no innocent, but she is shocked. She starts to shut her car window, but he shoves his arm in to stop her. She continues to press the electronic switch, but stops before it traps him. She does not want to be accused of assault.

Thank God, somebody from one of the cars behind them is approaching on foot. Please God, says Faro, shutting her eyes, let it be a reasonable person. And it is a reasonable person. It is a middle-aged Indian, a family man, serious and sober. He takes on the mad shouter. 'Calm down, sir,' he says diplomatically. The young man looks as though he is about to hit the Indian, but the Indian has an air of authority which deters him. 'Switch off your engine, sir, switch off your engine,' says the Indian to the madman. 'Mind your own fucking business!' yells the madman. 'Your car is leaking, sir,' says the Indian. Faro knows that although she is still trembling, this line will one day amuse her. The madman goes to switch off his ignition, and the Indian gentleman leans through Faro's open window and asks if she is all right.

'I don't know,' says Faro.

'The world is full of crazy people,' says the Indian philosophically.

Faro nods agreement. She is beginning to recover. She finishes unbuckling her seat belt and opens her car door. This sensible chap will defend her. A road-rager cannot murder her in broad daylight on a three-lane highway—well, he could, but if he does she will be very unlucky. She gets out, protected by the Indian's presence, and surveys the scene. Her own car is quite badly damaged, the bumper crushed, the rear lights in splinters, the bodywork crumpled. It had been a serious impact. Yellow and white and red glass scatters the road. The madman's car, a not-very-new Vauxhall, has come off even worse. No wonder he is a bit upset. It doesn't look as though he will be able to drive it away very easily. How can he have got up enough speed in such slow traffic to slam into her with such force?

The madman, having switched off his engine, returns to the attack. By now Faro has pulled herself together sufficiently to be able to say to him, 'I think the most sensible thing to do now would be to exchange our insurance details.' She says this in one of her many speech options, in a priggish middle-class voice which she judges suitable for the occasion, but the madman does not like it at all. His large face is still hot and glaring. 'I'll make you pay for this, you stupid cow!' he yells. He seems to be running out of language. 'Please, sir,' says the Indian, who is immediately dismissed as a black bastard. The wail of a police siren approaches, a sound that Faro has never before been glad to hear. It seems to drive the madman into a worse frenzy. Perhaps he really is mad, quite mad? Some people are. Faro is beginning to hope that she will soon be able to drive away from this mess, this metal, these refracting shards of glass. Her engine must be OK, unlike his. A dark fluid is seeping from his onto the roadway. She hopes it will not burst into flames.

Clearly he is in no state to exchange insurance details. Yet she feels obliged to mention the matter once more, for she knows her rights and her duties as a citizen-driver. But the subject of insurance inflames him yet further. He advances towards her, breathing hotly into her face, and suddenly leans down, past her, and into her car, and grabs her car keys. 'Hey, give those back,' yells Faro, but the red man, his features distorted and melted like something in a trick mirror, like a character from a medieval fresco of hell, starts waving them in the air, taunting her, and then, suddenly, with a wild gesture and considerable strength, he hurls them high over the roadway, in a glittering arc, over the stationary traffic, and into the green verge beyond. 'You bastard!' shrieks Faro. 'You stupid fucking bastard!'

'Don't you use language like that at me,' yells the madman, dripping with sweat, shining with anger.

Faro is beside herself with rage at the loss of the keys to her freedom, and fears moreover that she is about to burst into retrograde womanly weeping. Her face is hot, her eyes are hot, and her tight blue shirt is damp. Where are the police? The siren still sounds, more frantically, but the police car is not much nearer: it is stuck in the snarl-up. Other vehicles, trying to get out of its way, have created a barricade, and all lanes but the slow lane have come to a halt. And it is the slow lane that separates Faro from the verge and from her keys. Will she ever find them? Is she stuck here for ever?

A police officer at last approaches on foot. Faro is too wise in the ways of the world to expect much sympathy, but she knows she must look more credible as a driver than this man of wrath, this parody of a thug, who has surely committed a serious offence by chucking away her car keys? And damnit, her flat key, her office key, her key to Queen's Norton, and the key which lets her in to feed Peter Bantam's cat? They'd all been on the same ring.

Half an hour later, Faro is still on her hands and knees, crawling through the filthy grass of the verge. Her car has been towed to safety, the red man has been cautioned and his car removed, and the chivalrous Indian has gone home to Crouch End. But Faro has refused to leave without her keys, although the police officer has assured her he can fix her car so she can drive it home. Why, he tells her, he once drove himself all the way down from Glasgow with a screwdriver in his ignition, and he can do better than that for Faro with his box of tricks. Faro thinks the officer is getting frisky and taking advantage. Stubbornly, she insists that she wants to find her keys. She doesn't want them lying there for anyone to find. They must be there. She saw them fall.

The texture and composition of the verge prove weirdly compelling, and the debris that has collected there would make a fine art installation. Faro, trying to be methodical and to impose a grid system upon her search, notes a variety of vegetation and a rich sampling of the wind-borne and window-chucked litter of a late-twentieth-century summer. Plastic bags, cigarette ends, orange peel, broken sunglasses, sweet wrappings.

Garbage and waste, Rose & Rose. She thinks of their sweetly stinking and belching little landscaped hummocks of muck that Steve Nieman had pointed out to her on their route back to Northam. Where there's muck there's money, had been the old adage, and it seems it still rings true.

The police are getting impatient with Faro. They've twice been back to buzz her from the soft shoulder, to tell her she can't scrabble around there all evening. Faro has tried to argue that there's no reason why she shouldn't look for them all night if she wants, it can't be illegal, but they disagree. It *is* illegal. She's not really allowed on that verge at all. It's nice of them to let her be there. That's the line they seem to be taking.

Faro irritably reexamines a nastily familiar, nastily repeating patch of plantain and dandelion and dirty Kleenex. And, suddenly, her keys flash up at her. There they are, all of them, safe on their darling little gold key ring, safely attached to her Darwin Society medallion. Her little enamelled bird, her keys and her burglar alarm, all intact. All is well, and all shall be well. She wipes the medallion on her trousers, thanks her keys for coming back to her, and thanks St Antony of Padua, and sits on the bank, happy now, waiting for the police to swoop by once more to collect her and take her back to her car, in which, stupidly, she has left her mobile phone.

She has to wait for some time. The police seem to have forgotten about her, or maybe they have found more important things to do. But the weather is pleasant, and after ten minutes she gets up and starts to inspect the motorway vegetation with a happier interest. The verge has been coarsely mown for a yard or so, but beyond that yard grows a band of taller plants, waist high, a rich crop of thistle and nettle and dock and ragwort. Faro plucks herself a teasel and starts to gather herself a motorway bouquet. The hot breath of the stream of cars wafts towards her with a Phlegraen stink as she tugs at hairy stems, at woody twines, at hollow culms. She as-

314

sembles a pretty nosegay of yarrow and tansy, of daisy and cranesbill, of groundsel and camomile, of all the dusty white and yellow and purple survivors. Some she knows by name, some she does not recognize. Her fingers prick but she is happy. The resilience of these plants delights her. Darwin would have liked this grassy bank and its brave fuel-loving adaptations. Passing motorists gaze in wonder at the wayside maiden in blue and white, calmly stooping and bending as though in the fields of paradise.

She ties her bunch of flowers together with grass, and sits down again to wait. By her feet, a glinting object catches her eyes. It is a cheap little brooch of shells and of glass. She picks it up, and polishes it up on her trousers. Its catch is broken, and it is not really very nice. But she feels sorry for it, and she puts it in her pocket with her medallion and her keys. Faro wastes a lot of her time feeling sorry for all sorts of things, animate and inanimate.

When, at last, she gets home, she arranges her flowers in a blue-and-white-striped milk jug. They look surprisingly attractive, and they begin to recover at once from their dusty drooping thirstiness. She can almost see them drink in the welcome London tap water. She too is recovering. Despite the motorway disaster, and the sense that there is only a thin crust of kindness sealing in the violence of human nature, she is feeling pleased with herself and her day. Steve is an ace. She knows she will see him again soon. She can invent questions to ask him when she starts to write her article. She hardly needs an excuse to ring him. They are fast friends, and may become more than friends. Perhaps he will ring her. In fact, she knows he will ring her.

And the phone trills just as she has settled down to watch a spot of restful television. She leaps towards it eagerly, convinced it will be Steve asking her if she is safely home, eager to tell him about her motorway misadventure. But it is not Steve. It is her dark angel Sebastian Jones, who is pleased to inform her that he has just been told he is mortally ill with cancer of the pancreas, and that he expects to see her the next day.

ᏯᛏᛏᏯ

Faro sits underground on the Central Line between Shepherd's Bush and Holborn with a basket containing her motorway posy, a cold roast chicken, half a loaf of bread, a bunch of seedless grapes and a bottle of white wine. Invalid fare. She is Little Red Riding Hood travelling towards the wolf of death. And she is in a very bad temper. She really cannot believe that Seb is dying. It is some dirty manipulative game he is playing with her. How dare he sink so low? And why is she such a fool as to respond so promptly? She perches her large basket on her lap and stares crossly around her. None of the adverts down here are for products, they are all for financial services. Faro doesn't need any financial services. Amongst them is a poster with a Poem on the Underground, so she takes refuge in reading that. It is the end of *Paradise Lost*.

> *Some natural tears they dropp'd, but wiped them soon;*
> *The world was all before them, where to choose*
> *Their place of rest, and Providence their guide.*
> *They, hand in hand with wand'ring steps and slow,*
> *Through Eden took their solitary way.*

She is thinking about Adam and Eve and Cotterhall Man and Steve Nieman as the train comes to a standstill between stations. Nothing very unusual in that, though the Central Line is usually more reliable than the Hammersmith and City, which is always loitering in the dark. But the delay prolongs itself for minute after minute after minute, and her fellow passengers start to look at their watches. Faro can't see hers as both her hands are busy trying to stop the basket from slipping off her knees, but she guesses that over five minutes have passed, and still nothing is happening. Most people are sitting dully, like stunned cattle, but one or two are beginning to rustle and exchange anxious or irritable glances. Fortunately the carriage is not full of dangerous psychopaths or hysterics— the week before on her way back from the office Faro had found herself sitting opposite a youth with an enormous transistor and a broken bottle, with which he was systematically slashing the upholstery while muttering to himself in an unknown tongue. There's nobody like that on board today. A selection of men in suits, some middle-aged women, some tourist types, a couple of black girls laughing together over a film magazine. Nobody here will run amok.

Ten minutes pass. There is no announcement. A murmuring revolt seems about to begin. One passenger starts sniffing the air and says he can smell smoke. This is not helpful. Everybody, except for the tourists, is thinking of the King's Cross fire, in which so many lost their lives underground. Faro can't smell smoke, but she can smell a nasty black oily fuel-like smell. Perhaps it's only the stinking newsprint of the *Evening Standard* being read by the fat chap sitting next to her, whose bum and left elbow are encroaching on her body space. How long are they all going to sit without protest? Why had they come down here in the first place? Faro doesn't look forward to arriving at her destination, but she doesn't want to be suffocated or smoked or burned to death down here either. She resolves not to panic, and to think of higher things.

Henri Bergson argues, if she remembers rightly, that consciousness is a by-product of mobility. Most plants draw their sustenance directly and unmediated from the ground in which they live, but animals are obliged to move in search of food and prey, and they become conscious as they do so. The vegetable is condemned to rooted torpor, the animal to hungry movement. And thus we evolve, and they stay where they are. Bergson had made some interesting points about those halfway species, the fungi and the insectivorous plants, but Faro can't remember what they are. Was it Bergson who had called fungi the blind alleys of the vegetable world? Maybe the human species has evolved too far, maybe we all move around too much, too pointlessly, and consciousness will implode upon itself.

Faro doesn't know what Bergson would make of modern restlessness. Freud had thought that travel and transport were bad for the health, and on the present showing, he would seem to be right. It can't be good to spend too much time on the London Underground. But maybe Bergson would have argued that the impulse to travel is an evolutionary necessity, that we are seeking ways to jump the planet and escape entropy. We are working out our escape, even as we sit underground in the dark.

Bergson had suggested that we might learn how to escape death itself. Freud would have made short work of that suggestion. But Bergson may have been right.

Faro sits tight, and starts, despite herself, to think about Sebastian Jones and his pancreas. She has looked the pancreas up on the Internet, that twentieth-century magnet for the hypochondriac, and has found little comfort there. True, there are accounts of successful pancreas transplants, with prices given in dollars, and there are portraits of sections of benign tumours, but these are outnumbered and outweighed by grim statistics. Faro has stared at slides of marbled, blotted and blotched cellscapes, representing *Malignant Tumour, Ectodermal, Excellent* and *Malignant Tumour, Ectodermal, Good.* She can't see anything very good about them. The pancreas, which in its natural state is light tan or pinkish in colour, has been dyed in virulent laboratory shades of purple and green and red. Its cells splurge and cluster. A transplant, without an accompanying kidney, costs somewhere in the region of two hundred thousand dollars. Symptoms of a diseased pancreas include abdominal pain or pressure, relieved by leaning forward, which she supposes may account for Seb's habitually hunched and bowed posture. Also one may expect a yellowish skin, weight loss, weakness and darkness of the urine. Faro has never seen Sebastian Jones's urine, and does not wish acquaintance with it now.

Faro pictures Seb sitting on his couch, hunched into himself, as though his body would cave in upon itself and devour its own entrails.

Faro is not up to comforting a sick man, but she is even more incapable of refusing to try to do so. It is all very unfair. Why isn't his mother there, looking after him? Surely vicars' wives are trained for that sort of thing? Faro had had enough of deathbeds with the death of her father Nick Gaulden, the first anniversary of which is fast approaching.

The train moves on, eventually, and carries her onwards, towards the condemned man. When she gets there, she finds Seb isn't in bed at all, he's sitting, alert and intent, on his unspeakable couch, watching a video. He doesn't even switch off as she lets herself in, though he does grunt in acknowledgement of her arrival, then waits to the end of a sequence before pressing the pause button. He is watching an early black-and-white version of *Frankenstein*. The high-browed balding frozen monster peculiarly resembles Sebastian himself, Faro cannot help thinking.

Slowly, Seb heaves his feet off the couch, and sits there, leaning slightly forward, hunched, in what Faro must now consider his pancreatic position. Then he pats the fraying foam cushion seat next to him, inviting her to sit. She goes to sit by him, and takes his hand in hers. It is white and cold and dry. He lets her hold it. She massages it, gently, trying to impart warmth, trying to transmit the vital spark. Seb shudders and does not return her friendly pressure. She continues to squeeze and rub, and sighs heavily.

'Oh Seb,' she says, 'who would have thought it?'

'I'm sorry,' says Seb.

This uncharacteristic remark convinces Faro that he is not faking. But he follows it up with a request so dreadful that Faro is confounded.

'Descend with me,' says Seb. 'Descend with me.'

A pulse of hysteria leaps through Faro's head and flickers in terror. *Descend with me?* What can he want of her? A nerve twangs at the base of her skull, and the small sharp pain shoots upwards to lodge behind her left eye. Whatever she does, whatever she says, will be inadequate, trivial, risible. How dare he trap her and test her like this? Will he play with her as a cat with a mouse? Is this the waiting game he has been playing throughout their unsatisfactory and pointlessly protracted relationship?

Faro is a healthy young woman who does not want to have to think about the last things. She does not want to descend. She likes the light and the sun. She wants to sit on a sunny bank with butterflies about her. This gloomy apartment is as near the grave as she wishes to go. All the things that are in it speak of death—the unwashed sheets on the unmade bed in the poky little bedroom, the shower room with its dirty plastic curtain, the kitchenette with its unwashed plates, the piles of old sci-fi and horror magazines stacked in corners, the 1988 wall calendar portraying a street scene in Kampala. They all mark time for ever. The dust which lies on ledges, the London grime on the windowpanes of the old-fashioned broken-corded sash windows. Faro is not a tidy person, but her flat shines like an advertisement for Mr Muscle Home Cleaner in comparison with this place. Faro looks around her, desperately, as though the room itself will rescue her and give her some lines.

'I brought you a chicken,' croaks Faro at last, letting go of Seb's hand.

Seb grins, his skin stretching. His teeth look too big for his face.

'I'm not so ill that I can't get to the pub,' he says.

'I'm not going to the pub,' says Faro, suddenly leaping to her feet and going to stare out of the window. 'I hate that pub. I've always hated that pub. I've never been able to see what you see in that pub.'

Seb's flat is on the second floor back of an eighteenth-century terraced house which has seen better days. It looks out onto a small courtyard, in which grows a small thorn tree. It is overlooked by the backs of tall buildings of the sixties— an office block, the service area of a cheap hotel. It is a little corner of old London, and it is dying, even if Seb is not. Faro stares out stubbornly at the tree.

'OK,' concedes Seb. 'We'll have some chicken.'

So Seb and Faro sit at Seb's cluttered little table, which is almost as unhygienic as Auntie Dora's, though its layers are differently constituted. It is strewed with dirty ashtrays, cigarette packets (and yes, like all diseases, cancer of the pancreas is linked to heavy smoking), bottle tops, paperback books, a bruised apple, a spotted banana, ballpoint pens, paper clips and two potatoes, green and sprouting transparent waxy fingers from their many sickly eyes. Faro eats a mouthful of cold chicken and wonders if she dreamed those words she thought she had heard. *Descend with me.* No, people do not talk like that, in the late twentieth century. They talk and they live in the upper reaches, in the rapid shallows. Nobody goes down there anymore, not even the dead and the dying. There is nothing down there anymore.

Cotterhall Man with his long yellow shanks appears to Faro, as she silently chews on the dry white breast. He had been killed by a blow to the head. Seb, it seems, will die a lingering and medicated death. It's a sort of progress.

Nowadays, thinks Faro, as she clears up the dishes and piles them into the dirty sink, we go in for grief management and all that kind of nonsense. Or we write newspaper accounts of our mortal illness, or we die on camera. It's a very long time since people believed in God, and the Resurrection of the Body, and the Life Everlasting. If they ever did. All this horror trip, thinks Faro, is a religion substitute. *Descend with me.* Where to, for Christ's sake? Faro shudders, tosses her head, and splatters water from the balding washing-up brush, as she flutters about restlessly like a stuck moth trying to free itself.

Faro is vital, but Seb is guttering. Will it help if she tidies up? She busies herself. She cannot bring herself to sit down near him again. She knows that Sebastian can smell Steve Nieman on her. Seb will do his best to keep her from Steve Nieman. Seb is contagious: he will infect the spirit, if not the flesh. Seb's flat smells of sour milk. She pours herself another glass of wine, and stays on her feet, wiping, officiously rearranging, scraping at long-dried stains on the draining board, rinsing out the greenish deposit from a couple of dirty glass milk bottles. Her energy surges in little leaps through her body as she fights back against the scum and the silt. Seb has sunk into entropy. He is growing old and cold before her eyes.

'Have another glass?' says Faro, with a merry intonation. Her voice sounds almost convincing. Seb does not answer, but Faro has been cheered by the loud sound of her own self: she fills his glass anyway, places it by his side, puts the bottle on the floor with its fellow empties. She starts to sing as she rinses out the slimy J-Cloth. 'There's *you* and *me* and the bottle makes *three* tonight,' sings Faro, in her pleasing light contralto. Can it really be only a week or two since she first had her DNA tested, and swapped stories with Peter Cudworth from Iowa? Why, a week is a lifetime. For all she knows, her mitochondrial DNA may even now be unfolding wonders of cultured mortality in its Oxford test tube. What is time? We merely borrow from it. We are leasehold. Faro's spirits rise, she is restored, she can do it, and she will. All shall not perish.

She bounds across the room, and flings herself down upon the couch by Sebastian Jones. The springs move and rattle under her weight. She bounces up and down, deliberately, like a child. Then she seizes Seb's inert cold fist.

'Hey, come on, Seb,' she says, as she lifts his hand to her mouth, and kisses its tight clenched fingers. 'Come on, Seb, I'm not descending anywhere with anyone. You come back up here to me.'

Thus far Faro pledged herself, as she bent on him the dark lustre of her great eyes, as she stared at him with her hypnotic power. And Seb stirred slightly under her challenging gaze, and smiled a small dry smile from his sunken features, and uncurled his fingers, and grasped at hers.

So Faro Gaulden undertakes her journey to the underworld, willing to descend at least ankle-deep with Sebastian into the waiting trench. She is sure that she will clamber out again. Seb may not, but she will.

Over the next month, she rallies her troops. She enlists her friends, and she has many. But she is depressingly aware of the limitations of her thirty-something circle of unmarrieds. OK, they are kind-hearted, and they are free to drop in on Seb, to have a chat, to share a takeaway, to watch a video, to provide company. But they have no weight and no *gravitas*. They do not have homes fit to die in. Only the married friends have homes, and they are married because they have babies, and therefore they have no spare free time or free bedrooms. Their rooms are for serious living, not for dying. The shallow roots of Faro's bachelor London existence are exposed. She has done her best to make herself a life, but it is thin stuff, thin stuff.

Meanwhile, her new suitor Steve Nieman is besieging her with messages from Cotterhall. She does not tell him the full story of her deadly engagement with Sebastian Jones, but he senses it. He implores her to come up to see him again soon, as she had promised. He is building her a little gazebo of cedar wood and living willow at the end of the Wild Nature Park. He woos her on the phone, he writes her letters on real paper, he sends her postcards and peppers her with e-mail. His manner is as attractive as Seb's is repulsive. Who would not, of these two, choose Steve Nieman? There is no contest. They are the dark and the light. Hyperion to a satyr. Yet she finds she has not got it in her to abandon Sebastian. She is torn in two. Steve is persistent, but so is Seb. They both persist. She is tied to a stake between them. Seb plucks and gnaws. Steve threatens to come and rescue her and carry her away, but she forestalls him. They must weather it out, she cannot run away. Maybe Seb will get so ill he will have to go home to his mother. Maybe he will be interned in University College Hospital. Faro finds herself wishing he would get worse quickly, but he seems to hang on. It is bad to find oneself wishing worse health on a sick man.

Sebastian is full of strange fancies these days. They are his death row privilege. Is his medication making his mind wander? His fantasies attach themselves firmly to Faro. He thinks she ought to have a baby—not his, of course, for he is past that kind of thing—but somebody's. She ought to perpetuate herself. She owes her genes to posterity. He talks about this a great deal. This is a clear case of immortality-and-survival-projection, and Faro blames herself for having interested him in the subject of genes in the first place. Who cares if her mitochondrial DNA perishes? She certainly doesn't, and it's no business of Sebastian Jones.

His interest in reincarnation is more fantastic, and more far-fetched. He has become obsessed by the mummy portraits of ancient Egypt, and has tried to persuade Faro that she is the reincarnation of an unidentified Graeco-Roman Egyptian woman of the second century A.D., buried at Hawara and recovered by Flinders Petrie. Faro would like to tell him bluntly that he is raving, but now that he has pitched his tent in the fields of death she has to listen solemnly to any old rubbish he chooses to bore her with. That's how it is with believers. Patiently, she listens. She consents to turn over with him the pages of the illustrated catalogue of the British Museum exhibition of *Ancient Faces* that had first awakened this morbid interest. And it is true that they do speak across time. These young men and young women had been the contemporaries of Hadrian and of Marcus Aurelius, and yet they smile and speak. There is language in their eyes, their lips, their necks, their noses. Confidently they insist on resurrection, with the full polychrome glow of the fully human. They wait for the morning. They have never died.

Faro points out to Seb that her resemblance to any of these figures, even to the one that Seb has appointed as her soul twin and her foreshadowing, is only superficial. She grants that some of these Graeco-Roman Egyptians have their hair cut in a manner identical to the style intermittently imposed on Faro Gaulden by Carla at Crimpers: short, cut close to the head, black, tight and curly. Some of these fortunate dead beauties sport upon their brows a charming *bandeau* of small corkscrew or snail ringlets, such as Faro has always desired but never quite achieved. It is true also that some of these women display golden hoop earrings that echo precisely the design that she herself favours. And there is some similarity, she grants, in the general face-shape—a roundness, a fullness, an insistence on rings and globes and arches. These are not angular Cubist faces, she agrees. And she would like to think that she herself could smile through eternity with the enchantingly bold and wayward smile of her soul twin. But surely her mouth is not as wide, nor her nose so long?

Seb will have none of these doubts. It is the eyes. Look in the eyes, he says.

The eyes are dark lakes, lit with lustre. They stare and stare. It is nothing, says Faro. It is a trick of craft. It is art. These are not people, these are not even portraits of people. These are artefacts. They are works of art.

That is no answer, says Seb, as he stares into the liquid darkness. And, in a way, he is right.

Seb is mesmerized by the very language of these images. 'Portrait of a young woman in encaustic on limewood, with added stucco and gold leaf.' 'Portrait of a woman in encaustic on fir, with added gilding.' 'Portrait of a woman in tempera on a linen shroud.' The lively riches of encaustic favour the living flesh of Faro, Seb insists. Tempera is too pale and thin for her. 'The flesh is warmly tinted in tones of cream, apricot and rose pink with an ochre-green shadow by the nose,' intones Seb. Is not that pure poetry?

Seb suggests that in time the dead will be made to live again. Cloning will bring back the dead. He has been reading and writing too many horror stories, and his science is hopeless, says Faro. But, of course, he has a point. Even now, pigs are growing transplant organs for us, and Dr Hawthorn is busy with his swabs.

Faro, while all this is going on, tries to think of Steve Nieman and the butterflies. London is full of gloom and anger. Faro finds herself irresistibly attracted to the lodestone of the north. Something is calling her, and perhaps it is not only Steve Nieman, though she finds herself looking back to their picnic on the limestone outcrop as to a lost golden age of radiant light. When she cannot sleep, she summons up Steve Nieman and the grizzled skipper and the swooping swallows. She searches the papers and the Internet for news of Cotterhall and Breaseborough. There is not much. Breaseborough has its own Knowhere Guide on the Internet, constructed by rueful and self-deprecating cynics. It declares that whereas Breaseborough once had three cinemas, it now has none, and that it has no ten-pin bowling, no McDonald's, no Kentucky Fried Chicken—you name it, Breaseborough hasn't got it. There's a weekend disco at the Wardale Arms, and dodgy beer, karaoke and big-screen sports at the Glassblowers. The Full Inhalers will appear on Friday at the Prince of Wales, entrance free. Local crap like line dancing available at the Ferryboat, plus a barmaid with a see-through blouse who has caused the death by heart attack of three local lechers. The food highlight is Doug's Hot Hit Snax, E. coli guaranteed.

Somebody has written in to suggest that the best thing to do with Breaseborough is to blow it up and begin again. (Nothing changes: Faro remembers Grandma Barron saying exactly the same thing on several occasions.) Another wag has responded, more passionately, 'Why not blow up the human race and begin again with a silicon base?'

It seems that Auntie Dora, up in Breaseborough, is not too well. This doesn't matter so much, because Auntie Dora is pretty old, and what can one expect, but it's sad, just the same. Faro is fond of Auntie Dora.

The grizzled skipper, according to the butterfly page on the net, feeds upon wild strawberries.

ᘒᘎᘒ

While Faro has been worrying about the ill health of Sebastian Jones, Chrissie has been worrying about the ill health of her Auntie Dora. Dora, so recently and reassuringly reported by Faro at the Cudworth Reunion to have been in reasonably good spirits, has been sounding very miserable on the telephone. Of course, she complains more to ageing Chrissie than she complains to young Faro, because she feels she has a right to do so, but, even so, Chrissie suspects she really may be deteriorating. Her legs are not good, Dora says, and she is finding the stairs difficult. Her strength is ebbing and her natural stoicism is beginning to falter. Chrissie is not sure what to do—she is, as usual, very busy, what with one thing and another, and moreover in October she has to go to Australia with Donald for ten days to an archaeological conference. When she gets back, she promises herself, she will pay a brief November visit to Dora, and reassure her that she will be expected, as usual, for Christmas at Queen's Norton. Maybe she can persuade Faro to go up with her to Breaseborough to keep her company. Surely Dora can hang on that long? The prospect of Christmas always cheers Dora, though it mildly depresses Chrissie. It doesn't depress her as much as it did when Bessie was alive, and she's happy to have Dora to stay. But surely it's enough to do Christmas?

Chrissie is also acutely aware that the first anniversary of Nick Gaulden's death approaches, and that it is going to be disturbing both to herself and to Faro. She dreams about Nick constantly, and suspects that Faro does so too. So she has arranged for Faro to come to Queen's Norton for that week-end, so that they can be together. The date falls on a Sunday. Chrissie and Don get back from Sydney on the Friday. They can tell Faro their traveller's tales, and speak or not speak of Nick as they choose. It will be a comfort to have Faro there. Faro seems to have been having trouble with yet another un-suitable boyfriend. Chrissie wants to hear all about it.

On the eve of Chrissie and Don's flight to the other side of the globe, Dora rings, and says she is feeling really awful. Her legs are all swollen, and she hadn't been able to shut her bed-room window, and the rain had rained in on her bed, and she'd got all wet during the night. She'd caught a cold. She was mis-erable. She felt ill. She'd had an aspirin, but she still felt ill.

Chrissie feels guilty for suspecting that Dora is saying all this because she knows Chrissie is about to fly off to Australia. She prevaricates, says she'll be home soon, and urges Dora to see her doctor. Dora says she's too ill to go out. Then get the doctor to come to see you, says Chrissie. Oh, they won't do that anymore, says Dora. They will if you're really ill, says Chrissie firmly. Dora says that she will ring her doctor in the morning, if she doesn't feel better. Dora, unlike her late sister Bessie, hates seeing the doctor. Nor is she a hypochondriac.

So perhaps, thinks Chrissie, five miles up in the sky over Dubai, there is something new wrong. She sighs, heavily, and toys with her executive-class minimeal. Maybe she should have cancelled her trip and gone up north instead? But all the plans had been made so long ago, and the tickets were so ex-pensive, and the visas so tiresome to obtain, and Don would be disappointed, and so, to be honest, would Chrissie, who has never been to the Antipodes. Sydney Harbour is said to be one of the wonders of the world. Joe Barron had spoken of it with much admiration. He had enjoyed his visit to see his sister Ivy.

Don has been to Australia several times, but he too is looking forward to the trip. He is giving a paper on the new cave findings on Malta, entitled 'The Vulva, the Bird and the Chevron'. The conference has a feminist slant, and although there will no doubt be some fierce separatist hard-line women there, with extreme views on the essential placidity of the early paleolithic matriarchies, there will also be some interesting discussion. And Don will be made welcome by most, for his writings on the pre-Eleusinian mysteries have been famously well received by men and women alike. In fact, Don is an independent proto-feminist. Some women may shout at him, but most will be glad of his scholarly interest and support. And anyway, Don can look after himself. He doesn't notice when people shout at him. Or he pretends not to notice, which comes to the same thing. It's pretty odd of me to have ended up with an archaeologist, thinks Chrissie, but then, you just can't get away from your own past, can you?

Chrissie has left her hotel number with Faro, in case of a Dora health crisis, but Faro does not ring, so Chrissie assumes all is well. She doesn't ring Faro because it never seems to be the right time of day or night for a round-the-world phone call.

Chrissie likes Sydney. She attends a few sessions of the conference, and spends the rest of her time exploring. She catches a ferry to the suburb where Ivy Barron and Pat Parker had lived, but cannot find their house. It doesn't matter. She doesn't need to. She is satisfied that it is a far cry from Breaseborough, and she is satisfied that Ivy Barron had not wasted her life. Ivy had had pluck. This is a beautiful country. Ivy had escaped.

Chrissie sits alone at a quayside fish restaurant, sheltered from the sun by a striped awning. Donald is chairing a talk on

329

Stone Age food technology and the thirty-thousand-year-old Aboriginal grindstones of the Western desert, which will be followed by a luncheon sponsored by Electromix, but Chrissie has heard enough talks and attended enough luncheons. She is happy now, alone, quiet, with her book, and a glass of wine, and a bread roll. She has ordered soup and an unknown fish and awaits their arrival. She watches the traffic of the waterfront, and wonders if Harriet McGough from St Andrews ever married her marine biologist, and if she too is still connected to archaeology. The marine biologist was, if she remembers rightly, from Aberdeen, a city which has been transformed by North Sea oil. Both Scotland and the Faeroes are a long way away, in space and in time. Australia is blessed with a much more pleasant climate. It is surprising to Chrissie that the entire population of the Faeroes has not tried to emigrate to Australia. There is plenty of room for them here. This is a land of sunshine and of plenty.

At the next table to Chrissie sit a couple, a mother and a daughter. They have come from elsewhere, but Chrissie cannot guess their nationality. The child is about ten years old, and mother is in her thirties. She has a broad face, a flaring wide nose, and prominent, uneven, ill-dentisted teeth which sort ill with the expense of her clothing. She is wearing a tailored turquoise costume, and the child is wearing a Scottish pseudo-tartan dress with a white collar, the uniform of expensive children the world over. Both wear strings of pearls. They do not speak. They order a first course, which arrives as Chrissie's bisque arrives. Both mother and daughter are presented with what the menu had described as a Cold Seafood Platter, consisting of an open clam, half a crayfish and a few prawns in their shells, accompanied by a few fronds of dark olive-green seaweed and half a lemon in a muslin bag. Chrissie spoons down her soup, and mother and daughter, still without exchanging a single word, eat one mouthful each of each platter, and then sit back, pushing their loaded plates away.

Chrissie is sorry for them. Have they ordered something they do not like? Have they recoiled from the long red whiskers and cockroach-creatureliness of their choice? The waiter, impassively, removes their almost untouched plates, and returns for Chrissie's empty bowl. Some time later he returns with Chrissie's piece of fish, which is surrounded by the seaweed and half lemon of the house, and, for the mother and daughter, yet another seafood platter. It is hot, this time, but it is almost identical to their last servings. A hot half-lobster, a hot clam, a prawn or two and a large chunk of some kind of hash or mash or seafood pie. They survey their meals expressionlessly. Will this go down any better? The mother picks up a long silver surgical skewer, and prods, nibbles and picks. The daughter eats a forkful of hash. Then both lay down their implements, sit back and push away their plates once more.

Are they ill? What is happening?

Chrissie eats up her fish with gross pleasure. It is a solid, firm-textured, well-flavoured fish. She enjoys it. Chrissie was born during the Second World War. Chrissie thinks of how much Bessie had enjoyed her meals in the Queen's Grill.

Once more the waiter approaches, once more he clears the two adjacent tables, removing the full plates from the one, the clean plate from the other. Chrissie does not bother to look at the menu again, for she has indulged herself too much already, and will have to sleep it off or walk it off. She orders a cup of coffee.

The mother inspects the menu carefully, consults her daughter in the curtest of sentences, and orders dessert.

Chrissie's coffee arrives, and dessert arrives for her neighbours. Will the child be happy at last, as she receives a glass goblet containing ices white and pink and crimson, and an array of glistening berries black and purple and red? It seems so, for she smiles, briefly, and picks up her spoon. The mother delves into her leather handbag for a camera, and photographs her daughter with her colourful chalice. Click, quick, click, flash, click. The daughter eats a couple of berries, stirs the cream, nibbles at her wafer biscuit and lays down the spoon. The mother does the same. In silence.

The mother beckons the waiter. He brings her the bill. She pays. They leave.

Chrissie is baffled by this episode. She cannot interpret its meaning. Is it the quality of the nullity of the silence between these two that has distressed her, or is it the waste of good food? She thinks fondly of Don's careful habit of preserving every little leftover scrap in cling film in case he can eat it up another day. She thinks of herself and Faro, chatter chatter, natter natter. She thinks of herself and Bessie. At least she and Bessie had talked. Much of the talk had been unpleasant, but they had both made an effort to communicate.

When she returns to the hotel with its high view of botanical garden and harbour, she finds Don in good spirits. The paper on grindstones had been highly entertaining, he says, and it's a pity she missed it. The lecturer, a small fuzzy-haired Australian woman of Italian extraction, wearing a smart pin-striped suit, had been eloquent on the subject of female labour in prehistory, and she had given a vivid demonstration of the grinding process, which, she claimed, had been tough work. She had been clapped and cheered. Then Don had scored a triumph by claiming that he was entitled to one of the new baby-food mixers that the sponsors were distributing as samples to the female delegates. Why couldn't he have one too, he had demanded. It was sexist to deny him. Old and white and male he might be, but he had worked hard for his living and sung for his luncheon and he had a right to an electrical baby-food grinder. He had won his point, and here was the proof. He unwraps it from its gift bag to show her.

At midnight, on their return from a dinner sponsored by Don's publishers, they pour themselves a postprandial brandy from the minibar and play like children with Don's little machine. It is a wonder. Light as a leaf, smaller than a Coke can, at the press of a button this handy little plastic gadget slurries up a banana and an overripe nameless exotic fruit from the complimentary fruit bowl. The years of stone grinding are obliterated. Woman is released from labour. The fruits turn into a smooth disgusting yellowish pap. As Don and Chrissie are staring at this muck, wondering if it is their thrifty duty to eat it, or whether they may permit themselves to flush it down the drains into the Pacific Ocean, the phone rings. At this time of night, it cannot be anyone but Faro.

Faro is not ringing about Auntie Dora. Nothing bad has happened—well, nothing very bad. She is ringing to ask for Chrissie's advice about her Apple. It has refused to speak to its printer, for no reason that she can diagnose. It's giving her an incomprehensible message that she's never seen before. She needs to fix it right now because she's trying to print out an article on the new flu vaccine, and it's late already, and she's promised to deliver it in the morning. Help, Mummy, help, bleats Faro. Chrissie talks her through the possibilities. Faro presses this and presses that—Tool Box, Printer, Options, Acrobat, J-connect, Properties, Default, Colorbox. She goes in and out of programs, over the airwaves, through the satellites. In the end, Chrissie suggests she check the ink cartridges. Faro swears they are new. Never mind, check them, says Chrissie. Faro takes them out and puts them back in again, and behold, for no reason whatsoever, the machine begins to work again. Chrissie can hear the printer printing away in Shepherd's Bush on the other side of the world. Mum, you're a genius, shrieks Faro, delighted. So happy they are, the mother and the daughter, and Don too is happy, as he reappears from the bathroom in dressing-gown and pyjamas.

He has washed the baby food away. He tasted it, but it was too horrid, and after all, there isn't a war on, is there?

He has a word with Faro. They sing Chrissie's praises. He tells Faro about the pinstriped feminist archaeologist and the grindstones. They are all laughing. They will all meet soon, at the weekend. Faro longs to see them. Have they bought her an opal? Have they seen a koala and a duck-billed platypus? Is the sun shining, over there in Australia?

No, says Chrissie, it's after midnight.

Good God, says Faro. I'm sorry. Is it really? I'd no idea.

⬥

Chrissie was not feeling so cheerful when they all met again that weekend at Queen's Norton. Somewhere up in the under-oxygenated recycled air of the sky or in the hygienic vastnesses of Singapore airport she had picked up a flu bug. She sneezed all the way from Shanghai to Heathrow, while her throat began to prickle and her legs swelled. She hoped at first it was just aeroplane fever, but it accompanied her from Heathrow to the Cotswolds, and climbed into bed with her at Queen's Norton. She lay there, feeling sorry for herself. She didn't cancel Faro, because it was too late to do so. Faro could take her chance with the influenza. Faro joked over the phone that she hoped Chrissie hadn't got this new kind of Hong Kong flu which you get from pigs. Did they have pork on the aeroplane? They've been assassinating all the pigs of Hong Kong, hadn't Chrissie read about it? Singapore, not Hong Kong, croaked Chrissie. It's all the same, said Faro, and not to worry, she'd bring some nice boxed meals from the supermarket with her, and look after her poor old mother. She'd become very good at looking after people. She's a good nurse, these days, and she was sure Chrissie would make a very good patient.

The truth is that Faro is longing to tell her mother about Sebastian Jones and his wretched pancreas. If she tells all to Chrissie, it will go away, and she will be released from his encumbrance. Chrissie is a bright, strong, cheerful survivor, even though she's got flu, and she will obliterate the shadow of Sebastian. So Faro tells herself, as she drives along the M40 on a Friday afternoon.

She has made an appointment to call in at the Institute for Molecular Medicine in Oxford on the way, to find out what's happening to the Cudworth-Hawthorn project, and to get the results of her own swab. The super-mobile Dr Hawthorn is elsewhere, as usual, for he has more important things on his mind than inheritance patterns in South Yorkshire, but she is given a tour of the lab and the test-tubes by Dr Cooper ('Call me Tom') who loves all DNA, but the more ancient, the better. He speaks to her of the extinction of the moas and the monophyly of kiwis, of the evolution of the cave bear, of amber and insects, of glues and fungus, of prehistoric Amerindians and the peopling of the Pacific, of Nile Valley populations and mitochondrial polymorphisms in mummies, of the detection of infectious and inherited diseases from ancient human skeletal remains. He shows her slides and maps. She finds it hard to drag him back from the past to the present. He is nearly as past-oriented as Sebastian Jones, although he's working on the cutting edge of the fashionable field of molecular biology.

'I want to know about the Cudworths!' finally cries Faro, and he pulls himself away from the Nile Valley to hunt for the results of the Cudworth Convention in Hammervale. She trails after him, from room to room, until he finds a computer that gives them access to the Breaseborough data. Together, they sit and search the files. Faro, as usual, gets impatient and can't see why he can't just tap in the question 'Faro Gaulden, who is she?' There can't be anyone else in the world called Faro Gaulden. There has never been another Faro Gaulden on earth. But she'd better not interfere, she tells herself. Probably everything is coded, for reasons of genetic privacy.

Eventually she pops up. There she is. Gaulden, Faro, Flat 2, Etheredge Gardens, Shepherd's Bush, London W11, 8XX, e-mail address *faro@mimosa.com*. Date, year, place of sample. Tom Cooper scrolls, links and mousehunts her down. And there is the information that they have been looking for. It is as she had known. She is indeed a direct descendant of Cotterhall Man, as were Ellen Bawtry, Bessie Barron and Chrissie Sinclair before her. The sleeping prince in his glass coffin is their ancestor. Her genes had dwelled in Hammervale since the end of the Ice Age.

'Good God,' says Faro. 'I knew it. You should have let me know.'

Tom Cooper scratches his head, blushes engagingly, re-adjusts his spectacles. He mutters apologetically that letters to all participants would be sent out in the long run, they were just waiting for some of the more problematic findings to be sorted out. Some of the samples, unlike hers, had not been of Quality, Excellent.

Now Faro wants to know who else is directly descended, and Tom obligingly continues his quest. Auntie Dora must be, insists Faro, and Tom brings up Dora's name, but Dora's swab is one of those labelled Poor, and its result is not clear. Peter Iowa Cudworth is not related to Cotterhall Man in direct descent, though that does not mean he is not related.

'Well,' says Faro, over a cup of polystyrene in the canteen. 'I call that pretty interesting.' It was disappointing not to be the last of the Yorkshire Neanderthals—the result seemed to have ruled out that tantalizing possibility—but it was still pretty damn interesting to know where one's greatest of grandmothers had lived. Tom Cooper agreed. As far as he was aware, nobody had ever tried to track his branch of the Coopers back beyond the middle of the nineteenth century. His great-granny had been born in Islington. Before her, all was obscurity.

Faro drives on towards Queen's Norton with a folder full of offprints and gene maps. She is looking forward to telling all this to her ailing mother, who may well be appalled by this new evidence. She is feeling more and more cheerful, the further she gets from London. She is resolved, in her heart, that she will break away from Sebastian. All she needs is a little encouragement from her mother.

On the first evening, which is the eve of the anniversary of Nick's death, all goes according to plan. Chrissie feels well enough to get up for a couple of hours, and she sits by the autumn fire in the pretty rose-pink country drawing room and listens to Faro's stories. Faro relates first the story of the swab. Both Don and Chrissie, as archaeologists, find this fascinating. Don expresses satisfaction in finding he has married into so ancient a lineage. The Sinclairs go back a few centuries, but what are centuries to millennia? He congratulates his wife and his stepdaughter upon this momentous discovery. Will they hold land rights in Hammervale, he wants to know, and are there other claimants? Faro discloses that two others in the chapel test had indeed shared the same gene, but Dr Cooper hadn't told her their names—he said he'd better leave the revelations to Dr Hawthorn.

Faro shows Don and Chrissie some of Dr Cooper's charts. She shows them a little sketch of nuclear and mitochondrial DNA in a glob of frog spawn, about to be attacked by a sperm tadpole. She reads, aloud, to her small audience: 'There is a small possibility—about one in a hundred—that these minute changes that happen to genes with time might be happening under our very eyes in your family. This process is entirely natural and entirely harmless.'

'A chance of one in a hundred doesn't sound very small to me,' says Chrissie.

Don and Faro agree.

'And I suppose "change" is a polite word for "mutation", is it?' asks Chrissie.

'It certainly is,' says Faro. 'We try to avoid the word "mutation", in the media, except when we want to frighten people. Mutation's had a bad press, lately.'

'Ah well, poor old Mother,' says Chrissie obscurely.

Don, at this stage, tactfully absents himself, leaving mother and daughter together, and Faro abandons the subject of the static and non-mutant Cudworths, and embarks on her tale of illness and bondage. She tells Chrissie all about Sebastian.

Chrissie had guessed that something was amiss, for she can read her daughter's voice through every distortion of electronic and digital distance, but she is shocked to hear some of the details which Faro now imparts. She takes exactly the line that Faro expects, which is why Faro has been so anxious to come to see her in the first place. Chrissie thinks that it is absolutely ridiculous for Faro to be wasting her young life running around after somebody she doesn't even much like. Sebastian has no right to expect it, and she should tell him so at once. If Faro won't, Chrissie will. Chrissie, naturally, doesn't care tuppence for the misery or impending death of Sebastian Jones. Why should she? She's never met him and is sure she wouldn't like him if she did. She is much more concerned about her own daughter. Faro is far too kind-hearted. Look at all those years she spent shacked up with that old bookseller, simply because she felt sort of sorry for him. It is time she found somebody young, healthy and happy, with whom she can perpetuate Bessie and Chrissie's long-lived unbroken mitochondrial DNA, which is otherwise in danger of dying out for ever. If Faro has a baby, she and Don will give her the Australian baby-food mixer. Faro has no right to let all that evolutionary energy go to waste and seep away into a black hole of nothingness.

The baby-food mixer, she tells Faro, had nearly got them arrested at Sydney Airport. Apparently it looks just like the new kind of terrorist plastic bomb. Her hand baggage had been taken to pieces by the woman on the security conveyor belt. After causing all that trouble, it needs a baby. It's up to Faro to have a baby herself, or give it to a friend with a baby.

Chrissie delivers herself of these views with a somewhat fevered panache. Illness has fortified her and she speaks her mind. Faro laughs, and takes this maternal interference in good part. She agrees that she will have to break off her relationship with Seb. It is, like him, unhealthy. It is doing neither of them any good. He clearly isn't going to die quickly, in fact he may not be going to die at all. She's beginning to suspect that the whole charade really is something of a con trick. If Seb was as ill as he says he is, he'd be having chemotherapy, or something like that, wouldn't he? She treacherously betrays to her mother Seb's ghoulish necrophiliac Egyptian fantasies, and, treacherously, the two women laugh. The whole thing's absurd, says Faro. Seb has now reached a phase where he says he wants his organs extracted and stored in canopic jars. He doesn't want to be embalmed, thank you, but he would like his organs stored.

'What exactly *is* a canopic jar?' asks Chrissie. She had known once, but has forgotten. She'd never done the Egyptians, though Joe and Bessie had once given her Margaret Murray's *The Splendour That Was Egypt* for a birthday present. She still had it, somewhere.

'It's a sort of pot. They used to put the lungs, liver and intestines in it, and store them along with the embalmed body. You usually have four, but Seb says he'll be happy with two. He's particularly interested in preserving his rotten pancreas. He wants his sweetbreads pickled in formaldehyde for posterity.'

'What on earth does he want you to do with the jars?'

'I think he'd like me to *look after* them. Put them on the mantelpiece. Talk to them from time to time.'

Faro seems to find this funny, and so does Chrissie. Faro proceeds, with increasing hilarity, 'They used to remove the brain too, you know. Through the nose.'

'Of course they did,' agrees Chrissie, whose own nose is sore with sniffling.

'But they didn't keep the brain, Seb says. They threw it away. They didn't seem to have had much regard for the brain. Brains didn't rate, in Egypt. They didn't connect brains with thinking. Odd, isn't it?'

'I don't think we've any right to call the Egyptians odd,' says Chrissie. 'When you think what they did with Thomas Hardy's heart.'

'What did they do with Thomas Hardy's heart?'

'They were going to bury his body in Westminster Abbey, but they thought his heart should remain in Dorset. So they hacked it out. It must have been quite an old heart. Thin, *he* called it. He was well over eighty when he died. Anyway, they put the heart to one side on the table in the kitchen at Max Gate, while they were tidying up the rest of him, and the cat ate it.'

'No!'

'Probably not, but that's how the story goes. Hardy would have liked it. So I don't see we have much call to sneer at the Egyptians, do you?'

'I wasn't sneering. I was just laughing,' says Faro.

She hesitates, continues. 'In fact,' she says, 'there *is* something beautiful about the Egyptian cult of death and their belief in immortality. Perhaps. I know we think it's all a bit unscientific, and not even very spiritual, but maybe we're wrong. They believed in a real bodily afterlife, in a real place, with food and drink and household furniture and musical instruments. With jewels and jars and bowls of cosmetics. They believed you could live there, in that place.'

'So they believed the body was resurrected?'

'I think they believed that you had to survive death both in the body and the spirit. I mean, they *really* believed it, they didn't just think it was a nice idea. And I think that's why those Roman portraits are so startling and so beautiful. Because the painters truly believed that they could perpetuate life. They are so young, those young men and women. And they do live. The painters were right. Those people look at us. They tell us that they were beautiful, and that in life they were loved, and that they live on. I hate to admit it, but Seb is right. For those two centuries, belief fused with art. The believing artist created eternal life. Beauty was born of false belief. Eternal life was born of false belief.'

'Who says that?'

340

'I do,' says Faro. 'I do. I've just worked it out.'

'It may be so,' sighs Chrissie. 'It may be so.'

She is remembering the last time she spoke to Nick Gaulden, on the telephone, as he lay on his hospital bed: one year and three days ago to this day, she had said to him these words: 'Undying love.' Those had been her last words to him: 'Undying love.'

The Egyptians dined with the dead, relates Faro, in little pavilions. They sat among the mummies and conversed with them. And now, persists Faro, you can prise a bit of DNA out of a mummy, and find out who its closest relations were. Weird, isn't it?

A short silence falls. It is twenty past the hour, and an angel passes.

'Do you think,' says Chrissie, 'that DNA can suffer pain?'

It is just as well that Sir Donald has left the room, for he is a rational man.

'I think it might,' says Faro.

'Do you think the moment of mutation causes pain?' asks Chrissie.

'I think it might,' says Faro.

'Do you think that pain survives death?' asks Chrissie.

'I think it might,' says Faro.

They are both thinking that it is good that Nick Gaulden was cremated, and that he does not lie rotting in the earth.

If you were to look in at these two, like a spy in the night, through the uncurtained window, you would not mistake the relationship of these two women. You would see at once that they share the same flesh, and that it does not belong here. What are they doing here, in this well-mannered country drawing room, in a house built of yellow-grey seventeenth-century Cotswold stone? They are traitors and deserters, they are on the run. The walls are papered with a rustic print, and on it hang watercolours and small oils. The furniture is padded and deep and comfortable, and wears pleasantly faded linen loose-covers. A somewhat tarnished silver teapot shines dully on a silver salver by a polished oak dresser. A brown earthenware jug is filled with dahlias from the garden, and displayed on a ledge over the open fireplace is a large cream oval Spode serving plate, decorated with a tender display of dark pink passion flowers. This is a room of deep Middle England, with all its drag and all its allure. In the river at the bottom of the garden trout swim, perpetually breasting the current. If they swim with the stream, they drown and die. That is the way of fish.

Faro and Chrissie have abandoned the topic of pain and death, and are looking up the name of one of Faro's motor-way weeds in Chrissie's *Concise Illustrated Flora*. She has pressed a sample, and brought it with her. It has a thick ribbed stalk, alternate leaves and small platelets of yellow flowers. Faro and Chrissie are turning the coloured pages together. This is what people do of an evening in houses in the English countryside. And so Donald Sinclair discovers them, as he returns with a tray of tisane and decaffeinated coffee. He tells Chrissie that she ought to go to bed soon, and that she ought not to breathe germs all over her daughter. Faro stirs her apple and ginger, and Chrissie swallows a couple of aspirin, and Don goes back to the kitchen to look for the box of chocolates he had hidden from himself earlier in the evening. The telephone rings. Faro has not told Sebastian where she is, so it can't be him in pursuit of her. It must be for her mother. Maybe it will be Stella, or Moira, or one of those other Gaulden women, wanting an anniversary lament? Faro crosses the room, picks up the cordless receiver and hands it to her mother.

Chrissie listens intently, gravely, says Yes, says No, says Oh dear. Is it poor Eva Gaulden, bewailing the loss of her son? Faro cannot pick up the content of this interchange, but does not see why she should leave the room. She is sure that Chrissie has no secrets from her. The content is bad, whatever it may be. Chrissie is running her fingers through her thick dyed red hair, and looking miserable. Oh dear, oh dear, oh I am sorry. She waves at Faro to bring her pen and paper, takes down a telephone number, repeats it. It is a Breaseborough number, but Faro doesn't think it's Auntie Dora's. I'll ring back, says Chrissie.

Chrissie rings off, and blows her nose. 'Damn,' says Chrissie.

Auntie Dora has had a stroke. At least, her neighbour thought it was a stroke, though it could have been a heart attack. Anyway, she'd been taken into the Wardale Hospital in Breaseborough. The neighbour didn't know how serious it was. Dora had still been speaking as she was carried into the ambulance. You couldn't understand what she was saying but she was trying to say something.

'Oh God,' says Chrissie. 'I really ought to go. Poor Auntie Dora. Thank God she waited till I got back from Australia.'

But she concedes that she is not fit to drive, and Faro at once volunteers to go for her.

Chrissie and Don cannot understand why Faro is quite so keen to be helpful. Faro says that of course she will drive up to Breaseborough in the morning, visit the hospital, visit the neighbour, find out what's going on, feed the cat, do whatever needs doing. Faro's a kind girl, they know that, but she seems positively elated by the prospect of driving northward. Her eyes are glistening, her colour is high. Chrissie thinks that maybe she is keen to hit the road in order to keep moving in order to flee Sebastian Jones and Nick Gaulden, but Chrissie is wrong. Faro has, for the moment, forgotten all about her father and Sebastian. She is full of jubilation. Dora's illness is, for her, a bizarre stroke of luck.

Phone calls are made, numbers exchanged, and Chrissie manages to find her Yale key to Auntie Dora's house, entrusted to her last Christmas for exactly such an emergency. And in the morning Faro holds her breath while she cautiously kisses her red-eyed red-nosed mother, and is escorted to her Toyota by her stepfather. 'This is really very good of you, Faro,' he says, in his precise and gentlemanly Scottish way.

Bad weather and high winds have been forecast, but a luminous autumnal morning so far defies these prophecies. Breaseborough is almost due north as the crow flies, but the road system urges her towards Birmingham. She drives cross-country, along green roads, towards the M1. The wayside trees are red with a scattered mist of blood drops of scarlet berries, and silvery-grey old man's beard clambers through the hedgerows. She passes a ploughed field on fire with stripes of dazzling tawny-russet and orange stubble. It is the time of bonfires, and blue smoke rises from cottage gardens. When she reaches Chipping St Lawrence, Faro pulls into the verge, by the church, and to the sound of church bells reaches for her mobile. She hadn't wanted to wake Steve Nieman too early at a weekend, but he'll surely be awake by ten thirty?

He is awake. He is more than pleased to hear her. They will meet.

As she drives onwards, she scrabbles in her glove pocket for a tape, and hits on the Northam Choral Society's recording of *The Messiah*, directed by Sir Malcolm Sargent, with the Royal Liverpool Philharmonic Orchestra. Grandpa Barron had given it to her for Christmas, many years ago. It was his favourite, he had said. It seems appropriate for a northern journey. She starts to play it, but it makes her cry so much that she has to eject it, and turn to the tones of Joan Armatrading.

The Wardale Hospital isn't as depressing as it was when it was opened in 1906, or in the 1920s when it was closed for an outbreak of smallpox. The forbidding core of the old building remains, with its leaded pipes bearing the Wardale crest, and its tall despairing windows, but most of it is new, built in a cheerful red brick, with a glass and steel circular watchtower like the lookout-post on a liner. Even the old building is freshly painted. The staff are friendly. They conduct Faro to

Auntie Dora's ward, which isn't an intensive-care ward, so that's reassuring. And Dora, although she looks pretty decrepit, is conscious, and immediately recognizes her great-niece. Faro, boldly, kisses her. Dora hates being kissed, and always recoils from any adult bodily contact, but that's her problem, and now she's stuck in bed she can't protest very vigorously. Faro pulls up a chair, sits down and tries to ask Dora how she's feeling. Dora's speech has been affected, but not disastrously. One can still make out some sense. Faro explains that Chrissie is too ill to make the journey but will come when she's better, and Dora seems to understand this.

Faro stays for nearly an hour, during which she promises to go round to Dora's house in Swinton Road and make sure the cat is OK and pick up a dressing-gown and a few toiletries. Dora seems very set on being reunited with her own hairbrush, which must be a good sign. On the other hand she is not all that pleased to find Faro already has a key to her home. This makes her suspicious. Is Faro going to steal her treasures? The paranoia of helplessness is setting in fast. Faro speaks to some kind of doctor, but he seems to be an ill-informed part-time Sunday doctor, not Auntie Dora's regular GP, and she's not sure if she trusts him. He tells her Dora may well make a good recovery. Who knows? She's old, and overweight, and has a weak heart, but the stroke hasn't totally disabled her. They may get her back on her feet again.

Faro doubts this. Auntie Dora had looked ghastly. It's time for the old people's nursing home. Faro collects a list of them from the woman at the front desk, before driving off to Swinton Road.

She has arranged to meet Steve later, in Northam.

It is eerie, letting herself into Dora Bawtry's little property. Faro feels like an intruder. But the marmalade cat Minton greets her, and Faro strokes him. Somebody has already been in to feed him. His bowl is overflowing. It also looks as though it hasn't been washed in weeks. Faro throws away the old cat food, washes the dish, wipes it with a limp, threadbare and dirty tea-towel, and scatters a few dry pellets of Go-Cat into it. Minton politely crunches one or two morsels, but he is not very interested.

Faro looks around her, at the spider plants, the enormous television screen, the flowered wallpaper, the plastic lamp-shades, the dead-end casein relicts. Then she heaves a sigh and goes up the narrow stairs to look for the hairbrush and the dressing-gown and the flowery sponge-bag. While she is par-celling them up and tucking them into a plastic bag, she hears a knock at the door, and guiltily, like a thief, runs down to see who is there. It is the cat-feeding next-door neighbour, Mrs Sykes, worried that Faro is a burglar. Faro confesses that she has been taking possession of various personal items, and thanks Mrs Sykes for feeding Minton. They natter, for a few minutes, about Dora, and what-to-do, and Mrs Sykes de-scribes the details of Dora's collapse—the banging on the wall, the garbled phone call, the cry of 'Let yourself in!' It's a good thing Dora hadn't put the chain on the front door. Though she ought to have done—there have been a lot of break-ins lately, and only last week someone had come bang-ing on their doors asking for old furniture.

Faro finds it hard to credit that anyone could want any-thing belonging to anyone in Swinton Road, but conceals her scepticism. Mrs Sykes seems to be quite a nice person, best to keep on the right side of her, they may have need of her.

Dora is pleased to see her matted and battered old Mason Pearson hairbrush, and to hear good news of Minton. Faro stays for a while, chats for a while, says she'll keep in touch. She promises to try to speak to Dora's friend Dorothy in Wath, and let her know what has happened. She finds a cup of tea from the Friends' Comfort Room, and a vase for the de-pressing selection of ill-assorted and unnaturally tinted carna-tions and African daisies she has bought at the cemetery gates, then ruthlessly kisses her great-aunt good-bye. Steve Nieman will be waiting. It is already late afternoon.

Steve is waiting for her in the pub on the corner of his street, on the outskirts of the Breaseborough side of Northam. He lives on the top floor of a high block of council flats with a doorcode entry system which he says is always buggered, and he's said he'll wait for her in the Telstar, which he has described to her as a conspicuously unsuccessful establishment. And there he is. Faro, who has been thinking about him almost incessantly for a month, is so relieved to see him again that tears start up into her eyes. For he is even more what she needs than she had been imagining. He hadn't been a fantasy. There he is.

He seems to feel the same about her. Chivalrous, he makes sure she's parked her car safely—it's a bit of a dodgy district—and buys her a Guinness and a packet of crisps. They sit together, at a small round wet beery wooden table in a corner, and he strokes the back of her hand, tenderly, while she tells him about the hospital. The hairs on the back of her hand stand up at his touch. He radiates heat like a furnace. He glows tawny in the gloom. He has described the pub correctly. It is even gloomier than Seb's local in Holborn. It has a different genre of gloominess, impoverished, sparse, dark and mournful, and Steve and Faro are decades younger than the only other merrymakers, who are silently watching a football match on a large overhead TV screen.

Steve hopes it's all right with her, he's bought her some supper. Will she come up for it? Of course she will. Her heart sinks slightly at the sight of the graffiti-adorned entrance to his grim concrete sixties-built residence, and the smell in the lift is worse than the smell of Swinton Road, but Steve assures her it will all be OK when they get up there. She fears the worst, but tells herself that no bachelor pad can be as dreary and dirty as the second-floor back of Sebastian Jones, and that Steve would not invite her into a fouled nest. Even so, she is taken aback by the brightness and beauty of Steve's apartment. He is right to be proud of it. He tells her about it as he uncorks a bottle of Rioja. He gets it for next to nothing from the Council, through the Project, because nobody wants to live up here, it's too high and the lifts keep breaking down. Not many people can face ten flights of stone steps. And yes, he's done it up himself. After all, he is a carpenter. It's his job.

It is a two-bedroom flat, and he has painted it white and taken most of the doors off their hinges. It is spacious and airy. His bicycle stands in the corridor. There is no furniture, apart from a few wooden platforms with cushions, and some bookshelves. There are no curtains. But there are large pots of tree ferns and date palms, some of them ten feet tall. Faro admires the sharp green plumes of the phoenix of the Canaries, which is flourishing here in South Yorkshire. The apartment is light and minimal. Everything is clean. After Seb's horrors, this is like heaven. And the view is spectacular. Steve can see all the way up the valley, westwards towards Cotterhall and Breaseborough. In the distance lie the Wild Nature Park, and the Water House, and the gazebo he has built with his own hands for Faro. He shows her a balsa-wood model of it. It is octagonal, and looks in all directions. It is Faro's lighthouse, and he will take her to see it one day soon. Its official name is Goosebutt Gazebo, but Steve thinks of it as Faro's Folly, and so must she.

Steve and Faro stand by the window, shoulder to shoulder, gazing out over the landscape. The brilliant golden October day has turned into a dramatic evening, and the sun is sinking in a red glow, more lurid than the furnace fires that these two have never seen. Great slate-grey and purple cumulus clouds swell and grow on the horizon, shot with rays of orange and yellow light, and towers and castles of darkness mount and break and shift before them. They are watching black vesper's pageant. It is the moment of Nick Gaulden's passing, but neither of them is thinking of Nick Gaulden. The wind is beginning to whine in the double-glazing. It will be a wild night.

When Faro wakes, at three in the morning, she wonders for a moment where she is, and why, and what has woken her. Has the earth moved? Has she heard a faraway explosion? Something has happened. And then she remembers that here she is, with Steve Nieman, who is sleeping by her side. She breathes him in. He is warm and naked and hairy, and he smells of warm earth and resin and cedarwood.

It is nighttime, but there is enough light for her to find her way to the bathroom, where she pees as quietly as she can, and drinks a glass of water. A strange red light is still flowing through the high windows. The sun is long set, and the foundries have been dead for decades, but there is an unnatural and unearthly glow to the west. Faro, wrapped in a small towel, approaches the large window from which she and Steve had admired the post-industrial view, in front of which they had eaten their modest supper. Faro gazes forth in consternation, for, far away, the valley seems to be on fire.

Is it some trick of the light, some natural phenomenon? It cannot be an early dawn, for it is in the east that the sun usually rises. Should she wake Steve and tell him about it? She stares at the dull and distant flickering. Is it an industrial disaster? Is it the end of the world?

It is not the end of the world, but it is a conflagration. Faro wakes Steve, and they stare out together through Steve's binoculars. It is Steve's valley that is burning. 'Jesus Christ,' says Steve, in shocked amazement. What can have happened? They dial 999, and report it to a person who thanks them and says that fire engines are already on the scene. The person will not tell them any more details. They tune to an all-night local radio station, and at first get nothing but music, but after ten minutes a news bulletin reports that there has been an explosion at Bednerby, between Breaseborough and Cotterhall, and that high winds are fanning the flames. So far no casualties reported, but there may be an evacuation of adjacent buildings if the fire is not brought under control. There is an emergency number. Stunned, Steve rubs his eyes and strains his vision.

They cannot return quietly to their bed and wait till morning for more news. They ring the emergency number, and are told that police are on hand and assisting evacuation of Goosebutt Terrace and Rattenhole Edge. This is terrible news to Steve. This is the very edge of his own territory. Silently, Steve and Faro clamber into their clothes. Faro will drive.

Steve has worked out the best way to get near the Project, along what locals call the Road to Nowhere, which is a rarely used short stretch of expensive newly surfaced and expensively finished dual carriageway linking Breaseborough and Cotterhall. It had been built with European money in the days when a revival of local manufacturing industry was still a realistic expectation. They drive through the night, towards the blaze, and eventually reach a cordon of police vehicles. The police not surprisingly seem to think they are at best unnecessary intruders and at worst sensation-seekers, and try to turn them back. Steve gets out, argues with them, pleads with them, questions them. They become more friendly as he reveals his local credentials, and tells them Faro is an important and accredited journalist working for a famous scientific magazine. They tell him that the fire began just before midnight, and although a spontaneous explosion of methane and/or natural gas is suspected, arson has not been ruled out. Some of the site buildings of the Project have already been destroyed. Fifty firemen are fighting the blaze, and reinforcements are on their way from Doncaster and Sheffield. No, they can't let Steve through, it isn't safe. Steve asks if his boss, Charlie Henderson, has been informed. The police have never heard of Charlie Henderson. None of the emergency numbers of Rose & Rose are responding, they say. All is chaos.

Steve says he doesn't see the point of waking Charlie in the middle of the night with bad news. It can wait till morning. He gives the police some names and numbers, including his own. Then he gets back in the car, and asks Faro to reverse away from all of this.

There is soot on the air, and a smell of destruction.

Steve says they can drive up, round the back, and look down from the top quarry road at the back, above Coddy Holes. There's no point in watching, but he can't quit now. He wants to see the worst. So Faro follows instructions, and winds her way back down the valley, and up through some suburban 1930s terracing (Mount Pleasant, Quarry View, Bella Vista, Braeside, Crosswinds) and on to a high ridge looking down over the valley. There is a screaming of the convergence of fire engines, and below them leap the flames of hell.

They are not alone on the vantage point of the ridge. A little ragged band of spectators has gathered there to witness the day of judgement. A couple of first-shift firefighters, who have knocked off and are now taking a breather and drawing hard on their cigarettes, are staring glumly down at the scene of destruction. Their faces are blackened, as had in the old days been the faces of their forefathers the miners, and their teeth and eyeballs shine white in the darkness. The tips of their cigarettes glow. A small and wizened old man with a raincoat over his striped pyjamas stands with his hands in his pockets, muttering to himself. A group of whey-faced late-night local revellers is standing near him, representing the unemployed of Breaseborough. They have cans of beer in their hands, but they have stopped drinking. Will the fire spread and engulf the whole of Breaseborough? Steve goes to speak to the firemen, who shake their heads and say they cannot tell what will happen. You can't tell what's underground, in these parts. It's been building up for centuries. They speak of the great fire of Hatfield Moor, which had burned for over two weeks through the December snows of 1981, and which had at last been extinguished not by the firemen of Doncaster but by a Texan oil-well troubleshooter called Boots Hanson. Their jokes are as bitter as their faces are black. Boots is probably dead by now, and so is Red Adaire. Who will be flown in now to save Hammervale? And who will pay? Cheaper to let us all burn to cinders, says the old troglodyte in his raincoat. Who gives a fuck about Hammervale? If there was gas down there, or oil, now that would bring them in. But there's nowt down there but rubbish.

Steve watches the work of his hands go up in flames. Faro's gazebo has surely gone, and probably also the Water House and the Observatory. He seems to be in a trance. Faro leaves him standing there, and goes back to the car. She switches on the car radio, puts in the tape of Grandpa Barron's *Messiah,* opens the car doors, turns up the volume. The music floods out into the night sky. *And every valley shall be exalted, and every mountain and hill made low, and the crooked places shall be made plain...* The music fills the earth and the heaven. They all listen, the boys, the old man, the firemen, Steve and Faro. *For the people that walked in darkness have seen a great light...* On and on pours the music. There is no stopping it. *Rejoice greatly, O daughter of Zion! Speak ye comfortably unto Jerusalem...* Tears pour down Faro's face, streaked with smuts borne on the dying breeze. The music defies hell and soars to heaven, and it seems to Faro that all the caverns of the cliff will open and give up their dead, that the men of the ages of stone and bronze and coal will come forth from their subterranean mansions, and that they will be redeemed. For now is Christ risen, and hell has been harrowed, and those that sleep shall be awakened. The skeletons totter out into the blaze. Faro weeps and weeps, as she sits on the low wall, with the car doors wide open like a beetle's wings.

When the first track of the tape comes to an end, one of the firemen comes over to Faro. She half expects him to tell her to turn the fucking volume down or fuck off back down the M1 back to where she came from, but what he says is 'Is that the Northam Choral Society singing there?'

Faro nods.

'I thought it must be,' says the fireman. 'I could tell it was. My dad sang in that choir. He sang for that very recording. With Sir Malcolm Sargent, in the City Hall, in 1957. They could sing, in them days. Now, it's nowt but striptease and karaoke.'

'My Great-Grandpa Bawtry used to sing with the Breaseborough Chapel Choir,' says Faro.

He nods, as though this is what one would have expected and, less predictably, stretches out his grimy hand to her. 'Pleased to meet you,' he says. They shake hands, across the divide. His hand is hot and safe, his grasp is firm.

The pause ends, the tape reverses, and the second side of the tape begins to play. *I know that my Redeemer liveth, and that though worms may corrupt this body, yet in my flesh shall I see God.* The trumpets sound, and the ashes stand upright at the latter day. The joyful voices of the dead rise in impassioned and glorious unison. Cotterhall Man hears them, in his glass coffin. Their voices harrow hell and pierce the firmament.

The fire did not burn for forty days and forty nights, nor even for four days and four nights. The offspring of Red Adaire were not flown in to quench it. It burned for three days, and at first attracted national press and TV coverage. Interest waned quickly. The usual clichés were rolled out—'a miracle nobody was killed', 'a disaster waiting to happen'. But even as the valley continued to smoulder, the cameras moved on. There was one small human-interest story—old Mrs Clegg, who had for some years been stubbornly resisting efforts to rescue her from her endangered yet strategically desirable slum, had barricaded herself into her bedroom on that first flaming night, and had refused to move. She said she'd survived two world wars in that house and would prefer to die there. The Germans hadn't bombed her out, and she wasn't leaving now. Who'd won the wars? She had. She wasn't having any firemen giving her a fireman's lift. Her oaths were impressive. She was talked out at dawn by the only woman on the scene, a young London journalist called Faro Gaulden (or Golden, as some papers understandably misspelled her name). This person had persuaded Mrs Clegg to come forth, and had bullied her into taking shelter with a neighbour. Mrs Clegg was not a grateful or a pleasant survivor. She kept on saying she'd rather die than spend a night under the roof of a stranger. And as the danger passed when the wind changed direction, she was allowed home the next day. Not much of a story.

More was made of the reasons for the disaster. Was it the chicken shit? Was it the methane? Was it the curse of Cotterhall Man? Several column inches were devoted to the technology of energy creation from waste disposal, to the virtues of anaerobic digesters and the dangers of landfill. Faro, who wrote a good deal about the incident herself, became an instant expert in the acronyms of waste management, and her conversation became rich with references to LFG (landfill gas), MSW (municipal solid waste) and NFFO (non-fossil fuel obligation). Rose & Rose with their greendump sites were acquitted of any malpractice: in fact, it emerged that the claims made to Stella Wakefield at Nick Gaulden's wake, and relayed to Chrissie Sinclair, were not wholly false. Rose & Rose had considered the environment as well as their own profits. Mistakes had been made, but not mistakes worthy of the description of criminal negligence. It was the ancient poison that had broken out. Rose & Rose had cracked the crust by overeager excavation and let it out, but they could not be blamed for what was down there in the first place. It was not they who had been digging and rooting and undermining Hammervale all the way through the Industrial Revolution. They'd been far away, minding their own business, in a *shtetl* in Poland, in a tailor's shop in Austria, in the history department of the University of Heidelberg. Not guilty, was the verdict on Rose & Rose.

The discovery, on site, of two 45-gallon drums of depleted uranium was hushed up by the Environmental Agency. This volatile and dangerous substance, which can ignite spontaneously, burns at 1,000°C and vaporizes everything around it. Its presence on the Rose & Rose dump was inexplicable. It had been illegally dumped, but by whom? Investigators are still at work. Mrs Clegg had a lucky escape.

The valley and the Earth Project would recover, in time, and Steve said he would rebuild Faro's gazebo. Flowers would grow once more from the ashes. Cinders are good for the soil. There was a small sympathy vote from the Lottery distributors, and a little more money trickled back again—not enough, but a little. Hammervale would soon be forgotten again. The ragwort and the hawkweed would blossom in peace.

Dennis Rose's claims to an environmental conscience had some substance, but Sebastian Jones's claims to a cancerous pancreas did not. He had been lying to Faro. Faro, returning from the flames, had accused him of lying, and he confessed. He was ill, but not fatally ill. Faro told him he needed to see a psychoanalyst more urgently than a physician and recommended Moira, whom she had just met at a book launch to celebrate a new genetics-based study of mother-daughter relationships called *The Maternal Genie*. Moira, Faro said sharply, would be just the person to sort Seb out. Moira had been through hell and back again, and she would drag Seb out too, if she could. Seb expressed horror at this suggestion, but Faro had lost patience with horror. He had overstepped the mark, and he had lost her. She would not go back. Sebastian Jones had wasted quite enough of her time. She was sick of waste. The crudity of his death wish, she told him sternly, was unworthy of someone of his intelligence. He should think of something more sophisticated next time.

Sebastian Jones, perversely, seemed to enjoy her severity, and he began to perk up once Faro had finally quit him. Or so Raoul and Rona reported to Faro. She should have ditched him long ago, said Raoul and Rona.

A couple of weeks after the Breaseborough disaster, Faro received an e-mail from her distant cousin Peter Cudworth. It started mildly enough, telling her that he had seen her name on the Internet news coverage of the fire, and had read with interest her article on the history of municipal solid waste disposal and recycling techniques in the nineteenth century. Her e-mail address had been attached, so he had taken the liberty. It had been good to see her name, and to be reminded of their meeting in the summer. He felt he had to tell her that he had been through a very bad time. She had told him about her father's death, and now he had to tell her about his wife's. Two weeks ago, Anna had committed suicide. She had survived an earlier bout of severe depression, some five or six years ago, but this recent recurrence had proved intractable, and the drugs which had seemed to work reasonably well on a previous occasion had produced an unfortunate reaction.

Faro, reaching this point in the e-mail, decided to print out. She couldn't read stuff like that on the screen, it didn't seem right.

The printer clicked on and on, as it spewed out Peter Cudworth's long, sad story. No wonder the message had taken some time to retrieve.

Peter apologized for unburdening himself to a stranger, but he felt that Faro, because of her own family history, would understand. Anna, he wrote, had become obsessed by the history of the Holocaust, and had taken to reading nothing but Holocaust literature, of which there was now, in these recent years, so much. She had read her way through histories and diaries, through novels and poems, through Primo Levi and Hannah Arendt and Albert Speer and Gitta Sereny. She had read Daniel Jonah Goldhagen's *Hitler's Willing Executioners*, and convinced herself she came from evil stock. 'There's no need for me to tell you,' wrote Peter Cudworth, widower, 'that she wouldn't have hurt a fly. She was a good woman.' He had tried to persuade her that it would be a good idea, next year, for them to go back to the village, to look at her past, for it would prove either innocent or alien. He'd even suggested they should brave a tour of the death camps. 'She'd see it had nothing to do with her, I told her,' wrote Peter. 'But she was beyond reasoning. I hadn't realized it had got so bad with her.'

There had been other factors—medical, menopausal. But it was history itself that had weighed upon her. He was sorry to burden Faro with this, but it was good to be able to tell somebody. His friends and colleagues in Iowa City had been more than kind, but there were things he could not talk about to them. He signed himself off, *With all good wishes for your health and happiness, your kinsman Peter. Stemmata quid faciunt?*

Faro was sympathetic but cautious in her reply. She could not cope with another sick man. She did not want Peter Cudworth to arrive on her doorstep. She would keep him at a safe cyber-distance. She seemed to attract sorrow and sickness like a beacon. She would try to dim her light.

⊙〰〰〰⊙

Auntie Dora, the last survivor of the old world of Breaseborough, did not make a good recovery. It was soon clear that she would never be able to go home to Swinton Road and to her cat Minton. She would not be able to live by herself again. The list of registered care homes picked up by Faro at the Wardale Hospital came in handy. At first, Chrissie was surprised by how eager and helpful Faro continued to prove over the time-consuming and saddening administration of Dora's illness, but when she learned that Faro was having an affair with a nice Jewish boy up in Northam, she was surprised no longer. No wonder Faro was always ready to drive up and down the M1. Steve Nieman sounded just the right kind of chap for Faro, and she looked forward to meeting him one day soon.

Auntie Dora was moved from the hospital into a home in Cotterhall, where she had a small room to herself, with full-time nursing care, and was allowed to keep Minton with her. She did not at first adapt well to institutionalization, and objected strongly to being dispatched all the way from Breaseborough to Cotterhall, but eventually she accepted Faro's insistence that it was the only nursing home she could find which would

357

take pets. She was able to enjoy pouring good strong Bawtry scorn on the other residents, who seemed to her to be suffering from an exaggerated array of geriatric complaints, such as leglessness, toothlessness and witlessness. She still had most of her teeth, despite or because of the fact that she hadn't seen a dentist for thirty years: her teeth had protected themselves with a natural coating of tartar and plaque, and could still munch their way through a chop or a pork pie. She refused to do her exercises, but stroking Minton kept her thick and gnarled old fingers moving. Minton, a wily and sociable cat, soon found many other admirers, and was seen to spend much time eyeing Enid Love's powder-blue budgerigar. But he was polite enough to remain loyal to his old mistress, and always retired to the end of her bed for the night. Faro, secretly, was astonished that this was allowed, in this age of hygiene, but she was so relieved by the lenience of the regime that she kept her astonishment to herself. Minton, in her view, deserved a medal.

Faro got on well with the manager of the home, a fussy old gay called Ronnie, with a penchant for flowery wallpapers and upholstered toilet rolls, and a partner called Len who organized bingo and card games. Ronnie had once been a publican: he told Faro that there was more money in old folk these days than in beer. They were his little gold mine. He was, as far as Faro could see, very kind and gallant to his old ladies and gentlemen. He praised them and petted them and urged them to live on to the next millennium, and he iced cakes for their birthdays with his own hands. Dora, in time, came to like him, though she remained critical of many of her fellow inmates. Faro, watching Dora respond to Ronnie's flirtatious teasing, wondered, and not for the first time, if Dora herself was gay. Or had been gay. Clearly, by now, she wasn't anything along those lines. But she did ask, sometimes, after her friend Dorothy in Wath. Could Faro let Dorothy know where Dora was? She hasn't heard from Dorothy for a long time, not since her last birthday card. Faro promises that she will, but is hampered by the fact that Dora doesn't seem able to remember Dorothy's married surname and therefore can't find her address or phone number in her little address book. She'll get round to sorting it out one day.

Chrissie and Faro soon became familiar with the tiresome and complex bureaucracy of old age, with benefits and social services and care allowances. It was clear that it would be sensible for Dora to sell Swinton Road as soon as possible and get rid of her small capital, and Faro undertook to investigate the housing market. She was shocked by what she found. Prices were lower than she could have imagined. Whole houses were going for a quarter of the price of a one-room London flat in an undesirable area miles from the nearest Tube. In Breaseborough, you could buy an end-of-terrace for £26,000, and a mid-terrace for £19,000. Faro has fantasies of buying one, and setting up a little northern home of her own. Dora's house was valued at £30,000, but Faro thought that was optimistic.

The house would have to be cleared, and, again, Faro volunteered. She had already taken a selection of Dora's treasures to her bedroom in the Poplars, but there was a lot of rubbish still to go before the house could be put on the market. Faro and Steve made several trips to the Rose & Rose Greendump with the worst of the stuff. The contents of the freezer proved a problem. Steve, a Jewish vegetarian, was particularly worried about the pork chops, which looked as though they had been there for decades. It didn't seem right to chuck them in a greendump. A pity, said Faro, that Great-Grandpa Bawtry's Destructor had ever been decommissioned. They'd have roasted away nicely in there.

Faro tracked down the house of Dora's friend Dorothy, but she came too late, for Dorothy had died suddenly, and the house was for sale. Dorothy Cooper, née Clarkson, had lived in a house called Walden in Quarry View Road, Wath-upon-Dearne. If Faro had expected a picturesquely depressing residence, she was disappointed. Wath itself was depressing, because depressed, but Walden proved to be a pleasant 1930s building with stained glass in the panels over its bow windows, and a front garden full of rose bushes. Had it been named after Thoreau's *Walden*? Had Dorothy Cooper read Thoreau? A little island of peace, overlooking the quarries. Faro stood there for a two minutes' silence, watching the removal men as they heaved out the old furniture. In the garden next door stood an extraordinary and unlikely object, twelve foot tall, bristling with wires and spikes and crowns of thorns. Was it a sculpture? No, the removal men told Faro. It was a ham-radio transmitter. From this forgotten ridge, somebody was reaching out to the world.

Faro, amongst the leavings of her great-aunt's life, sits alone, one dark winter evening. She is once more going through the drawers of the living-room sideboard, where Dora had kept her papers and her photographs and her albums. It is a sad task, but Faro is not unhappy, for she is spending the night with Steve, and looks forward, as always, to seeing him. She has, at times, wondered if she should brave spending a whole night in Swinton Road, to see if the ghosts of her grandmother and great-grandparents will visit her, but she has not been able to face it. It is too unpleasant there, and she does not think the ghosts will come.

She has, however, on her various visits, found some evocative mementoes. She has found her aunt's little suede autograph album, and read its jokes, its poetic inscriptions, its pious exhortations. She has found the little brownish card from Breaseborough Urban District Council inviting George Albert Bawtry to a dinner at 6.30 on Monday, 2 June, at Hardy's Rooms to celebrate the opening of the Destructor and Electric Lighting Works in the year of the Coronation of King Edward VII, 1902. It is signed, *Obediently Yours,* by a committee of four. She has found *Little Henry and His Bearer* and *The Dairyman's Daughter,* and various inscribed hymnbooks and Bibles. She has found books of coloured scraps, carefully pasted in by tidy children. She has found postcards from her great-grandfather to her great-grandmother, dating back to the days when Ellen Bawtry was still Ellen Cudworth. She has found postcards from unknown Cudworths and unknown Bawtrys. Her aunt's old driving licence, and her postwar ration book. A sheet of Polyfotos of a much-replicated fierce-eyed Chrissie Barron, aged about ten, in a panama school hat, and a similar sheet of her Uncle Robert, staring solemnly at the camera and half-strangled by a large knotted school tie. A photograph of the little sisters, Bessie and Dora, in their Sunday best, all frills and embroidery and sweetness. A photo of Grandma Barron's wedding day, taken in Breaseborough churchyard. A photograph of Bessie and Dora, fair and young and pretty, sitting on a grassy bank in cloche hats, full of hope, smiling. A rather surprising portrait of Great-Grandpa Bawtry in drag, looking like Charlie's Aunt. A lineup of about twelve motorbikes and sidecars, off on a rally, the men in caps, with cigarettes bravely clenched between their teeth, the women in hats with earflaps. The Mongol hordes of South Yorkshire. They conquered nothing.

There are too many memories here. Impatience is overcoming Faro. She has several plastic bags full of rubbish, and she is sure she is about to discard something important. Though how could any of this be of any importance? These are such little lives. Unimportant people, in an unimportant place. They had been young, they had endured, they had taken their wages and their punishment, and then they had grown old, and all for no obvious purpose. And now she is throwing them all into a plastic bag.

Most of Auntie Dora's books, apart from the Victorian Sunday school keepsakes and Dick Francis hardbacks, are old *Reader's Digest*s or cheap book club editions, and Faro boxes them up for charity. She hesitates when she finds a novel by Georgette Heyer called *Faro's Daughter,* and starts to browse through it. It tells the story of the beautiful Deborah, spirited niece of an aunt who runs a gaming house in Regency Mayfair. Faro, skipping rapidly, is pleased to find that despite her professional disadvantages this daughter of the game marries the disdainful and stylish gentleman who had been so rude to her in the first pages. This unlikely romance is cheering. Faro admires the innovative boldness of Georgette Heyer, and her careless disregard of probability. She puts the book to one side. She reprieves it from Oxfam. She will hand it on to her mother. She glances at the rest of the Georgette Heyer collection, and finds another title of interest, a very early work called *The Black Moth*. It doesn't look as though it is about industrial melanism, but she puts that to one side too. Maybe Georgette Heyer is trying to tell her something?

Auntie Dora has asked her to look for her gold bracelet, her father's silver watch and her mother's engagement ring. So far, Faro has not discovered them. She will have one more look, in Auntie Dora's bedroom. She climbs the narrow staircase, lit from above by a dangling light bulb. Dora's bedroom is very damp. The window had been left open, letting in the rain, and now it will not close properly, for the old wooden frame is swollen. There are dark patches on the plaster ceiling, shaped like the billowing mushroom clouds of atomic explosions. The room smells of cat and human urine. Here is the very bed in which Chrissie and Robert would snuggle up to warm, buttery Auntie Dora when they were on their Breaseborough visits. These are the very stains at which they had stared, and of which Chrissie had spoken to Faro. They had frightened Chrissie, for those had been the days when children lived in fear of another Hiroshima.

Faro rummages in the chest of drawers and on the top shelf of the wardrobe. She discovers a cache of all the crisp new linen tea-towels that she and Robert and Chrissie have been giving Dora as Christmas extras over the years, emblazoned with representations of the counties of England, the wildflowers of Wales and country recipes from Somerset. She finds, in the bottom drawer, a forlorn pile of antique unused bed linen, and folded amongst it a pair of beautiful lace-edged pillowcases, embroidered, white on white, and enclosed in yellowing tissue: with them is a handwritten card, which says *To Dora, for your Bottom Drawer, with best regards from ABB.* She also finds a couple of promising boxes. One is square and wooden, one is round and lacquered. Both contain a touching jumble of what look like more or less worthless treasures—a glittering paste buckle, a chipped Wedgwood cameo brooch, some strings of pearls and glass beads with broken clasps, a rubber-banded scroll of out-of-date banknotes, a little leather child's purse of coins, a tortoiseshell hairpin, an amber cigarette holder and a silver napkin ring with the initials DCB engraved upon it. Faro spills the coins out over Dora's glass-protected kidney-shaped dressing table. There are bronze farthings, with their stubby little wrens, and octagonal three-penny pieces with their emblems of flowering thrift, and a silver sixpence dated 1951. The sixpence is discoloured. Faro has never seen a farthing before, but the sixpence reminds her of something. She can't think what.

She finds the gold chain, and the engagement ring. The ring is a clear and eloquent candidate for pity. Its slender golden band has worn thin and its shaft is broken. She tries it on, but even in its broken state it is far too small to encircle Faro's smallest finger. Can Ellen Bawtry's fingers ever have been so slender? This fragile circle bears a diamond-shaped cluster of eight small dull rubbed pearls, which, examined through Dora's bedside magnifying glass, look more like tiny teeth than jewels. In the centre of the pearls is set a tiny square of pale green glass. It does not even pretend to be an emerald. Faro feels sorry for the poor ring, and for her grandmother.

Bert Bawtry's round solid-silver watch is more robust. It has a heavy silver chain attached to it. Its face displays roman numerals, in a plain handsome black script, on a white ground.

Faro manages to prise open the complicated layers of its back, inspects its hieroglyphic hallmarks, and gazes into its intricate workings. She shakes the watch, holds it to her ear, and to her astonishment hears that it begins to tick. Its second hand moves. It lives again. It has waited patiently through all this time for her to come to discover it and reawaken it.

At the bottom of the wooden box is a brown envelope. Inside it is a photograph. It is of the two sisters, taken on Grandma Barron's wedding day, for Bessie is wearing her wedding dress, and Dora is playing bridesmaid. They are sitting in a backyard on a bench next to what is clearly an outdoor privy. It must have been taken at Slotton Road, before the sisters set off to the church to meet Joe Barron. Both sisters look happy, shy, hopeful and enchantingly pretty. Bessie's hair is charmingly shingled, Dora's is in ringlets. *The world was all before them, where to choose...* Faro stares at this photograph, in the belief that it has more to say to her than it can show. She examines it through the magnifying glass, and it seems that through the curve of the thick plastic lens, round the receding edges of the image, she begins to see movement. It is as though the frozen moment lives again. Somebody is standing behind Bessie and Dora Bawtry, in the shadows. Who is it? Will this person come out of the shadows? Who is there, with these young women? Is it their Redeemer?

On the way down the stairs, she remembers, with a sense of sudden shock, the last time she had seen a silver sixpence. It had been hidden in the Christmas pudding that Bessie Barron had served up at her last family Christmas at Woodlawn. Bessie, who had sliced the pudding, made sure that little Faro got the sixpence, and Faro, who had noticed the manoeuvre, had nevertheless been pleased and excited to find the little coin, hygienically wrapped in foil, half hidden in her rich brown fruity portion. Faro stands stock-still on the seventh step, for she can see Grandma's happy face, smiling, as Faro cries out and unwraps the silver treasure. Grandma Barron had always made a good Christmas pudding. Faro had always enjoyed the Surrey Christmas. She felt safe there, in that large, bright, clean house. Like a proper child.

After Bessie's death, Chrissie Barron had bought all her puddings from a shop.

Afterword

This is a novel about my mother, Kathleen Marie Bloor. The epigraph is a poem by my daughter, Rebecca Swift. Neither Rebecca nor her brothers appear in this volume, and my brother and sisters have also been excised. The later parts of the story are entirely fictitious.

My father died in December 1982, and my mother shortly afterwards, in April 1984. After her death several friends—mostly novelist friends—suggested that I should try to write about her. Use your mother's blood for ink, one of them urged me. So I tried, but it wasn't easy. I think about my mother a great deal, uncomfortably. Night and day on me she cries. Maybe I should have tried to write a factual memoir of her life, but I have written this instead.

I encountered great difficulties. The worst was the question of tone. I find myself being harsh, dismissive, censorious. As she was. She taught me language. One way of escaping from this would have been through comedy. And my mother did often teeter on the brink of appearing as a figure from an Alan Bennett comedy—opinionated, provincial, ridiculous. But I do not have the talent for that kind of comedy, and my mother was not a comic character. She was not funny. She was a highly intelligent, angry, deeply disappointed and manipulative woman. I am not sure if I have been able to find a tone in which to create or describe her.

I recognize that I appear to betray a bias in favour of my father, and that I may not have been able to bring him to life. I find myself repeating that he was 'a good man'. And so I believe he was.

The plot also presented difficulties. I knew something about the early lives of my parents, and drew on letters which my father wrote to his best friend. This correspondence began in their schooldays and continued through the period when my father was acting as travelling salesman for Drabble's Sweets, through his years at Downing College, through the early years of his marriage and the birth of my elder sister, and through the war, when I and my younger sister were born. On my father's death, that friend, also now dead, gave me these letters, and I think he would have wanted me to use them. They gave me many social details about raffia baskets and coffee sets and T. S. Eliot. So my descriptions of those early years are backed up by documentary evidence and by some research, though I have also filled out the record with invention. But the Drabble social background continues to mystify me. What are my father's sisters doing on skis in the Alps in the 1930s? Is the photograph a studio fake? Where did the money come from? How much money was there? And what was the family of Leila Das doing in South Yorkshire? How did they get there? I could spend years trying to answer these questions. Maybe, one day, I will.

I have checked some, but not all of my mother's stories. The trauma of her Tripos was, I believe, as she and I have described it. She often spoke of Miss Strachey, and she was taught by Dr Leavis: somewhere I have the reference he wrote for her when she began to apply for teaching posts. She admired Virginia Woolf, and in particular, curiously, *Orlando*, though she cannot have read this as early as she thought she did. Of course, she may have told different stories to my sisters and my brother. Each child has a different mother, as I believe Winnicott says somewhere.

I never visited Mexborough during my childhood, for my grandparents, unlike Chrissie's, had moved away during the 1930s to run a bed and breakfast business on what was then the Great North Road. The first time I visited Mexborough was with my aunt, after my mother's death. My mother hated Mexborough. I have not exaggerated her feelings towards Mexborough. She may have done, but I have not. My aunt liked the town, though she also moved away, to Doncaster, in the thirties, where she worked as a primary-school teacher. She inherited the bed and breakfast house on her parents' death.

My aunt, as I write, is still alive. I have sanitized my account of the old people's home where Aunt Dora lives. It isn't as nice as that. Nor is she as content as I have made her appear. Minton's alter ego, in the form of a small white dog, does not live with her, but is taken to visit her regularly, by neighbours whose kindness is beyond all praise.

I wrote this book to try to understand my mother better. I went down into the underworld to look for my mother, but I couldn't find her. She wasn't there.

It's all very well, imagining a happy ending, imagining Faro Gaulden's happy memory of a happy Christmas. It wasn't like that. For moments, it seems to me that it might have been like that. If I try very hard, I can induce in myself a brief, unconvincing, unsustainable trance of happy memory. My mother did enjoy Christmas, and she did make good Christmas puddings. I didn't, and I don't. She wasn't unrelentingly anxious and unhappy, as I have portrayed her. She had a capacity for enjoyment. I should have taken her across the Atlantic on a luxury liner. I tried, but I failed. I lacked Chrissie's courage.

There is an underworld story from another mythology about a woman who wished to enter hell to seek for her loved one. Only the dead could enter hell, so she made herself as one of the dead. She rubbed herself with dead rat water in order to disguise herself with the smell of dead rat, and thus she was able to pass the guardians of the dead. I feel, in writing this, that I have made myself smell of dead rat, and I am not sure how to get rid of the smell. I cannot remember if the woman from the rat story was able to release her loved one from bondage.

I cannot sing, my mother could not sing, and her mother before her could not sing. But Faro can sing, and her clear voice floods the valley.

ML

THOMAS CRANE PUBLIC LIBRARY

3 1641 00454 6770

Drabble, Margaret

The peppered moth

DUE DATE		D137	25.00

FICTION CATALOG

MAR 30 2001